D1594109

To Jane
best wishes
Sonia Buckley

Cliffs Edge

SONIA BUCKLEY

To my family with love

Prologue

S ilent and sleek, the yacht, Sea Nymph, sliced her way through the dark waters of the English Channel. Lord Reginald Spencer plied the wheel of his handsome craft with well-practiced skill. This night he carried with him a young Frenchman, Etienne De Vane, and a gallant English crew of five. Their destination, France. Their mission, one of rescue. Drawing ever closer to the French coast, all eyes were watchful.

Etienne stood motionless at the bow, his thoughts in turmoil. Had it only been four short weeks since his perilous escape from Paris? It seemed like forever. He still wondered if leaving the rest of the family behind had been the right thing to do. But there had been no choice.

Caught in the grip of a revolution, Paris was a city gone mad. Prisons overflowed. Royalists were executed daily. Young or old, it made no difference. Their only crime; an aristocratic name. Tumbrels, filled with the condemned, rolled endlessly through the streets. For them, it was but a short trip to the ever-hungry guillotine.

viii   Sonia Buckley

For the once proud family, De Vane, it was only a matter of time. They watched, helpless, as their friends were dragged away to face the tribunal. A mockery of justice. They lived in constant fear. Soon fists would pound on their door. They too would fall victim to the hysterical mob. They had to escape. But Ellen, Etienne's young English wife, had just given birth. The delivery had been difficult, and both mother and child were too weak to travel.

"We need help," Etienne's father insisted, holding up his hands to Etienne's protest. "No, my son, either we wait helplessly here to meet our fate, or we take our fate in our own hands."

Thus, it had been decided. Etienne fled to England with a pledge to return on the night of the next full moon.

"Soon, Etienne." Lord Spencer placed a comforting hand on his shoulder.

"I pray you are right," Etienne whispered. "It will be a miracle if they even make it out of the city." He slumped forward, grasping the ship's rail for support.

"All will be well," Spencer encouraged.

"I wish I could be as certain." Etienne looked toward the distant horizon. "There," he said, suddenly pointing out across the dark sea. "It's the coast of France."

"Are you sure this is the right place?" Spencer asked.

"Yes, see there?" Etienne pointed again. "It looks like a camel's hump. I know it well. If they are there, my father will light a flare."

"Martin, Quinn, to the sails!" Spencer commanded.

Hauling down the sails, the young Englishmen let the large vessel drift slowly toward the shore. They held their breath and waited. All was in darkness.

"There!" one shouted. "Look, Dewhurst, there it is again."

A dim light flashed from the shore.

"I see it too," Baily, the youngest of the crew, shouted.

"Thank God! They are there," Etienne whispered.

Soon, shapes were visible along the shore, silhouettes, large and small, moving in the moonlight.

"Come, Etienne. The boat is lowered. Let's go." Roger Downes rushed to join him, and together they scrambled down into the rowboat below.

"We've made it, Spencer." Lionel Quinn joined him at the rail. "We'll be back in England before you know it."

"I pray you are right, Quinn," Spencer answered.

Etienne pulled hard on the oars, an unexplained chill gripping his chest. He listened. Something was wrong. There it was again, the solid chink of harness. The steady beat of hoofs. A quick glance confirmed his worst fear. Horsemen! Black faceless shapes moved swiftly along the shore. Downes caught sight of them too and froze.

"For God's sake man, row," Etienne shouted. "If you value their lives at all, row."

From the shore, he heard his father's anguished cries.

"Go, my dears, go." He urged his little family into the sea.

Etienne added his voice to the plea. "Mother, Ellen, quickly. Here, here."

Hugging her child to her chest, Ellen ran into the rolling surf. His mother quickly followed, tugging his little sisters with her. Now only his father and his younger brother, Jacques, remained on the shore.

Desperate to protect their loved ones, they stood tall. Side by side, in the moonlight, they faced the foe, defenseless and alone.

The horsemen hesitated, uncertain. But impatient to move, horses pranced, sides heaving, hooves churning sand. Time had run out, and with one mighty arm raised above his head, the leader charged. Spurs dug deep into hairy sides, and loud voices rang out in unison as his followers gave chase. Closer and closer they came to the helpless little family. Etienne could only watch in horror as, one by one, the once proud family of De Vane fell. Like toys thrown from the hands of a willful child, they lay broken and twisted on the wet sand. Ellen and her child were the last to fall.

With blood lust still hot within their veins, the marauders urged their sweating chargers on. Steam rose in clouds, as wide-eyed and snorting, they plowed belly deep into the icy waters. Still, the leader pressed on. But further prey was denied him. Protected by the briny deep, the little boat was out of reach. Finally, angry, and frustrated, the man stood tall in his stirrups, shaking his fist and cursing the wind-tossed sea. Then, with no care for the carnage he had wrought, he whirled his steed around and galloped away. Regrouping, his men followed suit and thundered off into the distance from whence they had come.

Desperate to help, the crew of Sea Nymph threw themselves into the chilly waters and swam hard for the shore. They were too late. Nothing could be done. Numbed with shock, Roger Downes stood frozen, horror etched across his face. Etienne De Vane, eyes vacant, face ashen, sat holding his wife and child to his chest. With the rest of his family strewn around him, he rocked back and forth in the swirling red foam.

The moon was a ghostly galleon tossed upon cloudy seas,
The road was a ribbon of moonlight over the purple moor,
And the highwayman came riding-
Riding- riding-

The Highwayman.
by Alfred Noyes

Chapter One

"Stand and deliver!"

The loud command shocked the London-bound passengers out of their varying degrees of slumber. Confused and disoriented, they held on as the driver, swearing loudly, fought to control his frightened team.

Hooves skidded on the hard-packed surface of the road. Brakes squealed in protest. Dust flew from beneath large spinning wheels. Top-heavy and in danger at any minute of tipping over, the ungainly coach slowed, shuddered violently, and then came to a quivering halt.

From her seat in the corner, Madeline Carlyle saw her own fear mirrored on the faces of those around her. In the past few days, she had come to know her fellow passengers quite well. They were an odd lot. Under normal circumstances, they might never have met. But as so often happens with traveling companions, they had formed a tenuous bond. It would end with their arrival in London, but at least in this time of danger, they had each other for support.

"Everyone out and be quick about it," came the command. "Do as I say, and no one will be hurt."

"Oh my, oh my," whimpered Jeremiah Frye, the large balding salesman. His attitude now a far cry from the braggart of a short time ago. Clutching at his middle, he fondled the money belt hidden snugly beneath his clothing. "Hurry, hurry, don't keep the man waiting," he cried as he pushed the frail Mrs. Graves out through the door. "You next," he muttered, quickly sending her bewildered husband to join her. Ling Ho, the timid little Chinaman, then suffered the same fate. "Now me," Frye babbled. With an awkward heave, he raised his immense bulk from the seat. Then, tripping over Madeline's feet in his haste, he too exited the coach.

Madeline wiggled her trampled toes, a pained frown on her face.

"Nasty man!" Gloria Brownlow, the last remaining passenger, voiced her disapproval. "Never you mind, dearie." She patted Madeline's knee. "Just you stay close to me." The mother of four girls herself, Gloria had been shocked to learn that this young girl was traveling alone. From that moment, she had latched onto Madeline like a mother hen. Now, sensing danger, she was determined to protect her newly adopted hatchling. She defiantly crammed her silly little hat down further on her graying head, bending its long white feather in the process. "Just let this villain tangle with me," she bristled. "I'll soon set him down a peg or two."

Madeline smiled warmly at the feisty little woman. She had liked Gloria right from the start but, for reasons of her own, had tried to avoid her. There was something about her twinkling brown eyes that was unsettling. It was as if she could see right through you. But now, none of that mattered. There was something solid and comforting about her presence. Madeline was glad she was there. Taking a deep breath to calm her nerves, she grasped the woman's outstretched hand.

"Are you ready, child?" Gloria asked, giving her fingers a reassuring squeeze.

Madeline nodded, and together they stepped out into the bright afternoon sunlight.

Despite the heat of the day, Madeline shivered at the sight of him. From somewhere in the region of her left elbow, she heard Gloria gasp. What had they expected? Obviously not this. Dressed all in black, seated high atop a black steed, he looked more giant than man. It was a sight to strike fear into the heart of even the stoutest of souls. Except for Mr. Frye, who blubbered constantly, everyone waited silently. Breathing was difficult; the air was hot and heavy. Dust motes swirled. Flies buzzed incessantly. Time stood still. The man's dark eyes scanned their faces, coming to rest at last on Madeline.

"Step aside there." He waved his pistol contemptuously at Jeremiah Frye. "Make room for the young lady, if you please."

"Yes, yes." The salesman did as he was told, quickly giving the selected one a sharp shove with his elbow.

"Oh, you, you, simpering bowl of jelly." Mrs. Brownlow grew tongue-tied with rage. "Take him first, you bullying bandit, and leave this defenseless wee girl alone."

"I wish that I could, Madam," the man replied, "but you see, she is the reason I am here. Yes." He nodded at Madeline's surprised gasp. "It's you I came for."

"Th-there must be some mistake," she managed to stutter.

He seemed not to hear her. "Back inside with the rest of you, and hurry," he snapped. A mirthless chuckle escaped his lips as he watched the mountainous bulk of the salesman quickly disappear from view. Mr. and Mrs. Graves and Ling Ho soon followed suit. "Now you, Madam." He motioned to Gloria Brownlow.

"No, I won't leave this child alone," the woman insisted. She moved to Madeline's side and grasped her arm. "You must deal with me first, young man. I won't let you have her."

"Dear Lady, your courage is commendable," he voiced his respect, "but if I must, I will have you tied hand and foot and put in with the baggage."

"Nooo, Mrs. Brownlow, I beg of you." Madeline pried her arm free of the woman's grasp. "I will be all right. Really, I will. Please, just do as you are told."

Reluctantly, Gloria climbed back into the waiting coach, closing the door behind her.

"Don't worry, dearie," she called, sticking her head out of the window, "I will send help as soon as I can. I promise."

Frightened and unsure, Madeline gave the woman a half-hearted wave.

"On your way, driver!" To reinforce his words, the man in black sent a well-placed shot over the man's head. He needed no more encouragement. It took but a slight flick of his whip to put his frightened team in flight.

Shading her eyes, Madeline watched as the large vehicle careened dangerously off down the road. At last, it faded off into the distance, but until the very end, she could still see that silly crooked white feather at the window. She wished now that she had confided in Gloria, but it was too late. Besides, how do you tell a woman like her that you are running away?

A soft snort and the gentle nudge of the black's muzzle against her shoulder quickly returned her to the present.

"Time to go." The man's voice was gruff. "We've wasted enough time already."

Madeline looked up at him, heart pounding. "What do you want of me?" she demanded.

"Nothing, except to take you back."

"But I don't want to go back."

He shrugged. "Perhaps not, but I've had a long ride, and I don't intend to go back without you." He moved toward her and reached for her hand.

She backed away. Who was this strange man? Had he really been sent to bring her back? She found it hard to believe. He moved closer. She panicked, and giving no thought to her direction, she turned, raised her skirt, and began to run.

"Damn!" She heard the man curse and the soft thud of the horse's hooves as he gave chase. Then, without further warning, a powerful arm encircled her waist, and her feet were treading air.

"Stay still," he hissed as she struggled to escape. "Do you want to fall?"

But the warning came too late. The heel of one flaying shoe dealt a sharp blow to the horse's shoulder. With a startled whinny, the animal reared up on his hind legs.

"Easy, Samson!" The man barked the command as he fought to maintain his hold on the girl.

Madeline could feel herself slipping and squealed in fright. Trying to save herself, she threw her arms around the man's neck. But it cost her much. Her chin made solid contact with his shoulder, and stars spun before her eyes. A sharp, dizzying pain pierced her head. It robbed her of breath. She felt sick.

"Oh God!" she managed to gasp as darkness closed in around her and her body went limp.

"Damnation!" Tyler Wentworth looked down at the girl lying still in his arms. "Well, I didn't bargain on anything like this, Samson."

Calm now, the gelding snorted and tossed his head as if in agreement.

"It was one thing to say I would bring the girl back," the man continued, "but confound it, I never expected to have to play nursemaid."

Frustrated, he shook his head. Soft and disjointed as a rag doll, she lay in his arms, her fair head pressed close to his chest. Her delicate face was finely boned, the skin flawless. "Peaches and cream" were the words that came to mind. Absently, he wondered where the ridiculous saying had come from, but somehow, with her, it fit. She was small, her slim body warm and supple. He sensed a vulnerability about her, and for some reason, he found it oddly erotic.

"This is crazy, Samson," he muttered. "I thought finding her was going to be the hard part, but now I have a sinking feeling our troubles have only just begun."

Suddenly anxious to be on his way, he shifted the girl's weight to his other arm.

Errant strands of her long blond hair tickled his nose, and unable to suppress the urge, he sneezed. She uttered a soft sigh, her head rolling back against his shoulder. Long lashes fluttered open, and bewildered bright blue eyes stared up at him. His pulse raced.

"Are you alright?" he asked, a trifle shaken. Her face was ghostly pale, and no answer was forthcoming. "Are you alright?" he demanded, this time giving her a gentle shake.

"Please don't do that!" Madeline moaned.

She blinked her eyes, trying to make sense of the world she had just reentered. Bit by bit, it came tumbling back. The London coach, the hold up, her abduction, the unknown man. It was his voice she heard now. The warmth she felt wasn't fever but the heat of his body pressed close to hers. The pounding in her ears was merely the steady beating of his heart. She tried to move; her head hurt, and the world began to spin.

"Let me down," she squeaked, her stomach churning in protest. Certain that her last meager meal was about to resurface, she clutched her midsection and struggled to get free.

"What's wrong?" he demanded. But as her distress became apparent, he quickly lowered her to the ground.

Unable to speak, Madeline ran to the tall grass and fell to her knees. He was beside her in an instant. Large hands held her tight as violent spasms wreaked her small body.

"Deep breaths," he coached, his left hand now slowly massaging her back.

Madeline shivered, too weak to protest the intimacy of his touch. Instead, she followed his directions, and breathing deeply, found that it helped. Gradually, the queasiness eased. Her stomach settled, and the world around her slowed to a more leisurely pace.

"Feeling better?" he asked.

She managed a weak nod.

He looked at her face, now damp and devoid of color, and shook his head, muttering, "Of course, you are."

In truth she felt drained, unable to move, so she offered no resistance when he bent and picked her up. Then, as if she weighted nothing at all, he carried her to a nearby stand of trees.

"Don't move," he ordered, gently laying her down in the welcoming shade.

Still a trifle befuddled, Madeline said nothing. She lay still, watching the movements of the mysterious man who had entered her life so suddenly and violently. He pulled the kerchief from around his neck and dampened it with water from his flask. Kneeling beside her, he pressed the cool cloth to her forehead.

"Does this help?" he asked.

"Yes." With a grateful nod, she closed her eyes and exhaled.

"Good. But don't get too comfortable. We can't stay here long." He reached for his flask again and, slipping his arm around her shoulders, raised her to a sitting position. "Drink!" he ordered, holding the flask to her lips.

She stared solemnly up into his dark unshaven face for a moment, then slowly obeyed.

"I'm sorry you were hurt," he said, returning her gaze. Absently, he brushed the damp hair from her forehead. "But it was foolish to run."

"Why?"

"Did you really think to outrun me?"

"I didn't think," she admitted unwillingly.

"Obviously!" He ignored the slight tightening of her lips and waited.

Slowly, the color returned to her cheeks.

"Well, you look almost human again," he said with a grunt of satisfaction, "so now it's time to go." He came to his feet in a hurry and shoved the flask back into his saddle bag. Without further ado, he scooped her up in his arms, placed her unceremoniously onto his saddle, and swung up behind her.

Chapter Two

For England, the spring had been unusually hot and dry. This day was no different. By midday, the skies were brilliant. Heat shimmered down on the landscape in undulating waves. Grass, normally lush and green, was burnt to a drab brown. Trees forced roots deeper into the earth in a relentless search for moisture. Only the humble wayside weeds seemed unaffected by the drought. Somehow still able to cling to life, the nettles and ragweed proudly flaunted flowers of white and yellow.

As the day wore on, the heat only added to Madeline's discomfort. The clothing she wore was ill-suited to this mode of travel. Long sleeves clung to her arms, and fitted cuffs chaffed her skin. Perspiration trickled relentlessly down between her breasts, and she longed to loosen the collar of her dress. Damp tresses of long blond hair worked free of restricting pins to hang in ever-tightening ringlets around her small face and neck.

Her seat in the saddle was precarious. Wedged between the rock-hard thighs of her captor, she suffered ever-increasing distress. Muscles flexed and relaxed beneath her buttocks, sparking a strange, disquieting feeling in the pit of her stomach. Certain that the recent events were to blame, she again tried taking deep breaths. It didn't help. Trapped within the restricting circle of his arms, she inhaled only the warm, masculine, essence of him. Rugged and earthy. It did nothing to help her condition.

He spoke rarely. His mood appeared sullen. The only words to pass between them concerned the water flask they shared. On one such occasion, his hand brushed hers, and she quickly pulled away. Her skin tingled at his touch. Their eyes met, hers shy and embarrassed, his dark and brooding.

"Sorry," she murmured, quickly looking away to cover her confusion. But still feeling his intense gaze upon her, it was hard to slow the rapid beating of her heart. It seemed an eternity before he at last looked away.

Tyler gave little thought to his companion's discomfort. Their close contact was causing him enough distress of his own. She felt good tucked within his arms. Her blond head fit snugly beneath his chin. The faint smell of lavender clung to her hair. Drifting up in wispy threads, it left him wanting more. Only rigid self-control could help him in what otherwise might turn into a difficult situation. But a long journey still lay ahead, and the sky looked threatening. Dark clouds had gathered overhead, and thunder rumbled off in the distance. Was it possible that the long hot, dry spell was coming to an end at last? If so, he could be in trouble. He would be forced to seek shelter and could find himself confined in close quarters with this woman for days. He urged Samson to move faster, praying that the weather would hold.

Daylight was fading fast when, at last, he was forced to stop. A night spent on the road at any time was undesirable, but with a beautiful young woman in tow, it was downright dangerous. With that thought in mind, he chose a spot with care. A clear view of the road in both directions was needed, along with enough cover to hide them from passersby.

"We'll stay here tonight," he stated when he was finally satisfied. He slid quickly from the saddle and turned to help the girl dismount. She ignored him. "Suit yourself."

He made no further move to assist her but stood back and watched silently as she struggled. When, at last, her feet touched solid ground, her legs trembled and buckled beneath her. With a startled gasp, she grabbed a hold of the stirrup leathers and held on tight. Her face was ashen, but somehow, she had avoided disaster. With a shake of his head and a grunt of disgust, Tyler turned on his heel and walked away.

It was several minutes before Madeline was able to move, and even then, it wasn't easy. After hours in the saddle, her muscles were cramped and her back sore. She flexed her shoulders with difficulty, wincing as the stiffened joints complained bitterly. Freshly released blood surged swiftly down to numbed feet, leaving in its wake a trail of tingling nerve endings. Slowly, at first, she made her way to an inviting moss-covered mound and gingerly sat down. While gently massaging the circulation back into her legs, she took time to look around. How far had they come and in what direction? She wished she knew. She thought to ask her companion, but it was as if he had forgotten her very existence.

Silently, he first tended to his horse's needs, then turned his attention to his pistol. He checked and cleaned the weapon thoroughly before tucking it snugly into the belt at his waist. As she watched him, a million thoughts buzzed inside her brain. Who was he? More importantly, what did he want of her? He said he had been sent to bring her back, but that was hard to believe. True, she had left a note to say she was leaving—it would have been cruel not to—but she had made no mention of where she was going. It didn't make sense. Was it his plan to hold her for ransom? Perhaps, but why her? If it was money he was after, why had he let everyone else on the coach go? He would have to be blind not to notice Jeremiah Frye's desperate attempts to conceal the money belt beneath his clothing. It had been so obvious. Even Gloria Brownlow, her staunch supporter, had sported a large diamond ring on her finger. Yet he had taken nothing. It was puzzling. Then there was his horse. She was no judge of animals, but even she could tell it was worth a goodly sum.

Her eyes slowly traveled the length of him, from the top of his dark head down to his black-booted feet. Despite his casual mode of dress, the garments he wore were of the finest fabric. They were personally tailored, she guessed, to fit his tall frame. He was well over six feet. She studied him further. His handsome face, bronzed by the elements, was well-defined, with high cheekbones and an angular line to his unshaven jaw. The nose was short and straight, a trifle arrogant perhaps but well fitted to his other features. His hair was black. Thick and curling, it was worn short as fashion dictated. Dark brows topped bright green eyes, and even white teeth flashed when his full lips parted. Suddenly her face burned. Without realizing it, her gaze had returned to his lean hips and lingered now on the snug fit of his black britches.

"Oh!" Shocked, she covered her eyes. What on earth was she thinking! In one short day, this man had turned her little world upside down. Not only had he changed the course of her physical being, but now he was invading her mind as well. She didn't understand, and she didn't like it.

It hadn't been easy running away. To leave the safety of the place she called home had taken a great deal of courage. Now this man claimed he was taking her back. He had no right! Anger and resentment flared. She wouldn't let it happen. There must be a way, and with a little luck, I'll find it. When the moment is right, I will . . . Well, she wasn't sure yet what she would do, but she was determined to get away.

Shadows lengthened, and still her companion ignored her. Dressed as he was in black and moving in the semi-darkness, he was hard to see. Madeline sensed rather than saw him crouch down to set a fire. In seconds, the tinder, well dried by the unusually warm weather, crackled as flames took hold. Fascinated, she watched the sparks shoot skyward, higher and higher they flew, winking and blinking. Like a million tiny fireflies in the night they spiraled up into the darkness, bright shapes on a frantic dash to oblivion. With their energy quickly spent, one by one they faltered, flickered, and then sputtered out.

An errant breeze fanned the fire. The flames burned higher, catching her attention. There, amid the smoke and flames, for one brief heart-stopping moment, the man's face was captured by the glow. Startled, she suddenly realized that those unwavering green eyes had been watching her all the time.

"Come closer," he said, his gaze never leaving her face. "It's getting cold. You'll freeze way over there."

"I'm fine," she said, her voice taking on a defiant note.

"Have it your way," he muttered as he added more wood to the fire.

All too soon, she found he was right. As the sun slowly dipped further below the horizon, the air chilled. Tired, cold, and hungry, she hugged her knees to her chest, trying hard to stay warm. Tears dampened her eyes. Her lips trembled. Try as she might, there was no stemming the oncoming tide. Salty drops filtered slowly through soft lashes, and once released, they ran unhindered down her cheeks.

It took the unexpected rattle of dishes to divert her. Stomach grumbling, she watched as he brewed tea in a small tin pot. Busying himself by the fire, he appeared not to notice when she moved closer. Determined to resist, she gritted her teeth. But when he pulled dried beef and cheese from a sack, she weakened. With a reluctant groan, she joined him by the fire. It was impossible to ignore his smug grin as he handed her the plate he had already prepared.

"Beast," she muttered under her breath. But nevertheless, she took the dish and, sitting cross-legged on the ground opposite him, ate with gusto.

"You were really hungry."

She nodded and, inching closer to the warmth of the fire, kept on eating.

"You can leave the plate," he teased.

Questioning eyes flashed to his face.

"Never mind," he said, shaking his head. Adding more food to her plate, he watched in silence as she ate her fill. "Here, drink this," he said when she was done.

The tea he poured was strong and sweet, and she drank greedily.

"Easy!" He hurried to her side as she sputtered on the hot liquid.

"I'm not a child!" she managed to say, her face turning red.

"Really!"

"No!" Breathing heavily, she scrambled to her feet, dropping the cup in her haste. "I'm nineteen, a woman full-grown."

"Forgive me. I didn't know." He bent to retrieve the now empty cup. "But I thought only children ran away."

"What do you know of it?" she snapped. "I had no choice."

"We always have choices."

"Perhaps," she conceded, "but it was still my choice to make."

He looked thoughtful. "I'll grant you that," he said at last, "but there are those older and wiser than you who thought it the wrong choice. That's why I'm here."

Frustrated, she stamped her foot. "You know nothing of me or my—"

"I beg to differ," he cut her short. "I know all I need to know, and your childish antics are getting tiresome." Anger darkening his face, he strode toward her.

"Stay away!" she warned, holding up her hands, suddenly fearful.

With a menacing growl, he grabbed her arms. Trapping them behind her back, he pulled her to him, green eyes flashing fire.

"Listen to me!" He pulled her even closer. "I foolishly gave my word to bring you back so, like it not, you are going." Looking down into her frightened face, his anger quickly melted. Taking a deep breath, he released her and took a step backward. "We have a long day ahead of us tomorrow," he said softly, "so I suggest you try to get some rest."

This time, Madeline didn't protest, but later, as she lay on the soft bed of pine he had prepared, sleep was the farthest thing from her mind. By turning on her side, she could just make out the shape of him lying still beside the fire. At rest, he seemed quite harmless. But she remembered the strength of his arms wrapped around her and the ripple of hard muscles beneath his shirt.

Awake, she knew she was no match for him. If she were to have any chance of escape, it would have to be while he slept. Perhaps then she could slip quietly away, and with any luck, by morning, she could be well on her way to London. Once there, she doubted he would be able to find her.

She fought the urge to sleep, watching the steadily rising moon. Her head bobbed sharply, and she knew she could wait no longer. Across the clearing, her companion slept soundly beside the dying fire. Taking a deep breath to slow the rapid beating of her heart, she came to her feet and waited. He didn't stir. With a wary eye turned in his direction, she tiptoed slowly toward freedom. A twig snapped sharply beneath her shoe. She froze. Still, he lay silent. One more step, then another. Her breath came a little easier now. Freedom was within her reach.

"Going somewhere?" a soft voice asked.

Startled, she spun around. The silent shape still lay unmoving beside the fire.

Too late, she realized it was just a ruse.

"I asked if you were going somewhere?" he repeated.

Eyes probing the darkness, Madeline found him at last. Almost invisible, he sat with his back to a tree. Only the glow of his cigar betrayed him.

"What kind of a man are you to hide among the shadows?" she demanded.

"A wise one, I think," he answered. "Would you prefer I leave you unprotected? The countryside hereabouts abounds with thieves and cutthroats."

"Like you?" she blurted.

"Touché," he murmured softly, "but at least I won't sell you off to the highest bidder."

Madeline gasped.

"A harsh fact but a true one. Now, can I trust you to stay put for the rest of the night?"

She made no answer.

"Well?" he persisted.

Madeline nodded. Dejected and more than a little afraid, she returned to her makeshift bed. With his words still ringing in her ears: "at least I won't sell you off to the highest bidder." She doubted that she would ever find sleep this night.

For the first time, she realized what a huge chance she had taken by running away. But at the time, she had been so sure of herself. She had given no thought to the possible dangers she might face. Would it have made a difference though? She didn't think so. No matter what anyone said, she was nineteen now, old enough to follow her heart and live her life as she saw fit. She yawned, her eyes growing heavy. Snuggling deeper into the comfort of her bed, she breathed in the fresh sweet smell of pine. As she drifted off to sleep, she whispered, "Why, Father, why did you do this to me?"

Tyler tipped back his head and inhaled deeply on the stub of his black cigar. His mind was full of questions of his own. He glanced over at the girl, hoping she was asleep. She was proving to be a handful. It occurred to him again that, for the first time in his 28 years, he might have bitten off more than he could chew. "Damn it, Grandfather," he muttered, "what the hell did you get me into?"

Barely a week had passed since he and George, his best friend and self-appointed valet, had arrived in England from Boston. In fact, they were still unpacking when his grandfather came looking for him in a high state of alarm. It seemed his oldest friend, Sir Guy Ashton needed help in a personal and confidential matter. Apparently, the man's daughter had run away. She was an only child born to the man late in life, and she was the center of the old man's world. Since her mother's death, she had never heard the word "No." Recently, however, she had been introduced to a man who was apparently nothing more than a scoundrel of the worst kind. The two had quickly become involved, and despite her father's firm objections, the foolish female had agreed to travel halfway across the country to meet and marry the man.

"Bring her back, my boy," his grandfather had begged. "I am afraid if you don't, it will be the end of poor Sir Guy."

"But you aren't going to do this, are you?" George had asked him awhile later.

"What would you have me do?" He had wanted to know.

George shook his head and said no more.

Now, leaning back against the tree, Tyler stretched his cramped legs out in front of him. He knew that short of murder, both he and George would do anything for the old man. After all, William Searle, 5th earl of Marshfield, was the main reason for their visit to England. Shortly, the old man would celebrate his eightieth birthday. It was a milestone neither of them could ignore. The original plan had been to relax and celebrate the occasion with a much-anticipated round of horse sales. It was a passion the three men shared. Despite his age, William still kept a large stable, and nothing delighted him more than adding new blood to his string. But the last thing Tyler had expected was to find himself chasing halfway across England in search of a runaway girl.

"You were right, George," he said, glancing across at his sleeping companion. "I needed my head examined."

He took a last drag on his cigar and tossed its mangled remains into the fire's red embers. With a stifled yawn, he pulled his hat down on his forehead and closed his eyes.

Chapter Three

S he was running, running but going nowhere. Her legs were heavy weights dragging her down. She gasped for breath; pain pierced her chest. She took a quick look over her shoulder and glimpsed the dark shape still following behind. He was gaining ground, the space between them closing with every stride. A claw-like hand reached out toward her. She screamed and sat bolt upright, the echo of her scream still ringing in her ears.

"Hush!" Firm hands grasped her shoulders. "You were having a bad dream," he said not unkindly. "Your noise could wake the dead."

"Sorry." She shivered, still haunted by the ghosts of slumber. His grip tightened on her shoulder, and she slowly relaxed. Usually, when bad dreams plagued her nights, she woke alone and afraid. Now though, as he crouched beside her, she found his nearness oddly comforting, the warmth of his touch reassuring. The fear left her eyes, and she rewarded him with a wan smile.

"That's better," he said, grinning back at her. "It was only a dream."

She wanted to say, yes, I've heard that before, but why is it always the same horrible dream? Instead, she nodded and said nothing. He offered her his hand and pulled her to her feet. She made to move away.

"Just a minute," he said softly.

She waited as, with a distant look on his face, he gently picked pine needles from her hair. All of a sudden, his mood changed. A frown creased his brow. He took a step backward, then abruptly turned and walked away.

"It's time to go," he said over his shoulder.

Tea again bubbled over a small fire, and while her companion carefully removed all traces of their overnight stay, Madeline quickly poured some from the pot. With a grateful sigh, she held the cup between her cold hands. The cool air chilled her skin, and she breathed into the cup, luxuriating in the warmth as the steam rose and encircled her face.

"That was good," she said as she finished the tasty brew.

Her companion grunted in acknowledgment as he doused the fire with the remains of the pot. Madeline waited and watched as he quickly repacked his belongings into the saddle bags. When at last he appeared satisfied, he returned to kick dirt over the still-glowing embers.

At her curious look, he explained, "The ashes of a fresh fire could attract too much attention. We might find ourselves being followed as objects of interest."

She wasn't quite sure what he meant by that, but she had a strange feeling that she didn't really want to know. With a hurried look around her, she moved closer to his side.

His movements were easy as, once again, he checked his pistol before tucking it into his belt. He smoothed back his hair with his fingers, brushed off the wide-brimmed black hat, and crammed it down on his head. Then, picking her up, he placed her back on the saddle and, without a word, took up his place behind her.

For the next two days, there was no respite from the heat. They rested often, seeking out whatever shade was available. Knowing their appearance would create gossip, Tyler preferred to avoid villages and stayed far away from well-used roads. But it made travel slow and tiresome. Open countryside stretched out for miles around them like a giant, never-ending patchwork quilt. A splash of brown here, a touch of yellow there, an occasional triangle of bright poppy red, each joined to the next by hedgerows of green. Patch after patch, all carefully spread out to dry beneath a relentless sun and a cloudless blue sky.

As time passed, Tyler found his eyes drawn more and more often to the beautiful little creature he had captured. She was small, reaching no higher than his shoulder, with a waist he could span with his hands. Exposure to the sun had turned her skin to gold, and a dusting of freckles sprinkled her nose. He likened her eyes to the blue of summer cornflowers by day, but at night they turned the deep blue of star sapphires. Her lips were full and hypnotic in their power to attract him. His desire to taste their delights was so great it threatened to overwhelm him. He wanted to grab her, kiss her, and run his hands through the unruly length of her wild blonde hair.

Soon, keeping his hands off her was driving him crazy. He slept little at night, and during the day, he avoided her as much as possible. He could understand why, even without her father's money, a man would risk everything to possess her. But the thought that some other man might sparked a fire that burned his insides. He blamed the long sea voyage from Boston for his problem and cursed the lack of time needed to address his baser needs. It was something he intended to remedy just as soon as he was rid of the girl. Until then, he had to avoid her as much as possible.

Madeline no longer cared where she went. She just wanted the ordeal to be over. Each minute seemed an hour, each hour an eternity.

With the rising tension between them, she too became distant and withdrawn. Silence settled between them like a giant chasm. Her companion walked now more than he rode. He seemed tireless even in the worst heat of the day. His only concession to the elements was to roll up his sleeves and open the neck of his shirt. With nothing to fill her thoughts, her mind wandered. She noticed small things about her companion, like the way his hair curled over his collar, the muscle that flexed at his jaw, and how a faint sheen of moisture coated his arms and flecked the dark hair at his chest. Soon, no matter how hard she tried, he occupied all her waking thoughts.

At night, she resorted to a hasty little prayer. "Please, please," she begged, "let this be over soon." But there was no respite even in sleep because without her willing it, he found his way into her dreams.

Yet another day dawned, but this one came with a rising wind. There was a feeling in the air that caused creatures, large and small, to look at the sky with troubled eyes. They shook their heads, and with wisdom born somewhere deep inside them, they scurried away in search of shelter. The very land seemed quiet, waiting breathlessly, poised on the brink, it seemed, of some great happening.

Tyler swore under his breath and quickly broke camp. He could feel the change in the weather. This time, he knew there would be no reprieve. Distant thunder rumbled, and vivid lightning rapidly followed each shuddering boom. The wind gathered force, sweeping all before it. Giant pines swayed recklessly back and forth, dipping so low at times that they almost brushed the ground at their feet. Even the sturdy oaks, that paid homage to no one, were not immune. Like old men nursing arthritic joints, their sagging limbs creaked in loud complaint. But they knew in their hearts that time was their enemy. There is no cure for aging.

The young couple ate a quick cold meal, but long before they could get underway, heavy raindrops spattered down upon them.

"The girl's a jinx," Tyler muttered to himself. "Nothing has gone right in my life since I met her." Angrily, he tugged his rain gear from his pack and threw it around his shoulders. The source of his anger had already climbed into the saddle. He moved to her side and looked up, rain streaming down his face. "Shift over, Madam," he demanded. "I'll not walk today."

Her movements were slow.

"Come on," he urged, "it's getting late, and my patience is wearing thin." Quickly swinging up onto the saddle behind her, he held open his cape, inviting her inside.

She looked undecided.

"Alright," he shrugged, "suit yourself."

But water had collected in the broad brim of his black hat and now dripped down onto her head. She made a face, shook the drops from her hair, and quickly decided to accept his offer. He wrapped his arms around her, pulling her close to his chest. There, with her head resting snugly beneath his chin, he willingly shared the steamy warmth of his body.

The rain became heavy. Nature, it seemed, was making up for a careless oversight. As the parched earth gratefully drank its fill, the creatures of the land remained hidden. From hollowed trees and wooded burrows, large eyes watched silently as the three travelers took to the road. A man, woman, and horse shrouded in mist and moving ghost-like through the heavy downpour.

The lowlands quickly turned into a nightmare of mud. Roadways became impassable. Tyler sought higher ground, but climbing steeper paths made travel difficult. Rocks, loosened by the running water, became slippery and treacherous. By midmorning, even the sure-footed Samson was hard-pressed to continue.

"We have to walk awhile," Tyler said over the top of her head.

Snug and warm within his arms, the girl had dozed on and off. Now she emerged from inside of his cape like a butterfly from its cocoon. His arms felt empty.

Madeline slid to the ground. She yawned. Sleep still dulled her mind. "How much further?" she asked, rubbing her eyes.

"Too far," he quickly replied.

"I'm getting wet." She knew it was a stupid remark, but she couldn't help it.

"You won't melt," he replied sharply. "Here." Relenting, he removed his cape and placed it around her shoulders. "This might help a bit." Adjusting the large garment as best as he could, he fastened it under her chin.

Snuggling inside, Madeline yawned and mumbled, "Thank you."

Despite the bad conditions, her companion set off at a brisk pace, his horse at his heels. Madeline trudged along behind, the long cape dragging on the ground around her. Mud stuck to her shoes, slowing her down, and no matter how hard she tried, she kept falling further behind.

"Keep up," his words drifted back to her.

"Keep up," she repeated, childishly sticking her tongue out at his back.

But for him, she could have been in London now. Instead, she was wet and uncomfortable and miles from anywhere. She hated him and wanted him out of her life forever.

She stopped for a moment and, mumbling to herself, hiked up the hem of the muddy garment. By now, he was well ahead of her. But with a little less weight to slow her down, she should be able to keep up. Willing her legs to move faster, she trudged along, following his trail.

Thunder rumbled close overhead, and she shivered. Seconds later, vivid lightning zigzagged across the sky. In the brilliant flash, she saw her companion turn to wait for her. In the moments that followed, she could only watch the scene play out before her. Struck by lightning, a giant oak split asunder. Sparks flew. The earth shook beneath her feet. With horrified eyes, she saw the tree begin to fall. She screamed a warning. He looked up, but it was too late. The black horse reared and bolted to safety, but a large branch struck her companion and took him down. Trapped and unconscious, he lay now in a crumpled heap on the ground.

Terrified, Madeline struggled to his side. His face was pale. Blood oozed from an open wound on his head. Rain and blood mixed in a slowly spreading patch of crimson, matting the locks of curly black hair.

"Oh God," she cried, looking down at him, certain he must be dead but reassured by the slight movement of his chest. Slipping and sliding, she tugged at the branch that held him without success. With a sob, she fell to her knees. It was useless. Somehow, she had to find help, but where and how could she leave him like this?

Gently rocking back and forth, she fought against the rising tide of panic. Taking deep breaths as she had done once before, she slowly cleared her mind. With numbing fingers, she pulled the cape from her shoulders, folded it into a pillow, and placed it beneath his head. Blood, warm and sticky, coated her fingers, and her stomach churned. She knew nothing of wounds, but it seemed like a lot of blood. Quickly wiping it off with her wet skirt, she struggled to her feet.

"I'm going for help," she said, hoping he could hear. She waited a moment, but he showed no signs. Without waiting any longer, she turned and stumbled blindly away.

There was no telling how far she had gone. It seemed like miles. Probably not. The storm had eased—she hardly noticed. Mud caked her shoes, making walking difficult. Exhausted now, she made her way down the treacherous path. Suddenly, without warning, stones loosened by the rain gave way. She stumbled, struggling to right herself. For a moment, all seemed well, then her ankle twisted, and she lost her balance and fell.

Wild and out of control, she tumbled head over heels down a steep embankment. Brambles and vines ran rampant here, most undisturbed for many years. Thorns scratched her arms and legs and tangled her hair. Down she went amid a gathering pile of leaves and dirt, finally coming to rest, with a resounding splash, in the middle of a swamp.

Shaken and afraid, she struggled to escape. Arms thrashing, she grabbed at fallen branches, clumps of swamp grass, anything that might help her get free. But one by one, the objects sank from sight, sucked down by the mud that slowly closed in around them. She knew panic for the second time that day.

"Help, help." Her shrill cries sounded hollow, the only answer a distant echo. She didn't want to admit it, but she knew there was no one out there to hear.

Shadows lengthened. Night was falling. Wispy tendrils of mist drifted over the murky surface around her, covering it in an ever-moving cloak of gray. A thousand biting insects swarmed about her, filling her eyes and drawing blood each time they landed on her skin. Nocturnal creatures stirred. The raspy croak of one giant bullfrog quickly became a symphony. Countless things slithered and crawled, rustling among the quivering reeds. An owl, flapping on ponderous wings, hooted his lonely call. With yellow eyes, large and intent, he sailed low overhead in search of unwary rodents. A fox barked nearby. Seconds later, another answered its call. Madeline stared into the gloom, terrified. They were gathering out there beyond the swamp, circling slowly. All eyes were upon her. Red eyes that glittered in the dark.

"Calm. I must stay calm," she chided herself. "But what is to become of me?"

From somewhere in her childhood, she remembered hearing stories of animals trapped on the moors. One false step had sealed their fate. Only their bleached bones remained to tell the tale. Here too, life could end in a blink of an eye, but the struggle to survive was never-ending. She had become one with her surroundings and was suddenly convinced of the smallness of her existence.

"But I will survive, Lord. With your help, I will." As an afterthought, she added, "But please make it quick."

As time passed, an icy dampness drenched her clothing, numbing her extremities. Her teeth chattered. Chilled to the bone, she fought the urge to sleep by humming a tune. The sweet sound comforted her, so she added the words.

"Holy God, we praise Thy name

Lord of all we bow before Thee."

What was that? Her song trembled to a stop. There it was again, closer this time.

Something large was crashing through the undergrowth toward her. She froze, her mind quickly conjuring up a creature of terrifying proportions. Surely it must be at least ten feet tall with claws and fangs that could tear her to shreds. Frantic, she renewed her efforts to escape, but it was futile. Again, she prayed, "Lord, forgive me my sins and if this is to be the end of me, please make it quick." Perhaps if she stayed very still, it wouldn't notice her. It would go away. All around her grew silent too. This world was poised and waiting.

The creature broke from cover. Mist obscured it from her view. But she could hear its heavy breathing and sensed it watching her through the gathering gloom. A breeze fluttered around her. Slowly parting the mist as it went, it rippled its way over the water toward the shore. She cringed, steeling herself for the ordeal ahead, hating herself for her cowardice.

"Well, what have we here, Samson? Is she real or just a figment of my addled brain?"

Madeline shuddered and exhaled. His words were sarcastic, but it didn't matter. Not only was he here, but he was alive and well. Her heart rejoiced.

"You aren't dead!" She stated the obvious.

"Well, not the last time I checked." He dismounted and stood, hands on hips.

"How did you find me?"

"It was your melodious voice. Had you not decided to burst into song as I passed by, you would have been crowbait by morning."

"Ohh!" Relief sparked her anger. "Well, don't just stand there. Get me out."

"What, no 'thank you'? No 'glad you stopped by'? Tut-tut." He shook his head, quickly trying to disguise his own relief at finding her alive. "Now, if you were in her position, Samson, wouldn't you display gratitude?"

"If it weren't for you, I wouldn't be in this mess," Madeline retorted.

"But it could be argued that if you hadn't run away in the first place, neither one of us would be in this mess."

He pulled at a length of vine. Taking a knife from the top of his boot, he hacked it from its mooring.

"Catch," he called as one end sailed in her direction.

"You didn't come close," she yelled as it landed several feet away.

"I suppose you could do better," he yelled back.

"Well, I couldn't do much worse."

"Is that so? Perhaps we should just leave her there, Samson." He reeled in the vine and made as if to walk away.

"No, no, don't go," she cried. "I'm sorry!"

Pretending to relent, he returned and tried the vine again. This time, he was successful. "Hold on tight," he called to Madeline. Tying the other end of the vine to his saddle, he urged Samson with a "Go boy." Backing up slowly, the large black dragged his charge safely back to the shore.

"Don't look at me like that," Madeline begged a moment later.

"You should see yourself." He shook his head, trying hard to smother a grin. "You're a sight."

With her long hair a tangled mass and her fair skin swollen and red from vicious insect bites, Madeline knew he spoke the truth. Thick mud plastered her brown dress, and its long skirt clung to her legs, wet and dripping. She lifted her hem and stared down at her feet. A shoe was missing from one small foot, and its mate was ruined beyond repair.

"Oh, no." She sat down with a thump and stuck out her feet for him to see. "Look at that. I've lost a shoe!"

"Never mind, I'll buy you a new pair," he said consolingly. He crouched beside her and handed her his already soiled handkerchief. "Here, wipe your face, and you'll feel better." He waited, growing impatient as she dabbed at her tender skin. "Here, let me." He took the handkerchief back and rubbed briskly at the dirt.

"Ouch! That hurts." Madeline squirmed, twisting her head from side to side.

"Hold still!" he demanded. Catching her chin in a firm hold, he quickly scrubbed her clean. "There." Sitting back on his heels, he examined his handy work with a critical eye. "Yes," he said at last, "that looks much better." He stuffed the grubby handkerchief back in his pocket and came to his feet. "That wasn't so bad now, was it?"

"No," she admitted, pressing her hands to her cheeks, "but it stings!"

He shook his head in mock despair and quickly changed the subject.

"There's still just enough light to guide us out of here," he said, "so let's not waste any more time." So saying, he swung her up once again onto Samson's back, and then led horse and rider back along the narrow trail.

By the time he could secure them, another campsite the moon was high, and the storm had passed. It had been a long, trying day, and they were both lucky to be alive. Tyler cursed himself for his foolishness. He had allowed the girl to get under his skin, and as a consequence, he had taken far too many chances. But fate had been kind. Upon regaining consciousness, it had been easy, with Samson's help, to free himself from the fallen branch. The girl's whereabouts at that time were a mystery. He presumed she had gone for help, but where?

As it turned out, the sound of her voice had led him straight to her. His relief at finding her was so great, he vowed never to take such risks again. Right now, though, her condition worried him. She was indeed a mess. Sympathy softened his heart, but he quickly suppressed it when she started to complain.

"Look at me. My dress is ruined. And what of my hair?" She began tugging out the useless pins and running her fingers through the tangled locks.

"Stop whining and take your clothes off," he demanded.

"I will not!" Shocked, Madeline backed away, folding her arms tightly across her chest.

"Good Lord, woman, I'm in no mood for your foolishness. In case you've forgotten, I just came within inches of losing my life. I'm tired, and my head hurts. See!" He pointed to the gash on his scalp still oozing blood. "The only thing on my mind now is to get you dry and to get myself some sleep. So, take this," he said, handing her a blanket, "and give me your wet things." At her hesitation, he asked. "Shall I help you?"

"You wouldn't!"

"Wouldn't I?" With a raised brow, he took a purposeful step forward.

Madeline gave a frantic squeak, grabbed the blanket and quickly scurried off into the bushes.

Her clothing was difficult to remove. What should have been a simple task turned into a lesson in frustration. For all that her dress was of simple style, it fastened at the back. Even on a good day, the small fabric ties could prove difficult. But now, with the woolen fabric wet and less pliable, it was virtually impossible. Try as she might, the attachments refused to cooperate. With rising agitation, she pulled and tugged the harder, only to find the knots tied even tighter.

"What's taking so long?" he came closer.

"I'm stuck!"

"Does that mean you could use my help after all?"

Madeline remained silent for a moment, then managed a rather subdued "Yes, please."

Even with her back toward him, she could sense his approach. His footsteps were smooth and easy, almost silent in the damp grass. She closed her eyes, envisioning a large black cat, a panther. Yes, that was it, a green-eyed panther. You couldn't see it hidden among the trees, but from the tingle down your spine, you knew it was there anyway.

She tilted her head to the left, and hands shaking, pulled her hair aside. He moved closer still. His warm breath fanned her neck, and she shivered.

"Why you females choose to wear such foolish clothing is beyond me," he muttered as he grappled with the unruly ties. "Even a contortionist would be hard pressed to get out of this contraption." But for someone with such large hands, he proved surprisingly adept. In a matter of minutes, the ties were undone. "Sorry, I have no comb for your hair," he apologized softly, "but perhaps this will help a little." He ran his fingers gently through the tangled locks, smoothing and removing much of the debris that still clung there.

As he worked, Madeline wondered if he performed this task for his wife and timidly voiced the question.

"I have no wife, but I am one of ten children. I have four brothers, William, Todd, Ian, and Noah as well as five sisters, Clara, the twins, Sophie and Sarah, Carolyn, and Midge. Midge is the youngest, and she's the bane of my life. She is always coming home in a mess after some misadventure, and then she looks for me to help straighten things out."

"Midge?"

He chuckled. "Yes, she's a little bit of a thing, so we call her Midge. Her real name is Margaret."

"Oh."

"There, does that feel better?" he asked, carefully removing the last bramble from her hair.

"Yes, much, thank you." She made to move away.

"Wait!" He caught her arm. "By what name do they call you? No one thought to tell me."

"My given name is Madeline, Sir."

"Mmmm," he mused, "Madeline, yes, that fits. And mine, now that we have become acquainted, is Tyler."

"Tyler," she repeated.

"Yes. Tyler Wentworth." He introduced himself with a slight bow of his head. "And now, Madeline," he continued sternly, "you need to listen carefully. We both had a pretty narrow escape today, and I need your promise that you won't take off again." When she didn't answer right away, he placed a finger beneath her chin, tilting her face toward him. "I need your word," he insisted, green eyes intent and unwavering.

She met his gaze, a thoughtful frown on her brow. She knew how close she had just come to death, so it seemed foolhardy to refuse. "I promise," she said at last.

But he didn't release her right away. Rather, he slowly continued to study her face. Pulse thumping, she stared back. Moments passed. Then, no longer able to stand it, she pulled away.

"What's wrong?" she demanded, her face flushing.

"I was trying to decide," he mused softly.

"Decide?"

"Yes, if I can really trust you."

Later that night, wrapped only in a blanket, Madeline found sleep hard to come by. She tossed and turned, all the while thinking about her companion and the things he had told her. Five sisters, he had said. How she would have loved to have sisters. How different her own life might have been then. Perhaps if her mother had lived longer, but that was a foolish thought. She hadn't. Her death had been sudden and so very long ago that now she remembered very little about her. A soft smile, a gentle touch, a fragrant scent that lingered somewhere on the fringes of her memory. Were the memories she still carried with her real, or were they just conjured up by the mind of a lonely child? She wished she knew for sure. It was close to dawn before she at last drifted off to sleep. But it was a troubled sleep, one in which her old dream returned to haunt her. She awoke cold and trembling, and having no desire to return to the dream, she rose and went in search of her clothing. Hung on a bush overnight, they were still damp but stiff to the touch. Despite all her efforts, cleaning them proved useless. Finally, she gave up and put them on as they were. It was in this state of dishabille that her companion found her a short time later.

She was a sorry sight, limping around in her one shoe, her soiled dress dangling down around her ankles, but she said nothing. Her big concern now was the constant itching of her many insect bites. The stiffened fabric of her undergarments chafed her arms and legs, further irritating the affected spots on her skin. Try as she might, she couldn't leave them alone.

"Ouch," she muttered, frantically scratching the worsening red bumps.

"Stop that infernal scratching," Tyler demanded.

"But I itch!"

Exasperated, he threw up his hands. His mood was foul. There was a lump on his head the size of a goose egg, and somewhere behind his eyes, a drum beat out a steady tattoo. He grabbed his saddlebag and rifled through it.

"Here, try this," he said, tossing her a small tin. "It's salve. It might help."

Madeline took it without comment and quickly spread a thick layer of the greasy concoction over the affected area. When she was done, she handed it back.

"It smells," she said, wrinkling her nose. But after a moment, she sighed as her flesh cooled and the itching started to ease.

Tyler watched her from the corner of his eye and wondered again how he had ended up in this position. He could just hear George already saying, "I told you so." Playing nursemaid to a spoiled, young, society miss was way out of his league.

Apart from his mother and sisters, whom he adored, he preferred the company of older, more sophisticated women. Well, it was almost over. Today should see an end to it. By nightfall, he would deliver her, not too much the worse for wear, into the hands of his grandfather. Where she went from there would no longer be his concern. Hopefully, once she was back in the nest, her father would be able to curb her willful ways. But he doubted it.

As the day wore on, one weary mile followed another. Dark clouds rolled overhead; the storm had returned. No fierce lightening or rumbling thunder this time, just a light, steady, chilling drizzle. By late afternoon, Tyler was forced to make a decision. Soaked to the skin and exhausted, they were still some three miles from Marshfield Hall and his grandfather. Long Meadow, the house he had taken for himself for the duration of his stay, was a mere mile away. After a quick look at the girl half asleep in his arms, the decision was made. As much as he hated the idea, it would have to be Long Mead.

Chapter Four

One small lamp still burned in the window of the big old house. Its flickering flame beckoned as they made their way up the long tree-lined driveway. Rain-soaked branches swayed by the breeze sent icy splatters down upon their heads. Gravel crunched sharply beneath Samson's heavy feet. His senses told him he was close to home, and he picked up his pace, knowing there was a warm barn and sweet feed not too far ahead.

"Here at last," Tyler said, sighing as they finally came to a halt.

Weary beyond belief, he slowly lowered his stiffened limbs to the ground. Reaching up for his companion, he was just in time as, more asleep than awake, she slid from the saddle. With her limp form held close in his arms, he climbed the steps to the large front door. As if by magic, the door swung open before him, and he grinned at the sight of George silhouetted in the frame.

"You're a sight for sore eyes, my friend," Tyler greeted.

"Good to see you too, Gov," the man returned warmly. "Hurry up in now. It's not a good night out there for man or beast." He ushered them quickly into the drawing room, where the embers of a fire still glowed red upon the hearth. "Best get out of those wet clothes," he fussed, poking the ash and adding fresh wood.

Tyler set Madeline down by the fire and removed his cape. "I've never been quite so happy to see that homely face of yours, George," he teased, handing him the wet garment. "But we are chilled to the bone, my friend. Some hot tea for the lady and a stiff drink for me, if you please."

"Right, I'll be back in a jiffy," the man said, hurrying away.

As the door closed behind him, Madeline asked, "What is this place, and why did you bring me here?"

"This is my home at the moment," he explained, "and under the circumstances, I thought it better to spend the night here."

"Better for who?" she asked, blue eyes wide.

"For you of course," he snapped. "You looked half-dead."

"Why should you care?" she pushed. "You dragged me here against my will; why does my health concern you now?"

He sighed, shaking his head. "All right. If it makes you feel better, I'm tired, and my horse is tired. He carried us a long way today, so we are here because I thought it best. That's an end to it. I will hear no more on the subject." He grabbed a chair and pulled it close to the fire. "Sit," he demanded, taking her shoulders and forcing her down onto it. "Now, take off those wet stockings before you catch your death." His tone brooked no argument, but seeing her hesitation, he moved to a discreet distance. There he waited as she first removed her one ruined shoe, then struggled to discard the soaked stockings.

He took the garments from her and hung them over the mantle to dry.

"There, isn't that better?" he asked.

Her limbs were still stiff, and her teeth chattered with the cold, but the warmth of the fire caressed her bare skin, and vapors rose as dampness dried.

"Mmm." She murmured, her eyes closing.

"Good, then allow me." It was an order, not a request.

He knelt before her. Taking her frozen feet in his hands, he began a gentle massage. As shocked as she was at first by his boldness, Madeline shyly accepted his ministrations without complaint. His hands were large and warm, his fingers long and skilled in the art of manipulation. They worked in a slow circular motion and eased her tender, chafed flesh. Slowly, circulation returned. Blood surged through chilled limbs, and numbed nerve endings tingled with the sweet pleasure of pain. Tense muscles relaxed. With a sigh, she sank deeper into the comfort of the big chair.

Through her half-closed lids, she watched the man. Head bent, sleeves pushed up, forearms bared, he worked patiently, taking his time. What should she make of him, one moment angry and demanding, the next thoughtful and caring? She was struck by a strange urge to reach out and touch him, to brush back the hair that had fallen across his forehead—jet black hair turned blue now by the flickering firelight.

As if he read her mind, he looked up, his hands suddenly still. Green eyes, dark and brooding, focused on her face, impaling her with their intensity. She sensed the danger lurking in those smoldering eyes, and her heartbeat quickened. She shivered involuntarily, torn between a desire she didn't understand and the resentment that still simmered inside. Neither moved. The air grew heavy. Moments passed with only the sounds of their breathing to disturb the silence of the room. Then, slowly and deliberately, his hands went to work again, with a hypnotic effect, slowly growing bolder, moving higher.

Unnoticed, George entered the room, carrying a large tray. Discreetly clearing his throat, he made his way to the table.

Startled and embarrassed, Madeline quickly withdrew her feet, tucking them securely beneath her skirt.

"Good timing as always, George." Tyler came smoothly to his feet, a wry grin on his handsome face.

Still discreet, the man said nothing. Instead, he set the tray down, poured a brandy from the crystal decanter and tea from a large silver pot.

"Hope it's the way you like it, Miss," he stated, handing Madeline a cup of the steaming brew.

She took a sip and smiled. "It's just perfect, thank you."

"My pleasure." With a slight bow, the man returned her smile. "About the water, Gov," he said, turning to Tyler and handing him the brandy glass. "There was only enough heated for one bath. It'll take a while, but I can stoke up the stove."

"No, George, it's far too late. No need to wake the rest of the staff either. We can manage for the night. The lady gets the tub. I'll clean up in my room."

"Right you are," George acknowledged. "When you're ready then, Miss."

Madeline hesitated a moment, unsure.

"Go, go, Madam," Tyler urged, draining his glass. "Your bath awaits. Enjoy."

Again, she noted a touch of sarcasm in his voice, and she blushed.

"Sir, I have no desire to deprive you of—"

"This way, Miss," George intervened quickly. He took her arm and ushered toward the door.

"But I—" She heard the clink of the brandy glass as the door closed behind her.

George led the way across the hall and up the wide circular staircase to the landing above.

"Afraid you'll have to manage on you own tonight, Miss," he apologized. "The rest of the staff are all tucked up in bed, you see."

"Of course, I understand." Madeline hoped the relief she felt didn't show on her face. The one thing she wanted most now was to be left alone.

"Right then, this is it." He opened a door on his right. "You'll find everything you need here, Miss. I'll have food waiting downstairs when you're ready."

She thanked him and watched as he walked away. Alone at last, she entered the room, closing the door quietly behind her.

For the first time in days, she was completely alone. She had forgotten how good that could feel. She rested her head against the cool wood panels of the door, closed her eyes, and sighed. For several minutes, she didn't move, allowing her body the luxury of wallowing in total fatigue. Limbs grew heavy, and she drifted into a dark, half-sleep world. Without warning, her legs buckled out from under her, and she hit the floor with a thump. She sat still, shaken and disoriented. The delayed shock of the days just passed was beginning to take its toll. Afraid to move, she took a deep breath and waited for the world to settle. She was dizzy. Her head hurt, and she felt sick. With an effort, she pulled her legs to her chest, wrapped her arms around them, and rested her chin on her knees. Slowly, the world righted itself, and her trembling eased. Through blurry eyes, she watched as the room came into focus. It appeared warm and inviting. Soft lamplight cast shadows on pale yellow walls and the high white ceiling. Wood burned brightly in the green marble fireplace, and two welcoming wing-backed chairs sat close to the hearth. A large painting of bright-eyed cocker spaniels hung over the fireplace, and a gold-faced clock ticked quietly on the mantle. Tasseled green brocade draped the three long windows, and more of the same covered the big four-poster bed. A crystal bowl filled with fresh cut flowers sat atop a huge, hand-tooled oak dresser, and in a far corner, an ornate, full-length mirror captured the room in reflection.

Madeline gasped as she suddenly saw herself in such a disheveled state. She was barefoot. Gone were her stockings and her one good shoe. Her brown dress, she was sure, was beyond redemption. Her hair, missing most of its pins, hung in long, tangled strands down around her face. She struggled to her feet, her legs still unsteady. All she could think of now, though, was the promised bath. She went in search of the tub, wiggling her toes as they sank into the soft pile of the woolen carpet. At last, peeking around a door on the far side of the room, she found it. Its contents, still hot to the touch, were fragrantly scented with lavender. Overwhelmed with desire, she quickly discarded her soiled garments and climbed into the large copper tub. Giving her skin a moment to adjust, she took a deep breath, closed her eyes, and slowly sank down into the sweet-smelling steam.

Chapter Five

Deprived of the luxury of a bath himself, Tyler had done the best he could with his limited resources. Now washed and shaved, he felt almost human again. With only a towel to cover him, he went in search of George and clean clothing. Briskly rubbing the dampness from his hair, he watched as the man quickly attended to his needs. He was a tall, wiry man with a mop of red hair. His deep-set, intelligent, brown eyes looked out at the world from a rugged but quite pleasant face. How different their lives might have been if not for his grandfather. Some twenty years ago, on a foggy night in London, William had risked life and limb to pull a scruffy ten-year-old from beneath the wheels of a passing carriage. He had sought out the best surgeon to save the orphan's badly injured leg, then had taken him home to be raised as a member of his household. The boy had grown into a healthy and strong man loyal to the family and the old man who had saved him. But to this day, Tyler knew that in times of extreme fatigue, George still walked with a limp.

"What would I do without you, George?" he teased.

"For one thing, you'd have to learn to pick up after yourself," came the quick reply.

"Oh, I think I could find some pretty little wench to do my bidding," Tyler said, sliding his arms into the sleeves of a crisp white linen shirt.

"Ha, ha." George ducked just in time to avoid the wet towel that went sailing over his head. "Now you've got that out of your system," he grumbled, picking up the wet missile, "perhaps you can tell me where you've been. The old man's in a fair state. Expected you back a while ago. What happened?"

"All in good time, my friend, but first, I need a drink. I can tell you though," he confided as they made their way back down to the drawing room, "running the British blockade, as we did a few years back, was a picnic by comparison."

Although George had filled the table with assorted dishes, Tyler chose first to fill his glass.

"You should eat first," the man warned, eying the brandy bottle.

"Don't be such a mother hen. I'm fine." Tyler waved him away. "It's past eleven. Take yourself off to bed."

"What about the lady then?"

"Let me worry about her. After all, I've been doing it for days."

"Suit yourself." George hesitated a moment, then, shaking his head, he left his friend, glass still in hand.

Taking the brandy with him, Tyler flopped down in a chair by the fire. He stretched his long legs out in front of him and relaxed for the first time in days. The brandy warmed his insides but did nothing to dull the frantic racing of his brain. Every moment of the past few days played out in rapid succession. The London coach, the silly woman with the feather in her hat, the heat, the rain, the thunder, the swamp, and then there was those blue eyes. Those beautiful, unforgettable bright blue eyes. "Damn!" His fingers raked his hair. This wasn't like him at all. He had no room in his life for entanglements, especially none that included a spoiled rich girl and her doting father. Well, soon enough, she would be gone, and then, thank goodness, his life could return to normal. Happy with that thought, he did his best to settle down. But again, unbidden, her image came to mind. Angry with himself now, he attacked the brandy bottle with a casual disregard that was quite out of character. Gradually the intoxicating brew had the desired effect. His tongue thickened; his thought process slowed. As the brandy diminished, the room grew warmer. He struggled to loosen his shirt, rolling up the sleeves and tugging at the annoying buttons. At last, under stress, one by one, they popped from their moorings. Now the garment gaped open to the waist, leaving his bare chest exposed. He cared not. Through the fog that numbed his brain, he heard the hall clock strike twelve.

"Damn it all. Where is she?" he muttered, filling his glass yet again, unaware that his wait was almost over.

Another sound in the hall caught his attention.

"What the?" he demanded of the empty room.

Again, the sound. Closer this time. He struggled to his feet, blinking to clear his vision. The door to the hall creaked open on its hinges, and there she was.

Open-mouthed, he watched as she came toward him, the soles of her small bare feet squeaking on the highly polished surface of the floor. Wrapped around her, she wore a large robe of the deepest blue. Had she been a foot taller and some eighty pounds heavier, it might have fit perfectly. As it was, she had done her best to cope with its size, turning back the long sleeves and winding the wide sash two or three times around her tiny waist. Nothing could be done with the length of the garment, so as she walked, it trailed along on the ground behind her.

"What kept you?" he demanded.

"My dress. It was ruined. I had nothing to wear," she explained. "I found this." She indicated the robe. "I hope you don't mind."

He shrugged. "What's mine is yours," he muttered, moving closer. Now he towered over her, his dark face intent. "Besides," he continued, his fingers gently tracing the edge of the garment's blue collar, "I'm sure it never looked as well on me." His eyes met hers and lingered a long moment. "Well," he said at last, "now that you're here, Madam, dinner is sherved."

Madeline shivered. His speech was slightly slurred, and there was a strong smell of liquor on his breath. But with hunger worrying her insides, she allowed him to walk her to the table. He stumbled slightly but held out her chair.

"Thank you." Eager to eat, she maneuvered around him, took her seat, and waited for him to move. But instead, he lingered overlong behind her, his warm breath ruffling her hair. His presence was suffocating. She wished he would move. She sat stiff and still, her body tense. At last, his weight eased. Moving to the far side of the table, he landed with a thud in the chair opposite her.

For the first time, Madeline noticed that he was now clean-shaven. With the removal of the heavy beard, she found him even more ruggedly handsome than before. The black shirt she had grown accustomed to had been replaced by one of white linen. Although it was neatly pressed, it hung open to the waist and apparently was missing all of its buttons. He seemed unconcerned by his state of undress, but the mat of dark hair covering his broad chest brought a rush of color to Madeline's cheeks. Flustered, she lowered her eyes, centering her attention instead on the assortment of food set out before her.

"Eat!" he urged.

Cutlery flew as, needing no more prompting, she sampled each of the tasty treats one by one. Her only attempt at conversation was to offer him a large platter of cold meat. Quickly brushing it aside, he chose instead to refill his glass. An hour passed with only the clatter of silverware to break the silence. The fire in the hearth had long since dwindled to ashes. Nothing was left to brighten the room but the single candle burning low on the table between them. Madeline ate on, blissfully unaware that her companion watched her every move. The candle's flickering light captured the radiance of her face, framing it like a delicate cameo set against a backdrop of black velvet. Her flawless skin, still flushed from the warmth of her bath, glowed like a dew-drenched rose in springtime. Trailing down over her shoulders, her still-wet hair had turned the color of molten gold. Wispy curls dangled free about her ears, and errant strands fell in clusters to frame her small face. Her eyes, made even bluer by the heavy robe, sparkled like gems from beneath dark lashes, and Tyler watched, transfixed. But it was not just her beauty that held his attention. There was a spot in the center of the oversized robe, a spot where the two fronts met. Just inches below the base of her slim white throat, the garment had begun to drift apart. Slowly at first, little by little, with each movement she made, it slipped the smallest bit further. Soft curves appeared. Lower still, creamy white breasts thrust forth. His heart beat faster. Licking parched lips, he tossed down more brandy, unable to drag his eyes from the provocative display. His hand trembled, spilling large drops of amber onto the snow-white tablecloth. For a moment, he was befuddled. What the hell was he doing? Quickly pulling a handkerchief from his pocket, he made a valiant but futile effort to minimize the spreading damage. It occurred to him that, as usual, George had been right. Brandy was a bad idea, especially on an empty stomach. He knew his own limit, but tonight, for only the second time in his life, he had exceeded it. The first time was after the untimely death of his brother-in-law by a bullet. How do you explain to your sister that you held her husband in your arms and watched him die? But this time, apart from frustration, he had no excuse. Disgusted, he tossed the soiled handkerchief away, grabbed the brandy decanter, replaced its glass stopper, and set it aside with a thud.

Mystified by his angry movements, Madeline watched him through half-closed eyes. With her hunger satisfied, sleep became her sole desire. All she wanted now was a place to lie down. He said nothing, so she waited, her eyes growing heavy. With her elbows resting on the table, she propped her head in her hands. She tried unsuccessfully to stifle a yawn, but her eyes drifted shut, and the room slowly faded around her.

Tyler took a deep breath and leaned back in his chair. He had had enough. He wanted this thing over. The girl was back, as he had promised. He had done what was asked of him. He had stopped her runaway marriage and dragged her halfway across the country. Now he wanted her gone. Tomorrow his grandfather would take her back to where she belonged, and she'd be out of his life forever. That should make him happy, shouldn't it? But for some reason that he couldn't fathom, it just made him angry. He shot her a frustrated look and realized, for the first time, that she had fallen asleep. As he watched, her breathing deepened. Long lashes fluttered softly against her cheeks, and from time to time, her breath escaped in a gentle sigh. How did she do it? She had caused so much trouble, yet, relaxed in sleep, she looked the picture of innocence.

Exhausted and still feeling the effects of the brandy, he struggled to his feet, knocking over his chair in the process. Leaning heavily on the table, he made his way to her side.

"Got to get you to bed," he muttered as if she could hear him.

With an effort, he bent and gathered her up into his arms. She hardly stirred, but he breathed in a delicate whiff of lavender as her hair spilled down over his arm. Her head tumbled back against his chest, and the unruly robe slipped open, baring her neck and shoulders to his view. With an effort, he dragged his eyes from the sight, the longing to taste her sweetness almost overpowering him. On unsteady feet, he made his way through the darkened hall and up the wide staircase. Using his shoulder, he pushed open the bedroom door, passed through it, and kicked it shut behind him.

Chapter Six

Tyler moved quietly around the darkened room. Outside, the summer storm had returned to fill the pre-dawn hours with a symphony of sound and motion. Lightning flooded the room, bathing objects in ghostly pools of flickering light. Hidden corners jumped into view, then faded just as quickly back into darkness. He glanced toward the bed and pulled a face at the girl still lying there.

"I wish to God I had never met you," he muttered resentfully.

In the first gray light of morning, her soft white shoulders were visible above the covers. Her back was bared down to her waist. Somehow, during the night, the blue robe had slipped off and now lay in a heap on the floor beside the bed. His pulse quickened as visions of the last evening flashed before his eyes. With a strangled curse, he grabbed up the infamous robe and flung it onto a nearby chair. He turned away, cursing again as he stubbed his bare toes on the leg of the bed. Muttering irritably to himself he limped stiff-legged across the cold floor, grabbed another robe from the closet, and pulled it on. He caught sight of himself in the mirror. God, what a mess. He ran his fingers through his tousled hair and winced in pain. Last night, the brandy had dulled his senses, but now it doubled the discomfort of his wound. He groaned. He needed help. If he could just make it to the kitchen, he knew he would find coffee brewing there. With one hand shielding his eyes, he groped his way to the door. A light tap stopped him in mid-stride, and before he could answer, George was in the room.

"For God's sake, George," he snapped irritably, "what the hell are you doing here so damned early?"

"Got up on the wrong side of the bed then, did we?" Unperturbed, the man made his way to the table. "After all that brandy last night, I thought you'd be in need of this." Pouring the strong black coffee, he held out a cup.

It was their usual morning routine, but today the rattle of the dishes grated harshly on Tyler's ears. George's swift movements seemed over-exaggerated.

"Have mercy, man," he pleaded. "Can't you see I'm in pain?" Putting his hands to his head, he groaned softly.

"Drink the coffee," George instructed, then waited as the cup was emptied.

"Feel better now, do we?" he asked.

"No, we do not!" Was the disgruntled reply.

"Well, just wait a minute, and you will."

In all the years they had been together, George had seldom seen his friend drink to excess. Not that they hadn't had their moments when they were younger. They had first met when Tyler arrived at Marshfield Hall to enroll in school. At seventeen, he had had the reputation of being somewhat wild. George, who was three years older, had been given the task of keeping an eye on him. The young men soon found that they shared much in common, a love of good literature, a sharp eye for a fast horse, and a steady hand with both pistol and blade. They became close friends, and by the time Tyler's schooling was over and he was ready to return home to Boston, George had decided to join him. That had been some nine years ago, and George had never regretted his decision.

Now, as he moved to pick up the room, he caught sight of a slight movement in the bed. For the first time, he noticed the small blond head resting peacefully on the pillow.

"Well, what's been going on here then?" With raised brow, he looked Tyler in the eye.

"Shhh, don't wake her. Let's get out of here, and I'll tell all."

Closing the door quietly behind them, they made their way along the hall. It was early, but soon the staff would stir, and the house would become a hive of activity. For now, though, the men were glad of the time alone. George brewed fresh coffee and, making themselves comfortable, they sat by the warmth of the large kitchen stove. Neither man spoke for a while but then, without looking at his companion, Tyler began.

"Believe me, George, nothing happened with the girl last night. I did have far too much brandy and ended up putting her in the wrong bed. But I passed out in the dressing room, fully clothed, I might add, minus only my boots. I woke this morning, cramped and frozen, just minutes before you found me."

George shook his head. "Well, I won't say I told you so," he said at last, "but I did." He was silent for a moment, then finally asked, "So what did happen while you were away?"

Slowly at first, Tyler went on to describe his journey. In vivid detail, he told of his portrayal of a highwayman, of his brush with death beneath a tree, and of the girl's narrow escape from the swamp. "Now you know it all, George," he finished at last, "except to say that by the time we arrived here last night, I don't think she could have gone any further."

George exhaled, expressing his thoughts in a long hissing whistle.

"Exactly," Tyler muttered.

"Well, what do we do now?" George wanted to know.

"Better send for the old man, and while you're at it, someone should fetch her father too. The sooner we get this over with, the better."

It was no more than an hour later when Tyler climbed from the tub in his dressing room, refreshed and relaxed. He stood in front of the mirror and whistled as he tucked the white shirt into his black britches. He pulled on his boots, fastened his gray Marseille waistcoat, and slipped his arms into the sleeves of his new blue morning coat. The coat was the latest style, and the fit was perfection. He liked good clothes, and his Boston tailor was the very best. He took another moment to study his reflection with a critical eye. Then, with a grunt of satisfaction, he turned and made his way out into the hall. As he passed his bedroom, he quietly opened the door and looked inside. Except for the soft sound of gentle breathing coming from the bed, all remained quiet. The girl still slept peacefully. Satisfied that all was well, he carefully closed the door behind him.

By now, the rest of the household was on the move. He could hear the hustle and bustle of the servants as they scurried to perform their usual morning duties. At this time of day, the house was a hive of activity. Curtains were thrown open to let in the light, floors were swept, and furniture dusted. Loud sounds and inviting smells issued forth from the kitchen, and it occurred to Tyler that if he hurried, he would have just enough time to eat before the arrival of his grandfather.

A short time later, his meal finished, he added hot coffee to his cup and carried it into the study. Here he would await the arrival of the family's senior member. He liked this room; it was his favorite retreat. With its mellow oak paneled walls, high ornate ceiling, and thick oriental rugs, it was elegant and comfortable. Long shelves lined one wall, each filled with an assortment of gold-lettered, leather-bound volumes. The musty smell of their aging yellowed pages mixed pleasantly with the aroma of beeswax polish. Windows lined another wall, each one recessed with a cushioned seat that looked out over the vast flower gardens beyond. All was quiet. The stormy weather of the previous day had passed. This morning the windows had been left open to the elements, and a slight breeze fluttered the long linen curtains.

Tyler seated himself behind the large mahogany desk, and as he sifted through the pile of correspondence, his eyes were drawn to a letter written in a bold, vaguely familiar hand. Upon slitting open the envelope, he was surprised to find a letter from an old acquaintance. It was someone he hadn't seen since his school days at Oxford. He had no idea that anyone knew of his arrival in England, especially the beautiful Amanda. He waved the note beneath his nose and breathed in the sweet smell of Jasmine. He remembered the fragrance now as being so much a part of her. Surprisingly, her face flashed before him. Good Lord, had it really been close to ten years since he had last seen her? He wondered now about the others. There had been so many of them back then. All young and wild, with more money than sense, they had left their mark from one end of England to the other. From the gaming halls of London to the many racetracks, they were always greeted with open arms. Although not much of a gambler himself, Tyler wasn't adverse to a hand or two at the tables or an occasional flutter on a filly. But his luck was such that he seldom came away a loser. He tried to put names and faces together. Well, it might be interesting to see some of them again. But as hard as he tried, only one face came to mind. Amanda. He smiled. Well, now, this visit could turn out to be quite interesting. The sound of carriage wheels on the gravel driveway jolted him back to the present. His grandfather was here. He dropped Amanda's letter back onto the desk and banished the ghost of the past from his mind. Now his thoughts returned once more to the girl upstairs.

Coming to his feet, he straightened his cuffs and brushed some imaginary lint from his immaculate blue jacket. He was deeply fond of his grandfather, but he really wasn't looking forward to this meeting. With a grimace, he swallowed the cold remains in his coffee cup, took a deep breath, and made his way toward the front door.

Chapter Seven

A grin tweaked Tyler's lips as he watched the elegant carriage, pulled by a splendid pair of black horses, make its way up the long drive. He felt a sudden rush of pride at the sight. There wasn't another man in England, he thought, with a better appreciation for a fine-looking animal than the earl of Marshfield. With a crunch of gravel, the vehicle came to a stop in front of him, and the door flew open.

"Damn!" He cursed under his breath as he spotted the lanky form of his younger brother, Ian, and realized that his grandfather hadn't come alone. At nineteen, Ian, like his older brothers before him, was in England finishing his education. For Tyler, the unexpected appearance of his sibling this morning was too much. Explaining the happenings of the past few days to the old man was bad enough, but he'd be damned if he would do it in front of his kid brother.

"Good morning, Sir," he greeted his grandfather with an out-stretched hand. As he ushered the old man toward the study, he made a vain attempt to shoulder Ian aside, but the young man caught onto the ploy. With a devilish grin on his face, he sidestepped to avoid the block. He gained entrance into the room but grunted as he took a sharp jab in the ribs from Tyler's elbow.

"Out of the way, Sprout," Tyler snapped, using a nickname he knew his brother hated. Ignoring Ian's offended look, he urged William to make himself comfortable while he rang for tea. "You're looking well, Sir," he added as the old man sat himself down.

In truth, the passing years had done little to diminish William's good looks. Rather, they had enhanced them. Still tall and straight, he boasted a trim figure. His tanned face, though deeply lined, still appeared sharp and determined. His full head of hair had long since turned white but, in doing so, had intensified the deep green of his eyes. Like his grandsons, he had a good eye for style and was always dressed in the latest fashions. Today he looked dashing in a coat of forest green, a rust waistcoat, a white linen shirt, and fitted tan britches tucked into high topped black boots. Light gleamed brightly from the chain of his gold pocket watch as it hung across his still-trim middle. Gnarled fingers fidgeted with his cane. A gold lion's head with emerald eyes topped an ebony cane, a long-ago gift from his late wife, Sophie. He went nowhere without it.

Tyler sensed the old man's growing impatience. He was grateful when, at last, the maid arrived with tea. As he expected, William waited long enough for the maid to leave the room and then came straight to the point.

"Well, where's the girl?" he demanded, "I thought to have her safely back in her father's arms by now."

"Things didn't go quite as well as planned, Sir," Tyler explained. "We made no allowance for the weather, and that greatly slowed our return journey. But the young lady is here now and none the worse for the ordeal." By not going into a more detailed description of the perils they had encountered on the road or of his own indiscretion of the night before, Tyler hoped to ease his grandfather's mind.

"But where is she?" William insisted, color flushing his cheeks. "She is the daughter of my best friend, and I want to see her for myself." Breathing heavily, he slumped back into his chair.

"Calm yourself, Sir." Quickly pouring a brandy, Tyler handed William the glass. "Drink this," he ordered and waited till the glass was empty. "That's better." He relaxed a little as color slowly faded from the older man's face. "At your age, Sir, you should take more care of—"

"At my age!" William interrupted loudly, white whiskers fairly bristling with indignation. "What do you mean 'at my age'?" He pounded the floor with his cane. "As big as you are, I can still knock you down, and don't you forget it."

"I have no doubt, Sir." Tyler smiled when eyes as green as his own flashed from beneath shaggy brows.

"Don't patronize me, you young scallywag."

"That's not my intention, Sir." Tyler shot an exasperated look at his brother.

That young man, having found a chair, sat tipped back against the wall, arms folded across his chest. Being one of the younger members of a family of ten, Ian had long since learned the advantages of remaining silent. However, he was mildly surprised by what had taken place here. He had a feeling there was much more to the story than Tyler was telling. What it was, he could only guess at now, but he couldn't wait to get his brother alone to worm the truth out of him. But this, he decided, wasn't the time to get involved. Besides, he quite enjoyed watching his older brother squirm a little. He knew he would pay for it later, but for now, it was well worth it.

It took a moment, but at last William had calmed a little.

"So, she is here, and all is well." He sighed with relief, and leaning back in his chair, he took another sip of brandy. It warmed and relaxed him. After a while, he asked, "What do you intend to do now?"

"I have already sent a message to her father," Tyler informed him. "When he arrives, I will place the young lady safely back in his care. And I hope in the future, he will be able to curb her wandering ways."

"In that case," William said, holding out his glass, "pour me some more of that excellent brandy, my boy. Knowing Sir Guy as I do, I have a feeling I'm going to need it."

Tyler refilled the old man's glass, then, moving to the window, stared out into the bright morning sun. After the long spell of dry weather, the heavy rain of the last few days had turned the lawn into a carpet of vivid green. Flower beds had sprung to life in a profusion of brilliant color, so typical of an English spring. The scent of lilacs hung heavy in the air and drifted in through the open windows. Tyler took a deep breath and wondered what this day would bring. His thoughts strayed to the girl still sleeping in his bed, and it angered him. What was it about her that plagued him so? There had been no shortage of women in his life, most of them much more worldly and better suited to him than the little Miss he had just found. For one thing, she was way too young, at least eight or nine years his junior, and she irritated him. Yes, that was right; she irritated him. At eight and twenty years of age, he remained unmarried by choice, and he had every intention of staying that way. The world was in a mess, wars were being fought everywhere, and men were always being called away to fight and die. As a privateer running the British blockade in 1814, he had seen many a good man die. One of those was his sister Clara's husband, Henry. He had held the man in his arms and seen him draw his last breath. He knew firsthand the devastation it had caused. Left with three small children, Clara had returned home to be with the family. For the sake of the children, she hid her grief well, but in unguarded moments, he had witnessed her immense sadness. He had decided then and there that he would never put any woman through that. Well, soon, the present situation would be resolved. With the arrival of Sir Guy, the girl would be gone. She would be on her way out of his life, and that would be an end to it.

On the other side of the room, William sat and sipped his drink in silence. He watched his grandson's face and wondered what thoughts lurked behind those dark green eyes. He was sure there was more to the story of the girl than Tyler was admitting. But he knew it was best not to broach the subject now. Young people today didn't take too kindly to what they considered interference from their elders, especially when it came to matters of a personal nature. But what if something had developed between the two of them? Well, that wouldn't be so bad. It was time for this young man to settle down, and who better than Guy's daughter? After all, she wasn't a bad-looking girl. True, she wasn't too bright, but her bloodlines were good, and people had wed with less reason. Well, time would tell, but to William's way of thinking, the boy could do a lot worse.

What would his Sophie have made of it all? She had always been so much better than him at handling things. But it was different in their day. When you were twenty, you met a girl like his Sophie. You fell in love, and that was it. But where would you find another Sophie? He doubted you could. Even after all this time, not a day went by that he didn't miss her. Tears dimmed his eyes, and clutching his glass in his fist, he drained it quickly. The bite of the liquor burned his throat, and his hand shook. Damn it, he was a fool, and worse than that, he was an old fool. He was sure, knowing Tyler as he did, that nothing but the strongest love would entice him into marriage.

"Grandfather," Ian interrupted his thoughts, "I believe Sir Guy has arrived."

Loud voices sounded in the hall, and moments later, George admitted Sir Guy.

At little more than five feet six inches tall, Sir Guy was a rather insignificant-looking fellow. His frame was slender, almost to the point of emaciation. His thin white hair had receded from his forehead, leaving the top of his head quite bare and rather shiny. He sported a very large mustache, whose tightly twisted ends reached down to his chin. One might suppose that its purpose was to make up for the lack of growth on top. But it hadn't whitened like the rest of his hair. Rather it had remained a dingy shade of brown and looked quite out of place.

Today, however, it would have been hard to ignore him. His usually sallow face was flushed, and his watery eyes bulged. His breathing was heavy, and the mustache on his upper lip quivered.

Rather disconcerted, William pulled himself to his feet and, leaning on his cane, went to meet his old friend.

"Come in, dear fellow," he said, offering his hand. "We've been waiting for you."

Ignoring the offered hand, Sir Guy began to pace the room in an agitated manner.

"Calm yourself, Sir," William tried again. "Your girl is here, safe and sound, just as we planned. Sit down and have a glass of this excellent brandy." He beckoned for Tyler to hurry as Sir Guy seemed on the verge of collapse.

"No, no, please, you don't understand," the small man squeaked.

Suddenly, quite concerned, Tyler crossed the room in rapid strides. He grasped Sir Guy by the shoulders and propelled him into the nearest chair.

"Drink this," he urged, forcing a glass into the man's trembling fingers. "There's no need for alarm, Sir. My grandfather speaks the truth. At this moment, your daughter sleeps soundly upstairs."

But if he expected his words to give comfort, he was sadly mistaken. In fact, they seemed to have just the opposite effect.

"Listen, why don't you listen?" Sir Guy jumped to his feet, spilling drops of brandy from his glass. The room fell silent. At last, having captured their attention, he took a deep breath and faced Tyler. "I received your message this morning, young man, and came with all haste. I find it hard to tell you this, but the girl you have here isn't my daughter."

The front legs of Ian's chair hit the floor with a bang. Tyler remained rooted to the spot.

George stared open-mouthed, and William dropped his cane.

"What the devil are you saying, Sir?" William grabbed his friend by the arm.

"Of course it's your girl. My grandson took her from the coach as you requested. George, go fetch the girl at once."

As George made to leave, Sir Guy detained him.

"That's not necessary, George." He turned to Tyler once more. "I'm sorry, young man, but I can only repeat. The girl you have here isn't my daughter. You see, I just left her. She and her betrothed returned last night to beg my forgiveness. They will be married within the month." Desperate, he moved to William's side. "What could I do? She's my only child." He tugged at the end of his mustache, twirling it between nervous fingers. "For God's sake, say something, Marshfield."

He received no answer.

It was Ian who took charge now. He ushered Sir Guy to the door and called for his carriage. "Have no fear, Sir," he reassured him. "We do understand."

With one last agonized look over his shoulder, Sir Guy rushed from the room. Moments later, the rattle of gravel could be heard as his carriage made a hasty retreat down the driveway.

"She's not my daughter . . . not my daughter . . ." The words echoed in Tyler's head. He broke into a cold sweat. How could that be? A small blond girl, they had said. On the London coach. Well, she was there, just as they said. How could he have known it was the wrong girl? He could feel the noose tighten around his neck.

"Strewth!" George exclaimed, shaking his head as he quickly passed around the brandy. "I think we all need this now," he muttered, draining his glass.

"That's an understatement, my friend," Tyler agreed. "And to think that just this morning I thought the biggest problem I would be dealing with was her father."

"What's to be done?" William asked, looking stunned.

Taking a deep breath, Tyler pulled himself together. "Don't worry yourself, Sir, it's my problem. I will take care of it."

"Brave words, Brother," Ian said. "The only problem here is if she isn't Sir Guy's daughter, then who the hell is she?"

Chapter Eight

S ounds of loud voices and the banging of doors echoed up through the old house. Madeline grunted and rolled over, unwilling to lose the misty threads of sleep that bound her. The bed was soft and warm, and she snuggled deeper under the covers. But the sounds persisted, coming and going, heard yet unheard, strange and unfamiliar. A coldness clutched her heart. Something was wrong, very wrong. Her eyes blinked open, and suddenly all thoughts of sleep were gone.

Wide-eyed, she looked around her. There was nothing familiar here. No small window or stark white walls. No shuffling feet out in the hall or the clanging bell calling her to morning prayer. Not even the lumpy feel of her own narrow cot beneath her to give her comfort. Forcing herself to sit, she groaned. Sore muscles cramped—a painful reminder of time spent in the saddle.

"Oh Lord," she whispered, memory swiftly returning.

This was his house, but this wasn't the room she remembered. That room had yellow walls; this one had green. The fireplace was different here too, and instead of spaniels, the painting hanging above it was of a hunting scene. She gasped as she suddenly realized that this must be his room, his bed. The evidence of his presence was all around her. A half-empty brandy glass stood on the mantle. His white shirt lay in a crumpled heap upon a hamper. Black boots sat by the doorway, and a blue robe was draped over a nearby chair. Memory stirred again. Blue robe. She gasped, suddenly aware of her own nakedness. She grabbed the covers, and pulling them up to her chin, found herself surrounded by the fragrance of his cologne. Her heart beat quickened. What had happened? How did she get here? The last thing she remembered was the evening meal. Beyond that, everything went blank. Her thoughts ran in a thousand directions, all centering around the man who had brought her here. Had he really been sent to bring her back as he claimed? It seemed unlikely. No one knew of her plans to leave, not even her best friend, Mary, and they had shared everything.

Mary had cried when she told her of her mother's sudden death and how her life had changed that day. How the father she loved so deeply shut himself away from the world. How, when she was only five, he had sent her away. Sent her far away to live out her days behind the high gray walls of the convent. What would have happened when the nuns found out she was missing? Would they have questioned Mary? If so, would she remember the vow Madeline had made on that day so long ago? "As soon as I am able, Mary," she had told her friend, "I will leave this place and find my father. I will go to him and ask him why. Why, when I loved him so much did, he just cast me aside."

All at once, she realized it really didn't matter why she had been brought here because whatever happened, she would never stop looking for her father. If they returned her to the convent, she would just run away again and again. Nothing would stop her until she was able to look into her father's eyes and ask him why. Why did he suddenly stop loving her? What had she done to deserve it? Did he somehow blame her for her mother's death? These questions had tormented her for years. How many long, lonely nights had she lain awake crying in the dark? So many that she had lost count. Even now, just thinking of it brought tears of sadness to her eyes. A sudden sound distracted her, and she quickly brushed the dampness from her cheeks. Somewhere in the house, a door had slammed. There were voices too, loud and agitated, and the sound of hurrying footsteps. She rolled from the bed and followed the sounds to the window. Clad in nothing but a blanket, she watched as a small balding man hurried down the front steps. With one quick look back at the house, he climbed into a waiting carriage and raced away.

"Morning, Miss."

Madeline jumped. Spinning around, she was surprised to come face to face with a dark-haired young woman.

"Sorry, Miss," the girl apologized, bobbing a curtsy. "Didn't mean to give you a start. I'm Jeannie, your maid."

Dressed neatly in black with a stiff white apron tied around her waist, she was a picture of efficiency. Her thick dark hair was pulled back into a neat bun, and a frilly white lace cap perched jauntily on top of her head.

A maid! She had a maid. Madeline was incredulous. She stared open-mouthed at the pretty girl and suddenly became painfully aware of her own disheveled appearance. She clutched the blanket to her body with one hand while trying unsuccessfully to straighten her hair with the other. But Jeannie appeared not to notice her discomfort. Setting down the tray she carried, she poured the morning tea.

"Come on then, Miss," she said, pulling up a chair and patting the brocade seat. "Sit yourself down and have a nice hot cuppa while I see to your bath." So saying, the girl turned and left the room.

Hot tea and a morning bath. Madeline pinched herself to see if it was real.

Morning ablutions at the convent were a hurried affair, often taken in a small basin with cold water. Tea was only taken after the long morning prayers. Then, while the older nuns sat at rough wooden tables, she served them tea from a large metal pot. Only when their needs were met was she, at last, permitted to serve herself. But there had been no golden honey or fresh lemon slices like those that graced her table this morning. She spooned honey into her cup, and feeling almost guilty, she licked the spoon clean and sighed. She was still relishing the sweet taste moments later when Jeannie returned, her arms piled high with clothes.

"Sorry it took so long, Miss." She laid the items carefully on the bed. "Hope you're happy with them. They were a right old mess, but I did the best I could." As she spoke, she continued straightening and smoothing out imagined wrinkles. Madeline watched in awe. "How did you do it?" she asked, realizing this was her brown dress, her under things, and all the garments she had thought ruined and beyond repair.

"Well, it weren't easy Miss," the girl confessed. "Looked like you rolled around in the mud. Oh Lordy," she groaned, shoulders sagging, "there I go again. Beg pardon, Miss, for speaking out of turn." She giggled nervously. "Me Mum says I never know when to keep me mouth shut."

Reaching out shyly, Madeline touched her arm. "Please Jeannie, don't feel badly," she pleaded. "I did land in the mud, and I think you've done a wonderful job."

Jeannie's face glowed with pride. "Well," she said, standing back and admiring her own handiwork, "they do look pretty good, even if I do say so myself."

"Definitely," Madeline declared, and they laughed as if they had been best friends for years.

Suddenly, with all efficiency, Jeannie gathered the garments in her arms, then, directing Madeline to follow, she hurried away.

Not sure what to expect, Madeline waited, but when Jeannie called out that her bath was ready, she shivered with delight. The luxury of a hot bath two days in a row was downright sinful. But what would the maid think of her? Here she was in a strange man's bed chamber with not a stitch on under this wretched blanket. But when Jeannie called a second time, she just couldn't resist.

Once more, the copper tub awaited, but this time she found to her embarrassment that she wouldn't be alone. After helping her into the big tub, Jeannie went to work. With sleeves rolled up to her elbows, she wielded soap and cloth to best advantage. Before she knew it, Madeline was bathed and clothed in her clean brown dress. For the first time in days, thanks to Jeannie, she felt able to face the world.

"But I'm not done yet, Miss," Jeannie insisted. With a gentle shove, she sat Madeline down in front of a large mirror. She picked up a brush and comb and quickly went to work on the long fair hair. As her nimble fingers worked, Madeline questioned her about the house and the man who lived here.

"Well, I've only been here a few weeks myself," she explained, "just since Mister Tyler came to stay. Tyler Wentworth is his name. Cook says he came all the way from America with his man, George, to visit his grandfather. His grandfather's an earl. He owns most of the land in these parts."

"Does his grandfather live here too?"

"Oh no, Miss, he lives two or three miles from here at Marshfield Hall."

So the grandfather he spoke of was an earl. But that just served to confuse her more. What did they want of her? Again, she wondered why she was here. It was as if she had stumbled into the middle of a bad novel, the kind some of the girls managed to smuggle into the convent. A sinister man, a helpless woman, a plot that twists and turns. She shivered just thinking about it.

"What do you think, Miss?"

A hand shook her shoulder, and she jumped.

"What do you think?" Jeannie repeated.

For a moment, she just stared at the reflection before her. Vanity was frowned upon in the convent that had been her home. Just a small glass placed above the wash bowl, its surface scratched and distorted, was all she had to use. But her days had been busy, leaving very little time to worry about her appearance. So it was that she had grown from a child to a woman, never really noticing the changes taking place. Now as she gazed back into the blue eyes before her, a warm flush of pleasure stained her cheeks. She touched the soft skin of her face, marveling at its tawny suntanned hue. What would her father think of her now, she wondered. Would he find her pretty, perhaps regret letting her go? Why? Again, the question. Why had he sent her to live so far away, alone and forgotten?

"Don't you like it, Miss?" Once again, Jeannie captured her attention. This time, the disappointment in her voice was hard to miss. "Your 'air, Miss. Don't you like it?"

"Oh, I do, Jeannie. Indeed I do." Madeline turned her head slowly from side to side, trying to fully grasp her own transformation. Her hair, usually worn straight and pulled back into a bun, was now fashioned into a mass of golden ringlets. Swept up at her nape, they were entwined in a length of blue ribbon. Delicate curls encircled her face, and more hung softly at her ears. She gently fingered the wispy curls, marveling at the skill of the maid who had fashioned them. "I'm sure I never knew I could look so beautiful, Jeannie," she answered truthfully. "Where did you learn to do this?"

"I takes after me mum, Miss," the girl confessed. "Real clever she is with her 'ands. She was a lady's maid at one time, but when me dad deserted us, she had to give it up. Had to be at 'ome with me. I was still little, you see. Anyway, in the end, it worked out for the best. She took up sewing to make more money and become a seamstress. She's a real good one too."

"And what of you, Jeannie?" Madeline wanted to know. "Have you been a lady's maid for a long time?"

"Lordy, no, Miss. Right now, I just work in the kitchen. Cook says it's all I'm good for. But you should have seen her face this morning when Mrs. Carter told me to come up here."

"Mrs. Carter?" Madeline queried.

"Oh, she's the housekeeper up at Marshfield Hall," Jeannie explained. "Came rushing over this morning with this uniform, she did, telling me I was to 'elp you. Cook was fit be tied." Puffing out her cheeks, the girl did her best impersonation of the lady who ruled the kitchen. "'Don't get any 'igh faluting ideas in your 'ead, me girl,' she tells me. 'When they find out 'ow useless you are, they'll send you back down here with a flea in your ear.'"

Madeline laughed at the girl's antics but sensed the loneliness beneath the humor.

Although Jeannie didn't know it, they had a lot in common. Both lonely, both hard working, and both deserted by uncaring fathers.

"Listen to me run on," Jeannie apologized. "Me Mum was right. I talk too much, and by now, you must be starved." She took Madeline's hand and pulled her toward the door. "Oh, there's one more thing before I go." She grabbed a bottle from the table and added a dab of scent behind Madeline's ears. "Perfect," she whispered with a smile.

Deeply touched, Madeline gave the girl a hug. They stood a moment, one head fair and the other dark, rocking gently back and forth. Without either of them knowing it, a bond was formed that would last a lifetime.

At last, Jeannie moved away. "Get along with you now, Miss." She opened the door and urged Madeline through. "I 'ave to get back to the kitchen now, or Cook will have me 'ead." So saying, she bobbed a quick curtsey, and without another word, she hurried away.

Chapter Nine

Madeline suddenly found herself standing alone, looking down the long, empty hallway. She was instantly struck by a feeling of loss. It seemed that Jeannie's quick departure had drained all the joy from the morning. With that realization came the returning memories of the night just past and the man who had brought her here. She thought again of the things Jeannie had said. "His grandfather was an earl!" She had no knowledge of such people. What possible connection could he have with her? And what should she do now? She wished she knew.

All at once, her stomach complained loudly, and a growing need drove all else from her mind. She heard Jeannie's words from earlier on. "You must be starved," she had said. Well, she was, and it seemed as good a time as any to do something about it.

Slowly at first, she made her way down the stairs in shoes Jeannie had found in the back of a closet. How different everything looked today. Last night, the reception hall had seemed so dark and unwelcoming. But today, the sun shone down through the high glass ceiling, filling it with warmth and brightness. She could see now that the hall was circular and that gold and crystal lamps hung at intervals from the pale green wall. For incoming guests, red velvet chairs offered a place to sit and rest awhile. Or, for those so inclined, a discrete spot for a tête-à-tête. Giant ferns added a splash of green to the scene, cooling the air with an outdoor feel.

To her left, long windows framed the solid front door. Stretching halfway to the ceiling, they gave a clear view of the front drive. It was the doorway to freedom. Tempted to run, Madeline took a step toward it, then hesitated. No matter how badly she wanted to leave this place, she was sure being lost in the English countryside was no solution. Besides, without a penny in her pocket, where could she go? Common sense prevailed. If her years alone had taught her one thing, it was that she could survive. There must be a better way; somehow, she would find it, perhaps with Jeannie's help. Who could say, but at least for now, she felt better knowing Jeannie was there. With her mind more at ease, food again became a driving force. Turning her back firmly on the escape route, she set off again in search of breakfast. But where would she find it?

Last night they had eaten in the drawing room, that's what George had called it, so perhaps she should try there. But this morning, the room was empty. Neat and tidy with no remnants of the night before. No stained tablecloth, no empty dishes. But in a vivid flash, she saw it all again. The dark man across the table, chest bared, green eyes unreadable. She shivered, backed up, and shut the door with a bang.

Unsure, she moved on. Leaving the hall behind her, she passed into a wide gallery. Portraits as large as life lined its walls. Images of dashing young men in scarlet tunics and bejeweled ladies in gowns of silk and satin. She passed slowly before them, feeling rather like a general reviewing his troops. But as they stared down at her from their large gold frames, she knew they viewed her with disdain. So intent was she with her innermost thoughts that the door went unnoticed at first. Had it not been for the sound of muffled voices, she might just have passed it by.

She stopped now and moved closer. Who was inside? With her heart thumping, she pressed her cheek to the wooden panel. The voices, though louder, were still indistinct. Frustrated, she glanced up and down the hallway. She was alone. Without a second thought, she hiked up her skirt and went down on one knee. With her ear pressed to the keyhole, she could hear everything quite clearly.

The voice was unmistakable. "Have no fear, Sir," she heard him say. "It was I who brought her here. She is my responsibility. She'll remain here until I decide what is to be done with her."

Madeline gasped, hardly able to believe what she had heard. Was he speaking of her? He must be mad! In her agitation, she lost her balance. Quickly grasping the door handle, she steadied herself. All inside was silent now, and not wanting to miss a single word, she pressed her ear even closer. She thought she heard footsteps and a gentle "Shhhh." Then suddenly, the door opened. Caught completely off guard and with a surprised "Ohhh," Madeline tumbled headfirst into the room. With the wind momentarily knocked out of her, she lay flat on her stomach, gasping for air. Taking a deep breath, she raised her head and came eye to toe with a pair of shiny, black leather boots.

Upon being treated to a daring display of silk-clad legs, a soft voice taunted, "Well, Madam, a most appealing sight, I must admit, but nevertheless, not quite the way for a well-bred young lady to enter a room." With a condescending grin on his handsome face, he bent and offered her his hand.

Madeline eyed it scornfully, then, brushing it aside, struggled gamely to her feet. Red-faced with embarrassment, she straightened her dress with flustered hands.

"I tripped," she lied.

"Most assuredly," Tyler replied humorously.

Her chin came up, blue eyes challenging. Even at her full height, she came no further than his shoulder, but she confronted him, fists clenched at her sides. He made her feel like a fool, and she hated him for it. His green eyes narrowed, and for a moment she was sure he could read her thoughts.

In truth, all Tyler wanted was to take her hand, explain his mistake in bringing her here, and ask her forgiveness. But he saw no hope of forgiveness in those bright eyes, only anger. It jarred his already ragged nerves, and the words he had been about to say froze on his lips.

So instead of the apology he had planned to make, he snapped, "I see you've finally managed to rouse yourself from the bed."

Madeline flinched. "Believe me, Sir, your bed was the very last place I wanted to be."

"Forgive me, Madam." The muscle twitched at his jaw. "Perhaps you would have preferred the swamp!"

"At least the inhabitants there were honest in their intent. Can you say as much?"

He stepped closer, eyes gleaming wickedly. "Oh, how fast you forget." His voice was low. "If my memory serves me right, you begged to be pulled from that watery hell."

"Where your actions put me in the first place," she snapped back. "Had it not been for you, I would be safe in London by now, but instead—"

"Enough, I've heard enough!"

Suddenly Madeline remembered that they were not alone.

"It does no good to waste time on foolish recriminations," the voice said. "Better to deal with the problems you've created."

Madeline looked beyond her nemesis and saw the old man for the first time. He sat in a large leather chair on the far side of the room, and as he caught her eye, his face crinkled into a warm smile.

"We understand your distress, child," he continued, pulling himself forward on the seat. "This whole incident has been most unfortunate."

"I don't understand, Sir." Madeline moved quickly to his side.

"There will be time for explanations later," the old man said. "Right now, though, we must know who you are. Your family will be worried. We must tell them at once that we deeply regret what has happened and let them know you were brought here by mistake."

"Mistake!" Madeline still didn't understand, but it didn't matter. The cloud of mystery had been lifted. It was all a mistake. "My name is Madeline Carlyle, Sir," she hastened to tell him, "and there is no one searching for me. My father is my only family, and he believes me to be in a convent in France."

The men exchanged startled looks.

"Surely, child, you are not a nun?" William was dismayed.

"Oh no, Sir, I'm not a member of the order," she rushed on, unaware of their new concerns. "I taught English in the convent school. It was my home."

"Then what brings you to England?" Tyler asked. He wondered now why he had paid so little attention to her appearance. He should have realized from her mode of dress that she was no spoiled young miss. She wore no frills and fancies as one would expect of Sir Guy's daughter.

"I think that is my business, Sir." Madeline turned, her eyes steady. "All I want now is to continue my journey. I will travel on to London as I planned and will trouble you no more."

"Do you have family in London?" Tyler persisted.

"No."

"Then what awaits you there? You must know the city is no place for a woman alone."

Unsure, Madeline hesitated.

"You have to understand, child." It was the older man who spoke now. "We find ourselves in a very difficult position, and whether you like it or not, we need to know the truth."

When she didn't answer right away, Tyler grew impatient.

"Well?" he demanded, his voice harsh.

"Easy, lad." As the old man cautioned his grandson, he gave Madeline an encouraging nod.

She looked back at his kind, weathered face. Concern etched deep lines at his forehead, and eyes a familiar shade of green met hers in a troubled look. There was something about those eyes that touched her. She didn't know quite what it was, but she felt she could trust him. Perhaps he was right. London was a large city, and in truth, she had no idea where to begin her search.

She thought about it for a moment longer, then, at last, explained, "I came here to find my father."

"Well, child, now we have a place to start." He seemed relieved. "Why don't you tell us how you planned to find him."

"There is a solicitor," Madeline said. "I found his name in my records at the convent." Withholding only the details of how late one night she had broken into the little office at the convent, she explained what she had found.

"So, this solicitor, he sends money each year for your care?" Tyler's interest was roused. "And you have an address for him in London?"

"Yes."

"Then you must let us help you, child." The old man counseled her. "We have many connections in the city. It will be easy for them to obtain the information you seek."

Madeline hesitated, it sounded like good advice.

"A name," Tyler insisted. "We need a name."

"Edward Bailey. It's Edward Bailey," Madeline answered quickly before she had time to change her mind. There, it was done. For better or worse, it was done.

"Good girl." Satisfied, William patted her hand. "Well, child, you have displayed much courage, but nevertheless, your actions were fool-hardy. Now it's up to us to take care of things." He took a firm hold on his cane and rose stiffly to his feet. "There's much to be done, much to be done," he muttered and thumped his way out of the door.

For a few minutes, silence followed his departure.

Then Madeline asked, "What did he mean 'there's a lot to be done'?"

"If we are to help you, arrangements must be made."

"But what arrangements? I don't understand."

"You have no need to understand," Tyler replied. "Just do as you are told, and we will take care of everything."

"But what gives you the right?" Madeline faced him, fists clenched at her sides. She suddenly felt trapped and alone, and this wasn't what she wanted at all. "You speak as though I am to be given no choice in the matter," she persisted.

"That may be so." His voice softened a little. "But you must understand my position. Right or wrong, I brought you here—"

"By mistake," she interrupted. "You said so yourself."

"Yes, it was unfortunate, but it happened. Now we will have to make the best of it."

"We," Madeline snapped, her face reddening. "It seems to me that I am the one being asked to make the best of it."

Tyler stiffened. After all, he was as much of a victim here as she. More a victim, really, because now it was up to him to try to make things right.

"I can only repeat," he said, his voice harsh. "I regret the mistake that brought you here, but here you are, and here you will stay until I decide what is best to be done."

"Oh." Madeline gasped, angry tears filling her eyes. Upset with herself for showing weakness, she quickly brushed them away.

Tyler watched in silence, understanding her inner turmoil, his anger slowly ebbing. He handed her his handkerchief, and taking it none too graciously, she wiped away the tears.

"Just give me a little time," he said at last. "I'll leave for London in the morning, and by the time I return, I should have the information about your father that you hoped for. In the meantime, while I'm away, my grandfather will be happy to have you join him at Marshfield Hall." Without waiting for a response, he turned and left the room.

Madeline watched him go, suddenly cross with herself because of all the things she should have said. Who did he think he was anyway, ordering her around? What if she didn't want to go to Marshfield Hall?

He was a bully, and he had no right. She stamped her foot, muttering under her breath, "Oh, I hate him."

"Beg pardon, Miss, but breakfast is ready."

Startled, she spun around to find George waiting quietly by the door.

"Oh!" Pent-up air escaped her lungs in a rush. Like a hot air balloon that had just been popped, she felt deflated. Red-faced, she stared at the man as her anger slowly faded. "Thank you," she managed at last, stuttering as she tried to cover up her embarrassment.

George nodded. "It really wasn't his fault, you know," he said. Then as if nothing untoward had happened he beckoned her through.

Chapter Ten

At George's urging, Madeline followed him to the breakfast room. Here for the first time, she forgot about everything except the need for food. Wide-eyed, she made her way to the long buffet, where a multitude of covered dishes was set out before her. One by one, she lifted their silver lids, sniffing rapturously at the steam rising from each. Eager for the tasting and hardly able to wait, she gently spooned some of the content onto her plate and hurried to the chair George had pulled out for her.

The man smiled as he watched her attack the food. Without knowing anything about her, he found himself liking this young girl. He waited quietly for a while, then, sure that she had all that she needed, he excused himself and left the room.

Alone at last, Madeline focused her whole attention on the many new culinary delights awaiting her. A bite of fish, a taste of mutton, a delightful mix of eggs and cheese, and most surprising of all, white bread, unheard of in the convent. Not wanting to miss a single treat, she ate her fill, then, feeling rather uncomfortable, she leaned back in her chair and breathed a deep sigh. The thought struck her that sometimes being too full was as bad as being too empty. But now, with the need for food no longer uppermost in her thoughts, she returned her attention to the man who had brought her here. She had to admit he seemed genuine in his desire to help her. She had no reason to believe otherwise. After all, if his tale of mistaking her for someone else were false, why would his grandfather agree to it? She became so occupied with her thoughts that, at first, she failed to notice when someone else entered the room.

"Mind if I join you?" a pleasant voice asked, and without waiting for an answer, the owner of the voice came bustling in. About her age, he was tall and slender, fair of hair and handsome of face. "So you are the object of all this morning's carryings-on." He teased her as he poured coffee at the buffet. "Seems to me you are far too small to cause such a fuss." He grinned, pulled out a chair, and sat down opposite her. His brown eyes sparked with interest. "Allow me to introduce myself, Madam. I am Ian Wentworth, the handsomest and by far the bravest of all the Wentworth brothers."

Detecting his humor, Madeline smiled shyly. "I'm Madeline Carlyle, Sir, and alas, I have no way to prove or disprove your claim."

"You may believe the truth of it, dear lady, and as proof, I place myself at your service. No task too large or small." He leaned toward her in a conspiring manner. "Damsels in distress are my specialty. I have even been known to slay a few dragons in my time." He picked up a fork as he spoke, and stabbing wildly at the air, he pretended to avoid some imaginary foe.

Madeline laughed at his antics and quickly joined in the fun. "I would consider your words wisely, Sir Knight," she cautioned with a straight face. "Your services could be called upon much sooner than you think."

"Do tell, my dear." He leaned his head closer and took her hand in his. "I am anxious to know what horned beast doth plague your life that I may call it to account."

"This dragon breathes fire, my Lord, and I am in mortal fear for your life."

"I know the one you speak of well," he said, looking deep into her eyes, "and I think perhaps advancing years have dimmed the fire, and now he spouts nothing more than hot air."

"A touching scene." The voice dripped sarcasm. "My brother plays the jester, and the girl acts his fool."

Startled, Madeline freed her hand from her companion's with a jerk, upsetting her chair and dumping her in an unceremonious fashion onto the floor.

"Tut, tut." Tyler shook his head. "Just what is this penchant you have for the floor, my dear?" He walked to her side and looked down into her flustered face. "You seem to be constantly at my feet. As for you, young sprout," he said, turning his attention on his brother, "if you think age has dulled this dragon, you had best think again. Time only serves to sharpen the wits and make one more cunning, so I beg you, be warned!" He picked up the overturned chair and set it back in its place. "Now, Madam, if you can bear to drag yourself away from all of this frivolity," he said, pulling her to her feet, "we have much to do."

Madeline caught the younger man's wink of encouragement as she found herself whisked away. Moments later, as they passed William in the hall, she heard his words.

"All is well, child. We have taken care of everything."

"But Sir, I—" once again, Madeline tried to protest.

"Now, now, young lady," he interrupted, "it's all been arranged. You will come with me to Marshfield Hall. Mrs. Carter has been alerted, so let's hear no more about it." His last words drifted back over his shoulder as he disappeared down the hall.

Caught up in the whirlwind of activity, Madeline turned to Tyler, a confused look on her face.

"You want to find your father, right?" A questioning frown crossed his forehead.

"Yes, but—"

"Then so be it. As my grandfather said, it's all been arranged. I suggest now that you return to your room and prepare for your journey." With a stiff bow, he abruptly ended the conversation.

Madeline was left standing alone. Moments later, feeling very much in a huff, she pushed open the bedroom door. A jubilant Jeannie met her on the other side and almost knocked her off her feet.

"Guess what, Miss," the girl blurted out, "the master is sending me away with you. Won't that be fun?"

Madeline threw herself down on the bed, a sullen look on her face.

"I don't know about fun, Jeannie but it will be nice to have you for company."

"Don't you want to go Miss?" Jeannie's disappointment showed.

"To tell the truth Jeannie, I'm so confused right now I don't know what I want. But all I keep hearing is that it's all been arranged, and those men don't listen to anyone."

"Oh well, Miss, look on the bright side, at least there's not much to pack."

Jeannie was right. Clothes had been the least of her worries when she had planned her escape from the convent. All she had taken with her was a small bag, and it had been left aboard the coach going to London. She had carried a few coins with her, money she had saved from running errands for local vendors. Some she used to bribe her way onto a small boat headed for England, and the rest had paid her coach fare to London.

"You are right, Jeannie," she admitted. "What few things I did have are lost somewhere in London by now, I'm afraid."

"Oh, I did it again, didn't I?" Jeannie sighed. "Put me foot in it, I mean. Sorry, Miss."

"No, what you say is true, Jeannie."

Madeline took her hand and pulled her down on the bed beside her. They spoke of the upcoming trip with the earl. Despite her earlier misgivings about it, Madeline soon caught some of Jeannie's enthusiasm. So engrossed were they in their conversation that at first they didn't hear the noise out in the hall. But the sounds grew louder, and they exchanged puzzled looks. The shrill voice of a woman and the heavy tread of running feet came closer. With no more than a quick knock, the door was thrown open to admit a small flame-haired woman. Two weary-looking girls, their arms piled high with boxes, followed closely on her heels.

Madeline and Jeannie watched in awe as the fiery little woman took charge of the room. She issued orders left and right as the two harassed girls hurried to do her bidding.

"Well, now we can begin," she said in a broad Scots brogue. Mistaking Madeline's plain clothing, she addressed her in an overbearing tone. "Don't just stand there like a ninny girl. Run along and get your mistress."

Madeline stared wide-eyed, the woman's meaning quite unclear.

"Are you deaf, girl?" The woman's voice grew louder. "Your master wants his lady outfitted as soon as possible, so hop to it."

Jeannie stepped forward to explain, suddenly understanding the dressmaker's mistake.

"No, not you." The woman shook her head. "I need you to help my girls," she said, pointing at Madeline. "You, yes you, run along now before I box your ears."

"You mistake the situation, Madam," a cool masculine voice broke in behind her. Tyler moved to Madeline's side, and placing a hand beneath her elbow, he urged her forward.

The little dressmaker realized her error and hurried to make amends.

"My, what a beautiful creature she is, to be sure." Her effusive praise was such that her two young assistants snickered behind her back. "It will be a pleasure to work with the likes of her."

To Madeline's intense discomfort, the woman walked around her, looking her up and down, taking in the small waist and maturing bosom. Summoned at such short notice, the woman was pleased that she had brought only the latest of fashions with her. Always anxious for new clients, she had been pleasantly surprised at the sight of such a large estate. She knew wealth when she saw it and knew that if her garments were satisfactory, there would be more orders to come.

"Of course, Sir, you understand the selection is limited, but," she rushed to explain, "if I had a few more days—"

"The lady travels today," Tyler interrupted. "If you are unable to provide the services I seek—"

"Oh no, Sir." She hastened to reassure him. "Allow me to show you what is available." She clapped her hands at her two assistants. "Quickly, girls, show the gentleman what we have."

The boxes were swiftly thrown open, spilling their contents in a profusion of colors and fabrics. One by one, the dresses were displayed, and at Tyler's nod, first one and then another were placed in a growing pile upon the bed.

"Ah, the gentleman has exquisite taste," the woman gushed as only the finest of garments were selected.

There was a fashionable York morning dress in a becoming shade of blue, its high neckline and long sleeves adorned in a profusion of rich lace. There was a Russian wrapper in pale yellow and another in crimson trimmed with swans down, an evening gown of lavender crepe, and another of pink muslin. Next came a brown pelisse, fur-trimmed with a cambric lining, that fastened in the front with silk Brandenburgs. A riding habit in bright green was added to the collection, its front and cuffs ornamented with black braid, a la militaire. There was a small black beaver riding hat with a long green ostrich feather and a Pomona hat of blue satin. For her feet, there were walking shoes of nankeen, white satin slippers, and black half boots fringed with green.

Jeannie ooohed and ahhhed at each new acquisition to the ever-growing pile. But hot color flooded Madeline's cheeks. She wanted to run from the room and hide. How could he embarrass her so? She watched him silently from the corner of her eye. His dark face was relaxed and completely unconcerned.

At last, all the boxes stood empty. The little dressmaker and her helpers looked worn and exhausted. Still, the canny Scotswoman was well pleased; the day had turned out much better than she could ever have hoped.

"You may stay here for the fitting," Tyler told the woman. "Things that need no alteration will be packed for the journey. The rest I shall expect delivered by the end of the week."

His words invited no argument, and the woman was wise enough to stay silent. With mental agility acquired from years of practice, she tallied up the amount of her sale. So the girls would have to work through the night to complete everything. That mattered little. She would make sure all was ready in time.

Madeline felt completely ignored, and now Tyler was about to leave without as much as a word. She turned her back on all the confusion in the room and followed close on his heels until he reached the door. When he turned to close the door behind him, she ran smack into his broad chest.

"What the devil! You are supposed to be trying on clothes, young lady," he hissed. "Get your little tail back inside and stop wasting everyone's time."

"I will not." She objected so loudly that all activity in the room ceased as the women stared at her open-mouthed.

Tyler's green eyes glared at them over Madeline's head, and they quickly returned to their task. He took Madeline none too gently by the arm, and pulling her out into the hall, he closed the door firmly behind her.

"Now," he said impatiently, "tell me what this is all about, and make it quick. I have much to do."

"Those clothes must cost a fortune," she stormed, "and that is a debt I can never hope to repay."

His face lightened, her concern suddenly clear. "There is nothing to repay," he said softly. "The price is small, and under the circumstances it's the least I can do—"

"Oh, I see," she interrupted, close to tears, "you brought me here, turned my world upside down, and this paltry gift is a way to ease your conscience."

His face paled, the muscles tensing at his jaw. "You mistake my meaning, Madam." The words were bitter. "I sought only to repay the debt of your lost clothing. Although my humble gift may seem paltry compared to your present wardrobe," he continued, his eyes traveling the length of her plain brown dress, "I'm afraid it was the best I could do on such short notice. As to the larger debt you mentioned," he said, breathing deeply, "I rather suspect I may spend the rest of my life trying to repay it." He paused for a moment, then added, "If you have nothing more to discuss, I suggest you return for your fitting, if not for my sake, then at least for the ladies who have worked so hard on your behalf."

Madeline remained silent. He was right. She regretted the haste of her words. Not quite able to look him in the eye, she nodded her head, opened the door, and went quietly inside.

"Oh, Miss," Jeannie greeted her as if nothing had happened. "Come and try on some of these beautiful things."

Reluctant at first, Madeline allowed the women to fit her first into one dress and then another. Despite herself, she felt her spirits begin to lift. She was pirouetted in front of the long looking glass as the dressmaker made a small tuck here or pinned a tiny dart there.

Soon it became clear that most of the clothes were ready to travel right away, and the others required very little in the way of alterations. So it was that a good mood prevailed in the dressing room, and the hours ticked happily by. At the end of the day, the little dressmaker congratulated herself. She rubbed her hands together. All in all, the fitting had been a great success.

Chapter Eleven

S till disgruntled, Tyler made his way to the study, where he found his brother and grandfather waiting.

"How goes it with the dressmaker, big brother?"

"Delightful," Tyler replied sharply.

Surprised by the other's dark look and bad-tempered retort, Ian jumped quickly to Madeline's defense. "Well, don't blame her. After all, none of this was her fault, you know."

"Damn it, don't you think I know that!" Tyler growled.

"It does no good to lose your temper," William snapped. "As soon as the girl is ready, we will get underway."

Tyler nodded. "With any luck, Sir, George and I will see you in about two weeks."

"I can ride with you," Ian broke in. "With three of us looking, we should be able to make it in half the time."

Later, passing through the hall, Ian grinned to himself as, standing to one side, he watched the assortment of boxes being carried downstairs. One by one, they were loaded onto a waiting wagon. Jeannie ran back and forth, excitedly giving orders and throwing everyone, including

Cook, into a state of chaos. A now disgruntled Cook handed her the picnic lunch she had prepared, threatening her with dire consequences if she allowed anything to spoil.

"Silly old cow!" Ian heard Jeannie mutter under her breath as the woman disappeared back into the kitchen. He wondered if his grandfather was really prepared for the female invasion that was about to descend on his household.

At last, all was in readiness for the journey. It had been decided that a larger carriage was needed to accommodate all the extra baggage. George had overseen the arrangements, and now a spacious vehicle with a team of four waited in front of the house.

"Where's your mistress?" Tyler questioned Jeannie as the last of the bags was safely stowed aboard.

"She was right be'ind me, Sir," the girl assured him. "She won't be long."

He nodded his understanding and strode into the front hall to wait. Minutes passed, and he cast an impatient glance at the stairs. As all remained quiet there, he restlessly paced the floor.

Meanwhile, Madeline paced nervously. Her head hurt. She wanted nothing more than to see the last of the pushy little dressmaker. But the woman wasn't so easily put off.

"What would the fine gentleman say," the woman nagged, "if I was to let you travel in the likes of that?" She pointed in disgust at the plain brown dress. "And after him spending all his hard-earned money too." She turned to her two assistants, hands resting on her narrow hips. "Now I ask you, girls, did you ever hear of such a thing?"

Certain of the wrath that might be heaped upon them later, the girls rushed to agree. Their voices became louder and more animated until, in the end, Madeline could stand it no longer.

"All right, that's enough," she pleaded, pressing her hands to her ears. "I will do as you say, but only if you pack my dress along with the rest."

She watched, making sure, as the brown garment was swiftly folded and packed in the bottom of a box. A new gown had already been selected, and in next to no time, it was pulled on over Madeline's head.

"Now, turn around," the seamstress instructed with a flourish of her hand. As Madeline obliged, the woman stood back and surveyed her handiwork. "Perfect." She sighed at last. "just perfect."

Madeline took a quick look at her reflection in the mirror. A tiny "Ohh" escaped her lips at the sight. She swayed slowly from side to side, delighting in the gentle flow of the soft fabric. As she made her way toward the stairs, her shy smile of pleasure was almost enough to warm the hardened dressmaker's heart.

Tyler looked up and stopped short as the reason for his long wait came slowly down the stairs toward him. Cut in the French style, the dress she wore was pale yellow. The sleeves were long. Puffed at the shoulder, they fitted down to the wrist and were fastened there with a row of small pearls. The long, flared skirt seemed to add to her height and complemented her slim body to perfection. Curls peeked out from under the brim of the matching hat. Trimmed and fastened with a length of green ribbon, the low drooping sides made a frame for her small face. One white gloved hand grasped the banister while the other held the trailing skirt of her gown. The hem was raised just high enough to reveal a tantalizing glimpse of small white kid shoes.

"You honor me, Madam, by accepting my humble gift." He crossed the hall to meet her. "It gives me much pleasure." He reached for her hand, stopping her on the bottom step. "The color becomes you," he murmured, "and your beauty dazzles me."

He lifted her hand and pressed it to his lips. Their eyes met, and now he found himself hopelessly adrift in a sea of blue. Madeline quickly turned away. The intensity of his gaze left her weak at the knees. The warmth of his kiss still burned through the fine fabric of her glove, and with nerves already raw, she panicked. Quickly pulling her hand from his, she stumbled against him.

"Have care, Madeline."

His arm went around her as he hastened to steady her. Her hair brushed his cheek, and he breathed in the soft fragrance of lavender. He felt the rapid beat of her heart against his chest and instinctively pulled her closer. His body hardened, blood running hot in his veins. He gritted his teeth and waited till her heartbeat slowed. At last, reaching up to loosen her grip from around his neck, he lifted her gently and set her back on her feet. With one finger beneath her chin, he tilted her face toward him.

"Do nothing remotely dangerous for the next few days, my dear," he whispered close to her ear, "because I won't be around to save you."

Madeline's face burned. Oh, how she hated him for that and wished that she could smack his face. But instead, she placed her hands on his chest and pushed hard. He chuckled in an infuriating way and pretended to stagger backward. A shrill whinny interrupted their exchange, and the thud of impatient hooves suddenly reminded Tyler of the waiting carriage.

"I believe my grandfather is ready to leave," he said.

Lifting her from the stairs, he placed her on the floor beside him. Before she could resist, he took her hand, tucking it snuggly through his arm. She struggled to get free, but he held on tight. Left with no other choice, Madeline reluctantly gave in and allowed him to walk her to the door. Moments later, they found the rest of her party still waiting patiently out in the sunlit courtyard.

"Come, child," William called as he caught sight of her. "The day is wasting, and there is still much to do."

"Coming," she called back.

Tyler released her hand. Gathering up her skirts, she ran toward the carriage. With a quick glance over her shoulder, she saw his dark shape standing at ease, filling the frame of the open door. But although she heard neither sound nor movement, he was at her side as she reached the waiting vehicle.

"I wish you a safe journey, Madeline," he said as he handed her inside.

Then, standing back, he ordered the coachman on his way. Ian joined him and watched as the carriage trundled off down the driveway.

"Well, that's that," he said. "Now it's off to London, I suppose?"

"Yes. Here's to hoping Solicitor Edward Bailey will be easy to find and that he will have the answers we need. Then this whole thing can be done with. The girl will be gone, and life can return to normal."

"Mmmm, I wonder," Ian muttered thoughtfully, casting his brother a doubtful sidelong glance.

Chapter Twelve

The journey to Marshfield Hall proved pleasant. The weather was fair, and the earl, Madeline found, was a genial host. He enjoyed sharing points of interest and local highlights along the way. For Jeannie, who had never traveled in a carriage before, it was a magical moment, and her constant questions kept William on his toes.

Madeline was grateful for the much-needed time to collect her thoughts. She was upset and confused. She should hate Tyler Wentworth for what he had put her through. But if that was so, why did her heart race at the sight of him? Why, even now, with the miles growing wider between them, did her skin still burn at the thought of his kiss? Quickly rubbing at the offending spot on her glove, she tried to erase it. She must be strong and put him out of her mind. With any luck, if her father was found, she could soon put all of this and him behind her.

"What do you think, child?" William asked, bringing her back to the moment. "This is it. This is Marshfield Hall."

The sun was well past its zenith as they entered the large black iron gates. Madeline and Jeannie clamored in words of praise as they made their way up the tree-lined drive. William was so delighted his face threatened to crack if his beam of pride grew any wider.

Marshfield Hall was indeed magnificent. Sitting in the middle of a park-like setting, it was surrounded by wide green lawns, low stone walls, giant trees, and lush flower gardens. Reflected in the cool waters of a beautiful lake, the large house glowed like a rare jewel in the late morning sun. As the carriage pulled up at the front door, a plump woman with a jovial face rushed out to meet them.

"We have company, Mrs. Carter," William called to his housekeeper. "Be so kind as to show these young ladies to their rooms and let Cook know I will have company for dinner."

The organizing and removal of the luggage was soon carried out under the watchful eye of Mr. Wiggins, the butler. A short, stocky, stern-faced, middle-aged man, it was easy to see that he kept a tight rein on the household staff. Bags and boxes were moved from hand to hand with surprising speed and quickly made their way up the back stairs. Meanwhile, Mrs. Carter took charge of Madeline and Jeannie, shaking her head in mock distress as she hustled them into the grand entry of the big old house. With hardly a moment to catch their breath or a chance to take in the beauty around them, she led them across the Italian tiled floor and up the central staircase.

"Here we are, my dear." Mrs. Cater threw open the door to a large room at the front of the house. "Just look at the view from here," she said, rushing to the windows and pulling back the curtains. "Beyond the lake, you can see the countryside for miles."

The woman fussed around the room, smoothing imaginary wrinkles from the bedspread and adjusting the already perfectly arranged items on the dresser. As assorted bags and boxes began to cover the floor, she opened the spacious cupboards for Jeannie's inspection.

"Plenty of room for everything in here," she assured the girl, "so I will leave you now to make yourselves comfortable."

When they were alone at last, Madeline sighed and kicked off her shoes. At Jeannie's insistence, she sat herself down on the bed and watched as the mammoth job of unpacking began. A tray of small delights was delivered to the room about an hour later, along with a message from Mrs. Carter. Dinner would be served at eight o'clock sharp. Time passed pleasantly for Madeline. The room was cool in color and comfortable in design. It encouraged relaxation, and without even realizing it, her eyes slowly closed, and she drifted off to sleep.

"Sorry, Miss," Jeannie apologized softly as she gently shook Madeline into wakefulness. "It's time."

Accordingly, bathed and now dressed in pink crepe, Madeline made her way downstairs with a few minutes to spare.

"It's been a long time since I've had such a charming dinner guest." The earl greeted her in the hall, and offering her his arm, he escorted her to the table.

Whatever fears Madeline may have harbored about her visit to Marshfield Hall were quickly dispelled. She found that her host had a wonderful sense of humor, and soon the dining room rang with their laughter.

"Do you ride, young lady?" he asked suddenly as the meal was ending.

"No, Sir, I never learned," Madeline replied truthfully.

"Well, in this house, it's required, isn't that so, Wiggins?" he asked the straight-faced man overseeing the filling of the wine glasses.

"Quite so, my Lord," Wiggins replied sternly.

"Daft, if you ask me," Mrs. Carter chimed in as she happened to pass the door. "Up at dawn he is, racing around the countryside," she grumbled. "Should know better, a man of his age."

"Hush, woman," William scolded, "I'm not ready for the graveyard yet. Well, child?" He looked expectantly at Madeline. "What do you say, shall I teach you?"

At her eager nod, a wide smile spread across the old man's face.

Madeline awoke early the next morning, filled with a strange sense of excitement. It was several minutes before the reason became clear. A cock crowed in a distant barnyard, and the earl's words rang in her head. "Remember, my dear. I rise with the rooster, so don't keep me waiting."

She jumped from the bed, calling for Jeannie. "Quick, Jeannie, I'm late." Her excitement was catching. "My green riding habit. Where is it?"

All fingers and thumbs, and tripping over each other in their haste, they finally had everything on but the boots.

"Push, Miss, push." Jeannie insisted.

Bending over and out of breath, she struggled with the task. They pulled and pushed until the first one and then the other slipped into place.

"Good luck, Miss," Jeannie said, giving her a hug. Then as Madeline was about to leave, she added, "Wait a minute, we forgot your hat." Jeannie plopped it on her head, trying hard not to crush its long green feather as she quickly secured it with two long hat pins.

"Whew!" the girl exhaled loudly and collapsed against the door as she watched Madeline's headlong flight down the stairs.

"Best to hurry, Miss," Mrs. Carter advised moments later as the blond girl charged across the hall. "The master left some time ago. He said for you to find him out back at the barn."

"About time," the old man said gruffly as Madeline arrived, slightly out of breath.

"Sorry," she mumbled apologetically.

"Do you think that silly thing will stay put?"

Her companion pointed at the long ostrich feather stuck in her black beaver hat.

"I don't know," she answered truthfully, fingering the item in question.

"Well, we shall see." He smiled at the pretty girl in green. "But come now, young lady, the morning is wasting. Let's be on our way."

Eager whinnies welcomed him as he opened the heavy barn door. Large heads poked from darkened stalls, impatient hooves thumped, and warm air puffed from snorting nostrils.

"They look for this every day," William said, producing a big bag filled to the top with cut up carrots.

"Mrs. Carter?" Madeline asked.

He smiled and nodded. "From her garden." Dipping into the bag of treats, he placed one in her palm. "Hold it flat," he cautioned as the damp muzzle nuzzled her hand.

Large white teeth gently took the offered treat and quickly gobbled it down. They made their way slowly down the long barn, William introducing each animal to her in turn. At last, sitting on a bale of sweet-smelling hay, they listened to the comforting sounds of contented munching. Conversation flowed freely between the two, Madeline feeling right at home in the old man's company. He spoke mostly of his horses, describing each one with affection. Almost as if they were his children. The banging of the barn door and a cheerful whistle brought their conversation to an end.

"Ah, that sounds like Barnaby." William turned to greet the young stable boy.

Madeline liked his looks at once. A sturdy youth, perhaps a few years her junior, he had a round freckled face and a tousled mop of straight brown hair. Taller than her by at least four inches, he smiled down at her as William introduced them.

"Well, what say you, Barnaby?" William asked. "We need a good mount for this young lady."

"Only one I can think of, my Lord," the boy replied, pushing his cap back on his head. "But that's up to you, o' course."

"I think you're right," the old man said after a moment's thought.

Barnaby led the little gray mare from her stall for Madeline's inspection.

"Her name is Misty, my dear." There was a touch of sadness in William's voice. "She belonged to my wife, Sophie, but since her death two years ago, no one but Barnaby has ridden her."

"She's beautiful," Madeline whispered, gently rubbing the animal's soft muzzle. "You and I will be great friends, Misty," she promised.

"They make a good pair," Barnaby said, looking pleased. William just nodded.

From the first moment Barnaby boosted her into the saddle, Madeline fell in love with the sweet-tempered little mare.

In the days that followed, she proved an apt student. Soon the local villagers became accustomed to seeing the pretty young woman in green galloping confidently at the earls side.

"Well, my dear, you have learned everything I can teach you," he said one morning as they slowed to a walk. "All but one thing, that is."

"What?" Madeline asked.

"How to win a race. Last one home helps Barnaby to cool out the horses."

It was an unfair advantage, but he wheeled sharply around and headed home at full speed.

As if she knew the game well, Misty took off in hot pursuit, but despite her valiant effort, William had already dismounted as they pulled into the yard.

"No fair," Madeline called to him.

"All's fair in love and war, my dear," he called back. "I shall tell Mrs. Carter you'll be a little late for breakfast."

Madeline heard his hearty laughter as he made his way back toward the house.

"I haven't seen him do that since the mistress died," Barnaby confided as they rubbed down the steaming animals. "It was good you came, Miss."

Chapter Thirteen

The days drifted by pleasantly for Madeline. She had never felt happier in her life. William filled her mornings with activity. But in the afternoons, while he attended to business and, although he denied it, spent an hour napping in his room, she was left to her own devices. It was then that she sought out Jeannie's company, and together they spent time exploring the old house and the grounds around it.

On just such an afternoon, as they were relaxing on lawn chairs in the garden, dark clouds suddenly rolled in, catching them in a soaking downpour. With shrieks of laughter, they made a mad dash for the house, ending up in the kitchen.

"Just look at the two of you," Mrs. Carter scolded fondly. "Hurry up and dry yourselves off." She handed them towels. "It's almost four o'clock."

"It's teatime," Jeannie explained, pulling chairs up to the big kitchen table.

It was Madeline's first introduction to life below the stairs. She watched, fascinated, as cups and plates were lined up around the big kitchen table. Two large loaves of bread were placed in the middle, along with a plate piled high with slices of cold mutton and cheese. A glazed cherry cake, baked by Mrs. Carter herself, was then set out to complete the bill of fare. Mr. Wiggins, who presided over the affair, checked his pocket watch, and on the stroke of four exactly, the household staff were all assembled.

"Don't drip all over the clean floor, lad," Mrs. Carter called as Barnaby came in through the back door.

"There's someone 'ere to see you, Mam," the young man said, kicking off his boots and shaking the rain from his coat.

"Well, now, who might that be at this time of the day?" she demanded.

"Who do you think it might be, me old dear?" Reverting to the cockney accent of his childhood, George stepped into the kitchen to greet her.

With a hoot of joy, Mrs. Carter sprang to her feet and rushed to meet him. Encircling the plump woman's waist with his arms, George swept her off her feet and, much to the disgust of Mr. Wiggins, spun her around and around in circles.

"Enough, enough," she cried at last, all out of breath. "You've got me all wet, you bad boy."

He set her down and planted a hearty kiss on the top of her head.

"Why didn't you let me know you were coming?" she demanded, and before he could answer, added, "Let me get a good look at you." She held him at arm's length, regarding him with a critical eye. "You look thin," she stated. "Sit yourself down and eat."

"Your cherry cake, Ma?" he asked, eyeing the table.

"Of course, and who else's would it be?"

Happily fussing around him, she quickly poured tea into his cup and cut him a huge slab of the cherry cake.

"Calm down, Ma," he begged, taking a seat. "We came back yesterday, and the Gov told me to come here and wait for him. Is the old man upstairs?" he asked between mouthfuls of cake, and at Mrs. Carter's affirmative nod, he headed toward the stairs.

"How do, Miss," he said, noticing Madeline for the first time. "I'll be right back, Ma," he told Mrs. Carter. "And by the way," he said, winking affectionately at the woman, "you still make the best cherry cake in the world."

Basking in the glow of his praise, Mrs. Carter grinned from ear to ear and passed the cherry cake around the table.

"I didn't know you were George's mother, Mrs. Carter," Madeline said, surprised.

"Bless you, my dear," the housekeeper replied. "He's not mine by birth. But ever since the Master brought him here as a little bit of a thing, more dead than alive, it's been me who's cared for him."

"Tell us more, please," Jeannie begged, suddenly finding the slim man very interesting.

"An orphan he was," the woman explained. "Almost killed on the streets of London."

"And the Master brought 'im here?" Barnaby asked.

"That he did. Raised him here and sent him to school."

"Then why did he leave?" Madeline questioned.

Warming up to the subject, Mrs. Carter refilled the teacups, pulled up a chair, and joined the group around the table.

"Adventure," she said. "Always looking for adventure he was, and when Mr. Tyler came for a while, full of tales of America, well, that's all it took." She sighed. "Got along real well right from the start they did, my George and Mr. Tyler. So, when it came time for Mr. Tyler to go home, my Georgie went with him." She took a deep breath and cut herself another piece of cake.

"Go on, Mrs. Carter, tell us more," Madeline urged, her own interest growing.

"Merchants, that's what the Wentworth's are," the housekeeper continued. "Wrote me all about it, Georgie did. And when Mr. Tyler brought a trading ship, the letters were full of their adventures. Traveled around the world they did, fighting pirates in the China sea and a typhoon in the Indian Ocean—"

"What are you on about, Ma?" George asked as he returned to the room.

"She's telling us all about your adventures," Jeannie broke in, her eyes aglow with admiration.

"Is that all?" George laughed. "Well, move over, lass," he said, taking a seat beside her, "and I will tell you some tales that will make your pretty little head spin."

No one noticed when, a few minutes later, Madeline decided to leave. The rain had stopped, so, taking an apple from the large barrel by the door, she made her way to the barn.

"Oh Misty, I love you so," she said as the little mare gently nuzzled her hand. "But George is here now, and something tells me that I will have to leave soon."

She held the apple in her palm and watched the large white teeth bite delicately into the tasty treat. Her days at Marshfield Hall had been idyllic, and for a very short time, she had successfully blotted the past from her mind. With William and Misty to keep her company, even her father had faded a little from her thoughts. But with George's sudden arrival, she knew the fragile world she had created was about to crumble.

Tears gathered in her eyes, and she did nothing to stop them from running down her face.

William's thoughts were much the same that evening as he bade Madeline goodnight. They climbed the stairs slowly together as had become their habit. Conversation never a problem between them, they lingered overlong on the landing, each unwilling for the evening to end. At last, stifling a yawn, Madeline stood on tiptoes and kissed the old man on the cheek.

"Sweet dreams, Grandfather Searle," she said, using the affectionate title he insisted on. "May you stay safe until morning."

"Good night, child." He returned her kiss and waited until her door closed behind her.

Sleep proved elusive for him, and as on other such nights, he removed the old black velvet box from his dresser drawer and caressed it lovingly.

"Ah, Sophie," he said, sighing. "If one of us had to go so soon, why wasn't it me?"

He sat on the edge of his bed and opened the box. Light from the lamp sparkled brightly on the diamond and sapphire necklace that rested inside.

"Remember the night I gave you this, my love? I do. It was on our tenth anniversary." He ran his fingers gently over the gems. "That night, your eyes put these humble stones to shame. Oh, how proud I was with you on my arm. I was the envy of every man in the room when we walked out onto the dance floor." He reached for his ever-present cane, huffed on the golden lion's head, and buffed it carefully with his handkerchief. "You gave me this that night and called me your lion, your king of the jungle." He held up the cane and inspected his handy work. The emerald eyes winked back at him. "This girl reminds me a lot of you, my dear. Perhaps she was sent here for a reason. I sense something brewing between her and our grandson, even though they seem to fight a lot," he said, chuck-ling. "Come to think of it, you and I used to make the sparks fly a bit ourselves, didn't we, old girl, and no one was ever more in love than we two. Well, time will tell."

He turned the key on the bottom of the black box, and the gentle notes of a haunting refrain filled the silence of the night. With the cane lying beside him, he rested his head on the pillow and closed his eyes. As he drifted off to sleep, the years fell away. There was a soft rustle of a satin dress, and a delicate fragrance filled the air. He turned, and smiled, as the beautiful woman in blue floated into his arms. The music played sweetly on, and once again, the young lovers kissed and circled the dance floor together.

Chapter Fourteen

As Madeline prepared for bed that night, she listened to Jeannie's endless chatter. It was George this, and George that, and tale after tale about his adventures with Tyler Wentworth aboard the ship Gray Ghost.

"Enough, Jeannie," she cried at last. "One would think you have feelings for the man."

"Lordy, Miss," the girl exclaimed, covering her face with her hands and giggling. "I did get a bit carried away, didn't I?"

But she made no attempt to deny it, and for the first time since they met, Jeannie seemed at a loss for words. She remained deep in thought as she carried out her nightly duties. But when she picked up the brush and went to work on Madeline's hair, she began softly humming what sounded very much like the tune of an old sea shanty. At last, she wished Madeline a hasty good night and, with a distant look in her eyes, quickly left the room.

Despite her own unsettling thoughts about the future, sleep came swiftly for Madeline. But unlike William's, her dreams brought her no peace. It wasn't her usual dream. This time she wasn't running from a phantom figure. Tonight, she felt the roll of a tall sailing ship beneath her feet and sensed the acrid smell of gunpowder in her nostrils. A cannon roared in the distance, and the whistle of its shot came closer. The tall mast was hit, and splinter-laden wreckage crashed down around her. A second shot hit the broadside. Cries for help rang out as the ship shuddered and listed to starboard. Through the blinding cloud of smoke, a white sail appeared. The ship slowly drew alongside, and Madeline's blood ran cold. The flag it flew was the skull and crossbones. She watched in horror as the ragtag pirate crew quickly scrambled over the rails.

"She's ours for the taking, men," a voice called out.

Eyes burning, Madeline searched the smoke for the source. Her heart skipped a beat as she found it. High above the deck of the pirate ship, a tall man balanced upon the yardarm. Dressed only in britches cut off at the knees and a red kerchief tied about his dark hair, he trod his lofty perch with practiced ease. Black leather belts crisscrossed his broad bare chest; a sword hung from one, a pistol from the other. A scream froze on her lips when, grasping a length of rope, he jumped from his perch and swung out into space. Like a giant bird of prey, he flew through the air, quickly crossing the tossing waters that separated them. With the agility of a cat, he landed amidships, his sword drawn. Men scattered as he instantly joined in the fray on deck, wielding his weapon with expert precision.

He was one among many, but the very sight of him commanded Madeline's attention. Salty spray bathed his bronzed torso, and a sheen of silvery mist rose from the surface of his warm skin. He moved with an easy grace, quick and precise, taking all before him. Sword held high, he spotted her for the first time and hesitated. Green eyes on fire, white teeth flashing from the bearded face, he strode toward her. There was no escape.

"It's you I want, Madam," he said, his dark face looking down into hers. "You and only you."

He pulled her to him, capturing her lips in a searing kiss. Breathless, she tried to push him away, but he laughed at her feeble efforts. Grasping her hand, he led her through the smoke and flame till they stood on the very brink of the starboard bow. The doomed ship groaned as it rose and fell with the swell of the waves.

"Help!" Madeline cried, her heartbeat like thunder.

"Sorry, Miss, I'm 'opless," Jeannie called as she ran by.

"My tales will make your pretty little head spin," George said, running behind her, grinning as he emerged out of the fog.

"No need to fear, little one," she heard the pirate say. "Just trust me, Madeline, and I'll teach you to fly."

One strong arm encircled her waist. Her feet left the ground, and she held on tight. The wild rush of the wind tugged at her hair, and the salty spray soaked her skin. She buried her face against his chest, and together they flew away to she knew not where.

She awoke with a shuddering sob, her pillow clutched tight within her arms. Darkness closed in around her, and the silence of her room was deafening. She tossed and turned on her mangled bed, trying to banish the man and the dream from her mind. But suddenly, engulfed by a strange sense of loss, her heart demanded if that was what she really wanted.

Chapter Fifteen

I n spite of the restless night she had spent, Madeline enjoyed the
morning ride. She was excited because today, for the first time, she
had won the race home. But upon reaching the barn, her heart had
softened, and she shared the grooming duties with William. Holding
tight to the old man's arm, her eyes were bright and her cheeks flushed,
as they, laughing, made their way into the dining room.

"I must say, you look very well, Madam," a deep voice said.

Her heart skipped a beat as, looking across the room, she recognized
the tall man by the window.

"Oh, it's you." The words slipped from her lips as the laughter left
her eyes, and her face fell.

"I'm glad to see my return pleases you so," he said sarcastically, trying
to hide his disappointment.

While he had been away, he had found himself constantly thinking
of her. He had even urged his brother to set a faster pace all the way
home. The muscle at his jaw tensed.

"Had I known I would be greeted with such enthusiasm, I would
have endeavored to stay away longer."

"Hello, Princess," Ian intervened, quickly jumping up from his chair. "I don't know what you've done to this woman, Sir," he addressed his grandfather, "but I swear she is more beautiful than ever. The country air must agree with her."

With a bright smile, he took Madeline's hand and raised it too his lips.

"You are too kind, Sir," she murmured, quickly lowering her eyes to hide her embarrassment.

From his vantage point by the window, Tyler was only aware of the close proximity of the two young people. He noted the flush of pleasure that brightened the girl's face and the intimate way their heads moved near enough to touch. A low growl rose in his throat as he fought the urge to drag them apart. With an effort, he turned away, an unjust resentment of his brother burning in his chest.

Ian spared a moment to glance in his brother's direction, finding his behavior quite disturbing. He knew the man was no saint where women were concerned, but night after night, while they were in London, he had watched him ignore the blatant proposals of some of the city's most beautiful women. Yet now the simple lack of response from this innocent girl had triggered a burst of unnecessary anger. Could it be that she had succeeded where so many more worldly women had failed? Had she in fact done something their mother had long thought impossible? Had she captured his brother's heart?

"It's good to have you all back," William said, giving each of his grandsons a hearty hug. "We've been anxious for your news, haven't we, my dear?"

He sat down at the table, surprised at how easily the lie had slipped from his lips.

"Yes, Sir," Madeline addressed him formally, then, as part of her usual morning routine, she poured him tea.

"You shall have our news all in good time, Sir," Tyler said. "We have ridden hard this morning and could use a moment or two."

"Of course." William nodded his understanding. "I'm afraid that my grandsons have developed bad habits, my dear," he said, turning to Madeline. "They don't drink tea like civilized people. Would you be so kind as to ask Cook if we can have coffee?"

With a slight nod, Madeline hurried away to do his bidding.

"Now," William said as the door closed behind her. "Is the news of her father so bad that you wish to shield her from it?"

"Well, it took us awhile, but we finally located the Solicitor office," Tyler said, "but apparently the man is away. His clerk had no idea as to where he was or how long he would be gone. If he knew more, it was obvious he wasn't about to tell us."

"He did say he would notify his employer on his return," Ian broke in, "but he was very vague, and we were left with the distinct feeling it would go nowhere."

"So you know no more now than when you left," William stated.

"Not quite so, Sir," Ian replied. "We know now that there is a connection there. You see, I was able to distract the man long enough for Tyler to sift through some files that had been left on the desk. Madeline's name was mentioned and that of a Lord Reginald Spencer, a man who comes from some remote village near Exeter."

"I've already put some of our best people on it," Tyler continued, "God only knows who this man is, but at least it's a place to start."

"So we just sit back and wait?"

"Yes, Sir," Tyler confirmed. "After spending two uncomfortable weeks in London searching for the solicitor, we are still no closer to finding her father. I just hope the whole thing doesn't end up being a damn wild goose chase."

Madeline returned just in time to hear his disgruntled remarks.

"It was you who insisted on going to London, Sir." She confronted him, a resentful look in her eyes. "I neither asked for nor desired your help to find my father. I just wish ... oh, how I wish I had never met you." Her voice faltered, and turning, she ran from the room.

"Damn!" Tyler muttered, shaking his head. "What else can go wrong?"

The room remained silent. No one could give him an answer to his question.

Chater Sixteen

"**A**re you alright?" he asked as he entered the barn a short time later. "My grandfather said I might find you here."

Madeline didn't answer, but the brush she wielded moved even faster over Misty's already sleek gray hide.

"He tells me you've grown quite fond of Misty and that you ride very well."

"He is too kind."

"Believe me, he never wastes time on empty complements." He gently scratched Misty's ears. "Did he tell you my grandmother raised Misty?"

Madeline shook her head.

"It was in the middle of a bad storm when the mare started to give birth. The delivery was difficult, and with no hope of getting help, my grandparents spent the night right here in the barn. By daybreak, the storm had passed, but a heavy mist rolled in as the baby was born, hence her name Misty. Unfortunately, the strain was too much for the mother, and she died a short time later."

"Oh, how sad," said Madeline, burying her face in the silky mane.

"I didn't mean to make you cry," he apologized.

"I'm not crying," she protested, but she took his offered handkerchief anyway.

"If this keeps up, I will have to carry two," he teased.

Sniffing, she smiled up at him, her damp eyes bright.

"My brother was right, Madeline," he said softly. "The country air does agree with you."

He moved closer. She shied away.

"Have no fear, little one. I won't bite."

"It's not your bite I fear, Sir," she said softly, her troubled eyes meeting his.

Neither spoke for the moment, each unsure of the feelings they seemed unable to control.

"We need to talk," he urged.

Returning Misty to her stall, he offered Madeline his arm. Together they made their way across the lawn. It was a route Madeline knew well; she and Jeannie had traveled it many times. They paused a moment beneath the old arbor, breathing in the sweet smell of tea roses and listening to the gentle drone of busy bees. Picking one of the fragrant blossoms, Tyler carefully removed the thorns.

"A peace offering," he said, handing her the pink rose. "Do you think we could forget the past and just start over?"

After waiting a moment, Madeline took the offering.

"Can I take that as a 'yes'?"

A frown of doubt crossed his forehead. Without looking up, she nodded.

They walked on in silence, each absorbed in their own thoughts, neither one in a hurry to end this fragile moment of truce that existed between them.

Madeline watched his tall shadow dwarfing hers as they went on their way. She thought of George's words. "It wasn't his fault, you know." It was true; their meeting had been a mistake. She found she really didn't blame him anymore. But she was still confused, more so now perhaps than at the very start. Then she had felt anger, anger so fierce she wanted to strike out at him. But now, in moments like this, she felt what? Warm, comfortable, protected. Whatever it was, she didn't understand it and couldn't explain it. Maybe her growing fondness for William and Jeannie was to blame. Could her affection for them be overshadowing her need to find her father? The mere idea was shocking.

Tyler was at a loss for the first time in his life. He had been cast in a role not of his choosing, and it had turned out badly. Now it was left to him to put things right. The London solicitor had been a place to start, but he felt the man was deliberately avoiding him. His clerk had even hinted at it, suggesting he send the girl back where she belonged. Looking at her now, he knew that was unthinkable. He would do his best to find her father if that was what she wanted. He had no way of knowing how that would turn out. But the one thing he did know for sure was that she would never be behind those high convent walls again.

"It's hot. Let's rest awhile," he suggested.

The sun was high, and they found shelter, sitting among the gnarled roots of a giant willow. They sat in silence for a while, watching as a thousand insects skimmed the surface of a nearby pool.

"You must trust me, Madeline," Tyler said at last. "The words you heard earlier were spoken in haste. Believe me, I will find your father. Just give me a little more time. I have already set the wheels in motion."

"How much time?"

"I'm not sure, but in two weeks, my grandfather celebrates his eightieth birthday. We should hear by then."

"Two weeks!" Madeline exclaimed. "You don't understand. I have already waited so long."

"Then why quibble over a few more days? Besides, my grandfather will want you here for his birthday. I think it's the least you can do, don't you?"

For William's sake, she knew she couldn't refuse.

"In two weeks then. You promise?"

"I do," he said solemnly. "But perhaps you can help with the search."

"How?"

"Apart from the name of the London solicitor and the fact that you grew up in the convent, I know very little of your past. Anything you can remember might help."

"I was little when I left—only five."

"Yes, but even the smallest thing might help."

Closing her eyes, she thought for a moment.

"I do seem to remember someone, an uncle perhaps. He used to laugh because I couldn't say his name. Iggy, I think. Or Eggy. Yes, that was it. Eggy. Do you think that might help?"

"It might. I'm not sure. It gives us another place to try though. But we should be getting back." He helped her to her feet. "Grandfather will be sending out the troops to find us. Tell me first though, what do you want of your father when we find him?"

She took a deep breath, struggling to control her emotions.

"I just want to know the truth. I want to know why he sent me away."

Tyler heard the hurt in her voice and saw the pain in her eyes. He nodded.

"Alright." He promised, "I will find Edward Bailey. I'll track him from one end of England to the other if necessary."

Chapter Seventeen

Edward Bailey was a tall man, slim of build and distinguished of dress. His face could be called hawk-like, and his eyes, according to those who faced him across a court room, were piercing. Although thinning on top, his hair still retained its dark color. Slightly touched up perhaps, but he would never admit it. His facial hair, of which he was very proud, was always groomed to perfection.

At almost forty, he remained unmarried. Whether by choice or circumstance, no one ever knew. But he moved in the best circles, and his elegant London house was well-known for its large social gatherings. It was said that his only clientele were the rich and famous. In short, he liked the good things in life and knew how to get them.

Over the years, he had always made it a practice never to travel more than a few miles beyond the outskirts of the city. He hated the discomfort of it. Crammed into a small space for days, where the air was foul and the company worse, was something to be avoided at all costs. Add to that the bumpy, bone-jarring roads, the bug-infested accommodation, and the bad food that placed distress on his already delicate stomach. It was just too much. Not even to mention the internal upheaval he knew he would suffer for days afterward. So for these reasons, and many more if he thought about it, he chose to conduct all his business in his fashionable London office. But this case was different. It was personal, and it threatened to bring back events from the past that were best left buried, events in which he himself had played a large part. He pulled a letter dated two weeks ago from his pocket and read through it for the third time. According to the writer, rumors were circulating the city. Agents working for a young American were asking questions. Well, the time had come. In a way, he had always expected it. Now decisions must be made, and Edward was dammed. He wasn't about to make them alone. So reluctantly, he had submitted himself to the inevitable.

The long ride from London had proved as tiresome and uncomfortable as he had feared. He found himself wedged between two large ladies, one who smelled strongly of garlic, the other as if she had bathed in camphor oil. It did nothing to improve his mood. By holding his handkerchief close to his nose, he was able to endure the situation as far as Princetown. It was here that he decided to change his mode of transportation and hired himself a carriage. Although nothing eased the bumps in the road, occupying the carriage alone was a blessed relief. For days, his mind had been consumed with thoughts of the past, and now, in these moments of solitude, he tried to put them all into perspective.

It was over twenty years ago now when Lord Reginald Spencer had called upon his friends to sail with him to France. Young men, all ready for adventure. It was to be a rescue mission. Paris was in the grip of a Revolution, and those that could had sought to escape. But when the yacht Sea Nymph with Lord Spencer and his little crew set sail for France, how could any of them have foreseen what was to come? Strange how one impetuous act in your early years can chart your course for the rest of your life. Yet that had proved to be the case for these young men. They had been drawn into a web of circumstances by happenings beyond their control. Now fate, it seemed, was about to step in again in the form of one, Tyler Wentworth, and now, for the life of him, Edward had no idea how to prevent it. The closer he came to his destination, the more anxious he became. What was he letting himself in for? This place held too many memories, too many things from the past that could come back to haunt him. But it was too late now; the die was cast. For better or worse, he was here, and the time had come at last to face it.

The house at Cliff's Edge was much as he remembered it, sitting high above the beach on a long, lonely stretch of rugged English coastline. Alighting from the carriage, Edward took a moment to look around. Sunlight glittered on the calm blue surface of the sea. From a distance, it blinded the eyes to the obvious signs of neglect. But on closer inspection, Edward found there was no mistaking the wear and tear of the passing years. Obviously, very little had been done to counteract the harsh effects of time, wind, and sea. Sadness seemed to surround the house in a cloak of darkness. Ivy ran rampant over the old stone facade. Shuttered windows, like large, closed eyes, kept the world at bay.

The courtyard, once so full of color and activity, now sat gray and bare. Weeds pushed their way through cracked stonework and filled the beds where roses and other delicate flowers once thrived. The grand circular driveway that he remembered so well was no more. Gravel washed away by heavy rains had left it rutted and overgrown. But what of the inhabitants? Had time treated them as harshly? He shivered. It had been many years since he and his old friends had come face to face. For a moment, guilt engulfed him. His own involvement had been minimal compared with theirs. They had chosen to stay with Spencer and take care of things. Yet no one had ever called him to task for leaving. At the time, he supposed, they had all thought it for the best. After all, he had been the youngest member of the crew. Most of them had not wanted him along but he had begged, and finally, Spencer relented. Well, this was no time to be dwelling on the past. He took a deep breath to compose himself, then made his way up the worn stone steps to the door. He lifted the large brass knocker and let it fall. A hollow echo sounded inside. It was greeted by silence. He knocked again.

"I'm coming, I'm coming," an irritated voice called out from somewhere inside.

Edward waited patiently as the thud of footsteps came steadily nearer. At last, the sound of heavy breathing penetrated the wooden portal. There was a metallic rattle of keys as someone fumbled with the lock. Finally, the key clicked into place, and with a tired sigh, the old door creaked open.

"Well?" a woman asked.

Taken aback, Edward stuttered his name.

With suspicious eyes, she scanned the steps behind him. Satisfied at last that he was alone, she moved aside and let him in.

"Follow me," she said and led the way down a long, dimly lit hallway.

The clank of keys hanging at her waist echoed along the walls around them. Before Edward's eyes could become adjusted to the gloom, she stopped, opened a door on her left and instructed him to, "Wait here."

Edward did as he was told and she closed the door behind him with a bang.

It was obvious that the room hadn't been used for many years. Whatever furniture there was had been draped in dingy white covers. Curtains were drawn at all but one of the windows where light filtered in through the dirty glass. Brushing cobwebs from his face, Edward made his way toward it. Cleaning a small circle in the grime with his finger, he peered out. Memories of large wicker chairs and tall glasses of lemonade out on the terrace came back to haunt him. And then there was always Elizabeth, sweet Elizabeth. He still missed her. Deep in thought, he failed to hear the door opening.

"Bailey?"

Startled, Edward turned to face the newcomer.

"Yes," he confirmed, holding out his hand in greeting.

"Well, well. Is it really you, Bailey?" The man took his hand, though none too warmly. "It's been a long time," he mused. "You must excuse the housekeeper for showing you in here. She is new, and good help is hard to find. As you can see, this part of the house isn't lived in anymore. We seldom receive guests these days, and this place is much too big." He looked around, shaking his head. "But, enough of trivialities. What brings you to this far-flung corner of England, Sir? I thought you never ventured far from the comforts of the city."

His words sounded genuine, but Edward could detect an undertow of resentment.

Uncomfortable now, he cleared his throat. He knew the news he brought wouldn't be welcome.

"I'm sorry to say it's business," he said at last.

"Then let's move to more comfortable surroundings and fortify ourselves with a glass of brandy. For you to have come so far, I fear the news cannot be good."

Seated in a small room in the west wing of the house, the men drank a brandy in silence.

"You look well," Lord Spencer remarked at last. "The years have treated you well. But then I forget, you were so much younger than the rest of us. What are you now, thirty-eight or so?"

"Almost forty," he said, suddenly feeling self-conscious again.

He wished he could repeat the compliment to his companion, but the passing years had not treated Lord Spencer so kindly. Although still tall, graying hair and the loss of some twenty pounds caused him to look much older than his years.

Clearing his throat, he asked, "Where are the others? I thought we would discuss this together."

"Things have been difficult here of late, Bailey. Whatever you have to say you can say to me. We have no secrets here."

A little less than happy with the outcome, Edward nevertheless told his story.

"This man Wentworth is determined. He won't easily be misled. What would you have me do?" he asked when the telling was done.

"It seems obvious to me, Bailey. We all want the best for Madeline, so I suggest you urge this Wentworth fellow to return her to the convent. She will always be safe there and well taken care of."

"But I had rather hoped things might be better here after all this time, that perhaps you might see fit to let her return."

"Look around you, man. Tell me what you see." Not waiting for an answer, he continued. "What you hoped for is out of the question. It will never happen. Digging around in the past does no good. Now, I am sorry you had such a long journey, but," he paused, coming stiffly to his feet.

"Oh no. Hold on," Edward insisted as he too came to his feet. "I will not be put off this way. I came here to see you all, and I intend to stay until I do."

Silence followed his outburst. Moments ticked by. Then, as if a decision had been made, Lord Spencer turned and reached for the bell.

"In that case," he said, "we had best make you comfortable. It seems you are going to be here for a while."

Chapter Eighteen

Marshfield Hall had been in a state of chaos for days. Now plans were well underway for the eightieth birthday celebrations for the fifth earl of Marshfield. For days, Madeline and Jeannie had been swept along on a tide of excitement. It left little time to ponder personal problems. Despite Mrs. Carter's firm looks of disapproval, reminiscent of her days spent in the convent, Madeline insisted upon helping in any capacity she could. Dressed in her old brown dress, with the sleeves rolled up to her elbows and with a kerchief wrapped around her head, she polished brass and silver till they shone. Rugs were carried from the house and thrown over clotheslines, where they were thoroughly beaten to remove the dust. It was after one such expedition when, smudged and dirty, Madeline ran headfirst into Tyler in the hall.

"Well, now, who is this scruffy little urchin?" he asked, holding her at arm's length, his eyes full of fun.

"Out of me way, Mister." She played the game, bobbing him a curtsy and imitating the children from the village. Sniffing loudly, she wiped her nose along her arm. "I gots me work to do, see." She made ready to leave.

"Oh no, not so fast, young lady!" He stepped in front of her. "I would like to see what lies beneath this covering of grime. Perhaps a dip in the horse trough would suit my purpose."

She screeched as he made a grab for her, and dodging to avoid his outstretched arms, she took off at a run. Only a few steps behind her, a laughing Tyler chased her full tilt all the way to the kitchen. She finally found refuge behind a spoon-wielding Mrs. Carter. That lady threatened dire consequence to the man if he further delayed her help.

"Goodness, Mrs. C," he said, backing up, a wide grin on his face, "now I know why my grandfather is so terrified of you."

"Get away with you, you young ruffian," she replied, feigning distress.

"Don't worry, I'm leaving." He held up his hands as she swung the spoon in his direction. "But as for you, Madam," he said, wagging his finger at Madeline, "you can't hide out here forever."

"Oh, you think not?" Madeline said boldly but never left the safety of Mrs. Carter's sturdy presence.

The women chuckled as the young man gave in and retreated. They could hear him whistling as his footsteps echoed off down the hall.

Slowly the house was put in order to Mrs. Carter's and even Mr. Wiggins' satisfaction. One by one, the rooms on the first floor were thrown open and made ready. In answer to Madeline and Jeannie's eager questions, Mrs. Carter explained their purpose.

"This one," she said, "is where the refreshments will be served. We don't want the ladies to get a chill on the drafty stairs when they go for tea or lemonade between dances." Another room, she explained, had been set aside for the older guests who preferred a less active evening of cards. "This," she confided with a wink, "is where His Lordship will spend most of the evening."

Everything, it seemed, had been thought of, even a room to be used by ladies should they find their gown in need of repair. But by far the most exciting room in the house, the girls discovered, was the ballroom. Under the watchful eye of Mr. Wiggins, hours were spent with beeswax and brushes to polish the dance floor to a high shine. Long tables had been brought in, and these were placed at intervals around the room. On the night of the ball, they would groan under the weight of trays piled high with hundreds of delicacies. But for now, the gleaming crystal punch bowls and bright shiny silverware sat and waited expectantly. Large potted palms were carried in from the conservatory. Decorative in nature, they added an airy, outdoor feel to the room.

"I do envy you, Miss," Jeannie blurted out as they admired the room together. "Think how grand it will be, dancing 'ere with an 'andsom man like Mister Tyler." She threw her arms wide and drifted slowly around the floor, a dreamy look in her eyes.

"If only that could be, Jeannie." Madeline sighed. "But you see, I don't know how to dance."

"Oh my!" Jeannie's face fell, then she brightened. "But there's still time, Miss," she said. "Don't you worry. Leave everything up to me."

The next afternoon, much to Madeline's surprise, George knocked at her door.

"I've been told that you need instructions on the art of dance, Miss," he said formally, "and I am here to apply for the position, you might say."

Although Madeline still rode every morning, now when William took his afternoon nap, she too would disappear upstairs. At precisely one o'clock every afternoon, George would arrive for her lesson. She proved to be an adept student, and under the man's excellent tutelage, she quickly learned the intricate steps of the popular dances of the day.

At last, the day was almost upon them, and to Madeline's horror, His Lordship announced that she would join him and his grandsons to greet their guests.

"How can I, Jeannie?" she asked, panicking. "What will I wear?"

Together the girls emptied the contents of her wardrobe and laid them out upon the bed. One by one the dresses were quickly eliminated.

"This one will just 'ave to do, Miss," Jeannie said at last, holding up a demure gown of the softest lavender color. "It's not quite what I 'ad in mind." Shaking her head, she indicated the garment's high neckline and simple style. "But it's the best of the lot, so it will 'ave to do."

Madeline slipped on the dress, and they both agreed that, with a few small touches, it would be just fine. With that in mind, Jeannie did her best, finding a small pin and some earbobs in a little box, simple gifts her mother had given her.

"There," she said, as they put the things together one night, "that's perfect."

Madeline was deeply touched by her friend's generosity and vowed to return the treasured items as soon as she could. So now, all was in readiness for the big night, they thought. Together, they tucked everything safely away in a drawer, feeling happy that they had done such a good job.

Finally, the big day dawned, bright and sunny. The staff were awake early, each one ready for the busy day ahead. Large quantities of food were prepared in the kitchen, and as the clock ticked closer to the hour of eight, Mrs. Carter, in company with Mr. Wiggins, made their final inspection.

William, who had been absent during the days of preparation, now put in an appearance.

"This is just as it used to be, my dear," he told Madeline, his face beaming. "You know, I can almost see my dear Sophie standing in her usual place by the stairs. She always loved the crowds and the excitement. What fun we used to have."

"Tonight will be fun too," Madeline assured him, laying her hand on his arm. "Just you wait and see." Standing on tiptoe, she couldn't resist placing a kiss on his cheek. "But now I must run if I am ever to be ready in time."

The old man chuckled as he watched her race across the hall and take the stairs two at a time. He made his way into the library and looked at the portrait hanging above the mantle.

"Yes, my love," he said thoughtfully, "I think I did the right thing, don't you?"

He knew it was only wishful thinking, but he could swear that a smile lit up the beautiful face on the canvas.

Out of breath from her mad rush up the stairs, Madeline burst into her room.

"Look, Miss," Jeannie greeted her, eyes bright, "this arrived for you a few minutes ago."

A large box sat on the bed, its half-open lid displaying a dress of shimmering blue.

Hardly able to contain herself, Madeline pulled the gown from its box and held it up in front of her.

"It's beautiful, Jeannie," she cried, swirling around in circles. "But who is it from?"

"There's something else 'ere, Miss."

Jeannie pointed to a velvet box that had been hidden among the folds of the garment.

With trembling fingers, Madeline worked at the catch, and in a moment the lid popped open.

"It must be a mistake," she whispered, gazing at the brilliant gems inside.

"Oh no, Miss, there's a note inside, and it's addressed to you."

Setting the box down gently on the bed, Madeline read the written words carefully.

Wear this tonight child and make an old man happy.

Sincerely,

William

Sometime later, still in a state of shock, Madeline climbed from the tub and submitted herself to Jeannie's care. Before the finishing touches were made to her hair, the blue gown was quickly slipped over her head. One look at Jeannie's face sent her scrambling for the mirror. The gown was like none she had ever seen before. Although it fitted her to perfection, it exposed far more of her than she thought proper.

"Oh my," she gasped, fanning the heat from her face. "Do I dare?"

She looked doubtfully at her companion.

"Of course," Jeannie said emphatically. "There'll be some here wearing only half as much, just you wait an' see. Bend down," she commanded.

As Madeline obeyed, she placed the sapphires and diamonds around her neck. Then, sweeping the long golden curls to the top of Madeline's head, she tied them in place with a length of blue ribbon.

"There!" she exclaimed at last. "All done. Now you'd better hurry. People will be 'ere soon."

Taking a deep breath, Madeline pirouetted slowly.

"How do I look?" she asked.

"Too good, I'm afraid, so please take care," Jeannie cautioned, shaking her head.

Madeline wanted to ask her what she meant, but by the time she had pulled on her white gloves, the thought had vanished from her mind.

Despite her earlier concerns, she arrived in the entry hall early. After a quick look around, she realized that she was alone. Jeannie had said as many as two hundred guests were expected. What if they showed up now? What would she do? Her stomach turned a summersault. In an effort to calm herself, she paced up and down. At last, to her immense relief, she saw Ian coming down the stairs toward her. She turned to greet him, and if her appearance had caused her concern before, his words quickly dissolved her fears.

The young man clutched at his chest in dramatic style as he hurried to her side.

"Be still, my heart," he said, "or I will surely swoon away at her feet. Have you seen my brother yet?" he added, his eyebrows raising comically up and down.

"No, why do you ask?"

"Oh, I don't know, Princess," he said, chuckling, "but I have a feeling that this evening is going to be much more fun than I first expected." He took her hand in his and led her to a large silver salver filled with pretty fan shaped cards. "This is your dance card for the night, Madeline, and I suggest you choose your partners with great care."

So saying, he wrote his name on several lines, then, smiling into her eyes, he fastened the card around her wrist.

Once again, she was prevented from asking the reason why as William and Tyler came down the stairs toward them. Dressed as they were in formal evening wear, no one could fail to be impressed by these three handsome men. Madeline knew they would set many a female's hearts to pounding tonight, and an odd rush of pride came with the realization.

"You look beautiful, my dear," William said, kissing her hand. "I thank you for indulging this old man's whim."

If Madeline expected some comment from Tyler, she was to go unrewarded. After a long disapproving look in her direction, he planted himself solidly at her side, his eyes dark and unreadable. Ian gave her hand a comforting squeeze, but her happy mood had quickly vanished. She snuck a sidewise look at the man responsible, but his look was unchanged. He seemed angry, and the cause escaped her, filling her heart with consternation. Retreating into silence, she listened halfheartedly to William and Ian exchanging small talk as they all waited.

As the first carriages pulled up to the house, the big front doors were thrown open, and people began arriving in ever-increasing numbers. Madeline forgot at what point she lost count of the many hands she shook. Faces became a blur. But standing wedged between the two tall brothers it seemed that some of the younger male guests were hustled quickly from Tyler to Ian, missing her altogether.

Some half hour had passed when a sultry voice was heard purring.

"Tyler, darling."

"Amanda!" Tyler's surprise was evident. "It's been a long time."

"I know," the woman gushed. "So when Harry Manning told me about tonight, I was sure my invitation must have been misplaced. You know nothing would keep me away."

Madeline smelled the strong scent of jasmine and wrinkled her nose. She stiffened as the tall, well-endowed woman swayed perilously close to Tyler. Her mouth sagged as she viewed the woman's daring display, quickly recalling the fears she had harbored about her own décolletage.

She was still suffering from a state of shock when, at that moment, the first dance was announced in the ball room.

With a wink, Ian gently lifted her drooping chin with his finger.

"It's time for the first dance, Princess," he said. Then, taking her hand, he placed it on William's arm. "Your partner, I believe, Sir."

The old man acknowledged with a stiff bow.

Shy and unsure, Madeline took a firm hold of her partner's arm, and with the whole assembly watching, the handsome couple made their way out onto the dance floor.

Chapter Nineteen

Madeline's dance card was quickly filled. As the evening wore on, she found herself passed from one partner to another. William claimed her for one more minute, then departed to the back room for a hand or two of cards. Soon after, Ian grabbed her hand, and with spirits flying high, they joined in the lively steps of the quadrille. Forward and back, then promenade. With Ian's firm arm to guide their movements, the young couple adroitly worked their way around the square formation of dancers. When, at last, the music ended, they collapsed, breathless and laughing, into the nearest chairs.

"Oh mercy," Ian gasped, leaning back in a most ungentlemanly manner. "Fan me, Madi, or I swear I shall melt away."

"Anything to oblige, Sir."

With a quick flick, she opened her white lace fan, and with her head pressed far too close to his, they shared the cooling breeze. In the past few weeks, their friendship had blossomed to a point where they now shared confidences with ease. Such was the case now.

"While we have a minute, Ian, I'm dying to know, who is that woman?"

"I suppose by 'that woman' you mean the infamous lady Amanda," he ventured.

"You know that's who I mean."

Ian grinned. "No doubt you wouldn't be half as interested if she weren't hanging all over my brother. You really do care about him, don't you?" When she didn't answer, he sighed and said sadly, "What does he have that I haven't?"

"Oh you." Madeline tapped him playfully with the fan. "Why do you take such pleasure in teasing me?"

"Because, my sweet, it's so easy." He looked deep into her bright blue eyes and said, "Tell me, Princess, what is it you really want?"

The deeper meaning of his words escaped her.

"I just want to know who she is," she said, trying to sound casual.

"And where she fits into Tyler's life, right?" At her nod, he said, "I know her name is Amanda Alcott and that she and big brother were quite close at one time. Mind you," he hastened to add, "that was a long time ago. Tell you what, I'll go ask George. He knows everything. He has been around for—"

Before he could say more, the musicians took up their instruments, and the next dance was called.

With a squeeze of her hand, he whispered, "I see your next partner coming this way, so you will have to be patient for a while. But let me see what I can find out, and I will meet you in the conservatory at midnight."

"Midnight! That's forever," she protested.

"Take it or leave it, but be quick, my sweet. The general is upon us."

With an agitated glance at the portly gentleman marching purposefully toward her, she was forced to agree.

"All right, I'll see you in the conservatory at midnight, but don't you dare be late."

"My dance, I think, Madam."

Delicately mopping his brow, the elderly man presented himself with a stiff bow.

"Quite right, General," said Ian, relinquishing her hand with a wry smile, then quickly disappearing into the crowd.

With a small curtsy, Madeline took the general's arm, and together they moved out onto the crowded floor. It was then just ten o'clock.

Madeline soon found herself swept up in the gaiety of the evening. A quick succession of younger and much livelier partners followed the general. They were enchanted by her company. Her bright smile and merry laughter were contagious, and many a young man was loath to part with her hand.

As the hours waned, darkness crept in over the revelers. Candles were lit in the great chandeliers, and soon the big old house was ablaze with light. The room grew warm, and from time to time, melting wax dripped down onto the heads of unsuspecting guests. Couples sought temporary relief by gathering at the glittering glass punch bowls where champagne corks popped with great frequency. Harried servants, under the ever-watchful eye of Mr. Wiggins, scurried back and forth to the kitchen in the never-ending effort to replenish empty trays. Conversation became loud and raucous, and some among the crowd found their way out into the quiet haven of the gardens. Here, where the air was cool and heavy with the scent of roses, they wandered where they pleased or sat beneath late-blooming lilacs, listening to the gentle murmur of nearby fountains.

Madeline longed for a little relief from the heat but found herself with her dance card full. She was in constant demand. From time to time, she spotted Tyler through the milling crowd. Not once, as far as she could tell, did he venture onto the dance floor. Instead, he hovered at the edge, sometimes alone, sometimes in the company of the jasmine-scented woman. Madeline began calling her the woman in green. She grudgingly admitted that the woman was stunning. It was easy to see how any man would be enamored of her. A sudden thought came to mind. Had the woman's appearance here tonight really been unexpected? If so, had Tyler privately hoped she would come? Could that be why he had claimed no dance on her card? She strained to look around the shoulder of her current partner and sought him out again. Yes, there they were, still side by side, apparently engrossed in intimate conversation. As she watched, the woman placed a possessive hand on his arm, and the sound of her laughter drifted clearly to Madeline's ears. Fresh doubt welled quickly in her mind. Could she trust him, really believe anything he said?

Although Tyler's face appeared placid and unconcerned at a distance, he was far from it. He found Amanda's unwanted attention annoying. Her conversation was trite and boring, and for the life of him, he couldn't understand why he had once thought her so damned attractive. But he had been young then, he excused, and she was so well-versed in ways to please a man. It had mattered little that her past was less than pure. It made her who she was. Her zest for life had thrilled him. Her demands for his attention in her bed flattered and bolstered his youthful pride. But he had been very aware of her many other admirers, so when she moved on to greener pastures—a duke twice her age with a large estate in the north of England—his sadness was short-lived. He wished she hadn't come tonight. She was a part of his past, and that was where he wanted her to stay.

Irritation growing, he found his eyes constantly searching the ballroom. The hour was growing late, and by now the crowd had thinned on the dance floor. Many of the guests chose to rest for a while or to move on to other activities. Of a sudden, he found the one he had been looking for—a slender, fair-haired woman in a blue dress. Her face was flushed and her eyes bright as she and her partner circled the floor. His body tensed. Each time he had sought her out through the evening, she had been surrounded by an entourage of ardent admirers. He hated it, wanted to grab her and pull her away. With stormy green eyes, he watched her every move, unreasonable anger burning inside.

Blissfully unaware of the eyes that followed her, Madeline greeted her next partner with a bright smile. Completely dazzled, that hapless young man, to his utter embarrassment, tripped and lost his footing. She accepted his profuse apology for stepping on her foot but nevertheless excused herself and left the floor. She was hot and thirsty and grateful for a moment to cool down. Champagne flowed everywhere, and she took a glass from the tray of a passing waiter. It was cool, and the bubbles tickled her nose. She drank it down much too quickly. Still in need, she took a second, this time sipping it slowly to enjoy the sweet fruity taste. As she made her way through the crowd, scraps of conversation caught her attention.

"Just like old times," someone said.

"Wonderful evening," said another.

In fact, all the comments she heard were directed toward His Lordship and the great success of his party. Madeline glowed with pride. How much fun she and William would have discussing it all later! But long before that could happen, she had an appointment to keep. The large clock at the end of the hall showed almost midnight. She took a deep breath and cast a glance toward the conservatory. It was cloaked in darkness. Could Ian already be there waiting for her? If so, what would he have to say? Did George really know about the woman in the green dress? And even if he did, was it likely he would he tell all? Well, no matter what, the time for waiting was over.

With some difficulty, she worked her way around the edge of the ballroom. Behind a tall screen of sheltering palms, she came upon a group of hardworking musicians. With red faces and tapping feet, the overheated men suffered in silence. Madeline stopped a moment to praise their efforts and offered them cold punch to ease their discomfort. With a tip of the head and a grateful "thank you," the players rallied. They picked up their instruments with renewed vitality and broke into the delightful strains of the Sussex Waltz. After a quick farewell and still humming to the music, Madeline continued toward her destination.

The conservatory was dark and deserted. Ian was nowhere in sight. Since coming to Marshfield Hall, this beautiful glass room had become Madeline's favorite retreat. She took a deep breath, loving the delicious smell of damp earth and growing life. With the hustle and bustle of the ballroom far behind her, she wandered slowly among the large pots of tropical plants. Odd-shaped trees stood like quiet sentinels in the semi-darkness, their large split leaves silvered by the light of the moon. The air was cooler here, and tranquility reigned amid the orderly rows of lush green foliage. William had introduced her to the joy of gardening, and thanks to him, she knew the names of every plant and tree that grew here. There were large, leafed rubber trees, tropical palms, fruit-bearing papaya, lemon, and orange trees. All dwelled side by side with William's greatest passion, gardenias. Delicate, colorful, and fragrant, they thrived under his tender care.

With still no sign of Ian, she curbed her impatience by wandering among the beds of flowering shrubs. Touching them gently, she talked to them as William always did.

"My, how beautiful you look there in the moonlight," she crooned softly. "Pretty, pretty blooms. I just love you all."

"Well, I see we both had the same idea, child." The old man came up behind her. "They do look beautiful in the moonlight, don't they?" he asked.

"I didn't hear you coming, Sir," she said, turning to greet him. "But, yes, they do."

"I like to tuck them in at night." He smiled. "I don't admit that to many people, my dear. Afraid it makes me sound like a doddering old fool."

"Then I must be a fool too," she replied.

He took her hand and patted it. "Well, I'll tell you what," he whispered, "let's make it our little secret."

She looked into his smiling eyes and was filled with affection for the old man. He had welcomed her into his home and treated her like a member of his family. His kindness was never-ending, and he had become as dear to her as anyone she had ever known. On a sudden impulse, she threw her arms around his neck and kissed his cheek.

"It's our secret," she whispered back.

They laughed softly, enjoying the conspiracy.

"All right, child," he said at last, "enough of this foolishness. Run along now and enjoy the rest of the evening. I'm off to bed."

She watched him go, calling out after a moment, "Good night and sweet dreams."

With a quick wave of his hand, he exited the conservatory, leaving her alone.

Her thoughts quickly returned to Ian. Where was he? He had given his word he would be here. Well, there was nothing for it but to go and find him. Gently smoothing her hair, she headed back toward the ballroom.

"Well, here you are, Madeline."

Tyler emerged from the shadows.

"Oh," she said, jumping, "I didn't see you there."

"Obviously."

"What do you mean?" she asked, her heart still fluttering.

"Simply that I came here thinking to find you alone." He moved closer, green eyes intent. "But from the intimate whisperings I heard in the darkness a moment ago, I realize I was mistaken."

"How could you think such a thing?"

"How could I not, Madam, with the sounds of your passionate farewell still ringing in my ears? Sweet dreams! It's not every day one hears such a declaration of affection. It was quite touching. Tell me, simply as a matter of interest, which of your many admirers was it? Perhaps I know him."

"Oh! What a horrible thing to say."

Shocked, Madeline stepped back, the color draining from her face.

"Well, who was it?" he demanded again, moving closer.

Angered, she refused to answer, and with a toss of her head, she turned to leave.

"Not so fast, my dear." He caught her arm to stop her. "All evening I have been forced to stand idly by, watching you lavish your attention on every other man in the room. Now it's my turn."

He pulled her to him, his free arm encircling her waist.

"Let me go!" Breathless, she thumped her fists against his chest. "How dare you speak to me so when this entire evening, your attention has been focused elsewhere."

"If you mean Amanda, she's an old friend," he snapped.

"Obviously!" she mimicked him. "Ever since she arrived to hang all over you, you have left me to my own devices."

"Because I refuse to stand in line with the rest of your simpering admirers. But seeing the daring cut of your décolletage, I suppose it's no wonder they drool over you so. In fact, given the chance, I'd do so myself."

He pulled her even closer, teeth gritted and eyes narrowed.

"I don't believe you!" With a squeal of disgust, Madeline shoved him hard. Catching him off guard, she managed to break free. "For one thing," she said, facing him, chin up and eyes flashing, "this dress was a gift from your grandfather. I sought to please him by wearing it tonight. But what right do you have to criticize me anyway, when your overstuffed friend could spill her attributes at any moment for all to see?"

"So," he said, ignoring her question, "my grandfather provided the gown, the jewels too, I think. My grandmother's, I believe."

He gently fingered the jewels at her neck, his eyes never leaving hers.

Madeline nodded, her skin tingling at his touch.

"Apart from that, dear lady," he said softly, "I know of no other who could wear them as well."

They fell silent, neither moving, each torn by the feelings the other invoked. The air grew heavy around them. Their breathing slowed. A sudden rustling amid the leaves broke the moment, and Tyler's eyes flashed dangerously.

"Show yourself," he demanded. "Come out from there, whoever you are."

"It's just me, Guv." George made his way around the curtain of greenery. "The old man wanted you to have this, Miss," he said, handing Madeline a white lace shawl. "He said when he left you here a while ago, it was cool, and he was worried you might get a chill."

"Thank you, George," said Madeline.

She looked to Tyler, waiting for the apology she was sure must come. It didn't. Instead, he reached for her dance card.

"What's this?" he asked, his brow rising in mock surprise. "You've left no room for me."

He took her pencil and drew a line through the next name on her card, inserting his own instead.

"And what makes you think I would dance with you?" she demanded.

"As I understand it, Madeline, my valet was your tutor. If that was the case, you were taught on my time. I think it only fair I find out for myself if my money was well spent."

Before she could protest again, the orchestra broke into the lilting strains of a waltz, and she found herself being led back into the ballroom.

"I say, old boy," said an earnest young man, stepping up and tapping Tyler on the arm, "there must be some mistake. I believe this dance is mine."

"So sorry, old boy," Tyler said, affecting an exaggerated accent, "but I'm afraid the mistake is yours."

"Dash it all. That's not cricket, Sir," the startled fellow insisted, but he was left to stare open-mouthed as Tyler swirled Madeline out into the middle of the dance floor.

Her satin slippers scarcely touched the ground as her partner skillfully guided her around the room. She was completely unaware of how well they looked together or of the attention they were attracting.

Amanda was among those watching them, and the jealousy she felt was hard to conceal. Blending their bodies with the sweet notes of the music, they spun first to the right, hesitated, reversed, then spun to the left. With her sights set on the top button of Tyler's waistcoat, Madeline followed his lead. She saw the people around them come and go in an unending blur till her head grew light and she gasped for breath.

Tyler sensed her distress and tightened his arm around her waist. He hastened the last few revolutions of the dance and twirled her out through the glass doors and back into the darkened conservatory. The music ended, but he continued to hold her. Shrouded by shadows, his face was unreadable, his breathing heavy, his body on fire. It was a long time before he spoke.

"I must remember to thank George when next we meet," he said softly. "His talents as a teacher far outweighed my expectations."

Madeline's heart refused to stop its wild beating. Visions of the dashing pirate who had recently entered her dreams flashed before her eyes. Recalling his half naked appearance, her face burned. She backed quickly away, snapping open her fan to cover her embarrassment.

"I fear you flatter me too much, Sir," she whispered, knees weak, "but I'm pleased you feel your money not wasted."

"My grandfather's either, I think," he muttered.

The blue of her dress shone iridescent in a pool of bright moonlight. Giant lilies framed her where she stood, their large blooms rivaled only by the creamy whiteness of her skin. Regal in size, their overpowering fragrance hung heavy in the air.

In one swift movement, Tyler wrapped his arms around her.

"Your beauty dazzles me, Madeline," he said, "and truly, I can find no fault with those who seek your favors tonight." He pulled her closer, looking deep into her eyes. "But I must warn you," he continued, his voice hardening, "it isn't something I can tolerate with ease."

He could feel the steady beat of her heart against his chest. His body responded violently. All the frustrations of the past few weeks bubbled up inside. With a harsh growl, he tightened his arms around her. His breath escaped in a ragged sigh as his lips sought and found hers.

Madeline's first inclination was to resist, but he grasped her slim hips, pulling them closer to his, stilling her struggles.

"Don't fight me tonight, Madeline." He sighed. "I know I brought you here against your will, but I have tried to play by the rules these past weeks." His voice grew harsh. "I'm not a patient man by nature, so believe me, it hasn't been easy having you here right under my nose, seeing but not touching, always keeping my distance. If it's revenge you seek by driving me crazy, then rest assured, you have attained your goal."

"I have no knowledge of such a crime," she protested, looking up, eyes wide.

"I find that hard to believe." A frown furrowed his brow. "A thousand times I have tried to speak my heart but was dissuaded by the distance I saw in your eyes." He bowed his head and, leaning into her, whispered close to her ear, "How much longer must I pay for my mistake?"

His warm lips brushed her cheek, and she shivered. He nibbled at her ear. A thousand new sensations stirred deep inside, and without conscious thought, her arms reached up to encircle his neck. Her body relaxed, and with a quivering sigh, she melted into his arms.

Encouraged by her unexpected response, Tyler took advantage. Lifting her from her feet, his lips sought hers again, this time with a newfound urgency. Hot and demanding, his mouth moved over hers. The kiss deepened. He parted her lips and tasted the honeyed sweetness inside. Shivering, she clung to him, warm and pliable. With no small effort, he pulled away, smiling at the dreamy, faraway look in her half-closed eyes.

"Let's get away from here," he suggested, "and find somewhere to be alone."

Feeling her stiffen, his grip tightened at her waist.

"Ride with me, Madeline, down to the shore," he urged. "We can gallop along the sand and breath in the fresh salty air or just sit on the rocks at the point. The tide is low, and there's a full moon to light our way."

She looked up into his handsome face and hesitated, her legs unsteady. A muscle twitched humorously at his jaw.

"I dare you," he challenged, white teeth flashing, green eyes a-twinkle.

It only took her a moment. To feel the smooth flow of Misty's mighty muscles beneath her, racing along the moonlit sand, was a heady potion she couldn't resist. Excitement bubbled through her veins, and she nodded vigorously.

"Hurry then, love," he said. "Change into something more suitable, and I will do the same. Meet me in the stable as soon as you can." Brushing her lips with a fleeting kiss, he turned her around and gave her a gentle shove. "Be quick. Remember, I'll be waiting."

She stopped in the ballroom just long enough to exchange a few words with George.

At his nod, she urged, "Don't forget now, George."

He assured her he wouldn't. With a smile on her face, she raced up the stairs and burst into her room in a very un-ladylike fashion. As she ran to pull her riding habit from the drawer, she explained her haste to an ecstatic Jeannie.

"Oh Miss, how romantic," the girl babbled. "Here, let me 'elp."

She quickly unfastened the back of Madeline's gown, then reverently smoothed out the blue satin dress before going to put it away.

"Would you like to try it on?" Madeline asked as she tugged on her riding boots.

"Do you mean it?" the girl asked in wonder.

"Of course I do. Here, try on the slippers too!" She tossed them onto the bed.

"Well, look at me." Jeannie stared bright-eyed at her reflection in the mirror.

"You look beautiful." Madeline came to stand beside her. Then, catching sight of herself in the mirror, she squealed in disgust. "I can't possibly wear this silly hat, Jeannie. It has to go."

With an agitated jerk, she pulled off the offending feathered object and threw it aside. Fingers flew as she frantically removed the restraints from her hair. Curls tumbled in a golden mass around her face, and running her fingers through the long strands, she twisted them into a tight bun at her nape. She shoved in the last pin and turned quickly to Jeannie as if suddenly remembering something.

"My shawl, Jeannie. I forgot my white lace shawl. I must have left it in the conservatory. Do be a dear and fetch it for me. I can't go running through the ballroom looking like this," she said, pointing to her riding habit.

"But what if someone sees me in your gown?" Jeannie asked, mortified.

"Silly goose, no one will know it's you," Madeline assured her. "Do hurry, please, I would hate to lose it."

"All right," the girl reluctantly agreed, and heart thumping, she quickly made her way down the stairs. Reaching the ballroom, she stayed in the shadows, afraid that any minute her deception might be discovered. But, to her undying relief, she reached the conservatory without incident.

"Now, where is it?" she muttered, angry that she hadn't thought to ask. Nerves taunt, imagining hostile eyes watching her every move, she searched through the surrounding shrubbery. Suddenly, someone moved out of the shadows. She stiffened, hand flying to her throat. A man in evening clothes approached her, the moonlight at his back, his face unrecognizable at a distance. Terrified, she stood frozen on the spot.

"May I have this dance, Miss?" a soft voice asked.

"Lordy, George," she squeaked, faint with relief. "you gave me a right old start, you did."

Bowing deeply, George offered her his arm. With a shy giggle and a curtsy, she moved toward him. He took her hand firmly in his and swept her into his arms. By the light of the brilliant moon, amid the fragrance of tropical flowers, they drifted together in an unforgettable moment of pure delight.

Chapter Twenty

Tyler whistled to himself as he made his way toward the stables. Perhaps this evening would work out well after all. Knowing he had little time for conversation, he quickly skirted the garden and the many revelers that had gathered there. He spotted Barnaby among the crowd and knew he would have the barn to himself for a while at least.

A gentle whinnying greeted his arrival in the stable. Large heads poked over stall doors, their bright brown eyes inquisitive. He lit a lantern and, holding it high, quickly sorted through brushes and tack. Quickly slipping the leather halter over Samson's head, he led him from the darkened stall out into the lamp light.

"I know, old friend." He sympathized when the black snorted in disgust. "It's late, and you would much rather sleep. But, if tonight goes as I hope it will, I promise you an extra scoop of grain in the morning."

He hung the lantern above his head, and rolling up his sleeves, he quickly went to work. He brushed until the sleek black hide was clean and free of dust. Anxious now to be on the move, Samson stamped his foot.

"Be patient, my friend, not long now," Tyler assured the animal. "First, I must take care of Misty, then it's a good run for us."

He was making his way to the little grays stall when the barn door creaked sharply. He turned and peered into the darkness.

"Is that you, Madeline?" He called.

There was no answer. A frown furrowed his forehead, but shrugging, he returned to work.

With a gentle mewing, Tinker, the large barn cat, rubbed against his legs.

"So, it was just you, eh Tink? Been out on the prowl, have you?" Squatting down, he scratched the fluffy animal affectionately between his ears. "Run along now. There's a good boy."

He gave the cat a gentle tap on the rump to send him on his way.

Disgusted as only a cat can be, Tinker hopped in one agile move to the top of a pile of grain bags. His lithe body stretched, and he purred loudly while kneading a spot with his front feet. Content at last, he circled twice, laid down, and gazed at Tyler with unblinking, bright yellow eyes.

Again, the noise came from the far end of the barn. Coming quickly to his feet, the cat stood, back hunched, tail erect and quivering, staring off into the distance.

"It's alright, Tink, she's a friend," Tyler assured his furry companion. "I'm here, Madeline." He called out again.

The thought of racing across the countryside with her beside him pleased him. The elements were all in his favor tonight. A warm summer breeze, a brilliant moon and a star-filled sky. What more could he ask for? He hadn't sought this relationship. It had been thrust upon him. But now he had to admit his growing feelings were becoming hard to deny, and of late, she hadn't seemed too adverse to his advances. Only time could tell where this would lead them, but he was ready for the challenge.

Madeline smiled as she imagined Jeannie's surprise meeting with George. She congratulated herself when she thought how easily her plan had fallen into place. She hurried to the desk and searched the drawer for paper and pen. Then, with a flourish, she dashed off a quick note for her friend.

Jeannie,

> Hope your first ball was as much fun as mine. Let's talk later.

> Thinking of you, M.

As she propped the note in front of the lamp, she imagined the fun they would have later, sharing their secrets. She had no way of knowing what would happen tonight, but she had discovered one thing about Tyler: it was exciting to be in his arms. Breathless and flushed, she checked her image in the mirror one last time, then rushed out of the bedroom door.

"Ian!" She bumped into him in the hall. "What happened to you? We were supposed to meet at midnight."

"I'm sorry," he explained. "Grandfather begged out of a card game and insisted I take his place. When I finally made it to the conservatory, you were gone. I was advised by a very irate Walter Fox that you were most definitely otherwise engaged."

"Oh, poor Walter Fox. I had almost forgotten. I must apologize next time we meet. But I have to run." The words tumbled from her lips. "I'm going to meet Tyler now, but I promise we'll talk later."

They shared a brief hug before she turned and ran down the back stairs.

With her pulse racing, her feet flew over the dew dampened grass. Cool air fanned her cheeks, and a gentle breeze ruffled her hair. With enough moonlight to brighten her way, she avoided the partygoers in the garden and took the longer path around the lake.

Clear and still, the water glistened like glass beneath a cloudless, star-sprinkled, ebony sky. Swallows skimmed low over the silvery surface, feeding greedily on a constant swarm of humming insects. Large fish came rushing for their share of the tasty feast, mouths gaping. Splashing and bubbling, they sent ever-widening circles spinning out to shatter the glossy calm. A thousand chirping crickets filled the night with a noisy chorus, and for Madeline, the whole world was suddenly wild and alive.

At last, the barn stood before her. She paused a moment to catch her breath. A faint light showed at the half door and sounds of movement came from inside. Tingling with anticipation, she opened the door and stepped inside. Favorite, familiar smells invaded her senses—warm horseflesh, molasses sweet feed, and hay bales ripe with fragrant clover. With a happy shiver, she waited as her eyes became accustomed to the gloom. What little light there was came from a lantern hanging at the far end of the barn. She made her way toward it and was surprised to find Misty still in her stall. The mystery deepened when, further down the barn, she found Samson tethered to the hitch but still unsaddled. Suddenly, somewhere in the darkness, she heard muffled voices.

"Hello?" She called, but there was no reply.

Unsure now, she took a lantern from its peg and made her way cautiously toward the sounds. The voices grew louder. They seemed to be arguing, but she couldn't make out what they were saying. She waited, thinking it must be Barnaby, the stable boy. Should she go on? But what of Tyler? Had she mistaken his meaning? No, of that, she was sure. She held the lantern higher, and her heart almost burst from her chest. There was an angry hiss, and large yellow eyes flashed at her in the lamp light. "Oh!" She breathed a sigh of relief as the angry cat jumped up and scampered away. Still shaking, she leaned on the stall door for support. It slid open at her touch, flooding the stall with light from the lantern. Her eyes registered shock at the scene laid out before her. On a scattered pile of hay, half-naked, lay a couple seemingly locked in the throes of passionate lovemaking. Her shock quickly turned to horror as, startled by the light, the lovers looked her way. Two pairs of eyes, one green, one amber, flashed in recognition, the first in dismay, the second in triumph.

"Good God, Madeline, wait!" Tyler yelled, heaving Amanda from his chest. "Please wait!" he called again as he struggled to his feet.

But it was already too late. Madeline was gone. The only answer to his plea was the banging of the barn door as it slammed shut behind her.

"Let her go, darling," Amanda crooned.

Happy with the results of her plan, she laid back in the hay, flaunting herself enticingly.

Tyler threw her his tattered shirt. "Cover yourself, Amanda" he said in disgust. "What you offer holds no interest for me."

He stormed from the barn, and leaving her to fend for herself, he hurried away in search of Madeline.

"Whatever happened to you?" Ian demanded of his brother minutes later as Tyler strode across the lawn toward him bare-chested and black hair matted with hay.

Ignoring his younger sibling, Tyler brushed past him, eyes distant, face dark with anger. He shocked the servants by slamming his way into the house. He stormed through the kitchen and took the back stairs two at a time.

Once in his room, he pulled on a clean shirt, poured himself a large brandy, and paced across the floor.

"What the hell just happened?" he demanded of the empty room. One minute he had heard Madeline enter the barn, the next he was attacked from behind. He remembered flipping his attacker over his shoulder. There had been a loud "Umph" and together they landed head-first a pile of hay. He had swiftly stilled his opponent's frantic struggles and hissed, "If you wish to see the light of another day, my friend, I suggest you explain yourself in a hurry."

"Darling!"

His shock had been tenfold when, spitting dust, a disheveled Amanda sat looking up at him.

"Christ, Amanda. Explain yourself," he had snapped.

"It has been soooo long, my love," she had crooned, a sultry look in her amber eyes, "and this seemed like such a good place to make up for lost time."

So saying, she had thrown her arms around his neck and pulled him down, her eager mouth seeking his.

"Stop it!" he had demanded, pushing her away. "This is going nowhere."

"No, don't go!"

Breathing hard, she had grabbed a hold of his shirt, dragging it from his shoulders in the process. At that exact moment, the already over-stressed seams of her bodice had chosen to part company. Freed from all restraint, Amanda's ample bosom had spilled forth. It was in this compromising situation that Madeline had discovered them.

"God, what a mess," he muttered. "No wonder Madeline took off like a shot." He poured himself another brandy, drained the glass, and wondered out loud, "How in the name of all that is holy do I explain my way out of this?"

Chapter Twenty-One

Jeannie drifted on a cloud of pure delight. Never in her entire life had she spent such an unforgettable evening. If the earth opened up and swallowed her now, she wouldn't complain. She hummed softly to herself as she opened the door to Madeline's room. She put a light to the lamp and stopped short, suddenly realizing she wasn't alone.

"Sorry, Miss, I didn't expect you back so soon. 'ow was your ride?"

Madeline stood at the window, looking out at the lightening sky.

"I didn't get to go," she said, a catch in her voice.

"But why? What happened?" Jeannie asked, moving quickly to her side.

With Jeannie's comforting arm around her shoulders, Madeline told her of the happenings in the barn.

"Oh, Jeannie, it was awful," she said, ending the story at last.

At a loss for words, Jeannie could only hold her friend and help her dry her tears.

The two barely slept but spent the rest of the night sitting side by side on Madeline's bed.

By morning, the whole household was whispering. Rumors ran rampant.

"What happened?" they were asking each other.

"Well, they say Mister Tyler stormed in through the kitchen half-dressed last night."

"Steer clear of him this morning," someone muttered. "Staff upstairs say he looks black as thunder."

"But what of Mistress Madeline?"

"She's shut up in her room, not coming out. Only one allowed in is Jeannie, and she's not saying anything."

So the morning passed, everyone walking on tiptoe, just waiting for the outcome of whatever had happened.

Tyler found himself avoided by the whole household. His attempts to get close enough to Madeline to explain were quickly rebuffed. Constantly on guard, Jeannie ran interference at every turn. Even George, who knew all the facts of the case, was unable to get close enough to explain. Stung by such unfair treatment, Tyler became silent and withdrawn. He walked a narrow line between anger and indifference.

Hurt and humiliated, Madeline wanted no part of his explanations. Keeping to her room that day, she ranted to Jeannie about his behavior.

"What of his fine promises now? He can't be trusted. Just give me time, he said. He said he'd find my father after his grandfather's birthday. And like a fool, I believed him. Then what happens? This woman comes along, and all his fine promises fly out the window. Oh, I hate him!"

"But Miss," Jeannie said, trying to console her, "George says it's all a mistake. He says if you will just listen, he can explain."

"Explain! Explain what?" she cried. "I listened to George before. He said my coming here was a mistake. Now this is another mistake. How many more mistakes will there be? If you were there Jeannie, you would understand. Ooh!"

As if she were witnessing it all over again, Madeline clapped her hands over her eyes.

"So what will you do?" Jeannie asked, wanting to know.

"I'm not sure yet," she answered, "I need time to think."

That night, long after the rest of the household had gone to their beds, Madeline paced the floor, but try as she might, she could think of nothing.

The next day, at William's request, she emerged from her self-imposed seclusion, looking dark-eyed from lack of sleep. Though she joined the morning ride, her gaiety with William and Ian was forced, while she ignored Tyler completely.

"Whew!" William mopped his brow later as he and Ian returned to the house.

"Exactly," Ian muttered grimly, upset that his attempts to act as peacemaker had failed.

All he and William had been able to do was watch as Madeline cantered off ahead and Tyler rode silently behind.

Two more days passed in the same manner, the whole house tense, people wondering how long it would be before someone snapped. Everyone gave Tyler a wide berth, wary of his dark mood, preferring not to deal with the sharp edge of his tongue. Finally, on the morning of the third day, he waited in the upstairs hall. As Madeline made to leave her room, he blocked her way.

"We need to talk!" he said.

"Indeed, Sir, there is nothing to say. Your actions have spoken louder than words."

"Damn it all, Madeline." He grabbed her arm as she made to pass by. "Will you just listen to me?"

"No, I won't!"

She faced him, angry tears glittering in her eyes. With a sharp tug, she pulled her arm free, and without another word, she hurried away.

Later, after exchanging a few words with George, Tyler announced that he would be returning to Long Meadow.

"I'll be gone a few days, perhaps a week," he confided, "I'm expecting to hear from our agents in London. Hopefully, it will be good news. If not, then I shall head to Exeter myself."

As George, William, and Ian watched his departure that day, Ian put all their thoughts into words.

"Well, let's hope the news from London is good because I, for one, will be glad when this is all over."

"Me too, lad," William agreed. "I just wish he had told Madeline why he was leaving. I know he hopes to avoid disappointment for her if the news is bad, but I still think she had the right to know."

"Well, I suppose, this way, she'll be spared the worry of the next few days," George offered.

They all agreed. However, had they been privy to Madeline's thoughts at that moment, they would have felt quite differently.

"I'm leaving, Jeannie," she told the girl. "I can't wait any longer. I know my benefactor is somewhere near Exeter. I even know his name, Reginald Spencer, so I'm going to find him myself."

"Oh Miss, that's crazy talk. Please listen to me. It's too dangerous."

"I know I must be careful," she said. "A girl alone attracts too much attention, but I have an idea, Jeannie."

It had come to her that morning while talking to Barnaby. Suddenly, she had been struck by the shapeless cut of the boy's clothing. Dressed in such a fashion, with the large cloth cap he wore pulled down on her head, it would be almost impossible for anyone to know she was a girl. It was a daring plan, and she knew Jeannie would be difficult to convince. But if she were to succeed, she needed an accomplice.

"What are you going to do?" Jeannie asked.

"Before I tell you, you must swear not to tell a soul, not even George."

"Oh Lordy, Miss. George 'll really give me what for if 'e finds out."

"But he won't if you keep quiet," Madeline insisted. "All you have to do is get me some of Barnaby's clothes."

"Barnaby's clothes!" Jeannie squeaked, stunned.

"Yes," said Madeline, struggling to sound casual even though her heart beat quickened. "Don't you see? Dressed as a boy, no one will know who I am."

Jeannie still looked unconvinced.

"This is Saturday," Madeline persisted. "Barnaby will be going into town to visit Milly at the tavern. While I am at dinner, you must slip down to the stables. It should only take a few minutes. Take the things up to my room, and I will join you there as soon as I can get away."

"I wish you wouldn't, Miss," Jeannie begged.

"Please, for me?" Madeline pleaded.

At last, with a worried frown, Jeannie agreed.

The atmosphere at the dinner table was subdued. Although Madeline looked particularly lovely in a demure dinner gown of pale green satin, her usual sparkle was missing. Her heart was heavy, knowing that in all probability, this was the last meal she would eat in this house; that this might well be the last evening she would spend with William.

For a moment, her resolve wavered, but as her eyes traveled to the empty seat at the table, her anger sparked anew. Where was he? Why had he left without another word? It wasn't like him to give up so easily. Perhaps had he tried again, she might have listened this time. There was only one answer. He had gone to be with Amanda, the woman from his past.

Excusing herself early on the pretext of a headache, she hurried to her room.

"Have you got everything?" she asked Jeannie a moment later.

"Yes, but—"

"Did you have any trouble?"

"No, but—"

"Good! Let me see what you found."

She watched, breathless, as her companion pulled a large sack from under the bed. Dragging it across the room, she quickly emptied the contents out onto the floor. With a soft rustle of satin, her dress was quickly discarded and thrown down to join the pile at her feet.

"Now."

Shaking with excitement, Madeline grabbed up the oversized britches and pulled them on. They slipped down around her ankles. She pulled them up again, this time tucking a heavy shirt firmly down inside them.

"It's no good, Jeannie. They won't stay up," she groaned.

"Wait, I have an idea."

Dashing from the room, Jeannie returned moments later with a length of brown twine. As Madeline held the unruly garment in place, Jeannie was able to secure it by circling her waist several times with the twine. Big brown boots were fitted over several pairs of woolen hose, and although they were hot and uncomfortable, they filled out the boots quite nicely.

Jeannie giggled in spite of herself.

"Oh Lordy, Miss, what a sight you are," she sputtered, holding onto the cap as Madeline ran a brush through her hair.

She twisted the long tresses into a rope and wound them into a bun. With the bun securely pinned onto her head, the cap was perched on top.

"It just won't do, Jeannie," she fussed as the cap refused to stay put. "Bring me some scissors. Oh, don't look so shocked," she said when her purpose suddenly became clear. "It will grow back soon enough."

With that, she took a deep breath, squeezed her eyes shut tight, and chopped away.

"Well, how do I look?" she asked, stepping back, throwing her arms wide, and turning in a slow circle.

"Upon my word, Sir." Jeannie fluttered her lashes and dropped into a deep curtsey. "If I wasn't spoken for, I swear you could sweep me off me feet."

Madeline ran to the mirror and stopped short.

Her eyes never once leaving the strange reflection before her, she said in a trembling voice, "I think we've done it, Jeannie. Even I can't believe it's me."

Time moved slowly as Madeline waited in her darkened room. The house had long since fallen quiet, but still she waited, making sure no night owls wandered the halls. Thrusting her hands into her pockets, she checked the few coins she had borrowed from Jeannie. There was something comforting about the feel of them.

"No one could be a better friend than you," she whispered to the girl now dozing in a chair. "And I promise you I will pay back every penny."

Softly creeping to the door, she turned and blew a kiss to the sleeping girl. She hurried down the stairs, and brushing a stray tear from her eye, she walked out into the cool night air.

A bright moon shone down as she made her way toward the stable. It was almost midnight, and all was quiet. Even so, once in a while, she felt the urge to look over her shoulder. The unease stayed with her until, at last, she merged into the shadows blanketing the barn. At her touch, the barn door squeaked open, and she slipped inside.

"Quiet, girl," she whispered at Misty's whinnied greeting. "You will wake Barnaby."

As if understanding, Misty shook her head, then turned her attention back to the grain bucket. With one ear tuned for movement in Barnaby's room, Madeline quickly saddled the gray. Her fingers suddenly became all thumbs as she struggled to tighten the girth.

"Good girl, good girl," she soothed as the mare stomped her feet, growing restless. "I'm almost done." Her hands shook as she slid the bit between large white teeth and finally fastened the bridle. Then, with a sigh of relief, she patted the mare's soft warm neck and led her from her stall. She hurried out across the yard, too afraid to mount until they were well-hidden from view. At last, behind a stand of sheltering pines, she felt safe enough to stop and take a deep breath.

"We've made it, Misty. I knew we could."

With the newfound freedom in her male attire, she adjusted the stirrups and swung up into the saddle. Beyond her, the open road beckoned, stretching off into the distance. Despite her brave words to Jeannie, her resolve faltered a little. As she looked back at her beloved Marshfield Hall, her thoughts were all of William. How many happy hours they had spent together. But mocking green eyes lurked in the deepest corners of her mind. They pricked at her pride, spawning anger anew.

"Damn him!" she shouted to the night sky.

Bitter tears burned her eyes, and spinning Misty around, she shook out the reins.

"Go, girl, go," she urged, wanting to be gone before she could change her mind.

With no coaxing needed, Misty jumped into a fast canter. Soon, Marshfield Hall and William were left far behind.

The cool night air was exhilarating and, tossing her head, Misty picked up the pace. Caught up in the moment, Madeline pulled off her cap. She threw back her head and laughed as the breeze ruffled her newly cut hair.

Chapter Twenty-Two

Tyler spent a restless night. Finally, leaving his bed in disgust, he poured himself a stiff brandy. He paced his room late into the night. It was fast becoming a habit. His mood was sour, had been ever since the fiasco with Amanda. Damn it, how could he ever make things right with Madeline if she continued her high handed attitude. He had sought to distance himself from her by returning to Long Meadow, but it had proved useless. He thought of her now as he had last seen her on their morning ride, racing at full speed across the countryside, face flushed and glowing. Damn it, just thinking about her made his temper flare. Why wouldn't she listen? Why on earth, without ever giving him a chance to explain, had she tried him and found him guilty? It was unfair. Well, so be it, he decided, at last. But on his return to Marshfield Hall in a few days, she was going to listen to him, even if he had to sit on her to keep her still. The idea appealed to him, and he chuckled out loud.

The next morning, he dressed with care, regarding his image in the mirror with a critical eye. He cursed out loud as he retied his cravat for the third time.

"Damn it all, George, where are you when I need you?" he muttered, knowing full well it was his own doing that George had stayed on at Marshfield Hall.

A sudden commotion drew him to the window. It was his hope that the messenger he expected had at last arrived from London. Instead, to his surprise, it was his brother who burst into the room moments later.

"What brings you here so early, Sprout?" Noting the other's rather rumpled appearance, he added, "And in such a state too?"

"She's gone," Ian stated.

"What do you mean she's gone?" Tyler demanded, still struggling with the unruly neckpiece.

"Madeline, that's who." Ian landed in the nearest chair with a thud. "What do you plan to do about it?"

"Calm down," Tyler snapped, "and tell me what's happened. No!" He held up his hand. "On second thoughts, you can explain on the way." He tugged at the cravat he had just succeeded in tying. "I should have known she would try something like this."

Quickly changing into more suitable clothing for the ride, he berated himself. He was a fool. He should never have left with so many things unsettled between them.

Arriving back at Marshfield Hall, Tyler found the place in an uproar.

"She's not here, lad." William met him at the front door. He had a letter in his hand and his face looked drawn. "Her bed hasn't been slept in, and no one saw her leave."

His hand trembled as he handed his grandson a crumpled piece of paper. Tyler frowned.

"Well, this is no help," he said, quickly scanning the brief message. "She just says sorry, not to worry about her and that she will return Misty as soon as possible."

"Not to worry! Foolish, thoughtless child," William's voice faltered. "What could she be thinking?"

"Calm yourself, Sir. She must have confided in someone. What about Jeannie?"

"We thought of that, but so far the girl is saying nothing," the old man said.

"George has gone to speak to her. I just hope he can get something out of her."

"If there's anything to learn there, George will."

Tyler's words were designed to set William's mind to rest, but common sense told him nothing about this was going to be easy.

"What say you, George?" he asked the man a little later.

"Nothing to report, Gov." A tearful Jeannie sat in the parlor with George standing close by her side. "She knows something, but she's determined not to tell." He placed a comforting hand on the distraught girl's shoulder. "She's a loyal lass, and although she's wrong, I can't break her heart by forcing her to betray her friend."

Tyler nodded his understanding. "Truth to tell, I think we only have two choices anyway," he said. "As I see it, she either went toward London or Exeter."

George agreed and called on Ian to join them. They laid out their plans.

Despite William's desire to take part in the search, Tyler finally convinced him that his presence at the house was more important.

"We need you here, Sir," he insisted. "What if news comes from our London agent or, more importantly, what if Madeline decides to return on her own?"

Later, as they made their way to the stables, Ian remarked, "Well you managed to get the old man to stay, but I can tell you, Brother, he wasn't happy about it."

"I know, but I spoke to Mrs. Carter. She's been concerned about his health too, so she promised to keep an extra close eye on him while we're gone."

"Say no more," George said, chuckling. "I feel sorry for the old man though. Knowing Ma, she won't let him out of her sight till we get back."

"I think you're right," Tyler agreed, nodding.

Even though they wasted little time, it was almost noon before they left Marshfield Hall behind. Sure that Madeline must have a good head start by now, they decided to split their search. So, wishing each other well, they parted company. George and Ian headed toward London, while Tyler set his sights on Exeter.

Chapter Twenty-Three

Madeline had no idea of the upheaval caused by her departure from Marshfield Hall. She supposed, if she thought about it at all, that life there would go on as usual. Once she had decided to leave, she had given little thought to anything else. At first, it had been her plan to head for London, but she quickly abandoned that idea. The city was too large, and she was unsure about Solicitor Bailey. From what she had gathered from conversations between Tyler and William, the man had been hard to find. But Tyler had given her a name, Spencer, and a place to start, Exeter. With this knowledge to guide her, she would head west.

She had no idea as to how far she had traveled, but as the moon began its downward journey, she thought it safe to stop for a while. With the effects of her sleepless night taking their toll, she left Misty to graze in a nearby field, and creeping under a hedgerow, she closed her eyes and slept.

The warmth of the early morning sun on her face and the gnawing hunger in her stomach finally awoke her. She pulled a small bag from the inside pocket of her jacket and emptied the contents out into her lap. Her meager supplies consisted of a few pieces of dried bread, some cold meat, and an apple, all of which she had managed to secret from the dining table last evening. She knew she must stretch things to the limit, so she ate only enough to appease her hunger.

She bit off a chunk of her apple and offered it to Misty. "It's not much, I'm afraid, girl, but when we reach our destination, I promise I will make sure you eat like a queen."

Unperturbed, Misty tossed her head and chomped on her share of the treat.

As her journey continued, Madeline began to feel more and more at ease in her boyish garb. She traveled from village to village, spending just enough money to sustain her, and her passing went almost unnoticed. With a word here and a question there, she gathered information a little at a time. Never conversing long enough to arouse anyone's interest, she knew she was slowly getting closer to her destination.

"Where you be goin' then?" a farmer called out as she passed him on a narrow stretch of road. She pulled her cap a little lower over her face and waved her hand as if she didn't hear.

"Goin' to the fair then?" the man spoke louder. This time she nodded.

"Fine day for it," she said in her deepest voice.

"That it be, Mister," the man called back, and giving a sharp whistle to the dogs guiding his sheep, he trudged, unconcerned, on his way.

Madeline breathed a sigh of relief. All was going well, and as she began to encounter more people, her confidence soared. Soon she was surrounded by a lively crowd, all slowly wending their way toward the city. Dark-haired Gypsies drove gaily painted caravans, and peddlers navigated lumbering wagons with practiced skill. By listening to the gossip going on around her, she learned that this was the opening day of the fair. Excitement sparked the air, and she found it contagious. What difference would it make if she lingered here awhile? She felt safe. Even if

Tyler did come looking for her, which she doubted, he would never find her among this large crowd. So, upon finding a small stable, and dickering for a while with the hostler, she was provided with a night's care for Misty. She waited to make sure the mare was well fed, then rejoined the festivities, this time on foot.

"At the city square," someone told her. "The procession starts at the city square." She followed along behind the jostling crowd and was treated to the grandest sight she had ever seen. The procession was led by the head constable. He carried a parchment tied with blue ribbon. They said it was the charter granted for the holding of the fair. Behind him came two staff holders in tricorne hats, two fifers, a drummer, and a man carrying a long white pole. With much ado, they made their way to the old city gates. Madeline watched as the charter was read, and the three-day fair was officially opened. Musicians played, small children sang, and the ceremony finally came to a close amid the resounding cheers of the people.

Madeline mingled in, listening with interest to the lively conversations.

"Tell your fortune, young Mister." A raven-haired gypsy reached out to grab her sleeve. "Just cross my palm with silver and I—"

"No thank you," Madeline said quickly, without thinking. She saw a puzzled look flicker in the gypsy's dark eyes, and realizing she had made a mistake, she pulled her arm free and hurried away.

The slim gypsy climbed slowly back to her seat on the caravan. "There's something strange about that one," she mused.

"Bah! What will I do with you and your crazy ideas, little sister?"

"You never listen, Antonio," she spat back. "When will you learn that Roxanne, she sees everything."

Antonio shook his head in despair. He flicked the whip at his team, and they ambled slowly down the busy street.

Still a little shaken by her encounter with the gypsy girl, Madeline moved quickly to merge back into the passing crowd. She risked one last glance over her shoulder, and her heartbeat quickened when she again saw the dark-haired gypsy. Perched beside a man, on the high seat of a brightly painted caravan, the girl watched her movements from afar. Their eyes met over the heads of the other revelers, and although it was only an impression, Madeline was sure a sly smile spread slowly across the other's exotic face. Not caring now where she went, only trying to distance herself from the gypsy's prying eyes, she wandered back streets and alleyways. At last she found herself in an open marketplace where farmers jostled merchants, and rich men bargained with the poor. Tattered beggars vied for coins, while brightly clad jesters regaled their audience with comic stories and antics. Bakers and haberdashers, tinkers, and cobblers, all hawked their wares in shrill voices, each trying to outdo the other.

"Sticky buns, sticky buns, and sweet tarts right 'ere," cried one. Tempted by the sticky treats, Madeline parted with a penny and popped the delicious goodie into her bag.

"Pots to mend. I need pots to mend. Only one small copper coin. Pots to mend," called another.

Everyone, it seemed, had come to buy or sell, and momentarily forgetting her own mission, Madeline took time out to gaze in wonder at the exciting world around her.

"Ribbons for yur lady, young Zir?" a vender asked.

Her disguise was serving her well. But Madeline had never seen such a display of beautiful colors, and unable to resist the temptation, she gently ran her fingers through the pretty streamers.

"Make me an offer, Zir." The dealer pressed in hopes of making a sale.

But his disappointment was plain to see when Madeline shook her head and passed on by. Other merchants did their best to tempt her with their wares, but with a firm "No," she quickly turned them all away.

As the morning wore on, more people came out to fill the narrow streets. The nearness of their bodies and the dust stirred up by their passing feet soon made breathing difficult. In order to escape for a while, Madeline made her way to an open green. The sun had grown warm, and she sought shelter beneath the limbs of a big old oak. She ate a little of the food from her bag and watched, enthralled, as musicians and traveling actors performed on a makeshift stage. In her whole life, she had never seen such a wonderful thing. By now all thoughts of the strange gypsy she had met that morning had vanished from her mind. From her grassy resting place, she observed the many people around her. Coming and going, in groups or alone, they were looking to relax after a busy morning at the fair. Some drifted toward a tavern that proudly proclaimed itself The Blue Angel, while others chose to play silly games. There was one they called the grinning game. Madeline laughed as they took turns poking their heads through a horse collar and pulling the most ridiculous faces. Still others preferred to sit on the sidelines, drinking a glass or two of ale and just enjoying the antics of the players.

Later the colorful jesters came by, performing little acts of magic and begging coins from any who stopped to watch. An organ grinder joined them and strolled around the green. A monkey dressed in a blue suit with gold buttons and a red pillbox hat sat on his shoulder. Spotting Madeline, the furry little animal hopped down and ran to stand before her. He chattered away, flipped over twice, clapped his hands, and held out his hat.

Enchanted but having no extra money to give, Madeline offered him some leftover bits of her sugared bun. Quickly grabbing the prize in his tiny hands, his round black eyes shining, he jumped up and down, screeching as he stuffed the sticky treat into his mouth.

"That's all I have," she finally said, holding out the empty bag for his inspection. Not to be deterred, the little animal snatched it away, sticking his head inside in hopes of finding a few leftover crumbs. Madeline laughed and clapped her hands, delighted by the little creature and his crazy antics.

"I told you there was nothing left." She jumped up, and pulling the bag from his head, she shook it out to prove it was empty. As if understanding at last, he screeched out his disgust, flipped over once more, and scampered away.

Evening was upon her before she knew it. Lamps were lit, and the green was almost deserted. Tired revelers had slowly made their way home or inside to continue their party going. Music and loud voices came from the tavern, and for the first time, Madeline felt lonely. She missed Jeannie and wished her friend could have shared this day with her. What a fine time they would have had. A shadow of guilt crossed her mind. She had left Jeannie to bear the brunt, not only of Tyler's displeasure but of George's as well. But there was no turning back now, and tonight she was too tired to think on it further. Longing for company and with no one around to stop her, she crept into Misty's stall. The little mare greeted her with a toss of her head and gentle whinny.

"I love you too, Misty," she whispered. Wrapping her arms around the gray's neck, she breathed in her warm, comforting smell. Feeling a little better, she piled hay in the corner of the stall, curled up in a ball, and fell asleep.

Chapter Twenty-Four

Tyler Wentworth cursed his luck as he rode into the city. Today, he learned, was the start of the fair, and the streets buzzed like a frantic hive of bees. His hope of trying to find one small female at any time was difficult, but in such a crowd, it could prove impossible. As he passed the clock in the city square, it struck three. He had wasted little time getting here, knowing only too well that if he was ever to catch up with Madeline, he dared not delay. But what if he was wrong? Doubts were beginning to cloud his mind. How could she have come so far and not been seen? Inquiries he had made in each village and hamlet he had passed had proved fruitless. No one, it seemed, had seen a fair-haired woman. It was like chasing a beautiful ghost. He was of a mind to turn back. Perhaps by now she had already been found on the way to London. She might, at this moment, be safe back at Marshfield Hall.

"Damn it, Samson," he muttered, "I was sure she would come this way. I would have staked my life it."

Still unsure, he decided to go on for at least one more day. With his mind made up, he felt in need of refreshment. He asked directions from a group of noisy revelers, then joined them on their way to a tavern called

The Blue Angel. To avoid the crowd, he made his way to the courtyard out back. With Samson's needs in the care of the inn's groomsman, he now looked to satisfy his own. Thirst was uppermost in his thoughts as he entered the rear door of the tavern. The light inside was dim, but as his eyes grew accustomed to the gloom, he found himself in a long narrow hall. There was no one in sight, but the sound of music came from somewhere up ahead. It seemed there was entertainment here, and he made his way toward it. Ducking through a low doorway, he discovered a hot, smoke-filled room packed with people. The air was ripe with the smell of unwashed bodies, and had his thirst not been so compelling, he might have abandoned the idea altogether. But as it was, he moved further inside and discovered the reason for such a large gathering. All eyes were directed to a small dance floor in the middle of the room. There, bathed in the light of a dozen flickering lanterns, a beautiful dark-haired girl swayed sensuously to the soft throb of a gypsy guitar. She was a vision in red, and like moths attracted to a flame, men gathered all around her. Tyler stopped, his eyes narrowing from the smoke as he, like the rest, watched in silent admiration.

Her bright red dress was cut on the Spanish style. Worn low on the shoulders, it hugged her slim body down to her hips, where it blossomed out into a swirl of wide ruffles. Gold bangles glittered on her arms, and large gold rings dangled at her ears. A talisman, strung on black velvet, was worn around her neck, and a single red rose adorned her long dark hair. As she circled the room, castanets clicked at her fingers and the high heels of her black shoes tapped out a steady beat upon the floor.

Suddenly, spotting the tall man by the door, a smile curved her full red lips. Never once taking her gaze from his handsome face, she moved deliberately toward him. The musician's nimble fingers flew over the strings as people scattered to let her pass. With her dark hair flying out about her, she danced for one man alone.

Tension gripped the room. The air grew heavy. Bystanders held their breath as if under some strange hypnotic spell. No one moved. All eyes centered on the stunning couple. At last, the music trembled to a close. With the last notes still quivering on the strings, the girl threw back her head and fell to her knees at Tyler's feet.

"Bravo!" he cried, joining the applause of the crowd.

"You like, Senor?" she asked, chest heaving and eyes ablaze.

"I like very much." He chuckled as he gave her his hand and pulled her to her feet.

"My name, it eez Roxanne," she said, fluttering her long lashes. "You buy me a drink, no?"

"I buy you a drink, yes, pretty one." So saying, he tucked her hand through his arm and called out, "A table, if you please, landlord, and a jug of your best wine."

"Right this way, Zir." The portly man rubbed his hands together. It wasn't often he saw such a gent in his humble establishment, and he smelled money. "Sally," he roared at the little serving girl, "'urry with a jug fur the gent." With much ado, he led the way to the best table in the house. "Whatever you wants, Zir," he said, flicking remnants of the last customer's meal onto the floor, "all you have to do is ask."

Tyler nodded and dropped a coin onto the table.

"You are too kind, Senor."

Roxanne frowned as the landlord scooped up the money and stuffed it in his pocket. "See this poor girl," she said to Tyler as Sally served the wine. "'e works her too 'ard and pays her almost nothing. Big fat peeg!" As she sat down on the chair Tyler held out for her, she sent a withering look in the landlord's direction.

"You dance like an angel, querido." Tyler chuckled. "But your tongue betrays you, I think."

"Bah! These people. They are peons." She tossed her head in disgust. "But you, Senor, you appreciate Roxanne's talent, I can tell. So tonight, I danced just for you."

She smiled sweetly up into his eyes.

"Then I am in your debt, Senorita." As he sat down opposite her, he took another coin from his pocket and tossed it in her direction.

With an impudent grin on her face, she caught the coin in midair, tested it with her teeth, and slipped it into the neck of her dress.

"There's more where that came from, querida, if you can help me."

She moved closer and ran her finger along his arm. "Whatever you desire, Senor," she purred. "You have only to ask."

"You mistake my meaning," he explained. "I seek a woman."

"A woman?" She pouted, making no effort to hide her disappointment.

"Yes. She is small and fair and—"

"I have seen no such woman," she interrupted angrily. "Even if I had, why should I help you to find her?"

"You refuse me then?"

"Yes!"

He laid another coin on the table and made to leave.

"Wait!" She grabbed his hand, turned it over, and traced the lines on his palm. "Perhaps Roxanne, she can see something here."

Looking skeptical, he drained his glass and waited.

"Well?" he asked, an indulgent smile on his face.

Eyes distant, she studied the fine lines. "I see an old man with sad eyes," she said at last, "and a woman with hair the color of corn silk."

"Yes." His interest piqued.

"There is much danger for you with that one." Her face was anxious. "Forget her. Stay here with Roxanne. She is all the woman you need!"

"You tempt me, little one, but danger is no stranger to me, and the old man you spoke of would never forgive me."

"You are a fool then." Roxanne shook her head. "Just remember that I warned you."

Tyler nodded.

"Roxanne!" A sharp voice called from across the room. Roxanne's eyes narrowed as she watched the swarthy man hurrying toward her.

"Caramba!" she spat, throwing up her arms, her face darkening with anger.

Tyler came swiftly to his feet. Sensing danger, he turned to face the threat. With one hand close to his pistol, he listened while the two gypsies engaged in a violent exchange in Spanish.

"This ees my brother, Senor. He follows me around like a puppy dog. Go home, Antonio," she snapped. "I want no part of you." Her eyes roamed the room, looking for the musician, but he was nowhere in sight. "Bah!" she growled. "I see that peeg Carlos came running to find you. Just wait till I see him. I will slit his useless throat from ear to ear."

"Senor," Antonio said, ignoring her. "My sister, she looks like a woman full-grown, but in truth she is still a child. I must protect her from herself. You understand, si?"

The concern in the man's eyes was genuine, and although Tyler was the bigger of the two, it was obvious from the set of the Gypsy's jaw that he lacked nothing in courage. Tyler relaxed.

"Have no fear, friend. I have sisters of my own. Roxanne was kind enough to entertain me with her skill."

Unsure for a moment, Antonio held his ground. Then, with a nod, he stepped aside.

"Gracias." He bowed stiffly. "I pray you pay no notice to her foolish notions, Senor." Eyes narrowing, he scowled at his sister. "Come, Roxanne, you've made enough mischief for one day." He took her arm and, none too gently, marched her away.

But before she left, Roxanne called back her warning.

"There is danger, mi amore. Roxanne, she will pray for your safe return."

Tyler took his leave of the tavern by the back door. Grateful to be away from the oppressive atmosphere, he breathed deeply of the fresh air. From his darkened vantage point, he watched as the Gypsies passed by. Roxanne's shrill voice carried clearly to his ears.

"Ouch!" He flinched as he translated her scathing words. His knowledge of Spanish was limited, learned from dockside encounters. But as the long-suffering Antonio trudged stoically ahead of her, Tyler knew Roxanne promised eternal damnation to him and all of his descendants.

"Adios, pretty lady." He tipped his hat to her retreating figure. "As for you, Antonio, well, you have my sympathy, friend."

He had lingered too long, and now he wanted to be on his way. The crowds had thinned in front of the tavern. He took his leave, paying no heed to the old organ grinder or to the lone boy who played on the green with a lively little monkey.

Chapter Twenty-Five

Since leaving The Blue Angel, Tyler had ridden hard. Now he looked out over a bare stretch of the countryside. It was late, and daylight was fading fast. He was still angry with himself for having wasted so much time at the tavern. With still no sign of Madeline, he began to worry in earnest. He still found it hard to believe that she could have traveled this far. But where could she have gone? The conversation they had had in the gardens at Marshfield Hall kept coming back to haunt him. Could it be she remembered more about Lord Reginald Spencer that she was willing to share? The coast to the west of here, he had learned, was wild and untamed, and that would surely match her description of her father's home. But to wander out here with no real goal in mind was foolish. He was letting his emotions run away with him, and that was something he had always avoided. Frustrated, he decided at last to retrace his steps. Perhaps then he might be able to pick up a trail.

Dark clouds had begun to gather overhead, and the barren landscape took on a ghostly, gray hue. Raindrops spattered down on his head, and he cursed his luck when thunder rumbled ominously around him.

Reluctantly, he pulled up his collar and turned Samson back in the direction of Exeter.

"Mister, Mister!"

He wondered if his ears were playing tricks on him.

"Help, Mister!"

No, there it was again, a plaintive cry for help. Anxiously he scanned the rugged terrain and at last spotted the source. A small boy was coming toward him, waving his arms wildly as he ran.

"It's me Gran, Sir," the child explained, gasping for breath. "We was collecting peat for the fire and she fell. Over there." He pointed to a distant boulder. "I'm scared, Mister. She can't move."

"Stay calm, lad. I will do what I can."

With one last futile look at the road ahead, Tyler sighed in resignation. He dismounted, knowing his own mission would have to wait. The plight of this small boy and his grandmother left him no choice.

Though poorly dressed, the child's clothing was neat and well patched. His face was thin, and his limbs lacked the luster of a good diet. Tyler guessed his age to be about seven. Light as a feather, he lifted the boy up onto the saddle, gave Samson his head, and they followed the boy's directions.

"What say you, old woman?" Tyler knelt beside her, saddened by the pain he saw in her eyes.

"It's me leg, Sir." Her voice was little more than a whisper.

"Then with your permission, Madam." He lifted her skirt and examined the damaged limb. It was a sorry sight, and he winced at its distorted size and ugly color. "How long ago did you do this?" he asked.

"Early this morning, Sir."

"And you've lain here ever since?" He was appalled.

"The lad couldn't move me, Sir, and not a soul has passed by this way all day. Not till you came, that is."

"What's your name, child?" Tyler turned to face the boy.

"Charlie Tippit, Sir."

"Well, Charlie Tippit, if your Gran is ever to walk again, we must set this broken bone. Run now and find me two long, stout sticks."

While he waited, Tyler took a clean shirt from his saddle bag, tore it into strips, and tied them neatly together.

"Hold your Gran's hand, Charlie," he said when the boy returned. "This is going to hurt, and she'll need all the strength you can give her."

Charlie sat cross-legged upon the ground, the old woman's head cradled in his lap. She gave him her hand, and with tears running down his face, he took it and held on tight.

"Ready?" Tyler asked.

Charlie nodded.

Long after her shrill screams had faded and she had lapsed into unconsciousness, the boy's soft voice still offered words of comfort.

By the time they reached the tumbledown cottage the two called home, the dark clouds had fulfilled their promise of heavy rain. But the hovel offered little in the way of protection. Windblown rain cascaded from the roof to pour in through broken windows. The door, long since stripped of its hinges, hung limp and useless in its frame.

"Where's the rest of your family, Charlie?" Tyler wanted to know.

"Don't 'av none, Sir," he answered. "Never 'ad no dad, and me mum died when I was born. There's just me and me Gran."

Tyler said no more but did his best to make the old woman comfortable on a small wooden cot in the corner. He lit a fire in the open pit using as little of her fuel as possible and then set water to boil. With Charlie left to brew tea, he turned up his collar, rammed his hat down on his head, and went out into the elements to rummage through his belongings. When he returned, it was with two warm blankets, and even though it was only his traveling supplies, it was more food than his hosts had seen in days.

"Gran said you had been looking for help all day, Charlie," he said when the boy had eaten his fill. Charlie nodded. "And there was no one."

"No."

With a nod, Tyler moved to stand at the door. He pulled a crushed cigar from his pocket and struggled to light it. The rain had moved on, leaving behind it the sweet smell of damp earth. He inhaled deeply on the cigar, then threw it down in disgust, grinding it out beneath the heel of his boot.

"Damn it, where are you, Madeline?" he muttered into the darkness. Frustrated, he went back inside. Except for the sound of heavy breathing, all was quiet. Checking on the old woman, he marveled again at her courage. Through all her pain, her only concern had been for Charlie and how he would manage alone. In truth, he felt it might be the other way around. "You're a tough little one, I think, Charlie," he whispered, tucking the blanket firmly around the boy's small body. "I think, in favor of your Gran, you often go without." With a sigh, he settled down, his back to the wall. Stretching his legs out before him and pulling his hat down over his forehead, he shut his eyes and tried to sleep. Come morning, he would find a doctor for Gran, dispatch a letter to his grandfather, and decide how best to continue his search for Madeline.

"Will I see you again, Mister?" Charlie asked the next morning as he was about to leave.

"Perhaps," he answered. "But don't worry, Charlie. You and Gran will be fine. Just make sure you keep her still until the doctor gets here."

"Thanks, Mister." Despite the tears that welled in his eyes, Charlie did his best to look grown up.

After one more check to be sure the two were as comfortable as possible, Tyler made his way to the closest village. With help now on its way to the Tippets, he dispatched a hurried letter to his grandfather. It read:

> Sir,
>
> No sign of Madeline here. Think I must have been wrong. In hopes that's the case, I have decided to head back.
>
> Tyler.

It was still very early, and determined now to make up for lost time, he set out with all speed, back toward Exeter.

Chapter Twenty-Six

The sun had barely risen when Madeline awoke to the loud curses of the hostler. She waited with bated breath in hopes he wouldn't find her. Through a crack in the stall door, she watched as the man staggered from the barn. Doubtless, he was still befuddled from a night of heavy drinking. Once he was out of sight, she grabbed her jacket and cap and made a mad dash for the door. With her eyes wary, she ran to a nearby horse trough. There, she pulled off the oversized jacket and cap. Quickly dipping her hands into the cool water, she washed her face, then ran her wet fingers through her tussled hair. Cold droplets trickled down her neck and she shook her head to remove the excess dampness. Ablutions done, she struggled back into her jacket, jammed the cap back on her head, and pulled it down over her forehead.

Roxanne watched from a distance as she gathered herbs along the roadside.

"So, I was right," she whispered to herself, a smug smile on her beautiful face. "I told you there was something strange about that one, Antonio, but you wouldn't listen." Her brother always disputed her powers of perception. She thought him jealous because the skill had passed from their grandmother to her alone. "But this time, Antonio, you will see." She savored the thought. "As for you, little dove," she mused as Madeline made her way toward the tavern, "I shall make it my biznezz to keep an eye on you. Roxanne, she wants to know why you run from the oh so handsome man." She picked up her basket of herbs, and with the contented smile still on her lips, she made her way back to the caravan. Like a cat with cream, she licked her lips. "Oh, Antonio, how I will love telling you 'I told you so.'"

Unaware of the Gypsy and her close attention, Madeline entered the tavern. There were at least three other early risers in the dining room. Two men sat by the window, deep in conversation. They glanced her way briefly, then seemed to lose interest. The other, a small, rather shabby-looking man, sat alone in the corner. Although his eyes were closed, Madeline had the strangest feeling that he was watching all that went on around him. Not wanting to attract attention, she chose a table in the darkest corner of the room. Hunger was getting the best of her, so counting out her remaining pennies, she studied the morning's bill of fare carefully. It included such things as steak and kidney pie, poached eggs and bacon, partridge pie, cold ham, and Stilton cheese. Her mouth watered at the possibilities, but her limited funds caused her to set them aside.

"Make haste, young gent," the landlord boomed. "Just in time to beat the rush, you are. London coach due in at any minute," he explained. He took her order quickly and returned to the kitchen. There, he could be heard chastising his help for their lazy ways. It was no more than thirty minutes later when the distant sound of the post horn set the tavern into motion. As she rushed to finish her meager serving of bread and cheese, Madeline made inquiries of the landlord.

"Never 'eard of Lord Reginald Spencer," he answered with a shake of his head. "But ask around town. Lots of people 'ere for the fair. Someone might be able to 'elp you."

It wasn't much to go on, but it was a place to start.

In the courtyard a few minutes later, she watched the arrival of the London bound coach. Chicken squawked and scattered in a flurry of feathers as the team of four pulled up and came to a halt.

"Welcome, welcome, ladies and gents," the landlord called. He held his door wide to make way as the passengers rushed to disembark. They knew they only had as much time as it took to change horses before the coach would depart again. With that thought in mind, they made haste to attend to their needs.

"'Ave no fear, Madam." The landlord hurried to assure a harassed-looking woman with three small children in tow. "My good lady wife will take care of you with time to spare. Out of the way, Josh. You too, Toby." He pushed the yapping dogs aside, making way for a gray-haired man and the lavish young girl on his arm.

"Ho, I say, dearie," the girl said upon seeing the tavern for the first time, "I 'ope this ain't the posh place you said you was taking me to."

"Nothing but the best for you, my love, when we reach London," the man promised.

Madeline didn't hear the rest of his words, but the girl laughed shrilly and exclaimed, "Oh 'arry, you are a caution!" So nice of her father, Madeline thought naively as she watched the two hurry inside.

The hostler's mood was still surly as she reentered the stable.

"Git out of me way," he growled when she inquired about Misty. "If you wants 'er 'elp yurself. Can't you see I'm busy?" He bullied his way past her, forcing her to jump aside to avoid being trampled beneath the feet of a large bay gelding.

Glad to see the last of the miserable man, Madeline quickly removed Misty from her stall and hurried on her way.

The day was fine, and the streets of Exeter were full of people, but at the moment, Madeline felt very small and alone. During the night, her dreams had returned, and somewhere, deep inside, an elusive memory had stirred. She was standing, with the barren moors stretching out before her. Cold raindrops struck her face, and a wild wind whipped her hair. A large hand was holding onto hers, and the heavy gold ring on it bit deep into the flesh of her tiny fingers. Something bad had happened, and she was afraid. With a shake of her head, she tried to banish the image from her mind, but it did nothing to ease the icy chill that hovered around her heart.

"Mornin' to you, young zir."

Startled, Madeline spun around. Unheard, a man had come up behind her.

"Name's Pratt. Percy Pratt," he offered. He pulled off his cap to reveal a mop of straggly, unkempt hair. "Are you for the open road then?" he inquired.

Madeline nodded and made to move away.

"One moment then, if you please," the man insisted. "I couldn't 'elp but 'ear your conversation with the landlord of this 'er establishment a moment ago."

"Yes." Madeline took a closer look at the man, remembering him now as the customer sleeping in the corner. She was surprised to find him taller than he had first appeared. His clothes were coarse. They had seen much wear but very little in the way of cleaning. He had the look of a day laborer. The rolled-up sleeves of his shirt revealed arms more wiry than muscular. His hands were work-worn, the nails ragged and dirty. Sun had lined and darkened his face, accentuating his sharp, almost birdlike brown eyes. Those eyes met hers now in a cool, unblinking stare. With no wish to engage him in conversation, Madeline tried again to move away.

"Your pardon, young zir." He reached out and grabbed her arm. "But I 'eard you ask about Lord Reginald Spencer."

Madeline stopped short. "What do you know of it?" she asked, pulling her arm free.

"Not me, zir. It's me mate, 'arry. 'eard 'im speak the name before, I 'ave."

Madeline couldn't believe her good fortune. "Where is this man?" she asked. "How do I find him?"

"Why, he's just down the road a piece if you wants to 'ave a word."

"Yes, yes of course." With Misty jogging at her heels, she quickly followed along behind Percy Pratt.

"This way, zir," the man said, beckoning with his hand.

Excited, Madeline paid no heed when they left the wide, busy streets behind them and entered a warren of narrow back allies. Large buildings in varying states of decay crowded in around them. Doors and windows hanging sadly on broken hinges were thrown open to the elements. Large boxes littered the ground nearby, their rotting contents spewing forth in moldering mounds. Unseen creatures startled by the hollow echo of footsteps on time-worn cobblestones scurried to seek shelter in their own dark holes among the mangled wreckage.

"How much further?" Madeline called out, her breath coming in short gasps.

"Why, it's just around this next corner, Zir."

In his haste, the man stumbled, lost his balance, and landed with a thud against Misty's side. Flustered, the little mare kicked up her feet, pulled free, and raced off down the road.

"So sorry, young mister," the man whimpered.

Frustrated, Madeline turned her back on the man and made to give chase. But rough hands grabbed her from behind, jerking her backward. Struggling, she screamed as her arms were twisted painfully behind her back. Someone muttered a curse, and a gag was quickly stuffed into her mouth. Coarse sacking came down over her head, and she choked on the smell of rotten fish. Lashing out with her feet, she made solid contact with someone's body parts.

A yelp of pain was her reward for the effort.

"Watch out!" A voice yelled out as she tried it again. But this time she took a sharp blow to the side of her head for her trouble. Her feet went out from under her, and unable to save herself, the ground came up quickly to meet her. She landed with a harsh thud, and her world turned upside down.

"That'll learn ya. Now be still, ya little gutter snipe, or I'll break yur bleeding neck." It was the man named Harry.

Madeline whimpered and struggled to rise.

"All right, you asked for it, ya stinking little runt," he growled. "Now yur gonna get it."

A booted foot came down on her back, holding her immobile and threatening to break her spine. Her face scrapped against the harsh sacking, and the last thing she heard was the swish of a fast-moving object. A sharp pain pierced her head, and a dull roar filled her ears. Bile rose in her throat and dizziness overtook her. She tried to hang on, but it was useless. The world slowly drifted away, and darkness closed in around her.

"Stop it, 'arry," Pratt demanded. "'E's not worth a brass farthing to us if 'e's dead. We sat in that bleedin' tavern for three days waiting for 'im. If we lose 'im now, we're done for."

Harry grunted but said nothing.

Chapter Twenty-Seven

Madeline slowly returned from the depths of darkness. She lay still for a moment, trying hard to gather her wits. What had happened? Her mouth was dry. She tried to swallow. Something rough restricted her tongue. She gagged, and in a flash, memory returned. It was the man named Percy Pratt. He had led her into a trap. His clumsiness, the humble apologies, it had all been a sham. He had cleverly distracted her, giving his companion time to sneak up behind her. But why?

Though still tied hand and foot, the sack had been removed from her head. She tried to look around and groaned when her abused body complained. She could feel the rocking motion of a wagon and hear the metallic click of the wheels and the steady plod of horses' hooves. How long had she been unconscious, and where were they taking her?

"Don't ya see, 'arry?"

That voice was Pratt. Madeline was sure of it. Two men sat on the driver's seat, no more than an arm's length away from where she lay.

"If we deliver 'im to Cap'n Brown in one piece, then e's worth 'is weight in gold.

Once we 'ave 'im safe on board the Remington and collect the cash, we can wash our 'ands of 'im. Think about it."

"'Ow long will the cap'n be gone this time?" Harry wanted to know.

"'Bout two years, he reckons, so don't worry. Chances are this 'er lad won't never make it back. You know the cap'n. Has to have someone to warm 'is bed on a long trip. Likes 'em young, he does. This 'ere lad will suit 'im fine." They broke into a round of coarse laughter.

Madeline had heard of this practice before. When a captain couldn't get a crew by honest methods, he would resort to impressments. Press gangs waylaid able-bodied men and dragged them away against their will. Most died at sea of accident, disease, or at the hands of sadistic captains who overly enjoyed the use of the lash. Harsh floggings were commonplace aboard His Majesty's ships. Punishment of even the smallest infraction was the rule. But what did these men want with her? All at once, it became quite clear. Of course, they thought her to be a boy, and they intended to sell her. She wanted to cry out, "It's all a mistake!" but the gag in her mouth prevented it. Her heart beat faster, and she shivered in fear.

"'Ear who do you think you are then?"

It was Harry. He sounded mean. Suddenly the wagon stopped with a jolt. It swayed from side to side as first the driver, then his companion climbed down. Muffled voices were raised in argument. From what Madeline could hear, they were unable to agree on the conditions of her disposal. Voices grew louder as the fair division of the bounty they were about to collect caused conflict.

"This 'ere bloke is mine," Percy yelled. "I found 'im, and you get what I say."

The scuffle of feet told of the fight that ensued. There was a solid thud. Something hard had connected with its target. All went quiet.

Madeline lay still, ears straining, hardly daring to breathe. A loud grunt was followed by more scuffling. This time, it was as if something heavy was being dragged away across the ground. Footsteps returned. Someone leaned against the wagon, his breathing heavy. The hair at her nape prickled as he rested there, mere inches from her head. Moments later, the wagon sagged as he climbed back on board. Now, there was only one, and they were on the move again.

The pace was slow, and heat within the confines of the wagon soon became unbearable. Madeline's head hurt, and the ropes chaffed at her wrists and ankles. She closed her eyes in an effort to lessen the pain and soon drifted in and out of a half world where time ceased to exist. Mile after weary mile, the horses trudged on.

The air grew cooler and ripe with the smell of the sea. Screeching gulls circled low overhead, and Madeline guessed they were nearing their destination. Growing more desperate, she struggled with her bonds, but to no avail. Oh, how stupid she had been! William's kindly face flashed before her, his green eyes sad. Her heart constricted. How she wished she could reach out to him, speak to him, tell him what a fool she had been. Why hadn't she listened to Tyler and to Jeannie? They had been right; terrible things did happen. People could vanish without a trace, never be heard from again, and now apparently, that fate was about to be hers. But by whose hands would she be delivered, Percy Pratts or his infamous companion, the man named Harry?

Harry Bloom wasn't normally a happy man, but today he was as close to that state as possible. He had taken great pleasure in thumping Percy Pratt on the noggin. He had rid himself of his detested partner long enough to increase his own fortune by a considerable amount. By the time Pratt was able to track him down, the money would long be spent. Strong whiskey and a cheap woman. He even chuckled.

The bottom of his boat grated harshly on the pebbled beach. Wading in knee-deep, Harry pulled it back up onto the shore. As he made his way back to the wagon, he patted his empty pockets, thinking how good they would feel full of gold. He had no scruples about the task he was about to perform. He detested Pratt, but he hated Captain Brown. The man was vicious, cruel for the sake of being cruel, but his money was good, and there was plenty of it. Throwing back the canvas flap, he triumphantly dragged out his youthful golden goose. He pulled the sack back down over his victim's head and heaved him over his shoulder. All that remained was to deliver the boy to the Remington, collect his bounty, and be on his way.

"Pretty scrawny specimen," Captain Brown growled as Harry pulled the sack from Madeline's head and untied her hands and feet. "Hardly worth the price, I would say." But he slowly eyed his prize up and down. "Not up to Pratt's usual standards, but we sail too soon to wait for another. If he's the best you could find, I suppose he'll have to do. But if you service me again, I'll expect better or pay less."

Harry held his silence. He didn't care a fig about the huge, greasy-haired man's threats. He understood the captain's appetite, knew that no matter what, his services would always be needed regardless of the price.

The captain took a heavy purse from the drawer of his desk, hefted it in his hand for a moment, then tossed it to Harry. Stuffing the bag deep in his pocket, Harry bid the captain a good day and quickly took his leave. As he pulled his boat back onto the shore, he patted his pocket. He liked the feel of the heavy coins that rested there. This had turned out to be a good day. A very good day indeed. He knew exactly where he was going now and who he wanted to see when he got there. Flossie who tended the bar at The Black Swan. Harry thought of the joys that awaited him there. He knew he would have to prove to Flossie that he could pay the price. She was fussy that way, Flossie was. But once she saw the goods in his pocket, she would be his for the taking. He smacked his lips in anticipation. Whistling a toneless tune to himself, he made his way to the docks and The Black Swan.

"Whiskey, me girl," he ordered, thumping his fist down on the bar. "And make it yur best!" His eyes followed Flossie's every move as she made her way around the bar toward him, hips swaying.

"Not till I sees the color of yur money." Her bright red painted lips challenged him.

"No worries there, me gal." Harry pulled his money pouch from his pocket, and holding it close, he flashed his treasure trove for her to see.

Flossie's mood changed instantly. With a bewitching smile, she topped up his glass and, without bothering to ask, poured one for herself. Needing no more prompting, the perfumed woman kept Harry's glass constantly full. When her shift at The Black Swan ended some two hours later, Flossie wrapped her genuine fox stole around her neck. She took Harry's arm to steady him and led him out along the docks.

"Come on, ducks," she encouraged the inebriated fellow. "You've got money in yur pocket to spend, and the day is still young." With a knowing nod of her head to the many local venders, Flossie led Harry carefully from shop to shop. Soon, her wrist sported a brand-new silver bangle, and a sparkly clip adorned her bleached blond hair. A fancy silk handkerchief joined the bottle of cheap perfume she had stuffed in her purse, and a heart-shaped pin decorated the collar of her bright pink blouse.

By now Harry's pockets were almost empty, and Flossie was running late for another engagement. So at a sign that read "Nightly Rates," she thanked him with a generous kiss, pushed him through the door, and bid him a fond farewell.

Later, as Harry lay on a bed in the local flop house, his whisky-soaked brain remembered little of the time just passed. He reached into his pocket and found his money was gone. But as he wiped Flossie's bright red lip rouge from his face, he felt sure that Cap'n Brown's money must have been well spent.

Chapter Twenty-Eight

C aptain Brown pulled his personal ledger from its hiding place. He made a hasty entry, dabbed it with a blotter, and slammed it shut with a satisfied sigh. He had always kept two sets of books, one for himself and one for the company. He was no fool. He knew how to play the game. A man had to know how to take care of himself or suffer the consequence. It wouldn't be much longer now, then all his scheming would begin to pay off.

He poured himself a liberal shot of brandy and stood, glass in hand, apparently deep in thought. Now he could relax; he had what he needed most for his long journey. His cargo was safely stowed below deck, and tomorrow, with the tide, he would leave the town of Topsham and the Exe Estuary far behind him. He had grown up here, the oldest son of a wealthy ship builder. Their Dutch-style home, built on the Strand, was known to people for miles around. As a boy, he had grown up in the company of some of the most influential people in the land. But much good it had done him. Even his expensive education had proven to be a waste.

Silently, he cursed the affliction that plagued him, branding him an outcast, spurned and disowned by his family. By turning their backs on him, they had robbed him of his naval command, his rightful place, and condemned him to a life of no consequence. Now, because of his need for this boy, he had put himself in danger of losing even a tub like the Remington. But now he could sail on the next tide. Perhaps by pushing the old rust bucket till her rivets popped, he could make up time and still salvage something. He calmed a little. He would never come back here, never see his parents and siblings again. He hated them and wished them all to hell. His route would take him around the world to Singapore. From there, he would ditch the Remington and make his way to Australia.

A new life in a brand-new land was just what he needed, but it was going to take time, and right now he had other things to attend to.

"You are wet, boy." Turning around he noted the wet trousers clinging tight against the skin. He licked his thick lips. Beady eyes bright, he moved to run his hand slowly down the firm young thigh.

Madeline shivered, disgusted by the man's intimate touch. What did he expect of her? But afraid to speak, she bit her lip and said nothing. Her head was still spinning, and she wanted to be sick.

"God, but you smell of fish," the man said. He wrinkled his nose in distaste. "I shall have you stripped and scrubbed thoroughly before the day is done. Mmmm." The prospect excited him.

A sudden knock on the door was a distraction. Noticeably angered, he shouted, "Enter."

A sailor, hat in hand, entered at his command.

"Well?" he demanded of the man.

"Sorry, Cap'n," the man apologized, "but a man's looking for you up on deck. Says it's important."

"Gilroy with his usual complaints, I assume," the captain snapped.

"Afraid so, Cap'n," the man answered.

"Well, boy, it seems I must leave you for a while." He turned back to Madeline. "I might be gone for some time, but later we will have a chance to get to know each other better." So saying, he took a navy blue jacket from a peg on the wall, held it up before him, and examined it carefully. He huffed on its brass buttons, then took a rag and buffed them to a high shine. Finally satisfied with the results, he shook the garment out and pulled it on. With a critical eye, he checked his reflection in the gold-framed mirror above his desk. He turned his head from side to side, and with a grunt, he carefully straightened what was left of his hair. He picked up the ship's papers of lading, took one last look back over his shoulder at Madeline, and hurried from the room.

Madeline heard the key turn in the lock. Now she was completely alone. Suddenly cold and shaking, she felt numb all over. Every inch of her body cried out in pain. With a groan, she sank to her knees. Hunched over and too weak to move, she sat holding her head in her hands. Had the earth decided to split asunder at that moment, she would have been helpless to save herself. She would simply have closed her eyes and been sucked down into a dark oblivion.

"Breathe deeply." From somewhere in her subconscious mind, Tyler's voice called out to her. "Breathe. Breathe deeply." Those were his words to her on the first day they met. He had been angry then, but he had been right. She sucked in air, and it helped. Gradually, her shaking slowed, her stomach settled, and reason returned. She had no idea how long the captain would be gone, but she knew she must make good use of the time she had left. Still breathing hard, she struggled to her feet and took a quick look around. There had to be some way to get out of here. All she had to do was find it. The door was locked, but she tried it anyway, twisting the handle this way and that. It didn't budge. She tried again, this time throwing her whole body weight against it. All that did was add more injury to her already badly bruised shoulder. Tears of frustration dampened her eyes. She felt helpless. "Think," she scolded herself softly. "Think." Might there possibly be another key hidden somewhere, a spare? If so, where would someone as particular as the captain hide it? The desk! Obvious, but you never could tell. One by one, she pulled open the drawers, rummaging through them. They offered up nothing. She tried the large cupboard in the corner. It was neat. Freshly laundered clothing hung from wooden pegs. Without thinking twice, she quickly went to work, searching the pockets of each garment in turn. Jackets first, then shirts and trousers. As a last resort, she even tried each boot and shoe, but nothing. She did find an aging cutlass tucked away in the back of the cupboard. It was dulled with age and seemed quite useless, so she set it aside and returned to her task. There was a large trunk in the corner and a shelf full of books by the door. But a thorough search of both gave up no secrets to the hoped-for key. A small chest also proved useless but led to a wooden box tucked snuggly away beneath the captain's bunk. Pulling it from its hiding place, she was instantly intrigued by its mystical appearance. But time was passing quickly, and she was in a hurry now. She lifted the lid and found it filled with exotic things gathered from all four corners of the world, a treasure chest of sorts. There were silks from China, spiced tea, and oils from far off India, a finely carved set of ivory chess men, and an ornate silver snuff box. But to her dismay, the one thing Madeline didn't find was a key. Her distress mounted. What would happen to her now when the captain returned?

She went back to the old cutlass and hefted it in her hand. Its age may have rendered it useless, but nevertheless, she found its presence quite comforting. She thought again of Marshfield Hall. What she wouldn't give at this moment to see those dear faces again. Closing her eyes, she envisioned them all—William, Jeannie, and Ian. Even Mrs.

Carter and George. And what of Tyler? Did he miss her at all? Did he even think of her and wonder where she was?

Well, whatever fate awaited her now, she knew one thing. She would go down fighting. Her grip tightened on the old cutlass. Perhaps, with a little luck, it might still strike a blow for freedom. So armed, she waited, exhausted and shivering.

Chapter Twenty-Nine

"Will I see you again, Mister?" Those were Charlie's parting words to Tyler that morning.

"Perhaps, Charlie," he had replied, "after I find the lady on the gray horse."

The lady on the gray horse! Where the hell was she? It was like looking for a needle in a haystack. How could Madeline have disappeared so completely?

By noon, he was back in Exeter and once again made his way to The Blue Angel. In complete contrast to his last visit, the place now looked deserted. He entered and ordered a strong dark ale. Perhaps Ian and George had had better luck with their search for Madeline. He certainly hoped so.

"So, you come back to Roxanne, eh?" a familiar voice asked. "I tell you. You cannot resist me." Strong tanned arms encircled his neck, and once again the smell of wild honeysuckle filled the space around him. Smiling to himself, he grasped one slim arm and turned to face her. In a fake attempt to escape, the beautiful gypsy struggled playfully. Her laughter echoed through the empty room.

"You stay this time?" she asked at last, looking up at Tyler with large dark eyes.

"No, Roxanne." His voice was firm, "My purpose is unchanged."

"Then you are a fool!" A pout marred her flawless features. "Roxanne, she would never run from you."

"And what of your brother? He might have something to say about that."

"Bah! he doesn't own me."

"Perhaps not," Tyler replied, "but I'm not taking the chance, so little one, you had better run along." He freed himself from her grasp and firmly set her aside.

Roxanne stamped her foot, her gold-flecked eyes flashing fire. "I will go," she snapped, "but you will be sorry, Senor. Just you wait and see." With an arrogant toss of her head, she turned and ran from the room.

Moments later, Antonio stopped her on the street. "Roxanne!" He challenged.

"I see the gorgio has returned. Have you spoken with him?"

Roxanne made to push past him.

"No! Not so fast little sister." He grabbed her arm and pulled her to him. "Don't play games with me," he hissed. "I saw the man ride in a while ago. I ask you again. Have you spoken to him? Have you told him what you know of the girl he seeks?"

"No, why should I?" she snapped. "I owe him nothing."

"You owe him the truth," Antonio insisted. "Can't you see that this time your mischief could cause real trouble? The girl, she could be in danger. How much will this man hate you if she comes to harm?"

A frown darkened the girl's face, and for a moment she said nothing. Frustrated by her silence, Antonio shook her hard. "Think, Roxanne, think."

Shaken by her brother's unexpected rough treatment of her, Roxanne thought better of her actions. Resentment still burned her insides, but with a slow nod of her head, she reluctantly gave in.

"One moment, Senor!"

Tyler was preparing to leave the tavern when he heard Antonio's call. Not quite sure what to expect from the swarthy gypsy and his volatile sister, he watched their approach with a wary eye.

"It is Roxanne, Senor," Antonio explained. "She has something to tell you."

Tyler listened as Roxanne's story unfolded.

"Damn it!" When she was finished, he vented his frustration. "So, she's dressed as a boy! I should have known it. I was the one who told her it was too dangerous for a girl to travel alone."

"But that's not all." Anthony glared at his sister. "Out with it, Roxanne. Tell him the rest."

Roxanne went on to describe Madeline's abduction. How, after knocking her senseless, two men had thrown her into a wagon and taken her away.

"Which way?" Tyler demanded.

"West, they went west," Roxanne snapped back.

After a hasty word of thanks to the gypsies, Tyler saddled up Samson and headed west. At last, he felt he had something solid to go on.

He had traveled only a short distance when Antonio caught up with him.

"Where do you think you're going?" he asked.

"With you, my friend," Antonio answered. "I think when you find your lady, you will need all the help you can get."

Tyler nodded, and the two rode on in silence, neither one quite sure what might lie ahead. Roxanne's description of the wagon they sought was vague. Old and pulled by a mule was all she could offer them. Not much to go on.

The road they followed now was heavily traveled, and although both men were good trackers, they knew finding one particular set of wagon tracks would be difficult. They kept a sharp eye on the road ahead and moved at a steady pace. Despite his earlier misgivings about the gypsy, Tyler soon found himself at ease with the man. His dark eyes were intelligent, and there was an easygoing strength about him. He would be a good man to have on your side if the going got rough.

"Look, Senor!" Antonio sounded pleased. "I think this could be what we are looking for." They dismounted and examined a set of tracks. "See. These hoof prints. They are much narrower than those of a horse."

"Yes, my friend," Tyler agreed. "It seems we might just have found our mule. But something happened here. The wagon stopped, and two people got down."

"Over there," Antonio chimed in. "It looks like a scuffle took place." He moved a little further. "One man went down here, and by the looks of it, he was dragged off in that direction." He pointed toward the rocky terrain.

They found the man a short time later, partly hidden among a pile of rocks.

"I'm Percy Pratt," the man explained as they tended his wounds. "It was me partner, me ex- partner that is, who did this to me, Mister," the man explained, pointing at his battered face. "Knocked me out, 'e did, left me 'ere to rot. 'Arry bloody Bloom is 'is name."

"Well, Mister Pratt." Tyler's mood became threatening. "You had best tell us how this all came about, or you might find yourself in a lot worse trouble."

"So 'elp me, Mister. It was all 'arry's idea. Tells me this 'ere Cap'n Brown on the Remington 'll put gold in our pockets."

Enlarging on Harry's role in the scheme, Percy gladly answered all their questions. "But struth, Mister," he finally said. "I didn't know it was no girl. I swears it on me dead mum's grave. Besides," he muttered under his breath, "Cap'n don't take kindly to women."

Pratt was all willingness to help. To prove his good intentions, he revealed the whereabouts of the Remington and even gave up the key he had to Captain Browns private quarters.

"I stole this 'ere key, Mister," Percy confessed. "Cap'n don't know I 'av it. Kill me 'e would if 'e found out."

Tyler was inclined to believe the man, but dire consequences were threatened if his information proved to be false. Leaving Antonio to help the battered man, and with plans in place to meet up with him later, Tyler set out in search of Captain Brown and the Remington.

Chapter Thirty

"**W**hy, there she be, Sir. That's her out there in the harbor," a local salt told him some time later as he rode into the seaport of Topsham. "But she won't be there much longer."

"Why?" Tyler asked the obvious question.

"Well, I guess ya don't know, Mister, but she's due to sail on the evening tide."

"Damn." Tyler cursed his luck. His plan had been to scout ahead and then await Antonio's arrival, but now, with the imminent departure of the Remington, he dared not wait any longer. He lingered along the shore for a while, observing the comings and goings of the Remington's crew. Finally satisfied that the ship was indeed ready to sail and that most of her crew were enjoying their last hours ashore, he prepared to make his move. Carefully choosing a spot that offered him the most cover, he pulled off his boots and stripped to the waist. He hid his clothing among the rocks and slipped into the chilly waters. With a strong stroke, he swam out toward the anchored craft.

Soon, the giant wooden ship towered high above him, and the bold figure of a mermaid stood out proudly at the bow. He made his way slowly along the ship's side until he found what he sought. With a knife clenched between his teeth, he climbed hand over hand up the heavy rope cable. At last, dripping wet, he hoisted himself over the rail and dropped soundlessly down onto the Remington's deck. He took a moment to look around, familiarizing himself with his surroundings. Then, holding the key Pratt had given him, he followed the man's directions and made his way below deck.

Madeline trembled at the sound of a footfall outside the cabin door. She could feel the hair under her hat stand on end. He was back! She jumped to her feet. A key rattled in the lock. No more time to think. She had to move fast. With the dull old cutlass held high above her head, she hid behind the door and waited. The tumblers turned, and the lock clicked open. She held her breath, sure he must hear the wild beating of her heart. The door inched open. A moment more, then, eyes closed, she swung her weapon down. She missed her target completely, but the force of her swing carried her with it. She heard an angry growl as the intruder went down with her and hit the floor. For a moment they struggled in a wild tangle of arms and legs. But she was no match for him. This wasn't the captain, she was certain. This man was strong and lean, and she was hopelessly trapped beneath him. Angered and frustrated by her total ineffectiveness, she used the only weapon she had left. With his bare shoulder mere inches from her face, she sank her teeth into the warm flesh and held on tight.

"Ahhh! Damn it all." Grabbing a handful of her hair, the man rolled her over, trapping her beneath him.

"Tyler?" She looked up into a pair of bright green eyes and voiced her surprise.

"Good God, Madeline, it's you. Are you alright?"

"Yes, but I've never been so afraid in my life." She threw herself into his arms and held on tight.

"Calm down." He tried to reassure her. "I'm here now."

"But that awful man, he's coming back," she babbled. "Do you know what he planned to do with me?"

"Slow down, sweetheart." He grabbed her hands. "There will be time to talk later. Right now we need to get out of here." Filled with a feeling of relief, he kissed the top of her head. She was here, wet and dirty but feeling oh so good in his arms. He picked up the hat she had lost in their struggle and plopped it back on her head.

"There. That looks better," he teased. "Now let's get out of here, and you can tell me later what happened to your hair."

Madeline needed no more urging.

"Keep a safe distance," he warned, placing her several paces behind him. "And stay there until I get us out of here."

Madeline nodded her understanding and followed as he retraced his steps. They quickly made their way up the ladder and out onto the quarter deck. He paused for a minute, but all seemed quiet. Taking her hand, he guided her silently by open hatches and along a row of stacked cargo boxes.

"This is where we get off," he whispered as they reached the catwalk, "and by the way, I never thought to ask, but can you swim?"

"Better than most," she assured him.

"Good, then it's off with your boots my girl, and over the side."

"Hey, you there, stop!" a voice called out of the dusk.

"Damn it," Tyler cursed. "There's no time now." He gave Madeline a shove, and with one quick look behind him, he dove in after her.

He came up for air, relieved to see the small blond head, once again minus the hat, bobbing along in front of him.

A shot rang out. Narrowly missing him, a bullet whined past his head and landed in the water with a splat. Pow! pow! pow! Three more followed in close succession. He gulped in air and dove beneath the surface, pushing hard for the shore. More missiles whizzed around him, boiling and hissing in a cloud of steam and bubbles. Not much further and they would be out of range, but his lungs were already on fire. The bullet struck like the kick of a mule. Piercing his side, it ripped through his flesh, leaving a trail of white-hot heat behind it. The force sent him plummeting down as he fought against the darkness that threatened to engulf him.

Chapter Thirty-One

As strict as Madeline's upbringing had been in the convent, it did have its lighter moments. On long hot summer days, under the supervision of Sister Marie Louise, she and some of the other girls swam in a secluded, spring-fed pool. The sister, a strong swimmer herself, was happy to find Madeline such an eager student and encouraged her efforts. Now, as she sliced skillfully through the choppy water, she silently thanked the little nun for her hours of patient training. If only she could have known, that today, those lessons had helped to save her life.

Her feet touched bottom, and running up on the beach, she waited impatiently for Tyler. Voices echoed across the sea from the Remington, and hearing the steady splash of oars, she knew the crew were already giving chase.

"Where are you, Tyler?" She worried, pacing down to the water's edge. But there were no ripples to disturb the smooth surface. "Come on, come on. Where are you? It couldn't take you this long." she scanned the water, sure he hadn't been that far behind her.

"Madeline." The word was a hoarse whisper.

"There you are." She breathed a sigh of relief. "Hurry, I can hear them coming."

"Go," he hissed, "find a safe place to hide, and I will join you." He struggled to his feet, blood staining his side and pain distorting his face.

"Oh God!" Horrified, she rushed to his side.

"Go!" he insisted again, trying to push her away.

"You're a fool if you think I'll leave you. We go or we stay, but either way, we do it together."

"Stubborn wench." He shook his head. "Will you ever do as I say?"

"Perhaps, but not today."

"Let's away then, before those men get any closer."

Wrapping her arms around him and with most of his weight resting on her shoulders, she helped him ashore. Slowly they made their way along the rocky beach, feet slipping and sliding on damp green slime. Finally spotting a crevice big enough for two, they managed to crawl inside. Huddled together, wet and shivering, they waited while lanterns flashed their way across the sand. At times they came so close that Madeline was sure they would be found. When the men moved on by, she'd breathe a sigh of relief, grateful now for the green slime that covered the signs of their passing.

As night closed in, the rising tide rolled ever closer to their hiding place. Madeline watched as wave after wave lapped further up the sand. They had to seek higher ground or suffer the consequences. But Tyler's breathing was labored, his condition was worsening, and she was afraid.

Disgruntled voices drifted in the evening air.

"Capn's gone mad," one said. "Tides getting higher an if'n we don't go soon, we'll drown on this 'ere beach."

"Look out!" another yelled. "Our boats goin' adrift."

Picked up and carried by rising waves, their small craft was heading out to sea.

"Grab it lads and let's get out of here!"

They gave chase, wading hip-deep into the choppy waters. Quickly catching the wayward vessel, they all tumbled aboard in a wild frenzy of arms and legs.

"They're leaving." Madeline watched as the three men pulled on their oars. heading out toward the Remington.

"Good." Tyler's voice was strained. "They sail with the tide. By daylight, they'll be gone."

"We can't wait that long," Madeline insisted as water lapped at her ankles.

"We have to move now."

Tyler grunted his understanding, and with difficulty, she helped him to his feet. With Madeline again supporting most of his weight, they began the arduous trek to higher ground. Each time he faltered, she offered encouragement.

"Not much further, just a few more steps."

Luck was on her side when, close to exhaustion, they stumbled upon a secluded cave. Possibly well-known by locals, it was hard to see from the beach. Using all her remaining strength, she managed to get him inside, then, setting him down, she collapsed to the ground beside him. It took a moment to regain her breath.

Then she whispered, "I think we're safe here."

"Then listen to me." Tyler grasped her shoulder. "I must tell you this while I'm still able. I have a growing fever. Through the night, it will be much worse. There'll be nothing I can do to help you then."

"Then tell me now, what should I do?" Madeline had never felt so helpless.

"First, we must try to stop this bleeding. Look around, see what you can find. You need water, cloth, a lantern and, if possible, some brandy. We are not the first to use this place; my guess is it's well-known to the local smuggling trade. Let's hope they're not active tonight or we might give them a bit of a turn. They are not the most pleasant of men, and I doubt they would look upon us with kindness. So, go now, and please hurry."

Needing no more urging, Madeline made a quick search of the cave. It was much larger than she had first thought and, as Tyler had suggested, it had been well used. Several signs suggested recent habitation. In one corner, a crude table had been fashioned from empty boxes. Littered with dirty dishes and the dried up remains of unfinished meals, it also offered a lantern, primed and ready for use. A further search turned up a length of new rope, a shabby, well-worn blanket, and an assortment of tools. She also found a large wooden bucket and a dozen or more empty whisky barrels.

To the rear of the cave water dripped down from the high ceiling. The constant dripping had worn away at the rock beneath to form a perfect pool of clear water. Happy with her finds, she quickly returned to Tyler's side to show him the results of her scavenger hunt.

"Are you sure the barrels were empty?" he asked. At her nod, he sighed in disappointment. "Too bad." He managed a crooked grin. "Some brandy would have been useful right now, but you did well. Now what we need is something to bind the wound. Take this." He pulled the knife from his belt and helped as she slashed away the bottom of her oversized shirt. "That should do." He said at last. "Now clean away the blood and use this to bind me. I'll help as much as I can."

With the wick turned down low to avoid detection, Madeline lit the lamp. She had no knowledge of nursing, but she recognized the urgent need to plug the gaping hole in Tyler's side. Her first revulsion at the sight of his ugly wound quickly faded. With shaking hands, she gently cleansed the ragged flesh, flinching each time she heard his groan of pain.

"That's the best I can do," she said at last.

"Good. Now wrap the cloth around me as tight as you can. The bullet went right through, but with luck, the pressure should slow the bleeding."

With her head pressed against his chest and her arms encircling his waist, she carefully applied the bandage as tight as she could. Then, sitting back on her heels, she examined her handy work.

"How does it feel?" she asked anxiously.

"It feels fine. If I'd known all I had to do was get shot to get your arms around me," he teased gently," I would have arranged it a long time ago."

"It's the fever," she teased back, holding her hand to his forehead.

"Mmmm, do you think so?" He took her hand and pressed it to his lips.

Flustered, she pulled away. Rolling up the blanket, she made a pillow for his head.

"That feels better," he said, sighing. "Now woman, come lay beside me and keep me warm."

Madeline did as he asked. Wrapping his good arm around her, he pulled her close. Snuggling closer still, she offered him all the warmth her body could give. At last, he sighed and closed his eyes.

She nursed him through the long hours of darkness and found he had been right about the fever. It grew much worse as the night wore on.

Scared at times by the intense heat radiating from his skin, Madeline comforted him in the only way she knew how. Wetting lengths of cloth, she pressed each to his lips and to his burning brow. It helped to cool him a little as he drifted in and out of consciousness. His face was ashen, his breathing harsh.

In his quiet moments, she sat beside him, her knees hugged tight against her chest.

She heard the waves, dark and restless, pounding at her rocky fortress as shingle, helpless to resist the strong pull of the undertow, shifted and sighed softly in protest. Lulled by the constant motion, Madeline's eyes grew heavy, but ever aware of Tyler's condition, she slept only fitfully.

Each time his skin grew too dry or too hot to touch, she bathed him again with cool water from the pool. But when the fever raged and he lost control, Madeline feared he might do himself more harm. Then, not strong enough to stop him by other means, she placed her body over his and held him down. Thus, she passed the long night holding him tight and praying that the dawn would soon break.

"Water!"

At first light, she felt a tug at her sleeve and woke with a start. His eyes were open and seeing her. She breathed a sigh of relief.

"Water!" he said again.

"Easy," she cautioned as he rushed to quench his thirst. But he brushed her restraints aside and quickly drained the mug dry.

"How long have I been out of it?" he asked, breathing deeply and wiping his mouth with his hand.

"Most of the night."

A worried frown creased his brow. "What of the Remington?" He wanted to know.

From her vantage point, Madeline looked seaward. The tide had receded now, and still the Remington sat at anchor. There was no sign of life on deck, and her sails were still securely furled.

"What do you see?"

"They didn't leave," she answered.

"Then, this time, Madeline, you must do as I say. You can do me no good here. If you are the reason for the captain's delay, then I doubt his sanity. By missing the tide, he risks losing his ship. Owners don't favor such delays. He will seek us out, come hell or high water. Should they find us, and I have no doubt they will, there is no way in my present state that I can defend you. You have to go for help. No!" he held up his hand, anticipating her refusal. "There's a Gypsy. Antonio is his name. Find him and bring him here."

"Antonio?"

He nodded.

"How will I know him?"

"He will be waiting with a wagon on the hill that overlooks the town. He wears a red kerchief on his head and a large gold ring in his left ear." Before he could say more, his eyes closed and he drifted back into unconsciousness.

Distressed and uncertain, Madeline chewed on her bottom lip. She hated to leave him so, but common sense prevailed. They needed help, and if the gypsy could provide it, then she had to find him. But even so she lingered, taking time once more to place the cooling cloth against his forehead. His eyes fluttered open, and looking up at her, he urged her to go.

"Yes, I'm going," she answered quickly, "but I'll be back as soon as I can." First making sure he had fresh water at hand, she kissed his cheek and made her way toward the opening.

"Not that way, my sweet," he warned. "There must be another way out. When our absent hosts wish not to be seen, I doubt they use the front door."

Understanding and taking the lantern to light her path, Madeline ventured back into the dark unknown in her quest to find the gypsy.

Chapter Thirty-Two

Antonio had had a difficult day. But for his part, he had done all that his companion had asked of him. With money given to him by the man, whom he now knew to be an American, he had returned to Exeter and found help for the injured Percy Pratt. He had then sent a message to the earl of Marshfield that simply said, "Madeline located." His next stop had been the premises of a wily merchant, where he had acquired a rundown wagon with supplies and an aging team. Overpriced to be sure, but then town folk had no love for gypsies. Lastly, he had sought out his sister, Roxanne.

"No, I won't help," she said to his request for clothing. "Why should I? The stupid woman chose to dress like a boy. Let her stay that way."

"If not for her or the American, then do it for me, little sister. Is that reason enough?"

After much haggling, the girl had finally relented.

"Stupid, stupid!"

Antonio heard her mutter to herself as she rummaged through her things.

Then, throwing a bag of clothes into his wagon, she had turned and stormed away.

Despite all his efforts, Antonio had still arrived late at the meeting place. The slowness of his team had been to blame. He had been more than a little surprised, due to the lateness of the hour, to find no sign of the other man. Too many hours had passed since he and the American had parted company, so obviously something had gone wrong. Now he was faced with a new dilemma. Should he stay or should he go?

Darkness was already settling slowly over the town. As he watched, lights began to appear at the windows. The streets seemed unusually busy for the time of the day, and loud voices echoed up on the still evening air. Although he couldn't make out the words, it seemed as if something unusual was taking place. Confused and more unsure than ever, he decided to investigate further. He left the wagon and team behind and made his way, on foot, down the grassy slope.

Always alert to things around him, he sauntered down the main street. Passing the local smithy, he noticed a familiar black gelding stabled there.

"That's a fine-looking horse you have there, Senor." Running his hand over Samson's dark hide, Antonio played the innocent. "Is he perhaps for sale?"

"Not by me, 'e ain't. Some big furrin sounding bloke left 'im 'ere. Paid well 'e did too, so keep your thieving 'ands to yourself, Gypsy." Spitting on his hands, the blacksmith took a better grip on his large hammer.

"Have no fear, Senor." Antonio held up his hands, trying to allay the man's suspicions. "Is this man nearby? Perhaps I could have words with him."

"Don't know where 'e is, Gypsy. Now clear off." Once again, the man hefted his hammer, taking a threatening step forward.

"Sorry, my friend. I meant no harm." Antonio backed up, keeping the man in his sights until he was well away. He had learned what he needed to know. He was sure the American would never leave his horse behind, so he knew he must still be close at hand. But where?

At a nearby tavern, he tossed a coin down on the table, called for a bottle, and invited anyone close enough to join him. Long before his money was spent, he had learned of the daring escape from the Remington, and of the far-reaching wrath of Captain Silas Brown. From a group of disgruntled sailors, he added more to the story.

"Lost a cabin boy," they complained, "an' the cap'n, he's in a right old snit. Vows 'e wont sail till 'e finds 'im. Daft as a bedbug 'e is."

Antonio was certain that the escaped cabin boy must be Madeline Carlyle and that her rescuer was the American. But if they had escaped, where were they? And what should he do now? At last, he decided to remain where he was, at least for a while. That way, if they had run into trouble and needed help, they would know where to find him. The night sky was brightly lit by stars as he left the town and trudged back up the hill. Down below him, the tide rushed in, and inky waves quickly gobbled up the shore. With a sigh, he sat down, leaned his back against the wagon wheel, looked out toward the Remington, and waited for the dawn. He didn't know it at the time, but out in the darkness there was someone else watching. That same someone had been following Antonio's movements with a great deal of interest.

Percy Pratt was a happy man. His minor wounds had been attended to, and he had found a connection between the Gypsy and the American. Never one to miss an opportunity, the wily Pratt had been dogging Antonio's footsteps ever since. Now, he, like Antonio, kept a close watch on the busy comings and goings from the Remington. Having put two and two together, he was sure he knew what had taken place. There was no doubt in his mind now that if he just played his cards right, there might still be money to be made. With a satisfied smile on his face, he returned to his place of residence, a seaman's boarding house on the far edge of town.

News filtered quickly in and out of the dull little boarding house that was grandly named The Seaman's Arms. Most of the chatter here was provided by the illustrious landlady and her husband, a Mr. and Mrs. Henry Higginbottom.

Percy had entered unobtrusively through the back door and settled himself quietly down in the corner nook of what was laughingly called the common room. Here he had waited for the man he knew would come. And come he did, but now, as he sat across the table from Captain Silas Brown, Percy began to doubt the wisdom of his plan.

"A girl," Brown snarled, "you bought me a girl. You must be mad!" He slammed his fist down on the table in disgust, rattling the odd assortment of dishes resting there. "Is that what I pay you for, you scurvy little bilge rat?" he demanded. "Give me one good reason why I shouldn't wring your bleedin' neck?"

Percy cowered away.

"It weren't me, Cap'n," he blustered, watching the man's face turning red.

He feared the captain's wrath, but for the first time, he glimpsed the raw desperation driving the man. With the newly acquired knowledge came a strange sense of power. He had never questioned the right or wrong of his dealings with Brown before. He lived as he must, by his wits, and he felt no pity for the hapless souls he delivered into a life of slavery and degradation. The streets of England teemed with lost souls.

By removing a few, he did a service for the rest. One more bite of bread to go around, he reasoned.

"'Ow was I to know she was a girl?" he whined. "It was Bloom was to blame.

Ain't I always done good by you before?" Watching the man struggle to overcome his emotions, Percy suddenly knew he need never fear the man again.

From across the table Silas, looked into the weathered face he had come to know so well. His lip curled in contempt. He hated Percy Pratt. Pratt was a leech whose social standing was so far beneath his own that he deemed him unworthy to touch his boots. But he was joined in an unholy alliance with this man, and as much as he hated it, he needed him. He performed a service for a price.

"Well, it's over now, Pratt," he mused. "Still, I would pay a lot to get my hands on the girl. I'd make her pay dearly for her deception." How easily the girl had duped him. His anger flared again, dulling his senses. "Find the wench for me, Pratt," he demanded, "and I will put the jingle back in your pocket."

Percy tried to look humble. This was just what he had hoped would happen. "Well, she can't be far away, Cap'n," he said innocently, "and if the price is right, I can arrange it."

With remarkable speed for one his size, Silas reached across the table and grabbed Percy's collar. "Explain yourself, Pratt, if you want to go on breathing," he demanded.

"Easy, Cap'n!" Percy begged, clutching at his Adams apple, his face suddenly grown pale. "Give me a chance, will ya?"

"Make it quick then, or I'll wring your skinny neck," the captain said, growling.

"I followed the Gypsy, Cap'n. I know where he is," Percy blustered.

"But what makes you think he can lead you to the girl?"

"Take my word for it, Cap'n." Percy rushed to assure him. He had no way of knowing for sure about the girl, but right now he needed to buy time.

"So." Silas released him with a sigh of satisfaction and a glint in his beady black eyes.

Lowering his bulk back into the chair, he rubbed his chin thoughtfully. Perhaps he could still salvage something from this. In eager anticipation, he licked his thick lips. Revenge on the girl, he decided, would taste very sweet. As much as he hated to think it, sometimes it paid to know a character like Percy Pratt.

Chapter Thirty-Three

By the meager light of her lantern, sometimes bent almost double, Madeline made her way through the winding maze of tunnels. The ground beneath her feet was rocky, and the hollow sound of her footsteps followed along behind her. In some places, water dripped down from overhead, and at times, she splashed through puddles ankle-deep. The further she traveled, the more signs of habitation were apparent. Deeply rutted tracks told of the recent movement of heavy vehicles, and an oily film left by wagon wheels floated on the standing water. It all lent credence to Tyler's theory of smugglers, and it boosted her optimism. She could only imagine what went on down here. But surely, by the very nature of their trade, they would demand a ready escape route. Smuggling was a thriving business and a dangerous one. In fact, with the higher taxes on tea, coffee, and tobacco, it had become a way of life for many families. They grew brazen, willing to take bigger risks. Any number of gangs operated around the coast of Britain, wild and lawless men who lured ships to their doom on the rocks. They cared not for the lives lost in the wreckage; their sights were set only on the value of the cargo. She shivered, knowing the sooner they left this place, the better.

Pushing these unsettling thoughts aside, Madeline hurried on. Tyler's life hung in the balance. Every second counted. At first, it was so slight she hardly noticed, but the way grew steadily steeper. In hopes that the end of the tunnel was near, she willed her feet to move faster. Suddenly, she rounded a corner, and her heart sank. A large boulder blocked her way. She knew the bitter taste of disappointment. To have come so far only to fail now was too much to bear. Shafts of dusty sunlight filtered in around the rock, and warm air touched her skin. She pressed her cheek to the gritty surface and squinted out at the blue sky beyond. Freedom was out there just a few short feet away, but with no way to get to it, it might as well be a million miles.

She blew out her lantern and set it down. Without much hope but determined to do something, she began to dig around the rock with her bare hands. Each time she succeeded in clearing a small space, the shifting sand quickly rushed to fill it in. Pebbles skittered and bounced around her, striking her skin with the fierceness of a spring hailstorm. Dust billowed up in choking clouds, filling her eyes, nose, and mouth. At last, tired and dirty, she sat back on her heels. With nothing more to show for her efforts than skinned knuckles and bloodied fingernails, she let the pent-up tears flow.

"Ohhh!" She vented her wrath in a wail that echoed eerily along the tunnel walls. In pure frustration, she shoved the hated boulder. It moved. Startled, she pushed it again, much harder this time. With very little sound, like a well-oiled door, the boulder slid easily to one side. Hardly able to believe her good fortune, she sat for a moment, too stunned to move. Her eyes adjusted slowly to the sunlight, then, trying hard to contain her excitement, she scrambled to her feet and went in search of the gypsy.

Although the appointed meeting time had long since passed, Antonio continued to wait on the hilltop. He was worried. It had now been far too long. Just what had taken place on board the Remington? If the stories he had heard in the tavern were true, and the girl had been rescued, then she and the American could be miles away by now. He stood looking down at the town of Topsham, his thoughts in turmoil. Should he try the tavern again—make one last attempt to find the pair? But if that failed, what then? He had been away far too long already. He decided it was time to return to his family. With his mind made up, he turned back toward his wagon and stopped short.

"Not so fast, my friend," he shouted, his anger mounting as he spied a stranger snooping through his belongings. Galvanized into action, he lunged at the would-be thief, and catching him by the shoulder, spun him around. "Stop your useless struggling," he demanded, "or I'll box your ears."

"Antonio?"

Shocked, he took a quick step backward. How did this dirty urchin come to know his name?

"You are Antonio?"

He nodded.

"I'm Madeline Carlyle. I came to find you."

"Mama mia." He released her in an instant. "A thousand pardons, Senorita."

"Come quickly," she begged, brushing his apology aside.

"But I—"

"Please!" Madeline took his arm and pulled. "I will explain as we go."

Then, wasting no more time and with Antonio close on her heels, she rushed back toward the tunnel.

At first sight, Antonio thought the man dead, but at the sound of their approach, Tyler stirred restlessly.

"He was shot last night," Madeline hurried to explain. "He needs attention badly, but I am no nurse." Her face was grave as she watched Antonio unwrap the makeshift dressing. With a shake of his head, he washed away the blood and assessed the condition of the wound.

"The infection is bad," he muttered at the sight of the badly discolored, swollen flesh.

"What can we do?" Madeline asked anxiously.

"Here? Nothing. But my sister, Roxanne, she is very good with such things."

"Then why are we waiting?"

"It's not quite that easy, Senorita. First, we must move him, and in his present state, that will be difficult."

"But we can't just sit here and do nothing!"

"I didn't say we would," Antonio assured her as he retied the bandage.

"Will you two stop arguing and get me out of here?" Tyler attempted to sit up.

"Easy, my friend," Antonio cautioned, "I am glad to see that you are still with us, but please, let us try to keep it that way."

Tyler smiled weakly up into their worried faces. "It will take more than one bullet to finish me," he assured them. "But just the same, Gypsy, I am glad you came when you did. Now, if you can help me to my feet—"

"A moment longer, Senor." Antonio placed a restraining hand on his shoulder. "The wagon you requested isn't far from here. It will take but a moment."

"One more thing, Antonio. My horse is—"

"With the blacksmith," Antonio finished for him. "Do you want me to fetch him now? It may take a while."

"No!" Madeline cried. "There is no time."

But Tyler insisted.

"In that case." Antonio pulled a pistol from his belt and placed it in Tyler's hand. "This is just in case, my friend. Are you able to handle it?"

Tyler hefted the weapon for a moment, then, without too much difficulty, firmly clicked the hammer back. "I can still give a good account of myself," he said. Lowering the hammer once more, he set the pistol down safely by his side.

Pratt couldn't believe his luck. He had thought only to deliver the gypsy that day, but as he and the captain spied on the man from afar, the girl popped up out of nowhere. After a short tussle with the gypsy, she engaged him in an animated conversation. A moment later, they raced some distance away and disappeared.

"Best to wait and see what 'appens, Cap'n," he cautioned when his companion made to rush after the pair. "Last time I met up with the gypsy, he weren't alone. He was with this big American bloke. Believe me, you wouldn't want to run afoul of that un."

Never one to take unnecessary chances, Silas curbed his impatience. "All right, Pratt," he said, growling. "But if anything should go awry and the girl escapes, I will lash you to the yardarm and cut off your ears."

Percy had long since become familiar with the captain's threats. This was a new one, but he didn't doubt the truth of it for an instant. But he knew that if something did go wrong, he would rather face the captain's wrath than that of the American. His patience seemed to pay off when, a short time later, the gypsy reappeared. They watched as the man collected a rope from his wagon, caught one of his wandering horses, and rode off toward the town.

"Now, Cap'n," he urged his companion. Then, heart beating wildly, he followed in the girl's footsteps. With the captain close on his heels, he made his way into the dark underground tunnels.

Madeline heard the sound of approaching footsteps. "That didn't take long." She turned, expecting to see Antonio. The rest of her words were lost in a strangled gasp as she came face to face with Captain Silas Brown.

"So, we meet again, Madam." His lip curled as he sneered the word. "But what's this? You seem surprised to see me. Surely you didn't think that after deceiving me with your willowy form, there would be no price to pay. If so, let me correct the notion. There are places in the world where your fair skin will bring a high return." He stalked closer.

Madeline retreated quickly.

"Look around you." He spread his thick arms wide. "There is nowhere for you to hide, so just come quietly." Seeing the fear in her eyes, he trembled with excitement. Blood throbbed at his temples, his eyes developed a slight bulge, and his cheeks flushed a bright pink. "Grab her, Pratt," he demanded. Suddenly growing impatient, his mouth watered at the thought of what was yet to come. He could wait no longer. "Get her out to the Remington, man, and hurry."

"A moment, Captain, if you please," Tyler's voice broke in. "This lady is mine, and, believe me, I have no intention of letting her go. The only way to get to her is through me. Touch one hair on her head, and you will meet your maker in a hurry."

Percy stopped in mid stride, his eyes darting around the dark interior. Recognizing the soft American drawl, his heart threatened to leave his chest. How could he have made such a mistake? Hadn't he warned the cap'n of this very thing?

"I must say, Pratt, I'm surprised to see you," the voice continued, "I thought the money I gave you would see you safely out of my life forever."

Now Percy spotted him, sitting on the floor, propped lazily back against the wall.

"It's 'im, Cap'n," he squeaked in panic. "The bloke I told ya about."

Silas Brown turned on him, his voice filled with venom. "Liar Pratt." He stormed. "You vowed your pockets empty, but truth to tell they rattle with another man's gold. Just how many times have you played me false?"

"Never before, Cap'n." Percy cringed away. "I swears to God!"

"Bah, spare me your lies, Pratt," Silas demanded. "I will deal with you when our business here is finished."

"But Cap'n, the American!"

"Fool!" Silas roared, pushing the little man savagely forward. "Don't you see the bandage, Pratt? The man has been shot!"

"True, Captain." Tyler revealed the blood-soaked bandage. "One of your men deserves an extra ration of rum tonight. But whether it was good marksmanship or just a lucky shot, I can't say."

Silas's laugh was harsh. "That's why they have remained here, Pratt. Don't you see? He can't stop us. He's more dead than alive."

"Perhaps, Captain," Tyler said, "but I think this might improve my chances a little. What say you, Pratt?" He had picked up Antonio's pistol and waved the deadly piece threateningly in Pratt's direction.

Finding himself staring straight into the dark round eye of the pistol barrel, Percy was inclined to agree.

"Get the girl now, Pratt," Silas yelled. "The man has no strength to pull the trigger."

"Well, there's only one way to find out." Eyes bright with fever, Tyler clicked the hammer back. "But then Pratt, are you willing to take the chance? Get behind me, Madeline." He waved for her to join him. "Just in case. I don't doubt my own ability, but I can't vouch for our friend, Antonio, there."

"Bah! Do you hope to deceive me with such a ruse? The Gypsy has gone. He has left you to your own devises. What more would you expect from a gypsy?" His voice was filled with contempt.

"I would listen to him if I were you, Senor." The voice was soft but full of menace.

Percy felt the hair at his nape stand on end. The return of the gypsy was unexpected. The odds had changed. He wanted nothing more to do with it.

"Come on, Cap'n," he begged the man. "Let it go. The ship's waiting, and you need to sail."

"He's right, Captain," Tyler agreed. "I think it's time for you to go."

Still the man hesitated, gritting his teeth, eyes filled with hate. At last, reluctantly admitting defeat, he made to retrace his steps.

"Oh no, not that way." Tyler indicated with the barrel of the pistol. "That way would be far too easy. Take the front door, please, so we can keep an eye on you."

Percy needed no more prompting. Running headlong for the cave entrance, he began the rough climb down to the beach. Frozen on the spot, Silas still wasn't convinced, but as he watched Percy's speedy departure, he seemed to think better of it. With a grunt of anger, he eased his bulk out over the side. His voice could still be heard cursing the hapless Pratt long after they had disappeared from sight.

"Again you returned just in time, my friend." With a nod of thanks to Antonio, Tyler sighed, closed his eyes, and the pistol slowly slipped from his hand.

Chapter Thirty-Four

Later Madeline would remember every detail of that difficult journey. How, with Antonio bearing most of the weight, they somehow moved a still semi-conscious Tyler slowly from the cave. Antonio applied a clean dressing to the man's wound and dressed him in dry clothes. With Madeline's help, he fashioned a crude bed in the back of the wagon, and they did all they could to make the injured man comfortable. At last, close to collapse herself, Madeline leaned against the wagon wheel and sighed.

"What would I have done without you, Antonio? I shudder to think what our fate might have been had you not come when you did."

"Your man told me what to do, Lady, and luck was on our side."

"Just the same, thank you for being there." Madeline shivered, her teeth chattering.

Seeing her distress, Antonio apologized. "Forgive my foolishness, Lady. I must take care for you or I will have two invalids on my hands." He hurried away and returned moments later, his arms full of clothing. "These are for you." He held out the bright colored gypsy garb for her inspection.

"Oh!" Delighted, Madeline rushed to relieve him of his burden. With the garments clutched to her chest, she stood on tiptoe and placed a quick kiss on his cheek. "Thank you," she called, rushing away to find a secluded spot to shed her still wet clothing.

Antonio stood rooted to the spot for a full minute, his fingers gently touching the spot her lips had blessed.

"You are indeed a lucky man, my friend," he whispered to the still silent man in the wagon, "If she were mine, I would risk everything for her too."

Later, feeling as he did, Antonio found it difficult to deny Madeline's request but he did. "No, Lady." His voice was firm. "I understand your concern, but it is too late to travel tonight."

"But we must—"

He held up his hand to silence her, all the time thinking how well she looked in her bright gypsy clothes. "Have no fear. Antonio, he will take care of everything. Now rest," he insisted, spreading a blanket on the ground.

"Well, perhaps, but just for a moment." Still unsure, Madeline curled up on the blanket and fell asleep in an instant.

"Sleep well, little one." Antonio covered her gently. "And have no fear. I will never let you down."

It was the warm sun on her face that woke her. Unsure of her where-abouts, Madeline sat up with a start. Then, of a sudden, it all came rushing back. She jumped to her feet just as Antonio climbed down from the wagon.

"Ah, so you have joined us again, Lady. It must have been the good smell of my cooking that invaded your dreams."

"How is he?" She ignored his attempt at humor and ran to the back of the wagon to see for herself. At the sight of Tyler's face, ashen skin, and closed eyes, her heart constricted. She turned to Antonio, her eyes wide and questioning.

"Today, Lady." He promised. "See." He pointed to the front of the wagon where the horses were already hitched and waiting.

"Are you sure your sister can help him?" Madeline sought his assurance.

"Although I seldom give Roxanne enough credit for her skill, yes. So come, eat, and then let us away."

A little later, as Madeline climbed to her seat on the wagon, she turned for one last look behind her. The Remington no longer sat in the harbor. Shivering, she realized the captain had finally sailed without a cabin boy.

"It is over, Lady. You are safe." Antonio placed a comforting hand on her shoulder. "Shall we go?"

She took a deep breath and nodded. With a click of his tongue, the gypsy set his team in motion.

The morning dragged slowly by. Madeline spent much of the time at Tyler's side, administering to his needs. She knew her skills were limited, and she felt helpless. Her mood bounced from hopeful to downcast. At times, the feverish green eyes opened and her heart raced, but then his wild words and twitching limbs would dash her high hopes.

Later, as she sat beside Antonio on the wagon's high front seat, he did his best to encourage her. He told her of the injuries he himself had endured and regaled her with stories of the many cures brought about by his sister.

"So have no fear, Lady," he said at last. "Roxanne will heal your man for you. You will see."

The sun had long since started its downward decent, and although Madeline tried hard to remain positive, she wondered if they would ever find the gypsies and Roxanne. Suddenly the wagon came to a halt, jolting her from her solitary thoughts.

"What is it, Antonio?" she demanded, struggling hard to retain her seat.

"It's them, Lady. It's my family." Unable to contain his excitement, he handed her the reins, jumped down, and ran to meet them.

Madeline watched as the train of brightly painted caravans moved slowly toward them. Voices rang out in greeting, and soon Antonio was surrounded by a large, welcoming crowd. A pretty, older woman, whom Madeline decided must be Antonio's mother, was weeping openly. When he at last broke free, there was a look of pride on his face. With his arm firmly wrapped around the older woman's shoulders, he moved forward.

"Lady, may I introduce my mother, Maria, and the rest of my family?" he asked.

One by one, starting with his mother, the members of his family stepped forward and were acknowledged. Once the polite introductions were completed, Antonio's relatives rushed to surround him again, everyone talking at once.

"Antonio!" Madeline broke in at last, her concern quite plain.

"Yes, Lady, forgive them, but it seems they thought me dead." He turned and looked about him. "Roxanne," he called. "Come, little sister, show yourself." The family quickly parted, and from out of their midst emerged a dark-eyed gypsy girl.

Surprised, Madeline recognized her at once. So, Antonio's sister was the fortune teller from the fair. She had failed to make any connection before, but now as the girl moved slowly toward her, she could see the strong family resemblance. With her shoulder-length raven hair, large dark eyes, and full red lips, Roxanne was a living portrait of a younger Maria. Willow thin, she moved with the easy grace of a dancer, but her beautiful face was set in a frown, and there was an almost insolent sway to her narrow hips.

Antonio ignored his sister's obvious displeasure, and pulling her to him, he spoke softly to her alone. Long before he could finish, Roxanne's expression changed. She pulled herself free and rushed to the back of the wagon.

"Oh, look at you, my foolish man," she crooned, sounding close to tears. "The sight of you, it breaks your Roxanne's heart."

From her seat just inches beyond the canvas, Madeline's back stiffened at the familiarity of the girl's words. When had the two met, and just how close were they?

Minutes later, she could only watch helplessly as Roxanne gave orders left and right.

"Gently, gently," the gypsy girl warned as Tyler was quickly transferred to her caravan. Then, ordering everyone else away, she went inside and closed the door firmly behind her.

Madeline was only able to watch helplessly, her emotions running the gamut from relief to exhaustion to a resentful emptiness. Her eyes wide and questioning, she turned to Antonio.

"Trust me, Lady. This is for the best. Now, please," he beseeched her, "go with my mother. She will take care of you."

Too drained to resist further, she numbly submitted herself to Maria's care.

"Poor little thing." Maria fussed over her, greeting her with open arms and welcoming her into her pretty little home on wheels.

For Madeline, who could barely remember the warmth of her own mother's love, the woman's kindness was deeply touching. In the days that followed, bit by bit, her strength returned. During these days, she sat, mostly ignored, watching the activity that centered around Roxanne's caravan. Time and again, she had sought entrance only to be turned away.

"I must go to him, Antonio," she begged her friend at last.

"It will do no good, Lady. He will not know you. Give it just a little more time."

Madeline wanted to argue, but after a look at his face, she thought better of it.

"Alright," she finally agreed with a nod. "Perhaps it's best. Just a little more time."

Chapter Thirty-Five

Roxanne administered tirelessly to her patient, guarding him jealously and barring everyone but her brother from her caravan. Even Antonio was only tolerated because he would have none of her tantrums. She gave him little or no information to pass along, and Madeline's frequent inquiries were ignored altogether.

"That woman did this to you," Roxanne muttered as she removed the soiled dressing for the first time. "I tried to warn you." Tears filled her eyes at the sight of the ragged wound in Tyler's side. "But Roxanne, she is clever. She will make you well again, then you will belong to me forever."

She worked diligently both day and night. With an antiseptic solution of diluted oil of thyme, she cleansed the affected area. Dried leaves of agrimony staunched the flow of blood and flowers of honeysuckle reduced inflammation and lowered his fever. A fresh poultice of plantain applied every few hours helped the healing process. At night, when sleep eluded him and he tossed in pain, a brew of chamomile tea provided a good sedative.

As Tyler's body rested and fought to recover, Madeline moved freely among the gypsies. She quickly adopted their lifestyle, even their mode of dress. She grew close to Maria, who took her under her wing as they shared the older woman's spotlessly clean *vardo*. *Vardo*, she learned, was the Romany word for caravan. Soon she was accepted by all but one, Roxanne, and a strong animosity grew between the two.

Roxanne spent most of her time at Tyler's side, and she still refused Madeline access. As Antonio watched from afar, his concern grew. He was angered by his sister's actions, but knowing where her heart lay, he couldn't fault her. Bitter disappointment lay ahead for her, and he wished he could prevent it. One day, he caught her alone and tried to warn her.

"You are wrong, sister," he chastised her. "Do you think he will thank you for keeping them apart? No, and in the end, he will hate you for it. You must see, your love is wasted on him."

"And what of you brother?" she harshly retorted. He showed surprise. "Yes, you. I have seen the way you look at her." She tossed her head in Madeline's general direction. "You see, your eyes betray you too." With a toss of her head, she turned and stalked away, anger in her every movement.

As much as he wanted to shout a denial, Antonio suddenly realized that she was right. But at least he knew there was no hope for him. It seemed, the future held only heartache for both he and his sister. He knew now there was nothing more he could say to the headstrong Roxanne. But as he watched his sister enter her vardo and shut the door behind her, he whispered to himself, "I just hope, my American friend, when the time comes, you will be understanding with her."

Tyler had no recollection of his first few days among the gypsies. He was aware only of a raging fire burning deep within him, accompanied by searing pain. Blurred misshapen faces came and went with alarming regularity. They haunted his fevered dreams, even though he fought to keep them at bay. Strong hands restrained him, limiting his movements until, too weak to resist further, he again lapsed into unconsciousness. When that dark world engulfed him, time ceased to exist.

Gradually, with the passing days, his pain grew less, and faces became more distinct. He could tell night from day, and a ravenous hunger began to consume him.

"Food!" he muttered through parched lips.

Roxanne's heart skipped a beat.

"Food!" he repeated.

Not sure if she would laugh or cry, Roxanne rushed to his side, and for the first time in days, she looked into green eyes.

"So, my sister is right," Antonio said a short time later. "You have decided to join us again. For a while, my friend, I rather doubted that you would."

Tyler managed a rather sheepish grin and struggled to sit. He met with no success and so flopped helplessly back down on the bed. "Well," he jested, "if this is better, then I must really have been in a sorry state. In truth, I feel weak as a day-old kitten."

"Time, Senor. Time and my sister's care will soon return you to good health."

Despite his impatience, Tyler knew the gypsy was right. He was surprised to learn of the length of his illness and of Roxanne's constant care. In answer to his many questions, she gladly described in graphic detail his hours of fevered ranting and of her gallant efforts to revive him. She greeted his returning health with mixed emotions. Her heart grew light as she saw him improve, but with the improvement, he grew impatient. Soon, she knew, it would be hard to keep him abed.

"Not today." She checked his wound and shook her head. "Just a little longer.

Perhaps tomorrow. We will see."

As the infection slowly healed, the prolonged inactivity grated on Tyler's nerves. He began to chomp at the bit. All through his recovery, Madeline had been conspicuous in her absence. But in her daily prattle, Roxanne had slyly let slip that the girl's time was being well spent with Antonio. He had no choice for a while but to let that go. However, to say it did nothing for his peace of mind would have been a gross understatement.

It was more than a week later when he decided, with or without Roxanne's approval, he would leave his sick bed. That morning, he waited until she had absented herself from the caravan, then, throwing off the covers, he swung his feet to the ground. With one hand holding onto the bed for support, he gingerly tested his standing power. Not surprised, he found his legs less then steady. Moving slowly, he sought out his clothing, and with some difficulty, pulled on his shirt and britches. He bent to pull on his boots and cursed the pain that riveted his side. Righting himself with an effort, he waited for the spasm to pass. At last, breathing heavily, he emerged out into the bright sunlight and the unfamiliar world of the gypsies.

For Madeline, the days passed slowly. After helping Maria with the morning chores, she was mostly left to herself. Her daily efforts to visit Tyler were denied by an ever-vigilant Roxanne. With excuses that it was too soon or that he was still too weak, she found the door to Roxanne's vardo shut firmly in her face. Antonio soon became her only contact with the sick man, and always anxious for news, she would seek him out. They spent afternoons together, walking and talking of many things. Fascinated by the gypsies, Madeline plied Antonio with many questions. She learned that his people were Graiengers, horse traders, and that Roxanne was a dukker, fortune teller. Their leader was the Prima, and they followed the drom, the road. In particular, she loved the brightly painted vardos these people called home. Each wagon was alive with color and design, and Antonio did his best to explain their meaning. Thus, it was that afternoon, when with heads together, engaged in animated conversation, that Tyler came upon them.

At first, he watched them unobserved. Had it not been for the fair hair, he would have thought her a gypsy. She was dressed gypsy style with her golden shoulders revealed by the low cut of a bright blue blouse. A wide cloth sash encircled her small waist, and her bare feet were visible beneath the hem of her long full skirt. She sat beside Antonio, her eyes bright, her smile dazzling.

Tyler's heart constricted, and his face darkened in a frown. Could Roxanne have been right? Was there something between them after all?

Antonio was the first to see him, and startled, he jumped to his feet. Mistaking his surprise for guilt, Tyler stiffened, and walking with a slight limp, he made his way toward them.

"This is wonderful, my friend." Antonio rushed to meet him, hand outstretched. "We had no idea that your health was so improved."

"Obviously!" Tyler's eyes narrowed, and he ignored the offered hand.

Confused, the smile faded from the gypsy's face, and his hand dropped to his side.

"You look well, Madam," Tyler snapped, looking beyond the man to where Madeline waited. "I'm pleased that my condition caused you no great distress."

Madeline's eyes widened in surprise. The anger in his voice and the injustice of his greeting shocked her. But she faced him, unflinching.

"Perhaps you don't remember, Sir, but my nursing skills were sorely lacking." She came to her feet and moved toward him, her insides quivering at the sight of him. His skin was a little lighter and his face a little thinner from his convalescence, but he was as ruggedly handsome as ever. "I was told you had the best of care."

"Thank God, I did." His look was scornful. "For, without Roxanne, my bones might even now be bleaching in some shallow grave."

Madeline's face paled. "You judge me harshly, Sir." Her voice shook.

"Really, then how was it I missed your daily visits?" His words dripped sarcasm. "The wound is on my side, not my head."

Antonio stepped quickly forward, but Tyler waved him away. "No!" he snapped, "I have obviously intruded on a private moment, Sir. I will detain you no longer."

Roxanne, hunting for her patient, missed none of the exchange.

"There you are, you naughty boy," she scolded, a smug smile on her face. "Come, let Roxanne take you back to bed." She took his arm, tugging when he resisted.

With one last long look in Madeline's direction, Tyler allowed her to lead him away.

Madeline watched them go, still stunned by the injustice of his outburst. How had he phrased it? "Thank God for Roxanne," "How was it I missed your daily visits?" "The wound is on my side, not my head."

The joy she had felt at the first sight of him quickly faded. But as she watched him limp painfully away, her heart twisted.

"I'm sorry, Lady," Antonio was at her side. "I see my sister's hand in this," he said. "She has poisoned him with her lies." He shook his fist in the direction of Roxanne's vardo. "Leave it to me, Lady. My sister, she has meddled for the last time."

"No, Antonio." She grasped his arm. "If he has so little regard for me, so be it. I'll not beg for his understanding."

"But—"

She wouldn't let him finish. "Now that he is well enough to travel, I will soon be gone."

Antonio's heart was heavy. "No!" he pleaded. "Where will you go? What will you do?" At the shrug of her shoulders, he dared to suggest, "Then stay here with me." He took her hand. "You have been happy here. My mother loves you like a daughter, and my people will welcome you."

"No." Shaking her head, she pulled away. "Thank you, Antonio, you have been a good friend. But all I've ever wanted was to find my father. No matter what it takes, I will keep on looking. I hope you understand."

He nodded. "But give it time, Lady. Wait a while, I beg of you."

"I will stay until I am sure he is much improved," she said, "but that's all I can promise for now." Too miserable to discuss it further, she turned and hurried away.

Wanting nothing more than to be alone, Madeline sought the comfort of the little vardo she now called home. There, curled in a blanket, her face buried in a pile of pillows, she shed pent-up tears. For days, she had longed for Tyler's recovery, prayed for it, thought of nothing else. What could have prompted his hurtful outburst? Now Antonio's wish for her to stay had added to her distress. What on earth had she done to deserve this? It seemed that once again her world was turning upside down.

Chapter Thirty-Six

G lad to be on the move once more, the Gypsies gathered their belongings together, and with Tyler and Madeline at opposite ends of the procession, the little caravans took to the road. Travel was slow, and the days stretched out, quiet and uneventful. But when darkness fell and the evening fires were lit, no one in the little community was immune to the tension in their midst. The peace of their everyday existence was shattered by the stormy relationship of the tall Gorgio and the beautiful golden-haired girl. Each accidental meeting between the two became a charade played out for all to see.

As on one occasion, when rounding a corner, Tyler came up short, barely able to avoid a collision. Startled by Madeline's sudden appearance and temporally at a loss for words, he bowed stiffly. Then he managed to say, "Your pardon, Madam."

"Sir." She curtsied, her face flushed red, wanting nothing more than the chance to turn and run.

A strained silence stretched out between them. Uncomfortable, he fidgeted, clearing his throat.

"Is your health much improved?" she ventured at last, breathing deeply, struggling to slow the beating of her heart.

"Much, thank you," he replied, but her cool demeanor irked him, and he was driven to add, "Your belated concern is quite touching." Damn, he cursed himself as her back stiffened and the hurt showed in her blue eyes.

Madeline made no further comment. Instead, with another quick curtsy, she found herself once more hurrying away.

"Damn." With fists clenched and breath heavy, Tyler stood and watched her go. With the crop he carried, he struck a forceful blow to the side of his high leather boot. It did nothing to ease his dark mood. Finally, with a resigned sigh, he turned and strode angrily away in the opposite direction.

When his temper cooled, he became silent and angry. After all, he told himself, Madeline owed him nothing. There was no commitment between them. If Antonio was her choice, what right did he have to intrude? She was no longer his concern. Shortly he would return to Long Meadow, complete his business, and sail for Boston as soon as possible.

As he grew steadily stronger, he found Roxanne's constant fussing and the snail's pace of the wagons drove him to distraction. He took to prowling in the hours of darkness, casting a giant shadow in his wake, his soft footfall unnerving all those that heard his passage. By day, he saddled the sturdy Samson, deserted the slow-moving caravan, and sought out the freedom of the open countryside. As he galloped wildly away across the bleak landscape, the gypsies breathed a collective sigh of relief.

Madeline, still stung from Tyler's unkind words and not wanting to risk more uncomfortable meetings with him, kept to herself. Antonio's declaration of love had left her feeling awkward in his company. His sad eyes touched her heart, and now, instead of seeking him out, she found herself avoiding him. She seldom left her vardo; if she did venture out, it was to move like a shadow among her former friends. Everything had changed, and she was saddened by it.

Antonio bore his disappointment silently. He had known from the start that he stood no chance with Madeline, so why hadn't he remained silent? Didn't he warn Roxanne of the foolishness of her love for the American? So why hadn't he heeded his own advice? It seemed there was no logic when it came to matters of the heart. His own foolishness had cost him dearly. He seldom saw Madeline now and never alone. Their afternoons together had become a thing of the past, and he missed them deeply. Time had passed slowly for him too, but today, as he walked alone, he thought of her and the promise she had made.

"I will stay until he is much improved," she had said. Well, that time had come at last, and unless he did something to stop her, she might soon be gone. With his mind made up, he went in search of Tyler, knowing he must try to heal the rift brought about by Roxanne. He found the man tending his horse, and clearing his throat, he stepped forward.

"A moment of your time, Senor, if you please."

"Make it quick, Gypsy," Tyler answered, not turning as he tied a pack to his saddle.

"You are leaving?"

"It's time. My wound is healed. There's nothing to hold me here."

"What of Madeline?"

Tyler's laughter was harsh. "Do you want my blessing?" he snapped. At Antonio's show of surprise, his eyes narrowed. "Don't push me, Gypsy. Your sister kept me abreast of your actions while I recovered, so you should know there are no secrets here."

"Then you are a fool, my friend, I—"

Rounding quickly on the startled man, Tyler grabbed him by his shirt front. With muscles taunt and lips drawn back in an angry snarl, he drove the man backward, only stopping when he slammed into the side of a wagon with a solid thump. He leaned into the other man, their faces mere inches apart, and growled a warned.

"You've called me a fool for the last time, Gypsy. Take my word. Even though I owe you much of late, I am hard pressed not to plant my fist in your face."

"Kill me if you must, Senor." Antonio gasped for breath. "But if you believe all Roxanne says, then you are a fool. I mean no disrespect, but you should know my sister is not to be trusted. I love her dearly, but she sees things as she wishes them to be, not as they are."

Tyler frowned. "Go on," he urged.

"It was Madeline who saved your life. I would have given up on you, but she never did. It's true, Roxanne treated your wounds, but at the same time she kept Madeline from your side. For daily word on your health, she turned to me. Whatever feelings you thought there were, were mine alone. You hold the key to her heart, my friend. I know because she told me so."

Releasing the gypsy, Tyler exhaled. "So," he mused, "this was all Roxanne's doing."

"Don't be too angry with her," Antonio begged, "for as bad as she was, she too only followed her heart."

"Never fear, Gypsy. The fault is mine, but now the question is how to repair the damage I have done."

"Do what you must, my friend, but do it soon. Madeline has spoken with my mother, and now that she knows you are recovered, she too plans to leave."

"Do you know when?"

"Not for sure but perhaps as soon as tomorrow."

Deep in thought, Tyler thanked the gypsy, shook his hand, and walked away.

Antonio had been right. Madeline knew the time had come for her to leave. She felt the coward, but she had decided to wait until the last minute to say her goodbyes. The gypsies had been good to her; they had taken her in and accepted her without question. Then there was Maria, who was the closest thing to a mother she had ever known. How could she ever turn her back on all of them? It wasn't going to be easy.

Perhaps she could wait one more day. No! She decided, being firm with herself, the longer she waited, the worse it would be. She had thought long and hard about what lay before her and knew she needed help. To put her plans in motion, she turned to Carlos, the elder of the gypsy band, the Prima.

"Are you sure, child?" he asked of her request. "It would be best if you stay with us, at least until we can be sure you are safe."

Adamant, Madeline shook her head. "I will go with or without your help," she insisted, "but it will be much more difficult without it." She held her breath and waited.

His dark gaze rested thoughtfully upon her, and after what seemed like an eternity, he gave a reluctant nod of his head.

"Tomorrow, you may take what you need, child, and I pray your journey be a safe one."

Madeline thanked him, then made a mental note of what she needed. A horse and a few supplies, she hoped, would be enough to see her through. By this time tomorrow, she would be on her way, and this time, she vowed, nothing would stop her.

That evening, knowing it was to be her last in this place, she wandered the fringes of the camp site. Hidden among the trees, she watched the scenes she had become so familiar with of late. As the daylight faded, lanterns sprang to life at latticed windows. Glittering through small glass panes, their warm yellow glow brightened up the evening. One by one, campfires piled high with dry kindling, popped, and sparked into life. Excited barefoot children darted here and there, their voices shrill with their play. Grownups gathered together, their laughter mixed with a steady stream of good-humored banter. Large pots were carried out to hang above the flickering flames, and women, sleeves rolled high, went to work. Soon, steam began to rise from the heavy cauldrons. Spices were added to the bubbling ingredients, and delicious smells drifted up in the cool evening air. Tears gathered in Madeline's eyes, and for a moment, some of her resolve weakened. She sank to the ground, sniffing as she brushed the tears from her eyes.

"Here."

Startled, she gasped as a handkerchief was pressed into her hand.

"I'm overcome with a stranger sense of de-ja vu." Tyler's voice was soft.

Struggling to her feet, Madeline thrust the handkerchief back. "Thank you, but I don't need your help."

"Shhh," he hissed, and pulling her back into the shadows, he covered her mouth with his hand. While hunting for the elusive, Madeline he had managed to avoid Roxanne, but now he could hear the gypsy hot on his heels. "Promise to be quiet," he whispered, looking deep into her eyes, "and I'll let go." After a moment, she nodded. He dropped his hand, and they waited silently in their hiding place as Roxanne hurried by.

"Now." She turned on him, face pale and angry. "Please explain."

"I will I promise," he said, "but not here," He made to take her hand. She pulled away. "Please," he entreated.

Still uncertain, Madeline relented, and together they made their way to where Samson waited patiently.

"And now?" She asked.

"Not here," he replied, sweeping her up in his arms. She made no move to stop him as he placed her on Samson's back and swung up onto the saddle behind.

Chapter Thirty-Seven

With the sure-footed Samson as their guide, Tyler and Madeline had soon left the gypsy camp far behind. They had traveled in silence, each busy with their own thoughts. Madeline sat, stiff-backed and distant, behind her the man whose wellbeing had caused her so much concern of late. Beset by memories and feelings, she was ever conscious of his nearness. But his outburst had been hurtful and unfair, and her heart hardened.

Tyler was content, for now, with the turn of events. It felt good to have Madeline close to him again. He had, as Antonio had told him, been a fool. But in his own defense, his illness had dulled his wits, and Roxanne had been quite convincing. Now he was sure, given the chance, he could heal the rift that existed between him and Madeline.

At last, finding a secluded spot, they stopped to rest. The air was warm and scented with the earthy smells of the countryside around them. Still silent, they chose to sit side by side on a rocky knoll. Above them, the dark velvet of the night sky was dotted with a thousand stars. All was quiet, and to the young couple, it was as if the world stood still. For the moment, neither one seemed ready to break the spell.

It was Tyler who, at last, grew impatient. Jumping up and running his fingers through his hair, he began to pace. Not quite sure where to start, he finally said, "I was told your affections had gone elsewhere."

"And you believed it?"

"Well, your actions did nothing to disprove it," he defended.

"My actions?" she voiced disbelief. "But I did nothing wrong."

"Well, I know that now, but I didn't at the time." He stopped pacing and turned to face her. "Damn it all, Madeline. What I'm trying to say is, I was wrong, and I'm sorry."

Angry blue eyes now met green. "And that's supposed to make things right?" she demanded.

"Mercy!" He held up his hands, a sheepish grin on his face, "You may chastise me all you want later, Madam." He went down on one knee. "But right now, just tell me you forgive me."

Try as she might, Madeline couldn't keep a straight face.

"I suppose," she began slowly. "You were in a fevered state, and with a fever comes confusion. Not that I am making excuses for you, you understand."

"Of course not," Tyler wisely agreed, moving closer, "but now may I consider myself officially forgiven?"

"Under the circumstances," she hesitated a moment, as if deep in thought. Then, with a nod of her head, she said. "Yes."

"Whew!" he chuckled, "I'm glad that's over." Reaching for her hand he pulled her close. "I promise, I will never doubt you again," he whispered, drawing her even closer. His arms went around her, and their lips met in a tender, lingering, kiss.

By the time they returned to camp the evening meal was over. Small children had been sent to their beds, and grownups of the little community were gathered around a large crackling fire. The plaintive tremor of a gypsy violins filled the night with sweet sounds.

The young couple moved in quietly and took their place in the large circle. Smiles of pleasure greeted their arrival, and catching Tyler's eye, Antonio nodded his approval. They sat close, exchanging whispered words, seeming unaware of those around them.

For the Gypsies it was a happy sight. At last, the pretty lady and her man were reconciled. Peace would be restored and life in their camp could return to normal. But from the far side of the camp, Roxanne watched their intimacy with a heavy heart. Tormented and vengeful, she strode straight and tall into the circle of firelight. Lifting her arms high above her head, she clapped, one, two, three, one, two, three, and the musicians quickly picked up the beat. With her skirt held high, revealing her shapely legs, Roxanne began to dance. She moved slowly and deliberately around the circle, dipping and turning her movements seductive and inviting. Young men rushed to join her, but with a laugh and a toss of her head, she rejected them one by one.

Antonio watched his sister from afar. He guessed what she was about, and his face darkened in anger. He knew her actions could only end up hurting her, and he thought to stop her. But perhaps this was for the best. Now she would realize, once and for all, that this man was not for her. With a heavy heart, he followed her movements and waited.

Music swelled from the violin, sweet trembling notes that sighed in the soft evening breeze. As the musicians' fingers gently stroked the strings, the beautiful gypsy girl danced with wild abandon. Swaying and sensual, like a mystical sprite from some fairy tale, she held her audience spellbound. But she cared for none of them. Her dance was for one man and one man only, Tyler Wentworth.

Finally, she was there, face-to-face with the one she sought. Eyes soft and warm, she danced for him alone, pouring out her heart into every movement. It was as if they were the only two people left alive in the world. Her arms reached out toward him, beckoning for him to join her.

Tyler shook his head. Ignoring his refusal, Roxanne danced closer. Again, he resisted. But unwilling to give in, the gypsy grasped his hand and pulled him to his feet. At last, with an apologetic shake of his head to Madeline, he joined Roxanne in the circle of firelight. Flushed and triumphant, Roxanne gazed up into her partner's eyes. She circled him slowly, hands held high, clapping, challenging. He followed her movements step for step. Then, side by side, their movements fluid and graceful, they performed the intricate steps of the dance.

A hush fell over the camp. With all eyes centered on the stunning couple, the air was rife with tension. They moved with the music, the beautiful gypsy girl and the tall, dark georgio.

Madeline watched with her back stiffened. Eyes narrowed and fists clenched, she willed herself to remain calm. It was just a dance and would soon be over. But as the music drew to a shuddering close, Roxanne threw herself at her partner in a passionate embrace. For Madeline, after the anguish of the past few days, it was just too much to take. With a shrill "Ohhhh," she jumped to her feet and rushed at the couple. The music stopped short. Stunned onlookers watched open-mouthed, not sure what would happen next.

Surprise registered on Roxanne's face as her hair was grabbed and pulled. With a squeal of pain, she dragged herself free and turned around, fists flying. Madeline took a blow to the side of her head that sent her spinning. Roxanne pounced, and trading blow for blow, they scuffled back and forth in the dirt. Reacting in an instant, Tyler jumped into the fray. He caught Madeline around the middle and lifted her, kicking and screaming, into his arms.

"Stop, you little hell cat," he demanded, tightening his hold on her as he warded off Roxanne with his free hand.

Antonio rushed to his assistance, and with an angry growl, he quickly restrained his sister.

Faces flushed and eyes ablaze, the women struggled to break free. Neither was ready to end the animosity that existed between them.

"I said stop," Tyler roared. But, breathing hard, Madeline refused to listen.

"Put me down," she cried, thrashing wildly.

"No way, my dear!" Dodging her fists, he flipped her over his shoulder, and as she rained frustrated blows down on his back, he carried her away.

"Madeline, I need you to stop now." They had left the camp far behind them.

"Then put me down," she demanded.

"Gladly!" He winced as he slid her to the ground. "Your struggles do nothing to improve my wound."

Madeline was instantly contrite. "Oh, how could I have been so stupid? Please forgive me."

"Consider yourself forgiven," he muttered. "But right now, I'm afraid I need a minute." With a pained sigh, he leaned his weight against the nearest tree.

Madeline was at his side in an instant, but he gave her a reassuring grin.

"Don't waste your sympathy on me, love," he said. "I have lived through far worse than this. But you could spare a thought for Roxanne. I think she got more than she bargained for."

Madeline blushed. "I did behave badly, didn't I?"

He chuckled. "Let's just say you made your point. But then," he said, closely studying her blackening eye, "you fared no better."

"Oh!" Mortified, she buried her face against his chest.

"It's done," he said, kissing the top of her head, "and we have survived much worse these past days. But now the night turns cool, and I'm sure our friends grow anxious. Let's seek out the warmth of their fires before we both catch our death."

Chapter Thirty-Eight

In the days that followed, all remained quiet in the little gypsy community. The fact that Madeline sported a blackened eye was ignored. And if the incident that had occurred between the two women was mentioned at all, it was only spoken of behind closed doors. They traveled faster these days. Everyone, it seemed, was anxious to reach Marshfield Hall.

Roxanne was seldom seen at the evening gatherings, and during the days, she collected herbs and kept much to herself. Antonio did his best to sooth his sister's dark mood, but she would listen to no one. Even Maria's attempts were rebuffed by her daughter, and in the end, mother and son decided the girl was best left alone.

Madeline had expressed her regrets to those around her, and she found their quiet understanding touching. Now, with Tyler never far from her side, she longed for the first sight of Marshfield Hall and all the dear people waiting there. It seemed like forever, but at last the vardo she had called home in recent weeks was lumbering up the drive. As Tyler handled the reins, she bounced up and down on the seat beside him.

"Easy, love," he said, chuckling, "lest you fall off before we get there."

"But look, there it is." She clapped her hands in delight and bounced even harder. For her, it was like coming home. Marshfield Hall lay out before her, the ivy-covered walls of the big old house mellow and inviting.

Word had been sent on ahead of their arrival, and an anxious William paced the wide stone veranda. At the first sign of their approach, he gave a quick call into the house, and by the time the little cavalcade arrived, Ian and George had joined him there.

While Antonio and his family waited a short distance away, Tyler, still showing signs of a limp, helped Madeline down from her seat. The men of Marshfield Hall quickly greeted each other with glad words and hearty handshakes, but Madeline held back. Despite her joy at their return, she suddenly felt shy. Would these men forgive her for running away? Would they judge her and perhaps find her to blame for Tyler's injuries? Their concern for his health was obvious, even though he himself did his best to brush it aside. She had caused them so much distress, and all they had ever tried to do was help her. But William quickly banished her fears.

"I am so happy to see you, my dear," he said, his eyes bright as he took her hands in his. "Marshfield Hall hasn't been the same without you."

"It's good to have you back, Madi. I missed you." Ian placed a kiss upon her cheek. "But what's this?" He gave her a quizzical look as he studied her still blackened eye.

Madeline blushed, unable to hide her embarrassment.

"She's taken up fisticuffs," Tyler explained, a broad smile on his face, "and she's pretty good at it too."

Ian would have questioned them further, but then thought better of it.

At last, William broke up the little group. "Come, everyone," he urged and ushered them into the house. Once inside, they were greeted again, this time by the assembled household staff. Under the watchful eye of the stern Mr. Wiggins, their excitement was somewhat subdued, but no matter, a warm greeting was given by all.

William's dogs, Goldie and Prince, came skidding across the highly polished floor with their tails wagging, and soon it was a wild melee of barking dogs and everyone talking at once.

"Oh, Miss." Despite the disgruntled looks of Mr. Wiggins, Jeannie managed to make her way to Madeline's side. Their delight at seeing each other again was obvious. They hugged, and for them, there was no need of words.

"Mister." There was a tug on Tyler's sleeve.

"Well, if it isn't young Charlie." He smiled down at the boy. Dressed in a new suit, his face now full and rosy, he was almost unrecognizable. "What of his grandmother?" Tyler asked William.

"She is making good progress. The doctor thinks she will heal well in spite of her age. When we received your message, George went to fetch them. They are well-settled now in the little cottage by the river. This young man," William continued, fondly ruffling the boy's hair, "has been taken over by Mrs. Carter. Of course, he's being thoroughly spoiled."

"I've got a pony, and I can ride him," Charlie interrupted.

Mrs. Carter shook her head in mock distress. "He's already making a little hellion out of the boy, Mister Tyler, racing him around the countryside. But what can you expect? Your grandfather has never grown up himself."

"Quiet, woman." William squeezed her arm. "You're getting to be an old fuss budget." Shaking her head, Mrs. Carter hurried away.

"Come on, Charlie," George called and hoisted the boy up on his shoulder. "The two us will go out and show the Gypsies where to camp." A space near the barn had been offered to Antonio and his people for the length of their stay.

"We'll join you, George," Tyler said, and with Ian at his side, they left while things in the house slowly settled back to normal.

Making the most of a quiet moment, Madeline broached a subject that had been heavy on her mind. "Will you ever forgive me for loosing Misty?" she asked William.

He patted her hand. "The important thing is that you are safe, my dear."

"But I know how much she meant to you."

"Don't fret," he insisted. "We will talk of it later."

The conversation did nothing to ease Madeline's mind, but for the moment, there was nothing she could do.

By the time Tyler and the men returned from the gypsy encampment, the hour was getting late. As darkness fell, lamps were lit and tables laden down with food were set up on the terrace. Antonio and his family had been invited to spend the evening, and even Roxanne had consented to come. As the night wore on, food was consumed and conversation flourished. At last, ensconced in comfortable wicker chairs, their glasses filled with ice cold lemonade, the family relaxed, and the story of Madeline and Tyler's adventures unfolded. As the story came to a close, Tyler took Madeline's hand, and to everyone's surprise, he announced their engagement.

"Well, when did this all happen?" Curious, it was Ian who asked the question.

Tyler studied Madeline's face carefully for a moment, then, with a wink, he said, "I rather think it all happened on the same night as the black eye."

With hearty chuckles, the assembled group expressed their approval, and Madeline did her best to cover up her embarrassment. Lemonade was quickly replaced by champagne, and amid all of the congratulations, a toast was drunk to the happy couple.

Later as Jeannie prepared Madeline for the night, she revealed a secret of her own. It seemed that during Madeline's absence, she and George had also come to an understanding.

Madeline hugged her friend in delight.

"Well, it was all your fault, you know, Miss," the girl, at last, confided.

"How so?" Madeline inquired.

"Remember the night of the ball?"

Madeline nodded.

"Well, George, he just swept me off me feet."

Their laughter was spontaneous.

Chapter Thirty-Nine

Madeline opened her eyes and sighed. It was still early, so she lay for a while thinking about the day ahead. It was good to be back at Marshfield Hall, but a heavy cloud of guilt still hung over her. Wanting only to be alone, she quickly slipped from the bed and pulled on her clothes. The morning air was crisp as she followed the familiar path out to the stables. In her mind, she had gone over it a hundred times, but the words never seemed to come out right. What could she say besides "I'm sorry"? But it sounded so inadequate.

"How are you, child?"

She jumped. So involved had she been with her own thoughts that William's arrival had gone unnoticed.

"Let's walk together," he offered, and taking her arm, they walked on in silence. As they neared the paddock, William pulled an apple from his pocket. "A treat for Major," he said and gave a sharp whistle. With an answering snort and a toss of his head, Major came trotting toward the fence. "Good fellow." William greeted the animal with a fond pat as he quickly devoured the sweet morsel. "This one is for you, my dear." He pulled a second apple from his pocket and handed it to Madeline. "Look there." He pointed across the enclosure as a familiar gray shape trotted into view.

"Misty!" At that moment, choked with emotion, Madeline was unable to say more.

"Ian tracked her down and brought her back," William explained. "She was dirty and hungry, but apart from that, she was just fine."

Madeline leaned over the fence and hugged the little mare. "It was so wrong of me to take her, Sir, and I hope you will forgive me."

"All's well that ends well, child. There is nothing to forgive."

In the days that followed, Tyler and George again took up residence at Long Meadow, and, on the surface at least, life seemed to have returned to normal. At Madeline's request, the wedding would be held in the gardens at Marshfield Hall, and the date was set for four weeks hence. Work in the gardens intensified as, side by side, Madeline and William inspected the many plantings and the trimming of the rose arbor. The minister was hired, and the invitations were sent out. Jeannie kept a list, and one by one, each item was crossed off. Her mother, Isabel, was called upon to make the wedding dress, a task she was glad to assume.

"Oh Miss!" was all Jeannie could say when she heard the news, and she was on pins and needles until her mother arrived. George greeted his future mother-in-law with open arms, and he was happy to find that he really liked the soft-spoken little woman. But as soon as she was settled in, he retreated to join the men and took all their good-humored banter in stride.

In the days that followed, dress books were provided, and together the three women spent hours poring over every page. At last, Madeline's choice was made. It was to be a very simple gown of white satin. Cut somewhat low over the bust, its sleeves were long and fastened at the wrist with a row of small pearls. The skirt flared slightly at the hem, where Isabel's talented fingers would embroider white ivy dotted with more pearls. Measurements were taken and fabric was ordered, and for a while the activity slowed. For Jeannie, it was a welcome chance to spend time with her mother. While Madeline, with William and Charlie at her side, again enjoyed her morning rides.

Happy now not to be needed, Tyler took this time for a trip to London. With three things on his mind, he made his rounds of the city. His first stop was a visit with his agents, where he hoped to learn more about Cliffs Edge and Madeline's father. The next would take him to his tailors, where news of his impending marriage had already been received. Detailed instructions of his wishes had also been given, so he anticipated no delays. But upon arrival, he found he was wrong. Tape measures, chalk, fabrics, pins, and scissors soon covered a large worktable, and followed by a team of young apprentices, the elegant tailor practiced his craft.

At last, with more of the day spent than he had intended, Tyler made his last stop. It was the jewelers.

As the big day drew nearer, once again, Marshfield Hall buzzed. Cook ruled the kitchen with an iron hand, while the starchy Mr. Wiggins did his best to keep the staff of the earl of Marshfield's highly unusual household in order. But everything moved along quite smoothly, and now, the only question on everyone's mind was "What about the weather?"

All worries were quickly set aside when the day dawned bright and sunny.

"Mornin', Miss," Jeannie greeted as she set down the tea and threw open the curtains. "Perfect day for a wedding."

Madeline wasn't at all sure she agreed. She hadn't slept well, and her nerves were all on edge. "I don't think I can do this, Jeannie," she cried, and sliding down in the bed, she pulled the covers up over her head.

"Of course you can," her friend encouraged. "You just have a case of wedding day jitters. It happens to everyone."

"Are you sure?" the muffled voice asked.

"Very sure! Now be good and drink your tea. I added extra honey to give you a boost."

Jeannie was right; the tea did help. By the time Isabel arrived with her dress, Madeline was bathed and waiting. Together, mother and daughter attended to her every need until she stood before them, a radiant bride.

The nuptials were scheduled to begin at noon, but long before the appointed hour, carriages lined the drive. As she watched from her upstairs window, Madeline was again beset by nerves. A knock on the door diverted her attention, and at Jeannie's call, George entered with a box in hand.

"For you, Miss, and there's a note that comes with it."

The note read,

> Dear Madeline,
>
> I am told it's bad luck for me to see you before the ceremony, but on this our special day, I will be both honored and pleased if you would accept this token of my love.
>
> Tyler

With trembling fingers, Madeline opened the black velvet box. There, on a bed of ivory satin, fastened with a gold clasp, lay a string of creamy white pearls.

"Oh!" She was shocked and would have collapsed on the bed, but she feared she would crush her dress.

"Let me, Miss." Jeannie took the necklace from her still trembling fingers and placed it around her neck. "You look beautiful," she said, standing back to admire the effect. "The dress and the necklace, they are just perfect."

"See for yourself." Isabel, with Jeannie following close behind, led her to the mirror. Three expectant images looked back from the glass.

For a moment, Madeline gazed at her reflection in silence.

"Is that really me?" she asked at last, her eyes aglow.

"Yes, Miss." Jeannie gave an excited nod, while Isabel smiled and breathed a sigh of relief. Joyful hugs were exchanged, and the room was filled with much happy laughter.

"It's time, my dear," Mrs. Carter announced a short time later. "And my, what a beautiful bride you are." More hugs were exchanged, and with all their good wishes still ringing in her ears, Madeline made her way out of the room.

William met her at the foot of the stairs. "Are you ready, my dear?" he asked. At her nod, he placed a coronet of white orchids on her still shortened hair. "From our own green house," he said and kissed her cheek. He slipped his arm through hers, and together they walked out onto the sun-filled veranda. As on a previous night, the large wicker chairs had been placed here. All was in readiness for later in the day, when tired guest would come to rest awhile. Flowers in a multitude of colors bedecked the wide landing. Crimson and gold blooms spilled from large earthenware pots. Pink asters shared space with purple sage and long-stemmed goldenrod, while yellow and orange daisies partnered with blue monkshood and deep pink sedum.

Madeline hesitated at the sight, her eyes bright. William's love of his garden was evident everywhere, and together they took a moment to enjoy the beauty around them. Then, arm in arm, side by side, they slowly made their way across the lawn.

A large crowd had gathered in the rose garden, but for Madeline, their faces were just a blur. Only one stood out among the rest. Tall and handsome, in a coat of dark green and black britches, Tyler waited for her by the rose arbor. He greeted her with a smile and took her hand. Voices hushed as the minister intoned the opening line of the ceremony.

"Dearly beloved."

With eyes only for each other, Madeline and Tyler exchanged their vows. "With this ring, I thee wed." He slipped a diamond and sapphire ring onto her finger and whispered, "Sapphires will always remind me of you."

Madeline blushed, and her voice trembled as she said, "I do."

At last, the final words were spoken, the guests cheered, and the young couple shared their first kiss. With a bright sun overhead and the scent of roses in the air, Madeline and Tyler became man and wife.

Chapter Forty

Madeline was nervous. This was to be her wedding night, but secrets of the marriage bed were still a mystery to her. She had no idea what to expect. Her many whispered conversations with Jeannie had left great gaps in her understanding. After all, Jeannie's knowledge was as limited as her own. A tattered copy of Samuel Richardson's *Pamela; or, Virtue Rewarded* had been smuggled into the convent, and reading it at night by candlelight, Madeline had thrilled at the plight of Pamela Andrews and her nobleman master, Mr. B. But what could you learn when even the stoutest heroine swooned away at the hero's first kiss? What would this night bring? Fear tinged her excitement, and she wished so much that her mother was still alive.

Earlier, while holding tight onto her new husband's arm, she had made the rounds of their many guests. Her heart soared at the warmth of his touch and the pride in his voice as he introduced her as his wife. Now, however, with all the formalities taken care of, he had wandered off, deserted her, left her to her own devises. He had made no mention of his plans for the coming night. In fact, he had avoided the subject altogether.

Left alone, she wandered the garden, listening to the happy chatter of those around her. Dampness slowly penetrated the thin soles of her white satin slippers, wetting her feet. Finding a spot to sit, she kicked the shoes off and wiggled her toes. It felt good. She sighed and lingered awhile. Guest passed her by calling out congratulations, and a group of women from the village stopped to make small talk. Quickly slipping back into her shoes, she joined them and walked across the lawn. As they moved along, more women joined them. Village gossip was discussed with high humor and soon Madeline's laughter was added to the rest. But she was still jumpy and on edge. Her laughter seemed too loud. It didn't help when, on occasion, she turned to find dark green eyes watching her from across the lawn. Then her heart flipped, her hands shook, and the humor faded from her eyes.

"What puts such a frown on your face, new sister?" Ian whispered close to her ear. "This is your wedding day. You are supposed to be happy. Don't tell me you are disenchanted with big brother already. I told you you should have chosen me," he teased.

Glad to see him, Madeline smiled. "You can put it down to a case of wedding nerves," she confided.

He was silent for a moment, his gaze quizzical. Then, with a gentle nod, he offered her his arm. "In that case, I will play the good brother-in-law. My prescription for you is a little wine. It will help put some color back in your cheeks."

At the big silver champagne fountain, Ian filled two glasses and, standing shoulder to shoulder, they enjoyed the sweet taste.

He was right. After he filled her glass a second time, each bubbly sip spread fingers of warmth throughout her body, and for the first time that day, her insides ceased to tremble.

"You look better already." Ian smiled down at her.

She reached to fill her glass for the third time. "I do feel much better," she confessed with a giggle.

"Wow! No more." Taking the glass from her hand, Ian steered her in Jeannie's direction. "Take care of our little friend for a while, Jeannie," he said. "Perhaps a moments rest will do her good."

Jeannie nodded. "Come on, Miss," she urged, "a nice bath and a change of clothes will do wonders."

Later, refreshed and more suitably dressed in the garments of her gypsy days, Madeline joined William. A large chair had been placed on the terrace for him, and from there, with George at his side, he could oversee the festivities. Day dwindled into early evening. Lanterns were lit around the grounds, and the aromatic smell of roasting meat filled the air. Spirits were passed freely among the company, and voices grew louder. Madeline noted her new husband partook of more than his share as toast after toast was offered to the happy couple. It soon became apparent that the revelry would continue on through the night.

Madeline picked at the food Jeannie bought her and only half listened to her friend's happy chatter. Flushed and looking pretty in pink, Jeannie seemed unable to stay still.

"Oh, Miss, what a day" she gushed. "You look so beautiful, and Mister Tyler, he's so handsome. How happy you must be." Not waiting to say more, Jeannie skittered away in search of George.

"But he's ignoring me," Madeline muttered to herself. "Am I the only one to see it?" She twisted the ring on her finger. It felt heavy and strange. What have I done? She suddenly felt panicked. This whole thing was a terrible mistake. She looked around, wanting desperately to run away, but instead she hurried to William's side. There, in the company of the old man, along with George and Antonio, she felt at ease once more.

Meanwhile, Tyler, having made his way to the rear garden, now mingled with the partygoers he found there. As was his custom, William had provided food and entertainment for his many estate workers, and it was here that they welcomed their friends and families from the village. Gaily colored paper streamers fluttered in the breeze, and bright lanterns strung high in the trees shed light on the happy throng below. Large barrels of beer had been tapped, and glasses were flowing with the dark frothy brew. The enticing smell of roast meat came from the open fire where a suckling pig now turned slowly on a spit. A fiddler sat hunched over his instrument, his bow quickly working back and forth across the string, his right foot tapping in time with his tune. Older couples sat close together on the grass, and small children held hands as they danced around in circles.

A multitude of people pumped Tyler's hand and thumped his back as he met up with old acquaintances. A large mug of ale was pushed into his hand, and after quickly draining it, he wiped his mouth on his hand.

Slowly, the evening sky turned to a mottled salmon. It was now that Tyler came at last to Madeline's side. Also, now dressed in gypsy garb and looking quite dashing, he showed no sign of overindulgence. His eyes were bright and his smile engaging. Ignoring her obvious miff, he took her hand.

"Many weeks ago, my love, on the night of my grandfather's ball, we planned a tryst, you and I. Do you remember?"

Did she remember! Her back stiffened. How could she forget? "If you seek to curry favor," she said, "I give fair warning. Thinking of you in the arms of that woman does no good for my mood."

Tyler couldn't suppress a grin. "Jealousy does not become you, Madeline," he chided, "and on our wedding day too."

"Jealous!" She gave him a shove. "What makes you think I am jealous?"

"Wow!" He grabbed her hands and pulled her close. "Forgive me, my mistake, love."

She made to make a sharp retort, but he silenced her with a finger on her lips.

"Shhh, enough. It was unfortunate that our plans went awry that night, but the promise I made you then is still good. Will you let me fulfill it tonight? Just say the word, my love. Your moon awaits." He held out his hand.

"What will your friends think, Sir?" she asked, for the moment still unwilling to bend. "Is it right that you desert them?"

He chuckled. "Believe me, my sweet, no one will know we have gone."

But he was wrong. As she took his hand and ran with him toward the stable, from across the lawn, four pairs of eyes watched them go. William, Ian, George, and Antonio raised their glasses in silent salute.

Chapter Forty-One

"I was taking no chances this time," Tyler explained when they found Misty and Samson tethered and waiting. He bent, and clasping Madeline's foot, boosted her up onto Misty's bare back. Then, grabbing a handful of Samson's mane he swung himself aboard the big gelding. "Race you!" he offered with a twinkle in his eye.

Madeline's head shot up. Without a word, she took the challenge. Leaning low over Misty's neck, she urged the mare forward. Ready to run, the little gray kicked up her heels and the pair streaked off, away from the barn.

With a hoot of laughter, Tyler spun the gelding around. Samson pawed air, then hit the ground running. As one, man and animal set off in hot pursuit of the game.

Grazing cattle raised their heads in casual interest. Skylarks rose from the ground in a flutter of wings as the pair thundered past. With the sweet evening air blowing warm against their skin, they galloped together at breakneck speed. Through fields and over hills they rode, leaping hedges and fences in unison, blood pounding in their ears and hearts soaring in wild exhilaration. It was the whispered rush of the ocean that eventually ended their headlong flight. Breathing hard, the horses slowed to a walk. Side by side, with his leg brushing close to hers, the man and his bride rode in companionable silence.

At the crest of a hill, Tyler reined in and bade her to stop. He pulled a kerchief from his pocket and waited for her to dismount.

"What are you doing?" she questioned as he made to bind her eyes.

"Wait a moment, and you will see," he said. "Now here, take my hand and follow me."

"But I can't see!"

"Good, just trust me." Moving slowly, he led her, one step at a time, to the very edge of the hill side.

"Now." With one swift movement, he removed the blindfold.

Madeline blinked rapidly and opened her eyes.

"Oh!" She sighed, turning to him in wonder. There, below her, waiting on the white sandy shore, was a beautiful, brightly painted vardo. So, it was here that they were to spend their wedding night.

"It's yours," he answered simply, "my wedding gift to you."

Madeline could find no words. "Oh, she whispered. Suddenly, ashamed of her earlier outburst. He had always been good to her, even when she had been nothing more than a nuisance to him. Instead of showing her gratitude, she had chosen to berate him at every turn. Now, at the tenderness of his gift, her heart overflowed and tears dampened her cheeks.

"Well, this isn't quite the reaction I had expected," he said softly.

"Why do you put up with me?" she asked, dabbing at her tears.

"Perhaps it's because I love you." He smiled and kissed the tip of her nose. "Now, finish drying those tears, and let's go get a closer look at your gift."

Madeline took his hand and let him lead her down to the beach below. There, bright-eyed with wonder, she circled the pretty vehicle several times, then darted inside.

It was just as she would have wished it to be. Blue and white gingham trimmed the sparkling windows, and more of the same covered the roomy bed. Corner shelves housed a large copper kettle, some shiny pots and pans, and a set of bright blue dishes. Two chairs sat beside a small round table that had a large oil lamp hung above it.

Madeline stood and looked around her. It was all hers. He had said so.

"It's really mine?" she asked at last.

Tyler nodded. "All yours."

She ran her hands over the table's shiny surface, still unable to believe that it was true. Everything here had been planned with her in mind, even the vase filled with her favorite yellow and white daisies.

"Well!" he asked at last, "does it meet with your approval, my lady?"

His anticipation was almost childlike.

"Oh yes, it does indeed, my lord." She was breathless. "But how can I ever thank you?"

He took her hand and brushed it with his lips.

"Just give me a moment, my love." His voice was husky and warm. "And I am sure I can think of something."

Madeline's heart fluttered. His veiled implications sent a tremor through her, setting her insides on fire. Standing on tiptoe, she impulsively pressed her lips lightly to his. It was no more than the touch of a butterfly's wing, but the feeling was electric. With a sigh, he caught her in his arms and pulled her to him.

Suddenly pliant, she melted against his broad chest, thrilling at his groan of pleasure. He pulled her even closer, his open mouth finding hers in a hot, urgent kiss. She tasted the salt on his lips, smelled the hint of brandy on his breath, and the cologne on his warm skin. Her arms quickly encircled his neck, and she held on tight as her knees turned to jelly. Tentatively following his lead, she answered his kiss with one of her own. She clung to him, exploring the warm recesses of his mouth, willing the kiss to last forever.

Finally, Tyler reached up to free himself from the tangle her arms. His breathing ragged, he took a step back, holding her at arm's length.

"Madeline," he teased, "I think you have the makings of a wanton woman."

"Why, Sir, what do you mean?" She batted her eyes, grinning mischievously.

"Keep behaving that way, my dear, and you will soon find out what I mean. But first," he said, sitting down on the vardo's steps and holding up one booted foot, "come help your husband, woman."

Giggling, she grasped the offered boot.

"Pull!" he urged.

She tugged without success. Then, taking a deep breath, she tugged again. This time the boot offered no resistance, and tumbling backward, she hit the sand with a plop. While her husbands laughed, she made to repeat the task with the second boot. This time, though, she turned her back to him, and with his bare foot pressed firmly against her buttocks, the task was made much easier.

Her own slippers were quickly discarded, and barefoot, as in their gypsy days, they strolled hand in hand along the sand. With no need for words, they stood side by side, waves gently lapping their toes, watching the moon rise slowly over the horizon.

"There it is, right on time, my love, and front row tickets, just as I promised," Tyler whispered close to her ear.

"Thank you." Clutching his arm, Madeline leaned into him, shivering with pleasure. "It's just beautiful." Bathed in the light of the great silver sphere, they gazed up in wonder, feeling very small and like the only two people alive on the planet.

Playfully, Madeline kicked at the surf, startling Tyler as the cooling spray doused him.

"Why you little—" He went to grab her, but with a shriek of laughter, she turned and dodged his grasp. With her bare feet slapping hard against the wet sand, she began to run. Quickly overtaking her, Tyler caught the edge of her flying skirt, stopping her short. She turned to face him, her feet thrashing as she held on tight to the threatened garment.

"Truce," she begged when defeat became a certainty. "Let me go. Let me go!"

"Oh no, my dear, not so fast," Tyler warned, a wicked grin on his face. "You may have begun this battle, but I fully intend to finish it." Still holding on to her skirt, he slowly worked his way nearer. Hand over hand, ducking to avoid her flaying arms, he reeled her in like a fish on the end of his line. Finally, dripping wet, he gave a sharp tug and a hoot of triumph as he won the fight. Scooping her up in his arms, he lifted her high above his head, spinning around in dizzying circles. Their shouts echoed along the empty sands, disturbing no one but a flock of disgruntled seagulls. Round and round they went until, out of breath and weak from laughter, they collapsed in a heap upon the sand.

In a wild tangle of arms and legs, they tussled back and forth, waves washing over and around them. Hampered now by his wet clothing, Tyler stripped off his shirt and tossed it carelessly aside, muscles flexing.

"Ah! I have you now." Grabbing her, he rolled her onto her back. Straddling her middle, he pinned her to the ground.

"Help, help," Madeline choked as he shook water from his hair down onto her face. But only the indignant gulls heard her cries. With squawks of their own, they puffed up their chests and waddled away at a fast clip.

"Unfair, unfair!" Madeline renewed her struggle to escape.

"All's fair in love and war, my sweet." He chuckled "And to the victor goes the spoils."

Trapped beneath him, his wide shoulders blocking out the night, Madeline ceased her struggle. But for the rapid rise and fall of her chest, she lay still. Their laughter ceased. A frown crossed his forehead and, for a long moment, green eyes stared down into blue. No longer able to resist, he took her lips with a fierceness that rocked them to the core. They clung to each other, trading kiss for passionate kiss, oblivious to all around them, tossed by the ever-increasing rush of the sea. Suddenly overwhelmed by the intensity of the moment, Madeline pushed away. With a shaky laugh, she rolled to her feet.

Tyler made no move to stop her. Resting on one arm, he fought to gain control of his own emotions roiling inside. Through narrowed eyes, he watched as she waded knee-deep into the rolling surf. The gentle breeze plucked at her hair, and her head bobbed slightly as she met the incoming waves head on. He pulled the crushed stub of a cigar from his pocket, and after a few attempts, managed to bring it back to life. As the spark caught, he breathed in deeply, willing his tormented body to behave. Completely besotted with his new bride, he knew nothing would help until he had her completely. But not here, not like this. Tonight, he must bide his time. Tonight of all nights, everything must be perfect. He waited patiently as she made her way slowly back to the shore. At last, she stood, hands on hips, legs slightly spread, looking down at him. In the moonlight, her damp skirt became transparent, revealing every inch of her long, shapely limbs. Tyler groaned, his eyes feasting freely on the sight set before him. He quickly tossed the cigar aside, and in one lithe movement he came to his feet, the sweet agony of desire raging hot within him.

Even in the semi darkness, Madeline saw the fire that burned in his eyes. Her heart beat faster. A shiver of anticipation trickled down her spine. She moved into his arms, offering herself to him, all reservations forgotten.

"I love you," he whispered as their lips met again. The kiss deepened, and reaching down, he swept her up in his arms. With the bright moon lighting the way, he retraced their footsteps in the sand. Quiet and secluded, the little vardo welcomed them back. With Madeline still in his arms, Tyler stepped inside, closed the door behind him, and left the rest of the world outside.

Chapter Fourty-Two

"Y ou're cold!" he stated, setting her down, then lighting the lamp.

"A little, and very wet." She held out her damp skirt, teeth chattering.

"Well, that won't do." He chuckled as he turned and bumped his head. "Our cozy little retreat is just that, my love—little."

Until Tyler had first entered the caravan, Madeline hadn't realized how small it really was. Most gypsy were shorter and slight, and she smiled fondly as her husband tried to adjust to the cramped quarters.

"Here, drink this," he said, quickly filling a glass and handing it to her.

She took a sip and wrinkled her nose. "Ugh, it tastes horrid," she complained. "What is it?"

"It's just brandy. Drink up. It will do you good." Hands on hips, he stood over her, making sure she drank every drop.

Despite the taste, Madeline had to admit it was warming. "You were right." She giggled. "I do feel better."

Tyler smiled indulgently. "Well, now that we've taken care of the inside, let's see what we can do about the rest of you." Opening a cupboard, he rummaged around among the contents. "Ah!" he exclaimed, holding up a large towel. "It would seem we are prepared for everything." He sat on the bed side, legs spread wide. "Come, my love," he invited, patting the space between. Silently, she accepted his offer, her arms resting on the hardness of his thighs.

Wrapping the towel snugly around her, he gently massaged her shoulders.

"Better?" he asked.

"Mmmmm," she nodded, her eyes dreamy.

With slow deliberate movements, his hands traveled her body, her back, her neck, and her arms. Strong efficient hands gently kneading and warming. Madeline closed her eyes and sighed.

"Why the sigh?" he asked softly.

She looked up into his face and smiled. "I was just thinking what a perfect day this has been."

Tyler's heartbeat quickened. "And just think," he whispered, his breath warm against her ear, "the best is yet to come."

Madeline's spine tingled. She was jumpy and on edge. Her head grew light, her breathing shallow. Trapped in the steamy cocoon of his arms, she longed to break free.

Tyler's iron-clad reserve began to crumble. Dampness dotted his forehead. With a shaky breath, he cast the towel impatiently away, afraid that at any moment he might grab her by the hair and ravish her. Setting her quickly aside, he came to his feet. With no room to pace in their cramped quarters, he chose to distance himself from her.

"I'm sorry," he said at last, pouring himself a stiff brandy and pulling a cigar from a box on the table. He rummaged in a drawer for a match. Sulfur flared and tobacco glowed red as he sucked in a deep breath. Seconds later, he exhaled, and aromatic smoke curled in wispy trails around his head.

Madeline waited.

When he spoke, his back was toward her. "Madeline," he began, then cleared his throat before continuing. "I have discovered of late that I have been a rather selfish man. I have lived life by my own rules, taken my pleasure where and when I saw fit, with no ties and no regrets. But love is a different matter. This is a two-sided affair, and I need to know that you want me as much as I want you."

All was quiet in the little vardo. Seconds passed, then Madeline moved to stand behind him.

"I have little knowledge of the way of things, Sir," she whispered. "But if it helps, I promise to be a most willing student." Wrapping her arms around him, she leaned her cheek against his bare shoulder. She could hear the steady beating of his heart and feel tense muscles flex beneath her touch. His skin smelled of salty air and the fresh, clean smell of the sea. She breathed in deeply, never before feeling as safe as she did now, here with him.

He turned toward her, his face dark and unreadable. She offered him her hand, and he took it. His eyes never once leaving hers, he placed a kiss upon her palm, then another at her wrist. Her body warm and pliant, Madeline drifted eagerly into his arms.

Breathing heavily, he pulled her close, his fingers tangled in her hair. He kissed her ears, her eyes, her lips, her chin, and the valley of her throat where the pulse beat wild and out of control. All the while whispered words of endearment passed between them, and Madeline shivered as the heat of his lips etched his own indelible brand upon her flesh.

Impatient now, Tyler's large hands fumbled with the laces of her blouse. A frustrated groan escaped his lips as he struggled with the hopeless task. At last, with a smile, Madeline set his hands aside. In the soft glow of lamp light, he watched with hooded eyes as she slowly loosed the stubborn strings herself. At last, the garment slipped from her shoulders, for the first time revealing her young woman's body to his hungry gaze.

Gently, he cupped her small firm breasts, his caress slow and tender.

"Easy, love," he whispered as he felt her body tremble.

Trusting but unsure, she looked up at him, color again tinting her cheeks.

He kissed the tip of her nose and smiled. "Have no fear, my beautiful little gypsy wife. Our life together begins now, here tonight."

He nibbled her shoulder, his breath warming her skin. Madeline's head grew light, her breathing ragged. In an almost drugged state, she marveled that his hands were everywhere: her back, her hair, and her breasts, touching and teasing each rosy peak till he tempted them to hardness. Eyes wide, she responded, all shyness suddenly forgotten.

Now she welcomed him, delighting in his touch and eager for his lovemaking. The ties of her skirt proved no obstacle for him, and she hardly knew when it fell to the ground at her feet. His male heat pressed hard against her belly, and she found that somehow, in the tumult of the moment, he had managed to shed his remaining garments. In one swift movement, he swept her from her feet, and with her arms clasped tight around his neck, he carried her to their bed.

Gentle in his quest to enter her, he parted her thighs.

"Have no fear, my sweet." His words were soft against her ear. "For pain is part of our first joining."

But of necessity, a sob came to her lips.

"Sorry," he whispered tenderly. For a moment, he lay still, just holding her tight, hoping to ease her discomfort. Then, slowly at first, he began to move.

Her pain faded in an instant, and a hitherto unknown need crept in to take its place. Instinctively, her body responded, urging her on. She moved with him now, welcoming him as the smoldering embers of desire quickly fanned to flame. Swept along as by the rising tide of molten lava, she clung to him, accepting the hard thrust of his manhood deep within her. Her nails raked the skin on his back, and he pulled her closer still, his breath harsh against her ear.

Her eager reception thrilled him, and no longer restrained, he drove home hard. The heat of their passion consumed them, driving them on, both breathlessly seeking the release that would eventually set them free. At last, it burst upon them, draining them of strength and shaking them to the core. Sated, they lay unmoving, still wrapped in each other's arms, amid the waning embers of their union. Gradually, their breathing slowed, and the world righted itself.

Still warmed by the glow of their lovemaking, Madeline curled up close to her husband's side. Her fingers idly trailed through the damp hair on his chest.

"Me thinks you tempt fate, Madam," he murmured, his eyes closed.

"Then you think me too cowardly to wake the sleeping dragon, Sir?" she asked, blowing gently against his ear.

"Behave woman or suffer the consequences," he warned, tightening his grip around her.

For a moment, she lay quiet, listening to his slow, even breathing. But then her fingers wandered once more, this time to tickle the end of his nose. With a low growl, he rolled over and grabbed her. He silenced her laughter with his lips, and once again they rode a comet to the sky.

Chapter Forty-Three

Their days passed in blissful solitude, neither wanting more than the company of the other. They galloped to the beach in the early morning and swam in the heat of the noon sun. At low tide, as children might, they drew hearts in the wet sand or climbed the jagged rocks in search of periwinkles. Reluctant to try them at first, Madeline soon found the little snails quite tasty when sprinkled with salt. In the afternoon, they gathered driftwood for a fire and walked the shore, skipping rocks and playing tag in the tumbling surf. They caught small crabs in a warm tidal pool and laughed as they watched them race helter-skelter back toward the sea. Tyler grinned indulgently when Madeline collected shells to save in an old glass jar, but he helped her to wash them and sort out the ones she liked best. In the evening, they sat by a warm campfire and watched as the sun slowly turned the sky to flame. But at night, tucked safely away from the world in their little home on wheels, they shared whispered words and unending acts of love.

Although they never saw a soul, each day a large basket of fresh food awaited them at their door. At Madeline's quiet question, Tyler replied, "George and Mrs. Carter."

"I must be sure to thank them," she said, popping a grape into his open mouth.

The week drifted by much too quickly, and they knew the idyllic days were soon to come to an end.

"It looks like a change in the weather," Tyler said when they awoke to darkening skies. "Perhaps it's just as well we leave on the morrow."

Ominous clouds gathered low overhead, and a brisk wind whipped up the choppy sea. The rain was light at first, no more than a sprinkle here and there, but then as the force of the wind increased, the clouds opened in a downpour. For the first time that morning, Madeline caught a glimpse of the elusive George. Heavily wrapped in oilskin rain gear and casting a wary eye at the sea, he engaged Tyler in a lengthy conversation. Then, with a hasty wave of his hand and his head bent low, he left, and Tyler ran back to seek shelter.

"Look, wine!" he exclaimed. Shaking himself off, he held up the basket. "Good old George. He thinks of everything." He popped the cork from the bottle and filled two glasses.

"What will happen to my vardo now?" Madeline asked wistfully.

"Well, I guess it will reside in Grandfather's carriage house. After all, we could never part with it now." He winked at her. "Just think of all the stories it could tell."

"Do you think we will ever come back here again?"

"Oh, perhaps on our fifth wedding anniversary," he suggested, clicking his glass to hers, but her sad face arrested him. "What's this? Such a face," he scolded. Setting the glasses aside, he tipped her chin toward him. "Tell me."

"They are crying, you know." She said.

At his baffled look, she pulled away and pressed her nose against the windowpane. "The clouds," she explained. "They are sad to see us go."

"Silly goose," he chided her softly, and moving to stand behind her, he slipped his arms around her waist.

"I wish tomorrow would never come," she whispered.

"Well, in that case," he said, his teeth nibbling her ear, "we must make the most of today."

With a soft moan, she turned in his arms, weak with desire and consumed with a hunger only equaled by his own. Her fingers tangled in his thick dark hair, holding him fast as his hot open mouth covered her face with kisses.

He grasped her hips, grinding them hard against his own, no longer able to deny the raw male need that drove him to distraction. In a heated frenzy, they tore at their clothes, ripping them asunder and tossing them carelessly aside. Madeline lay on the bed, welcoming him with open arms. Her sighs of pleasure mounted as he settled heavily upon her. His quicksilver tongue traveled along her eager body, circling each hardening nipple and arousing feelings that made her shudder with anticipation. His hands slid lower, following the swell of her slender hips, her flat tight belly, and her silken limbs. Then, parting her thighs, his hands worked a brand of magic that was all his own.

"Take me. Take me now," she begged, her body arching to meet his.

But his movement slowed, his eyes heavy with lust. Prolonging the sweet torture, he carried her to a higher level of ecstasy. Panting, she writhed beneath him, seeking relief from the growing pressure and longing for the tingling waves of sensation that would soon surge up from her loins.

Tyler's own need quickly became apparent, pushing him to the brink, threatening at any moment to overtake him and spill his seed. His hands slid beneath her hips, lifting her to him. He plunged deep within her silken sweetness, and their moans of pleasure mingled as he took her with a fierceness that left them both weak and trembling.

They laid locked tight in each other's arms, heart beats slowing as they listened to the steady patter of rain on the roof.

"Our wine is still waiting," he said with a lazy yawn, and he rolled from the bed to retrieve it. Wiping a small circle in the steamy window, he peered outside. "I fear the rain will last all day," he said over his shoulder.

"Really." Madeline sighed. Openly admiring her husband's physique, her eyes glazed with rekindled desire. He joined her back on the bed, and sipping the wine, he dribbled it into her mouth as he kissed her. Scarlet drops dripped from her chin to spill upon the pale white skin of her breasts. The breath caught in his throat as she sat up on her knees and drew his head to her chest.

"Oh, you are indeed a wicked woman," he whispered, voice hoarse, his body hardening as he gently licked away the errant drops.

"Are you drunk, my Lord?" she teased.

"Drunk with love, my sweet," he growled, "and the brew is so heady I can never get enough." Quickly setting the glasses aside, he pushed her back down on the bed and proved his love over and over again.

The skies had cleared with the early morning light. The tide was low, and puffy white clouds dotted the distant horizon. A fresh breeze blew in from the west, gently ruffling the calm surface of the deep green sea. They packed up their belongings. Madeline cleaned and straightened the caravan, then stood, hands on hips, breathing in the fresh sweet smell of the salty air.

Tyler harnessed the horses and then, hand in hand, they walked the beach once more. Together they bid a final fond farewell to this special place and then they turned and went on their way.

Chapter Fourty-Three

Madeline was surprised when they didn't return to Marshfield Hall, but instead continued on to Long Meadow. They were greeted by an excited Jeannie who, with George and Mrs. Carter, had prepared everything for their return. Warm hugs were exchanged, and the two young women chatted on incessantly as they made their way into the house.

"Come on, Miss." Jeannie grabbed Madeline's hand and tugged her up the wide staircase. "Look," she cried. They had reached the top landing, and she threw open one of the many doors there with a flourish. "We did it all, George and Mrs. Carter and me." She laughed as Madeline stepped inside and gasped. The room was large and unfamiliar. With windows overlooking the flower garden, it had obviously been decorated with Madeline in mind. "And look at this, Miss." Jeannie ran and threw open the closet door to reveal a large collection of dresses styled for every occasion.

"All of this is for me?" Madeline marveled, letting her hands trail through the multitude of colored fabrics.

"Yes, me mum's been busy," Jeannie explained. "And just think," she added with a smile, "not so long ago, you didn't have one dress to wear to the ball."

"You're right," Madeline said, the enormity of it all suddenly hitting home. "It's hard to believe just how much has happened since that night."

They fell silent for a time, each one absorbed with their own thoughts. Jeannie was the first to break the silence.

"Are you worried, Miss?" she asked suddenly. "About going to America, I mean.

It's so far away, and I've heard stories about Indians. Although George says I won't see any in Boston, and he should know, don't you think?"

"I'm sure he does, Jeannie, but just remember," Madeline said, comforting her friend, "whatever happens, we will see it through together."

After leaving the women to their amusement, Tyler, with George at his side, had returned to Marshfield Hall. To Tyler's surprise, he learned that Antonio and his family had moved on. In a letter, Antonio had tried to explain.

"Never before have we been made as welcome as we were here," he wrote. "Gypsies are seldom greeted with open arms, and so it's our nature to wander. I live with the hope that one day we too will find a safe home of our own. Perhaps then, we might meet again. Until that time, I wish you peace and happiness, my friend."

"I wish I had been here to see him before he left," Tyler said, tucking the note into his pocket.

"He knew that had you been here, the parting would have been much harder."

"Mmmm, I think you are right George," Tyler agreed. "Well, let's get to the task on hand." With their shirt sleeves rolled up to their elbows, and with much more help than they needed from William and Ian, they set to the job of storing Madeline's vardo. Heated words were passed back and forth as the four men struggled with the cumbersome vehicle.

"Easy, lad!" William shouted at Tyler as a rear wheel narrowly missed running over his foot.

"Please, Sir, step back while we straighten this thing out. Ian, swing it a little to the left. No, damn it, I said to the left, not the right."

"Sorry!"

"Can you handle that end, George?"

"Got it, Guv, don't worry."

More than an hour had passed when, at last, worn out and hot and dusty, they completed the grueling task. After one last quick look inside the little house on wheels, Tyler closed the doors of the large carriage house and bid a fond farewell to the gaily painted caravan.

"All is well, my love," he assured Madeline upon his return to Long Meadow. He placed a kiss on her forehead, then, with a chuckle, he whispered in her ear, "Your wedding gift, with all our memories locked up inside, has been safely stored away."

Just the mention of the time they had spent together in the little vardo brought a rush of warm color to Madeline's cheeks. With a drawn-out "Ohhhh," she lowered her eyes and fanned her face furiously with her hands.

Later in the day, the men gathered in William's study. A pile of papers were taken from a drawer, and drinks were passed around.

"Well, what news from London since I've been away?" Tyler wanted to know.

"Well, see for yourself," George said.

Tyler studied the information set down before him. "It seems," he said, "the deeper we dig into the whole thing, the more confusing it gets. As much as I hate the idea, I will have to return to London again myself."

There was a nod of agreement from his companions, but each of them wondered in their own way just how this would all turn out. What should they expect? What kind of secrets did Cliffs Edge hold locked away, and why was it proving so hard to find them out? But before any of these plans could be carried out, George and Jeannie were united in a small ceremony attended by the family and staff. Tyler stood up with George, and Isabel, who fashioned her daughter's wedding gown, also gave the bride away. The gardens of the Hall once again took center stage, and Mrs. Carter presided over a lavish luncheon she had prepared for the occasion. Toasts were raised to the bride and groom, and even the starchy Mr. Wiggins was seen to partake of the fruity beverage. It was a sight William vowed he thought he would never live to see.

"Speech," Tyler called out, and much to George's chagrin, everyone took up the chant.

Still shaking his head, the man reluctantly came to his feet. He raised his glass and thanked all those assembled there for their good wishes Then, looking Jeannie straight in the eye, he winked and said, "Just think, it all began with a waltz." Jeannie blushed, and everyone cheered. He gave a special thank you to Isabel, his new mother-in-law and lastly to Mrs. Carter. "To you, Ma." He turned and raised his glass to Mrs. Carter. Later, slipping his arm around that lady's shoulders, he took her to one side.

"Look, Ma, it's about time you took it easy," he scolded. "Why not come back with us and let me take care of you for a change?"

"I couldn't do that, love," she answered, "not now anyway. I have far too many responsibilities here, you see." She ruffled Charlie Tippet's unruly hair.

"Bring 'im along too," Jeannie urged. But they knew that as long as William was living, nothing could persuade her to leave Marshfield Hall.

Chapter Fourty-Four

Madeline awoke with a contented sigh. She stretched like a lazy cat in the noon sun and rolled to her husband's recently vacated side of the bed. Pulling his pillow into her arms, she hugged it close. Still bathed in the glory of their lovemaking, a slow smile captured her face. Closing her eyes, she relived the night just passed. The sounds of their lovemaking still echoed in her ears. Without the least effort, she conjured up his image, her flesh tingling at the mere thought of his touch. Headier than wine, the tenderness of his kisses stole her breath away.

At first, coming back to Long Meadow had seemed strange. So many memories still lingered here. But, looking back on those days now, it was hard to believe that she was still the same person. When Tyler entered her life, it had changed forever. The only part of her that remained unchanged now was the continuing desire to find her father. With all the excitement of the past few weeks, she had been able to put it aside, but in quiet moments like this, the need crept back to haunt her. Of late, her old dream had returned to plague her. Again, she was running, and again a hand reached out to catch her. Her cries in the night had been stilled by Tyler, who wrapped his arms around her and held her tight.

"Easy love, it's just a dream." His whispered words calmed her. Tucked safe in the warm curve of his arm, her head pillowed on his chest, she found peaceful slumber.

She rolled from the bed, and shaking the unwanted thoughts from her head, she went in search of Jeannie. But the girl was nowhere to be found. However, her tub was ready and waiting, so, humming to herself, she climbed in and slid down into the warm, scented water. She soaped up her arms with a sponge, and at the sound of a hand on the door, called out, "Come in, Jeannie."

Moments later, water cascaded down on her, leaving her gasping. "Why you!" she sputtered, shaking her head. "You are a scoundrel," she shrieked, wiping water from her eyes as she looked up into her husband's laughing face.

With a hasty movement, he pulled his shirt off over his head, and kneeling beside the tub, he took the sponge from her hands.

"No!" she admonished him as he slid the soapy sponge across her shoulders. "Jeannie will be here in a moment. What will she think?"

He laughed again. "I believe she will think it perfectly fine, but don't worry, my love, she won't dare to come in. I gave her my sternest frown, and she left, trying hard not to giggle."

Madeline joined in his laughter and decided that this was a wonderful way to start the day.

"Alright, lazy bones." Holding out a towel, he helped her from the tub. "Now you can come and see my surprise." With much fanfare, he escorted her back into the bedroom. In her absence, she discovered that three large traveling trunks had been delivered.

"For you," he explained. "I must be away for a while, and I thought these might help you to pass the time. By the time we sail for Boston, you will probably need even more, judging by the size of your wardrobe."

Madeline suddenly grew quiet. The laughter left her eyes. There had been no talk of their departure date before, but this suddenly made it seem very real.

"Will you be gone long?" she asked softly.

"Not too long, my sweet, but there are business matters in London that need my attention." Tyler watched her for a moment, a silent war raging inside him. Should he tell her the real reason for his visit to the city? That, through his agent, he had at last had word from Solicitor Edward Bailey.

"Surely there's nothing to be gained by taking her there," he had reasoned with William. But his elder didn't agree.

"Take her, my boy," William had said. "Let her close that chapter of her life, no matter how painful it might be. Believe me, she will never rest easy until she does."

That night as they prepared for bed, Tyler asked, "Would you be much distressed, Madeline, if you were unable to see your father again?" She sat before the mirror, brushing her hair. He saw her back stiffen. "I'm sorry." He moved to stand behind her, his gaze meeting hers in the glass. "That was unfair of me, I know, but I worry you will only find sadness at the end of your quest. You have family here now, my love. There's grandfather and Ian, and when we get back to Boston, you will have more brothers and sisters with all their assorted families than you can ever wish for."

Madeline turned to face him. "You gave me your word," she said, a determined look in her eyes. "How could I ever trust you again if you break your word?"

Tyler sighed, knowing he was beaten. "Well, then, my love," he said, "you had best read this." He handed her a letter headed "Edward Bailey, Solicitor." Madeline's hand shook as she read the neatly printed lines.

Sir,

After much consideration, I have decided to answer your request for certain information. I am prepared to meet with you in my London office Tuesday next at 10 am to discuss the matter.

Sincerely,

Edward Bailey.

Madeline read the letter through a second time, and her insides churned. At last, this could be the answer she had been waiting for.

Chapter Fourty-Five

Edward Bailey paced the floor of his elegant London office. From his window, high on the third floor, he kept a watchful eye on the busy street below. Sounds he very seldom heard echoed in the hot summer air. The sharp clatter of horses' hooves upon the hard surface of the road and the rattle of carriage wheels as they went spinning by. There were the cries of city hawkers selling their wares, and even the distant sound of ships' horns as they traveled the busy waterways of the Thames.

He pulled the watch from his waistcoat pocket and checked it again. The gold hands registered ten minutes to the hour, but he already knew that before he checked it. His nerves were getting the better of him, and he moved to straighten papers on his desk, even though nothing there was out of place. Responsibility sat heavy on Edward's shoulders since his last interview with Lord Reginald Spencer. His recent stay at Cliffs Edge had not gone well. By the third day, there had still been no word from Spencer, and he was growing impatient. His business in London was going unattended, and he had wondered how much longer they expected him to wait. When at last the word came, he had entered the room feeling very much on edge. They were all there: Quinn, Dewhurst,

Martin, and Downes, the whole crew of that ill-fated rescue mission to France. His first thought was how much they had changed, but then it had been some twenty-odd years since that terrible night. They had been mere boys at the time. Edward waited. At last, Spencer spoke for them all. Without giving a reason, he simply said, "We've given it a lot of thought. We don't all agree, but it's been decided that the girl can't return to Cliffs Edge."

"But why?" Edward insisted. "Don't you think her father would want to see her?"

"Sadly, Etienne's state of health makes that impossible. We will leave whatever arrangements need to be made, up to you."

It was the last straw. "It had all been such a waste of time," Edward grumbled. The problem of the girl had been placed squarely on his shoulders, and he didn't like it. He had endured the journey back to London, all the while vowing he would never set foot in Cliffs Edge again. But the matter of Madeline Carlyle still laid heavy on his mind. Spencer had no right to treat him as he did. The close friendship that had once existed between them was over; it had been for a long time. His recent stay at Cliffs Edge had done nothing to ease the situation. Yes, he had seen the others, but what good did that do, it had just stirred up old resentments. Reminded him of things he would rather forget. He owed no one, only Elizabeth. It was for her sake that he had taken it upon himself to correspond with the American, Tyler Wentworth. For a moment, his confidence wavered, but no, it was done, and it was too late for doubts. For her own sake, the girl must be returned to the convent.

As the clock on his office mantle chimed ten, Edward witnessed the arrival of a hansom carriage. A well-dressed young couple quickly exited the vehicle. The man was tall and dark-haired, the woman slight, and although her bonnet covered her hair, he could tell it was light in color.

The pair lingered a moment at the curbside, in conversation, it seemed, with those still sitting inside.

Madeline had accompanied Tyler to London along with Jeannie and George, who were to spend several days in the city. As their carriage stopped on the busy London street, an excited Jeannie had found it hard to stay in her seat.

"Oh, Miss." She grasped onto Madeline's arm. "Can you imagine me seeing all the sights in the city?"

Madeline smiled at her friend who had been chattering on for days about The British Museum and the Theatre Royal at Drury Lane.

"Easy, lass!" George had warned, placing a restraining hand on his wife's arm.

"Or you'll never last the day."

"Best keep a tight rein on her, George," Tyler teased, "or you may be the one who won't last the day."

Jeannie blushed at the friendly banter, but she joined in their laughter. After promising to meet later for dinner, the couples bid each other goodbye, and seconds later, the carriage pulled away. Tyler and Madeline waited a moment watching its departure, then turned and entered a door with the words Edward Bailey, Solicitor written across it in large black letters.

Madeline took a deep breath to calm her nerves, and with a reassuring smile, Tyler took her hand. "Hold on tight, love." He encouraged, and together they made their way up the narrow stairs.

From inside his office, Edward listened to the sound of their footsteps on the stairs, not knowing what to expect from this meeting. He found it hard to disguise his feelings as he met Madeline Carlyle for the first time. It was as if the clock had suddenly been turned back to another time and place. Elizabeth stood before him again, just as she had on that Sunday morning over twenty years ago. His eyes darted to the framed portrait that sat on his desk. It was not that he needed to confirm the likeness, but rather to confirm that his eyes were not deceiving him. Anger welled up inside him. Had things gone differently, he might have spent time with the girl. With an effort, he pulled himself together. Hand outstretched, he greeted the young couple, but his eyes never strayed far from Madeline's face. They exchanged pleasantries, but Tyler was in no mood for it and came straight to the point.

"You said in your letter that you were at last ready to give my wife the information we need, Sir."

Wife! Edward was shocked. That was something no one had bargained for. It was obvious the girl would never return to the convent now. Well, Spencer had left it all in his hands. So be it.

"You must understand, my dear," Edward addressed Madeline alone. "The story isn't mine alone to tell."

"Please, Sir, whatever you can share, I need to know." Madeline implored, her blue eyes dark and intense.

Again, her likeness to Elizabeth struck close to Edward's heart. Why had he never met her before? For years, he had been responsible for her welfare at the convent, but she had been just a name on a piece of paper. She had been a duty that he had carried out, and that, to his shame, none too willingly.

"Sir!" Tyler's sharp voice cut into his thoughts.

"Forgive me." Edward cleared his throat, then continued, "Your father's name is Etienne De Vane, my dear."

Madeline sat silent as he told her the story of the long-ago failed rescue mission.

"Oh." She voiced her distress. The room was quiet for a moment, then Edward continued.

"Etienne blamed himself for our failure. In a state of shock, he retreated into a dark world inhabited only by himself and the ghosts of his dead family. Spencer took it upon himself to care for the man. We all helped as much as we could. I think we all felt the weight of guilt. If only we had arrived sooner, perhaps they would have been saved. Anyway, it seemed Etienne would never return to normal, but on one of my visits, I took a young lady with me. Her name was Elizabeth Carlyle."

Madeline caught her breath.

"Yes, child, your mother. Etienne took one look at her and spoke for the first time in months. Spencer was convinced it was fate and begged her to stay. I was not pleased. I did my best to discourage her but she wouldn't listen. She stayed on, and within the month, I was told that she and Etienne had wed." His voice faltered a moment, and rising from his chair, he walked to the window. "I know now I was wrong," he continued, "but at that time, I broke off all my ties with them. You see, Elizabeth was my cousin. We had grown up together. She had been about to become engaged to my best friend." Again, he hesitated. "I heard of your birth, and later of Elizabeth's death. The facts surrounding it were never revealed to me." Turning back to Madeline, he said, "I'm afraid this is all I can tell you, my dear. If you wish to know more, you must go to Cliffs Edge and find out for yourself."

"A moment Sir." Unwilling to end the interview just yet, Tyler reached for the portrait on the desk. "I take it this is Madeline's mother." He held it up to the light. "The likeness is quite remarkable."

"As you see." Edwards voice was suddenly brittle. Quickly retrieving the portrait, he wiped it clean and carefully put it back where it belonged. "Now I must bid you good day my dear." He moved toward the door. "As distant as it is, we are related, and I wish you well. I will notify Lord Spencer of our meeting, but beyond that, I can do nothing."

He watched as the young couple made their way back out onto the busy street. "Well, Spencer," he muttered, "now it's all up to you."

Later that evening, as Jeannie excitedly told Madeline of all the wonderful things she had seen in the city, Tyler discussed the days happenings with George.

"Well, at least we know the right name now. It's no wonder we had a hard time finding the man, Gov."

"Yes, George, let's hope now we can get to the bottom of it all."

Chapter Forty-Six

I t was early on a Monday morning, when, with her husband at her side, Madeline set off from Long Meadow. They broke their journey in Exeter and took up lodgings for the night in a very grand hotel. As they entered the elaborate front door, liveried attendants rushed to assist them. Madeline couldn't suppress a little giggle as, with her husband at her side, they were escorted across the dark green tiled floor and up the wide carpeted staircase.

"Now, what was that all about?" Tyler wanted to know when they were at last alone in their room.

Madeline threw herself down on the soft feather bed, and this time, she laughed out loud.

"I was just thinking how different this is from my last visit to Exeter," she told him. "That night, I slept in a barn with only Misty for company and shared a penny bun with a little monkey on the common."

"My God, was that you?"

Madeline looked puzzled.

"I remember seeing a boy and a monkey on the common that night. Was that you?"

"I think perhaps it was."

Tyler shook his head. "Just think how much pain could have been avoided if only I had known," he said.

Dark clouds gathered overhead the next day as they continued their journey. The countryside around them was rugged, and the wheels of the carriage bumped and clicked over the rough surface of the road. For Madeline, they seemed to be saying, "Almost there, almost there." Her emotions flipped from excitement one minute to blind panic the next, but even so, she strained for the first glimpse of the house she had left so long ago.

At last, there it was. Cliffs Edge. But gone was the home she remembered. In its place sat a rundown shell, just a sad reminder of what it had once been. Not that she had expected it to be unchanged, far from it, but still, this sad, decaying façade came as a shock. She grasped Tyler's hand and held it tight, tears dampening her cheeks.

"Don't expect too much, love," Tyler warned her. "Remember, it's been a long time."

Only half listening to his words, Madeline nodded. The horses stopped, and taking her hand, Tyler helped her from the carriage. For a moment, she stood looking, taking everything in. The stone steps were chipped and in need of repair, but the two white lions she remembered still stood guard at the front door. Suddenly overwhelmed, she wanted to turn and run. Tyler had been right. It was a mistake to come.

Seeing the panic in her eyes, Tyler took her arm. "We are here now, Madeline," he said, "You have to see it through." With a shiver, she straightened her shoulders and nodded.

The door opened before he could knock. He had a feeling that their progress had been carefully watched for some time. They were greeted by a woman who called herself Anne. She was a tall, solid-looking woman with a well-weathered face. Deep set brown eyes and heavy brows topped a broad chin and a straight colorless mouth. Lank blond hair and a dowdy style of dress made guessing her age impossible.

"You must be tired and hungry after your journey," she said, helping them inside.

The greeting was cordial enough but lacked any warmth. Tyler had the feeling it had all been very well rehearsed.

Anne rang a bell, and from out of nowhere, a strange-looking little man appeared. No more than five feet tall and elf-like in appearance, he had large, rather inquisitive looking gray eyes and a thatch of graying brown hair.

"This is Walter," she said. "He will show you to your room. As soon as you have made yourselves comfortable, tea will be served downstairs."

Before they knew what was happening, Tyler and Madeline were being hustled up the narrow staircase and into a large, cold bedroom. The strange fellow, named Walter, followed close on their heels. Silent as a ghost, he quickly set their bags down on the floor and then, just as quickly, turned and disappeared. As he went, whatever warm air might have been trapped in the room seemed to be sucked out with him.

Madeline shivered.

"Well, that was rather strange," Tyler said, looking a trifle perplexed.

Madeline only nodded. She had no idea what to say.

They found warm water placed in a pitcher for their use, and after washing off some of the dust from their journey, they made their way back downstairs. Once again, the mysterious Walter appeared. With only a nod of his head for acknowledgment, he led them to a room at the back of the house. It was dark and cold, but a small fire had been lit in the grate, and a tray of refreshments was already laid out for them.

They waited awhile, thinking that someone might join them, but when at last it seemed unlikely, Madeline served the tea. Deep in thought, she looked around. She had wanted so badly to come home, to be in the place that still dwelt in her heart. But this wasn't it. She was no more than an unwanted stranger here. She glanced at her husband. He stood straight and tall in front of the fire, a delicate China teacup in his hands. He looked out of place. She was about to ask him what he was thinking when the door opened, and they were no longer alone.

Madeline wasn't sure what she had expected. Her memories of her father were vague, but like any little girl, she had always thought him tall and handsome. This man could fit the part, older of course, face lined, shoulders slightly bent, but yes, he could fit the part. He came forward, hand outstretched.

"Welcome back to Cliffs Edge, my dear." Madeline hesitated. He frowned. "You don't recognize me, do you, child? I'm Spencer, Lord Reginald Spencer," he introduced himself with a formal bow. "Of course, it's been a long time, and you were very small. But" he said softly, his eyes never leaving her face, "I would have known you anywhere."

Madeline looked up into cool blue eyes. The hand that took hers was large and strong.

"Oh, I thought perhaps . . ." She hesitated.

"You expected your father, of course," he said. "Unfortunately, Etienne is not in the best of health. I thought it better if we delayed your visit for a while."

"Oh." Madeline's disappointment was clear. "Of course Sir, I understand." But she didn't.

Tyler watched the exchange in silence. The man seemed genuine, but beneath that calm exterior, he detected a growing sense of unease. Just what was he hiding and what would it take to find out?

"I'm sure you understand, Sir?" Spencer turned to him. "It is for Madeline's benefit that her father should be at his best."

"Of course," Tyler agreed, "but also I hope, for all concerned, that you won't keep her waiting too long."

An awkward silence settled over the room.

"Yes, well," Spencer said at last. "Right now, my dear, you should rest for a while after your journey. Dinner will be served at seven sharp." He waited a few moments, and then, with a stiff bow, he turned and abruptly left the room. As the door closed behind him, Madeline turned to her husband.

"Oh, Tyler, why did I come? This isn't going well at all."

"Don't worry, love." He took her in his arms. "It may not seem like it right now, but I guarantee you, everything will turn out just fine."

Chapter Fourty-Seven

I t had taken Madeline some time to dress for dinner that evening. Although Jeannie had made much effort with the items she had packed, at this point, nothing seemed quite right. She pestered Tyler to help her, holding up one gown first and then another.

"Please," she fussed. "I want to be sure it's right."

"Whatever you wear will be just right." He did his best to assure her. But Madeline still wasn't convinced. At last, frustration growing, he spread the garments out on the bed.

"Now," he said, "close your eyes."

She looked at him suspiciously but did as he asked.

He spun her around twice and said, "Pick." As a frothy lavender creation found its way into her hands, he said, "Perfect!"

At seven o'clock precisely, the young couple made their way into the dining room, and once again, they found themselves alone.

"Well, we didn't need to hurry," Tyler remarked. "He did say seven sharp, didn't he?"

"Mmmm," Madeline agreed, taking the time to look around. It was a large room, she noted, with a stone fireplace filling the far wall. It's unkempt grate, piled high with dead gray ash, spoke of many a fine blaze. Today, however, despite the chill in the air, no fire had been lit to warm the hearth. The furnishing was sparse. An elegant buffet displaying the opulence of bygone days, dominated the room. Above it, the aging glass of a decorative mirror quietly recorded the comings and goings of the generations. A harvest table, flanked by high-backed chairs and set with a crisp white cloth, ran the center of the room. Madeline made her way toward it, her footsteps sounding hollow on the old wooden floor. Candles lit the length of the board, flickering and glinting on what one could see was well-worn silverware. Even the pretty blue and white dishes betrayed their many years of use—a chip here, a stain there, a faded blue flower still struggling to be seen. It seemed to Madeline that this was very much a male domicile. No woman worth her salt would allow her guests to be served in such a way.

Movement sounded in the hallway, interrupting her thoughts, and she turned in time to see Lord Spencer arrive.

"I am sorry to have kept you waiting," he apologized. "Some of our guests were delayed, but everyone is here now." He introduced them, one by one, as they entered and took their places at the table.

"Sir Roger Downs, Lord Harry Dewhurst, Sir Richard Martin, and Sir Leonard Quinn."

Madeline found it hard to disguise her disappointment, when, once more, it seemed her father would not be in attendance. She had been told these men were her father's friends, but she searched their faces, and they betrayed nothing. At her enquiring glance, Lord Spencer explained once again that her father felt too ill to join them. Although not satisfied, she nodded her understanding.

Tyler wondered at the purpose of this meeting and watched Spencer's face closely.

He could tell the man was nervous, but why? What was he trying to hide? Earlier, when he greeted Madeline for the first time, there had been something odd about his manner. It was hard now to determine just what it had been. An intake of breath perhaps, or a certain look. Whatever it was, he needed to get to the bottom of it. By remaining vigilant, listening, and asking the right questions, he might soon be able to make some sense out of it.

The evening proceeded much as it had started. During the meal, conversation was lackluster, mostly about the weather and the state of the roads. The voices became a dull drone, and Madeline found her mind wandering. Her father was somewhere in this big old house, but where, and what was the real condition of his health?

"Madam." She was jolted back into the moment. "I inquired as to the state of your journey."

Madeline blushed, realizing her lack of attention.

"Please excuse me." She turned toward Lord Harry Dewhurst.

Brow raised, he observed her closely, but with a slight nod, he asked again.

"Uneventful, I am glad to say, Sir."

"Lucky indeed, given the state of the countryside these days. Cutthroats lurking at every turn." Silent humor curved the corners of his wide mouth, and an insolent look lurked within his bright eyes. With a quick glance at Tyler, Madeline wondered just how much of her history these men were familiar with.

"You would do best to remain silent, Sir." The deep voice of Sir Lionel Quinn demanded attention. A snicker came from the short-sighted Sir Roger Downes, and Dewhurst's grin quickly faded. A tense, uneasy silence settled over the room, lightened only by Sir Lionel's loud demand for more wine.

Tyler admired the timely intervention. But, even so, an undercurrent of unrest lingered on throughout the remainder of the meal.

Madeline felt the evening wasted. She learned nothing from these men, and far worse than that, nothing of her father.

At last, Lord Spencer came to his feet, signaling the end of the meal. He begged Madeline's pardon if the men partook of a glass of brandy. But before she could answer, a disturbance erupted in the hall. Seconds later, the door was thrown open and Walter entered, pushing an old man in a wheelchair before him. The room went silent, shock clearly etched on every face.

"What is the meaning of this?" Spencer demanded.

"It was the master's wish," Walter muttered, pushing the chair further into the room.

Tyler was sure Spencer was about to say more but changed his mind. At last, he said, "My dear Etienne, are you sure this is wise?" Focusing his attention on Madeline, the man seemed not to hear.

Madeline didn't move but nodded as she felt Tyler's reassuring hand upon her shoulder.

Could this old man really be her father? Gray hair, face thin and drawn. He bore no resemblance to the handsome man she had long remembered.

He reached for her hand. "Is it really you, child?" he asked, a distant look in his eyes.

"My dear Etienne." Spencer stepped forward, his voice harsh. "This is not the reunion I had wished for you. Madeline has had a long day, and I think we should postpone it until tomorrow." No one moved. "Now Walter." This time, it was an order. With a slight nod, Walter turned the chair around and headed for the door.

Madeline was about to object, but Tyler's hand tightened on her shoulder.

"Not now, my dear," he whispered in her ear. "It's better this way."

Later when they had returned to their room for the night, Madeline asked him to explain.

"I think that whatever your father has to say to you is better said when you are alone."

Chapter Fourty-Eight

They had talked until midnight and now Tyler slept soundly in the bed beside her. But there would be no such peace for Madeline this night. Instead, she lay looking up at the ceiling, her breathing shallow, her thoughts in turmoil. Seeing her father had been a shock, but why had Lord Spencer been so angry? Why had he insisted he be taken away? Then there were these men. Who were they really, and why were they here? And what of this house? Had it ever really been her home? She felt no connection. Would she ever get the answers she so desperately needed? Unable to stand it any longer, she threw back the covers and slipped from the bed. After a quick look back at her still sleeping husband, she pulled on her robe and slippers and tiptoed from the room.

"I should have brought a candle with me," she muttered, making her way along the dark passageway. But there was no going back now. There was too much risk of waking Tyler, and if that happened, he would never let her go.

She waited awhile, trying to get her bearings, letting her eyes become accustomed to the gloom. Moments passed. The silence was oppressive, the air hot and stuffy, making it hard to breathe. She shivered, trying to pull herself together before moving on. At the end of the hall, moonlight filtered in through a small window. Slowly at first, taking small steps, and with one hand pressed firmly against the wall, she made her way toward it.

"Ohhh." She tripped. Only the wall saved her from a fall. "What on earth am I doing?" she whispered, rubbing at the tender spot now on her shoulder. "What can I hope to find, stumbling around out here in the dark?" Discouraged, she thought for a moment of retracing her steps but stopped short as the light from the little window revealed an open landing. Just beyond it, there were stairs. Memories surfaced. She was a child again, her patent leather shoes clattering as she ran up these same worn wooden treads. There was a gentle swish of a starched dress, and the delicate fragrance of a pretty woman drifted in the air. Voices, once known, echoed along the walls of the dim hallway.

"Into bed with you now, child, and none of your nonsense." The sharp words of her nanny, Mrs. Jarvis, rang in her ears, followed by the shrill sounds of her own childish laughter. Again, she heard the rustle of the starched dress, felt a gentle touch, smelled the perfumed air, and knew in an instant that it was her mother. For a moment, she sank down on the stairs, too overcome with emotion to move. Determination alone drove her on.

The door at the top of the stairs was closed. Did she dare to open it? What awaited her on the other side? Perspiration dotted her brow, and the hand that reached for the big old doorknob was shaking. Stubborn at first, she tried again, a harder twist and then a push. This time, the door creaked open, and Madeline took a step back into her past.

Here, time had stood still. It was as if the clock had suddenly stopped the day the little girl had gone away. Since then, the room and all of its inhabitants had sat silent. Holding their collective breath, they had waited patiently for her return. The small white iron bed still stood by the window, its frilly pink spread, now dust-laden, sat waiting to be turned down for the night. Curtains, once so bright and fresh, had faded with time and drooped sadly from disjointed rods. What little light filtered in through the grimy windows cast shifting shadows over the once brightly dressed monkeys climbing the papered walls. In a far corner, Dobbin, her large dappled gray rocking horse, sat motionless but ready and willing for his young rider to climb aboard. The bright red runners would need no urging to take them off on a jolly chase.

Dolls, their dresses looking a little worse for wear, still sat side by side on the wide window seat. Their eyes bright and glassy, their lips a worn-out shade of red. Smiles, forever frozen in time, upon their delicate porcelain faces. A large brown teddy bear with one ear missing leaned drunkenly upon the pillow beside them.

"Teddy!" She spoke lovingly to the ancient bear. Once she had named them all. They were the friends of her childhood. But that was a long time ago now, and it was hard to remember. But she did remember Teddy. When she was sad or in trouble, he was the one she ran to. Many nights, she had lain awake in this little bed, hugging him to her chest, telling him all of her deepest, darkest secrets.

Bending down, she touched him gently. These were the remnants of her childhood. The childhood that had been so cruelly stolen from her. What had happened all those years ago? What had happened to take all of this away from her? Sitting down on the side of the bed, she took the soft brown bear in her arms. His large black, shoe-button eyes looked questioningly up into hers. Her breath caught on a sob.

"Oh, Teddy, I swear, I'll never, ever leave you alone again," she promised.

Her thoughts returned to Tyler, and she wondered if he had awoken to find her missing. There could be no doubt of his reaction if he had. He would be angry and demand to know why she had gone alone. Still hugging the willing Teddy to her chest, she took one last look around the nursery before closing the door behind her.

Suddenly, she was no longer alone. The narrow hall was filled with noise and movement. Voices raised in anger. Footsteps running on the stairs. Again, the soft swish of silk, the same gentle fragrance filling the air. Lamplight flickered. Giant shadows climbed the walls, locked in a desperate struggle for life or death. A shrill scream rent the air. Sounds of falling. A little girl crying, "Mama." Strong hands holding her back.

As quickly as it had come, the moment was over. Shaking uncontrollably, Madeline slid to the floor. Teddy tumbled from her arms, landing in an undignified heap at her feet. Minutes ticked by. The night had returned, and all was as it had ever been in the dark little hallway. She sat, her back to the wall, her knees hugged close to her chest. Now she knew the horror her mind had kept locked away all these years. It wasn't just a bad dream. It was all really true.

With an effort, she pulled herself together. Her heartbeat eased, and her breathing slowed. Reaching down, she picked up the rumpled little bear.

"Sorry, Teddy dear," she said, comforting the toy. Coming to her feet and holding him tight in her arms, she made her way slowly back toward Tyler and the safety of their room.

"Where the hell have you been?" The anger on Tyler's face quickly changed to concern as he looked into Madeline's eyes. Still in a state of undress, he grabbed her and led her toward the bed.

She listened quietly as questions tumbled in quick succession from his mouth.

"Where have you been? What happened? I told you to wait till morning. Why didn't you wake me?"

Holding up her hand and begging him to give her a minute, she sank down onto the bed.

Impatient but biding his time, he poured water from the pitcher, waiting quietly as she drank her fill.

"Now," he said, "tell me what happened."

"I couldn't sleep. I found it hard to believe that that was really my father we met today. Everything was so different, not at all how I remembered it. This house, these people. You have no idea how awful that felt. It was as if that time had never existed. As if my life had only begun when I entered the convent at five years old. I had to find something, anything that I could connect to."

"And did you find it?"

"Yes, I found my old nursery. And Tyler, it was just as I had left it. Nothing there had changed."

"So, that was your connection?"

"Yes, but that's not all. Just as I was leaving, my nightmare returned, but this time I was wide awake. I know now that something terrible happened there, and I was a part of it."

"I think you have always known that. Something had to cause those memories."

Sitting down beside her, he took her hand. "I am beginning to think it was a mistake coming here, Madeline."

"Oh no." She grabbed wildly at his arm. "Please, don't think that. I must know. I just have to."

"Very well. As you wish." He took a deep breath. "But you have to promise me something first."

"Yes, anything."

"There must be no more taking off on your own." He looked stern and stressed his words. "I mean it, Madeline. If we are right and something bad did happen here, then there could be danger." Her eyes grew wide. "Try not to worry," he said, comforting her. "George is on his way here, and he is bringing Jeannie with him. If I must leave for some reason, I will feel better knowing you're not alone. Now, let's hear no more of it tonight." Picking her up, he tucked her into bed and climbed in beside her. But despite being snug within the safe, warm circle of his arms, it was a long time before Madeline was able to fall asleep.

Chapter Fourty-Nine

Because of the unsettling night, Madeline had slept longer than usual. Even so, she was upset to find that Tyler was no longer there. She hurried to dress, all the time wishing that he had waited for her.

"Breakfast is being served, Madam." Once again, it was Anne who greeted her in the downstairs hall. "It's this way."

Madeline nodded, and together they made their way out onto a wide stone terrace. Bathed in bright morning sunlight, it looked out onto a calm, blue-green sea. The rugged coastline stretched out before her as far as the eye could see. For a moment, she stood watching the comings and goings of small boats on the water. Once again, memory stirred. Picnics on the beach, wading in a salty pool.

"Madam." Anne called her to the table. She took her seat, disappointed it was only set for one. A note in Tyler's bold hand waited for her there. It simply read,

Sending a message to George. Will return shortly.

George and Jeannie were coming, and she suddenly realized how much she missed them. Without ever really being aware of it, the inhabitants of Marshfield Hall had become her family. The only family she had ever really known. She read the note once more, then slipped it into her pocket. So she would eat alone and idle away the time until Tyler's return.

Pouring another cup of tea, she lingered long after Anne had cleared the table. Dark clouds gathered along the horizon, and she watched as they swiftly moved to gobble up the sun. A sudden gust of wind swirled around her, loosening her hair and tugging at the hem of her dress. Dead leaves, caught up in the grip of the mischievous prankster, twisted and tumbled at her feet.

Sensing the coming storm, gulls circled high above with their wings spread wide. Sharp black eyes scanned the choppy sea below, watching for the hidden bounty soon to be theirs. Loud screeching filled the air as one by one they dove deep into the tossing waves, snagging tasty morsels of fish to fill their empty gullets. Lightning streaked across the sky, and thunder rumbled close behind. Madeline made a dash for the house just in time as dark clouds split asunder and rain came splattering down. Safe inside, she stood for a moment, shaking the dampness from her hair and looking at the graying world outside. As she watched, puddles spilled out across the terrace, and she wondered if Tyler would be delayed by the storm. Did he have to seek shelter somewhere? The house behind her was quiet and still. No movement. No sounds of life. It seemed strange, but then everything here was strange. She shivered, suddenly feeling very alone.

"Stop it," she scolded herself. "You are letting your imagination run away with you, it will—"

"Can I help you, Madam?"

"Oh! Anne." She jumped. "I didn't hear you coming."

Unfazed, the woman smiled. "The Master said to take care of you, Madam. A fire has been lit in the library. It's this way."

Once again, Madeline followed in the woman's wake. In this room, for the first time since entering the house, she felt at ease. Here, at least, there were signs of life. A small fire burned in the grate, books were scattered around, and the curtains had been thrown open to let in the light. She moved to the window, unhappy to see that the rain was still falling. Left to her own devices, and sure now that Tyler must have been delayed, she ran her fingers along the books on the shelf. Titles jumped out at her, some she had heard of but never read. She pulled one out at random, the cover said, "Full of Mystery and Suspense." After one more look out at the rain, and in the hopes that it would help to pass the time, she took it, and settled down in the chair by the fire to wait. The book tweaked her interest, but the warmth of the fire was comforting. She fought to resist it for a while, but at last her eyes lids closed and the book slowly slipped from her fingers.

She awoke with a start. "Who's there?" She asked, straining to hear. "Tyler, is that you?" No answer. All was quiet. But someone had been there, she was sure of it. Even now the air still stirred as with someone's passing. She shivered, certain she was no longer alone. A board had creaked… There, it did it again. The hair at her nape stood on end. "Who's there?" she called out again, louder this time. Still no answer. But someone had been watching her she was sure of it, and suddenly the room no longer felt warm and inviting.

Sounds erupted in the courtyard outside, and still shaking, she ran to the window. Tyler had returned. Relived, she watched as, garbed in heavy rain gear, he dismounted, and headed toward the house.

"Sorry I took so long." He apologized as he entered the room. "The damnable rain slowed everything down."

"That's alright." Madeline helped him remove his wet garments. "I'm just glad to see you."

He looked concerned. "Is all well with you?"

"It's nothing, just an overactive imagination."

Tyler said no more.

Chapter Fifty

"Why was this allowed to happen?" Lord Spencer demanded.

"I don't know." Walter tried to explain. "I only left him for a few minutes. But he knows she is here. You have to let him see her."

"Very well," Spencer agreed. "But it's not my decision alone. I must speak to the others first. I know Wentworth won't be put off much longer."

Later that evening, Spencer put the question to the men gathered around the table.

"God, haven't we gone through enough all these years? Must it start all over again?" Sir Richard wanted to know.

"But we don't know for sure if she's still in danger. Surely after all this time—"

Dewhurst offered.

"Let him see her, I say." Sir Roger Downes spoke up.

"What say you, Quinn?" Sir Lionel acquiesced with a nod of his head.

"So, that's the decision of you all." Spencer wanted to know. It was agreed.

"You must understand," he later tried to explain to an irate husband. "This is not a well man."

"If his health is a concern, Sir, we are more than willing to follow your directions. But my concern is for my wife's welfare. All she is asking is the opportunity to see her father. Surely a short, planned visit can do him no harm. Don't you see, until she sees him, she will never be willing to leave."

Madeline took the note from Tyler's hand. "It's from Lord Spencer," she said, looking up at him, doubt in her eyes.

"Well, go on. Read it," he urged.

"It says my father will be on the terrace at ten in the morning," she whispered.

"So, my love." He took her hand. "In a little while, your wait will be over. Let's hope then you can put all your ghosts to rest."

After yet another sleepless night, Madeline again found herself out on the terrace, this time with Tyler by her side. Once again, the quiet Anne served tea, but Madeline's stomach was in knots.

"Just stay calm." Tyler tried to reassure her.

"I'll be alright." She gave him a shaky smile. But she was nervous and on edge, suddenly very unsure of how she felt. Yet, this was the moment she had waited for, wasn't it? Even prayed for. At last, she had a chance to learn the truth.

Tyler watched her closely. "What's troubling you?" he asked. "I thought this would make you happy."

"I'm afraid," she admitted.

"Of what?"

"I suppose it sounds foolish," she admitted, "but in my mind, I have come up with a thousand reasons why I was sent away, and each time, I come back to the same thing."

"And what's that?"

"I wonder if, somehow, it was my fault that my mother died." There, she had finally said it out loud.

"Now that's foolish. You were just a child."

"I know, but something bad happened in the nursery. I told you that."

"Yes, but no more now, Madeline, because your father is here."

Madeline watched as the odd combination of the funny little man, Walter, and the invalid in his care made their way toward her.

So here he was at last. Her father. This was the moment she had waited for, for so long. But now that he was here, she was at a loss for words. Faded blue eyes looked up from the aging face, a sad reminder of the years lost. Overcome, she knelt before him and took his hand.

"It's me, Father," she said. "Madeline."

"Madeline, you say." A thoughtful frown wrinkled his brow. "There was a Madeline here once, a long time ago. A pretty little thing she was."

For a moment, a gentle smile lit his face, and the blue eyes softened. But the instant passed. The eyes went blank, and he turned away.

"I'm cold, Walter. Why did you bring me here? Take me back. Take me back," he demanded in a petulant tone.

"Sorry, Madam," Walter mumbled, tucking the blanket more firmly around the old man's knees. "The master's not himself today."

Madeline could only watch as they turned and trundled away. "I don't understand," she whispered.

Chapter Fifty-One

"I'm glad to see you, George. Things have not gone well here," Tyler confided as they unloaded the couple's baggage. "Jeannie will be a good distraction for my wife." He smiled at the sounds of happy chatter coming from the two women.

"That little lady could distract anyone." George chuckled affectionately. "She hasn't stopped talking since we left Marshfield Hall. But believe me, most of it was out of concern for her friend."

"Please, Jeannie," Madeline begged, "I want all the news from Marshfield Hall."

"Well, now, let me see. Where should I begin?" her friend said.

"Alright, George." Tyler made a move. "Let's leave the ladies to catch up on all the gossip while we dispose of the luggage. I found you accommodation close by, and I don't think we will be missed for a while." They left with the happy sound of Jeannie's voice ringing in their ears.

"Did you find the elusive nanny?" Tyler questioned a short time later.

"Elvira Jarvis? Yes. I did with the help of Solicitor Bailey as you suggested. We stopped on our way here. She lives in a small cottage in the country, where she cares for her older, bedridden sister."

"And did anything come of it?"

"No, not really. She had nothing to say. Silent as the grave she was, but according to Bailey's excellent records, upon leaving Cliffs Edge, certain payments were made to the woman. So I think you were right. She was paid to keep quiet."

"Well, that's something I suppose, George."

"Yes, and I confronted her with it, but all she would say was 'That was a very long time ago, young man,' and then she shut the door in my face."

"Well, once you get settled in, my friend, go scout around the village. Make yourself known among the locals. Who knows what you might find out there. Meanwhile, I intend to push Spencer for another meeting with Madeline's father."

"But how long will he be gone?" he demanded of Anne upon finding out that Lord Spencer had left for parts unknown.

"I'm sure I couldn't say, Sir."

Frustrated by the delay, Tyler passed the days with his wife and her companion. Lunches were packed by the ever-present Anne, and time was spent picnicking along the sandy shore.

George used the time to travel the local gathering places, and in the days that followed, he became a familiar face in a place called The Black Cat Inn.

The Black Cat Inn was small, hardly worthy of the name Inn. Those who came in through its doors were mostly unsavory by nature, the dregs of society. This night, George called for his favored brew and took up a seat with the widest view. The crowd was small and the conversation limited. Even the buxom barmaid seemed too distracted to share her usual banter. By chance, he took note of a small, scruffy-looking individual occupying a table in the darkest corner of the room.

From time to time, the man cast a sly glance toward the door and muttered something unintelligible under his breath. He was becoming uneasy. His feet shuffled restlessly on the floor. He was waiting for someone but wasn't happy about it.

George moved closer. He checked the time. It was getting late, and he knew Jeannie would be anxious. But draining his glass, he called for another. He wondered if this was going to be just another wild goose chase. He had no reason to suspect the man of anything, but all of his instincts told him otherwise. A door opened. Cool air flooded the room. The wait was over.

Percy Pratt shivered. He didn't look up. No need. He knew this man and hated him.

Dressed in a long black cape with the collar turned up over his chin, he concealed his identity quite effectively. A wide-brimmed hat pulled well down on his head did the rest.

"Well," the man demanded of Pratt as he took a seat at the table. "Explain yourself if you can."

"Honest to goodness, Mister, I did me best." Hoping to calm the man, Percy slid a glass in his direction. "You said to get rid of 'er. Stay with 'er and get rid of 'er you said. And that's what I done. Followed 'er everywhere I did. If 'n it hadn't a bin for the damn Yank, she would a bin gone with the cap'n long ago, never to return."

"Well, it didn't happen, did it? And now she's here, and all you give me are excuses. I'm sick of listening to your excuses." Eyes like ice, the man slammed his fist down on the table. "What of the money I put in your pocket?" he demanded.

Percy Pratt shied away. He had never dealt with any one like this before. He had known how to deal with the captain, but this man was different. He could see it in his eyes. Cold and deadly, with the wild look of insanity. The money he had offered had sounded good at the time, but now Percy just wanted out. But how?

"Give me another chance, Mister," he begged. "I can still get the job done if you give me one more chance."

"I'll give you one more chance," his companion said, "but this time, get the job done, or suffer the consequences." He drained the contents of his mug in one swift move and slammed the empty container down on the table. This meeting was obviously at an end. The legs of his chair scrapped the floor as he came to his feet.

"But Mister." Percy made a grab at his sleeve, hoping in one last ditch effort to make a better deal. "If I have to deal with the Yank too, how much more will you pay me?"

With lightning speed, the man twisted, pulling his arm free. Percy choked, gasping for breath, as strong fingers wrapped themselves around his neck and began to squeeze. Percy heard the words through a descending fog.

"You are a clever little man. Use your imagination."

The fingers relaxed, and Percy slowly slid to the floor. From a distance, he heard the Inn door slam shut, leaving a chilling silence in its wake. With shaking hands, he quickly drained the remains of the ale from his glass. Throwing a coin down on the table, he called the landlord for another. He needed time. He had to think. There could be no approaching the girl, not after their last encounter. She might remember him. Then there was the Yank, the big fella. He had seen him in action a few times, and he had no intentions of tangling with him again. No matter how he looked at it, things did not bode well for Percy Pratt, he decided. But then, on second thoughts, he had been in tight spots before, and the money was awful good. He chewed on his bottom lip. He needed time to think. "You got to take ur time, Percy me boy," he muttered, "You just got to take ur time."

From his vantage point, George had taken it all in. Only fragments of the conversation reached his ears, but the fact that the little man was badly shaken was obvious. He thought to offer the man a drink, but the barmaid called time, and the chance was lost.

Chapter Fifty-Two

"No one seems to know much," George told Tyler the next morning. "One old man did remember an accident a long time ago. A pretty lady, he said. The locals heard she had died in a fall."

"Well, that seems to fit with Madeline's recollection of that night. Was there anything else?"

"Only that afterward, all these strange men arrived, but they keep to themselves. Never bother anyone."

"I don't know what to make of them myself, George. Spencer said their friendship goes back a long way. But what on earth could have bought them all here, and why do they stay? Keep digging, my friend, and see what else you can turn up."

"I've found The Black Cat is the place to go. Last evening, there was a bit of a rumpus in the bar room. No one seemed to know what it was about, but some odd little fellow was being picked on quite badly. I couldn't hear much, but I did get the man's name. It was Pratt."

"Pratt!" Tyler voiced his surprise. "I wonder what he's doing here. I had a run-in with Percy Pratt a while ago, George. It's a long story but suffice to say he's a thoroughly bad lot. It will take some looking into, but in the meantime, look at this. It came today. Could be nothing, but I thought it worth looking into, and if we leave early, we can be back before dark."

Surprised, George read:

Sir,

Something has been brought to my attention, and I think it might be of help to you. I await your convenience.

Sincerely,

Alvira Jarvis.

As he kissed his wife goodbye in the morning, Tyler had a word of warning. "Stay close to Jeannie. Make sure you stay with her until I get back. Don't wander off. We won't be late."

Madeline nodded, but the note she had found under her pillow had said, "Wait in your room. Must see you alone. Tell no one. Father."

"I'll be fine, Jeannie," she explained. "I'm a bit tired. I promise to stay in my room and read. What on earth can go wrong?"

Reluctantly, Jeannie finally gave in. "Well, I won't be far away," she said. "Please call if you need me."

For the past few days, Percy Pratt had familiarized himself with the outside of Cliffs Edge. He had been patient, waiting and watching, taking his time. Today, he was almost certain that the house was empty. He had watched them all leave. Only the girl and the old man remained. Even the old man's constant companion had left for parts unknown. All he needed to do now was get inside. No problem.

"Alright, Percy me boy," he congratulated himself. "This is your chance." All his hard work was paying off at last. The old man was powerless and taking out the girl would be no problem. He had no thought of killing her. Killing wasn't in his nature, but he was sure that once he got his hands on her, he could dispose of her for good. No one the wiser.

Entering through the old servant's door at the back of the house, he made his way swiftly up to the first floor. All was quiet, so he took a moment to grasp the layout of the rooms. He was used to this sort of thing; he had been doing it for years. His tread was light; he made no sound. Stopping in the hallway, he detected faint sounds from above. Certain this must be his quarry, he continued on.

Madeline looked out of her bedroom window. The day was dark and overcast, a promise of more rain to come. She was on edge, had been since hearing from her father. What should she make of the strange message? "Must see you alone. Tell no one." Why? She hated deceiving Tyler, but she convinced herself it wasn't really such a big fib. After all, she was staying in her room. Jeannie wasn't far away, and perhaps now, at last, she would learn the truth. The book she had found in the library lay open on her bed. It offered no comfort, but lighting the lamp, she picked it up anyway. Unable to concentrate, she flipped through to the last page.

"Well, that was foolish," she muttered after reading the end, and snapping it shut, she threw it down. It was getting late. Agitated, she paced the floor. Checking the clock for the third time, she wondered how much longer she would have to wait. At last, a footstep in the hall.

Eagerly, she ran to open the door but stumbled back as a dirty little man pushed his way into the room. "Who are you?" she demanded, heart pounding. "And what are you doing here?"

"No need to worry," Percy said. "Calm yourself, Lady. You and me are going to take a little ride is all."

That voice! She gasped, her mind quickly returning to the horror of it. The stinking sack. The smell of fish. The bone-jarring journey in the rotting wagon. The frightening encounter with the demented captain. This was the man responsible for it all.

He moved toward her now, arms outstretched. She backed away, eyes wide, hands grouping, reaching out for something, anything to protect herself.

"Oh, come on now, Missy, don't be shy," Percy urged with a toothless grin. "I ain't gonna hurt ya if you're a good girl."

The book. Her fingers found the book. Not much, but she grasped it firmly behind her back and waited. He moved closer. She watched him come. A few more steps. Shock registered in his eyes as the full force of the blow hit him. Arms flaying, he hit the floor with a thud.

Madeline ran. Yanking open the door, she stopped.

"Father!" Open-mouthed, she stared at the man standing there before her.

Supported by a cane and held upright by a man behind him, her father looked about to fall.

"Madeline, I . . . I . . ." he managed to stutter before the man behind him gave him a shove that sent him sprawling on the floor at her feet.

"Oh!" Madeline rushed to his aid. "What's happening, Father?"

"What's happening? I'll tell you what's happening." The voice was excited and high-pitched. "It means that, at last, your father is getting what he deserves. He is going to see you die."

Clinging onto her father's arm, Madeline looked up into a face she didn't recognize.

A dazed Percy scrambled to his feet.

"You fool, Pratt," the other man snarled. "I emptied the house of everyone, and once again, you ruined my plans." He pulled a pistol from his belt.

Fear galvanized Percy Pratt. "No, Mister," he begged. "I can still help you. I can get rid of her, and once she's gone, the Yank will give up and go away."

"You think that, do you, Pratt?" He sniggered. "Get out. You are useless. An even bigger fool than I imagined. For all the money I paid you, and I still have to do the job myself. Get out! Get out!" Yelling wildly, he waved the pistol in Percy's direction.

Frantic to help her father, Madeline reached for his cane.

"Oh no, you don't." Knocking her senseless, the gunman kicked the cane aside.

At that moment, Percy lunged, catching the other off guard. The pistol fell from the man's grasp to spin wildly across the floor. Furniture scattered as both men hurled themselves after it. Chairs toppled and tables upended, spilling their contents asunder. Madeline's lamp crashed to the ground, oil running unstopped across the floor, soaking everything in its path. Tongues of flame quickly followed, hungrily licking up the trail of precious nectar. With a low roar, the curtains flared. Still locked in the fight for the pistol, Percy was more afraid of the fire now than the gun. Gathering his remaining strength, he struggled to break free, and with no thought for anyone but himself, a horrified Percy took to his heels and ran.

Still dazed, Madeline struggled to her feet. She felt the heat, saw the flames, and saw her father lying helpless on the floor. "Lean on me, Father," she begged, trying to drag him to safety. She heard an angry growl and screamed as strong hands grabbed her, hanging on and spinning her around.

Still red-faced but drawn up to his full height, she saw him for the first time. Sir Roger Downes. The eyes, no longer short sighted, flashed bright and dangerous. Red whiskers bristling, he slammed her against the wall. Oblivious of the fire burning around them, he hauled her back to her feet, his large hands reaching out to encircle her throat.

"Why?" Madeline managed to ask, clutching at his fingers, trying to pry them loose.

"Why! Ask your father. He took everything from me." His face twisted in pain.

"I don't understand," Madeline pleaded.

"He married my little sister, Ellen, and took her to Paris. It was against my family's wishes. He knew the risk but wouldn't listen. They had a child, and again we begged him to bring her home. But by then, the city was in the grip of madness. When he finally came looking for help, it was too late. I was there. I saw my sister and her child die on that accursed beach. I felt her pain." His eyes clouded at the memory. 'Oh, poor Etienne,' they all cried. His whole family was lost. But did they think of my family?" His grip on Madeline tightened, his fingers digging into the tender flesh.

"The shock was too much for my poor mother," he went on. "She never recovered. But hers wasn't a quick death. Oh no. She lingered. My father and I watched as, day by day, she slowly wasted away. He was devastated. Within a month he took his own life."

Unconcerned for the ever-growing blaze around them, he spoke to the man at his feet. "The day I buried him, I made a vow Etienne. I promised him I would make you pay. I didn't know how I would do it then, but you yourself gave me the way. You married again, had another child. What right did he have to take another wife?" he now demanded of Madeline. "It was as if our poor Ellen and her child had never been, and I knew then what I had to do. Oh yes, I killed Elizabeth, almost got the child too. They all thought you did it, Etienne, in one of your crazy blackouts. I encouraged them to think that, and they've spent all these years protecting you for nothing." He laughed at the irony. "As for you," he told Madeline, "I knew if I waited long enough, that one day you would come back, and now you have, and my promise to my father can be fulfilled."

His face just inches from hers, Madeline saw the hate in his eyes and knew stark fear as his fingers began to squeeze. In a desperate fight for her life, she pulled his hair and scratched his face, her nails leaving thin red lines in their wake. With a bellow of rage, he threw her down. She hit the floor, sucking smoke into her complaining lungs. Somewhere a window shatter. She heard glass splinter and hit the ground. Curtains, fanned by the breeze, billowed in a shower of glowing embers. Swirling around in mad abandon they delt the final kiss of death to the already dying room.

Sparks singed her hair and blistered her skin. She struggled to her feet, crying out in pain. He grabbed her arm. She bit his hand. He cursed, striking her face with his open palm. The taste of blood filled her mouth. Semi-conscious, she fell. Again his fingers sought her throat, squeezing tighter. Her world grew distant. The crackle of fire faded from her ears. Her eyes dimmed. Life dwindled. Weightless, she drifted, looking down at her own body lying prone upon the bed below. Suddenly, the pressure eased, and she gasped for breath.

"Run, child, run," a voice called out through the fog. Tumbling from the bed, she tripped. On the floor, with only his cane to assist him, her father engaged Sir Roger Downes in a trial of mortal combat. Chaos reigned as the fire continued to burn out of control around them.

"Father!" She ran toward him, flames plucking at the hem of her dress and heat burning the sole of her feet.

Chapter Fifty-Three

The letter had seemed legitimate enough. There had been no reason to question it. There had always been the question of how much Mrs. Jarvis, the nanny, knew. The fact that she had recalled something of interest was plausible. But now, Tyler and George were returning from what they could only consider was a wild goose chase. Mrs. Jarvis had disavowed quite strongly any knowledge of the communication. Tired and more than a little despondent, they were both anxious to see an end to a wasted day.

Tyler was the first to sense something wrong. The horses were restless, and a strange stillness had settled over the landscape. The afternoon sky, usually alive with swallows returning to their roost in the eaves, was quiet. A light breeze drifted in from the west, carrying with it a slight whiff of smoke. It was awhile before he recognized the significance of the ever-growing orange glow in the sky.

"George!" he shouted, pointing in the direction of Cliffs Edge. As one, they spurred their mounts onward. People had already begun to gather as they skidded to a halt in the drive. The fire was spreading rapidly, swiftly gobbling up the aged timbers of the old house. Paint blistered, and glass cracked.

Like the talons of some raging beast, the fire clawed ever higher up the sides of the defenseless edifice. Bright tongues of red and orange licked hungrily at the slowly weakening structure. Like a living being sensing its own demise, the once grand old home trembled and sighed.

"Thank God the house was empty," Tyler shouted, seeing Jeannie among the crowd.

"But it wasn't." Frantic, she ran to his side. "Madeline decided not to go. She stayed here in her room."

"Dear God!" Tyler threw himself down from his horse and rushed toward the burning house. "Stay back, George," he yelled as the man followed him in hot pursuit. But it took two to break down the door. Heat blasted their faces as, unheeding, Tyler raced inside.

"Madeline!" His cry was desperate. There was no answer. Smoke billowed down the wide stairs, stinging his eyes and burning his nose and throat. Fire was spreading rapidly along the upper landing. Soon the stairs too would be engulfed in flames.

"Madeline!" Panic gripped him.

"Help!" He heard her scream. Struggling out of his coat, he pulled it over his head and raced for the stairs. "Thank God." Seeing her, he offered up thanks.

"No, no!" she struggled, desperate as he tried to pull her to him. "My father! My father!" she cried, pointing back into the blazing room.

Through the open door, Tyler saw two men locked in battle on the floor amid the smoke and flames. "Take her, George." Lifting his wife off her feet, he bundled her into the man's arms. "Get her out of here."

"No, George, no!" She fought against his restraining grasp. With little thought of dignity, George tossed his charge over his shoulder and descended the stairs two at a time.

"Don't let her go," he shouted to Jeannie as he deposited Madeline on the ground beside her. With that warning, he turned and raced back into the burning building.

Visible for miles, the flames brought people rushing from distant farms and villages. Voices shouted, bucket brigades formed, but they knew it was a useless endeavor. Surrounded by the mad melee of activity, two young women clung to each other, watching, desperate as the seconds slowly ticked by.

Suddenly, a loud cry went up from the onlookers. "There! There they are!" someone shouted. Men raced forward as two smoke-blackened figures staggered from the crumbling structure. Many hands relieved them of the burden they carried, and the exhausted men threw themselves down on the cool green grass.

In the days that followed, the story of Madeline's terrifying experience and of Sir Roger Downes' confession were foremost in every conversation. Madeline had been moved to a small cottage some miles away, where she was placed in Jeannie's care.

"Oh Lordy," the girl muttered as she applied fresh dressings to the blistered feet.

"Don't fuss so, Jeannie," Madeline scolded. "It could have been so much worse, and I am getting better every day." Her concern for Tyler and George had been quieted by their many visits. They assured her they had been well cared for by Anne, who had quickly stepped in to help. But, ever anxious for news of her father, she gave those around her little peace.

"Your father is in good hands," Tyler said. The news calmed her a little, but she was still on edge.

"He saved my life," she kept saying to anyone who would listen. "I must see him for myself. I have to."

Tyler prolonged the moment for as long as he could, but seeing her ever-growing distress, he finally gave up his objections. "But you must speak to the doctor first," he conditioned.

"Your father has suffered much from the fire, my child. His health was not good beforehand," the elderly man told her. "You must be strong. I'm afraid the outlook is uncertain."

"I understand," she assured him, and later, in the company of Lord Spencer, she sat by her father's bedside. Still attended by his constant companion, Walter, he lay unmoving, his flesh blistered and his breathing labored. She looked to Walter. At his nod, she whispered, "Father." His eyes opened. She could see his pain.

"My child," he muttered, his voice hoarse. "It's been a long time. Your mother and I have missed you."

"Oh!" Dazed, Madeline turned to Lord Spencer, tears staining her face.

"Not now, child." He took her hand. "Not now."

Madeline watched as her father's condition slowly worsened. She seldom left his room. With Tyler's close attention and the help of Jeannie and George, she made it through the difficult days. It was on a cloudy day, almost two weeks later, that Etienne was laid to rest beside Elizabeth.

Curiosity seekers watched as the handsome young couple in black walked side by side across the windblown cemetery. Joined by Walter, Anne, and the men who had silently frequented the halls of Cliffs Edge for years, they gathered at the grave site.

As the short service ended, Madeline laid flowers on the uneven plot. "I remember this place," she recalled softly. "It was raining that day. People came to the house dressed in black, their voices hushed. Carriages with black plumed horses lined the drive. I rode in one of them with my father. I stood at his side and watched as a long box was lowered into the cold damp earth. I was small, and I don't know how I knew it was my mother, but I did." She turned to Lord Spencer, a frown creasing her forehead. "But it wasn't my father, was it? It was you. That ring you wear. You wore it that day. You held my hand so tight that it bit into my fingers. It hurt, and I wanted to cry, but Nanny Jarvis said I shouldn't cry. My father wanted me to be a big girl, be brave she said. But that night, when my mother didn't come to kiss me goodnight, I did cry. The next day my bags were packed and I was sent away. I have always thought it was because I wasn't brave enough, or that somehow, I was to blame for my mother's death."

Without a word, Tyler took his wife's arm and escorted her away, but later he faced Spencer and demanded the truth.

"Now is the time, Sir. We will wait no longer. My wife has shed enough tears. She deserves to know the truth."

"And she will, tonight," he confirmed.

That night, one by one, they came, these strange men who for years had shared the secret of Cliffs Edge.

"I'm afraid we did your farther a grave injustice, Madeline." Once again, Spencer spoke for them all. "But at the time, we truly thought he had caused your mother's death. We never suspected anyone else. Even now, I find it hard to comprehend the magnitude of Downes' deception." There was a murmur of agreement.

Madeline looked into their uneasy faces. "But why would you think him responsible?" She wanted to know. "He loved my mother so."

"Yes, but he was a sick man. He never really recovered from the loss of his family in France. There were bad dreams, nightmares, times when he would retreat into his own dark world for days. No one could reach him, not even your mother."

"Even so, that could have meant nothing. I don't understand."

"That day, there were only four people here, you, your mother and father, and Mrs. Jarvis. Mrs. Jarvis said your father had been in one of his dark moods, the worst she had ever seen, so she stayed in the nursery. Later she heard loud voices. She saw two people fighting on the stairs. Your mother called to her, 'Take the child. He's trying to kill her.' She pulled you into the nursery and kept you locked in there until I came, but that was hours later. By then, your father had locked himself away. He remembered nothing."

"So, what did you do?" Tyler asked.

"We didn't know what to do at first. Etienne was our friend. He was a good man, and he had suffered enough. The courts would have found him insane, sentenced him to be locked away with other poor demented souls. That was unthinkable. We all felt that we shared the burden of guilt for that night in France so long ago. Had we arrived sooner, had we not been delayed. Oh, who can say for sure." His voice faltered. The anguish of the years showed in his face. It was a moment before he could continue. "So we claimed it an accident. The nursery stairs are steep. She tripped and fell."

"You were all of the same mind?" Tyler questioned.

"Yes." There were nods of agreement. "We have remained here, taking care of him ever since. But our concern for you was real, Madeline. With only Mrs. Jarvis words to go on we had to assume you might still be in danger. What if, in another dark moment, something bad should happen again, but to you this time? We would never forgive ourselves. With Edward's help, in his capacity as a solicitor, he made all the necessary arrangements. So you see, my dear," he said, taking Madeline's hand, "it wasn't your father who sent you away. It was I. I only hope you can understand and find it in your heart to forgive me."

As the carriage pulled away, Madeline turned for one last look at the burned-out shell of Cliffs Edge.

"Can you put it all to rest now?" Tyler wanted to know.

"I think so. My father gave up his life for me. What more could I ask of him? And how can I blame the others? They thought they were saving him from a horrible fate. They have suffered too. They've been tied to this place for years." She was silent for a moment, then said softly, "I wonder what will happen to them all now."

"I doubt we will ever know, but they were loyal friends, and all we can do is wish them the best. But Spencer's last words to me were that you had saved them all."

"What did he mean by that, do you think?"

"Well, they are no longer tied to Cliffs Edge. Now they are free to live their own lives again."

Chapter Fifty-Four

A month had passed since the young couple's return from Cliffs Edge, a month filled with activity. The time to leave was fast approaching, and everyone was busy in his or her own way. Tyler and George spent their days on board, preparing the ship for the long sea voyage. Knowing how hard the coming farewells with William and those at Marshfield Hall would be, they buried themselves in work and did their best to avoid the subject. Tyler went about hiring a knowledgeable crew, while George oversaw the loading of the cargo, along with large water barrels and enough food to see them safely to their destination. At least six weeks, if the weather was favorable. They worked from dawn to dusk, but at the end of each day, they relaxed with a glass of ale and spoke of the days ahead.

"For the women's sake, I hope we will be blessed with fine weather, George."

"Amen, to that," George said, nodding. "But after making it through the last few weeks, I think they can handle just about anything."

"Yes, we did cut it pretty close in that fire."

"Speaking of that, I've been meaning to ask. When you handed the father to me, you went back for Downes. What happened?"

"Nothing. He wasn't there. Not only that, but Spencer told me later that they searched after the fire but found no trace of him."

The halls of Long Meadow were piled high with trunks. Madeline viewed them with mixed emotions. Much of her time now was spent with William at Marshfield Hall. They rode through the countryside together and tended the delicate plants he loved so much. Her father was still on her mind, and in quiet moments in the conservatory, she shared her thoughts with her companion.

"I wish I could have known him better," she confessed. "We lost all of those years."

"It's history, my dear," William said. "Nothing can change it. Take it from an old man: don't waste your tears on the past. You are young. Look to the future. It's what your father would wish for you."

"But what of the future?"

"None of us knows what lies ahead. All we can do is make the most of what's given us. With my grandson by your side, live your life in a way that would make your father proud."

"Thank you." She took his arm. "You always make me feel better."

Jeannie and her mother, Isabel, found their time consumed in a far different way. Having decided to join her daughter in her new life, it was necessary for Isabel to dispose of her small business. She had first set up shop in her basement room, and it didn't take long for news of her skill to spread.

"Mother." Jeannie was amazed. "I can't believe how much business you have here."

Ladies of high society frequented her shop, and many came to express their dismay as they watched the removal of her sewing chest, the one thing that she would take with her. However, when the word "money" was mentioned, Isabel was glad to have her spunky daughter close by. Soon, they were pleased to write "Paid in full" next to the long list of overdue accounts. Mother and daughter enjoyed several days shopping together.

Ian made the rounds of his favorite haunts, meeting up with friends. Their school days were behind them. Studying was over. It was time to celebrate. They drank too much and slept little. But unbeknownst to anyone, Ian had another side. There were days when, dressed in the most elegant of style, he visited a big house in the city. At his knock, the door would open, and a little dog would jump into his arms.

"There, there, Peaches," he greeted the wiggling creature as he stepped inside. With a warm smile, he moved toward the pretty girl at the other end of the hall.

"Katherine." He loved the way she blushed when he kissed her hand. They had been introduced some months earlier by his best friend, Mathew. She was a little wisp of a thing with porcelain skin, hair the color of ebony, and soft brown eyes. He had been enamored with her since that first meeting. But she was only sixteen, and he would soon turn twenty. In a moment of despair, he had confessed to Mathew his undying love for his sister.

"Good Lord," Mathew responded, wondering what on earth someone as intelligent as his friend could ever see in his sister. But he did suggest when he came to the house that he might express an interest in horticulture. He was granted afternoon visits to the house, where he drank tea with Katherine and her mother and listened to the latest remedy for fruit flies. Now he was returning home without ever having had a chance to declare himself. But he had extracted a promise that Katherine would write.

At the first sight of the ship, the ladies found it quite exciting. This was to be their home for weeks. It looked quite grand as its tall mast swayed gently back and forth with the swell of the sea.

Tyler ventured to say that they might well change their minds by the end of the journey.

William, with Mrs. Carter and young Charlie in tow, joined them on their last night ashore. Candles lit the stained-glass windows of the little chapel as they bowed their heads in prayer. Later that night, after all of the champagne had been drunk, all of the tears had been shed, and all the promises to visit again soon had been made, Madeline stepped on board for the first time.

"Well, what do you think, my love?" Tyler wanted to know.

"It looks so big."

"After a few days, it won't seem that way," he promised.

But as she prepared to spend her first night aboard, unaware of how much trouble her husband had taken in the preparations, she marveled at the comfort of their sleeping quarters.

A large bed was piled high with comforters. Books and writing material filled a shelf in the corner, and red and blue cushions covered a small window seat. The closet held warm clothes, and waterproof gear hung from a hook on the door. As she lay beside her husband in the comfort of the big bed, she wondered at the strangeness of her new surroundings. The smell of salt water in the breeze, the gentle splash of wave against the hull, and the constant rolling motion with the movement of the tide.

"Tyler." Her words broke the silence.

"Mmmmm." He sounded sleepy.

"I want to thank you for everything. I know it's been difficult."

"No more bad dreams?"

"No."

"Then it was all worth it." He moved closer and nibbled her ear.

"Stop it," she giggled. "It tickles."

"I know it, but you should know better than waking a sleeping lion."

She sighed as his mouth followed a familiar path.

"What if someone comes in?" she whispered.

"They wouldn't dare disturb the captain," he growled. "They know better."

"Even George?"

"Especially George. Besides, he has his own troubles to deal with. So come here, woman. There won't be much time for this once we are underway." Rolling over, he pulled her to him and through the night, like the pirate of her dreams, he taught her much of the seafaring ways.

When she woke, it was to a chorus of unfamiliar sounds. The harsh blast of a horn, the clank of heavy chains, fast-moving footsteps, and a loud voice shouting out orders. Just as she was sliding from the bed, the door burst open.

"Hurry, hurry." Jeannie rushed into the room. "The tide has turned, and we are sailing."

Madeline jumped up, and with a little confusion and much chatter, she managed to get dressed. Running up to the deck, they joined Isabel and Ian. Standing side by side, shivering in the chill morning air, they watched as the coast of England slowly faded from view.